THE STONE

The Stone lay on a black stone altar that had been cut from the stone of the crag. It wasn't just something Jimmy saw with his eyes. He could feel it, feel its electric fire on his skin. And the evil, dripping and oozing and spattering from it, almost as though the Stone were a sponge overfull with every meanness in the world. It was alive...

Jimmy stooped over and pushed on the Stone. The Children screamed. It rolled forward, tumbling off the stone platform, pounding the rocks just below the ledge. The Stone shattered. The Children collapsed.

He scrambled down the almost sheer rock face of the crag. And saw that the shards of rock that had been the Stone were *moving*. Moving toward each other. And slowly but steadily reassembling themselves. The Children were beginning to wake...

BLOOD OF THE CHILDREN

— by —

ALAN RODGERS

BANTAM BOOKS

NEW YORK · TORONTO · LONDON · SYDNEY · AUCKLAND

For Shadow,
with apologies

BLOOD OF THE CHILDREN
A Bantam Book / January 1990

ISBN 0-553-28335-9

Published simultaneously in the United States and Canada

Bantam Books are published by Bantam Books, a division of
Bantam Doubleday Dell Publishing Group, Inc. Its trademark,
consisting of the words "Bantam Books" and the portrayal of
a rooster, is Registered in U.S. Patent and Trademark Office
and in other countries. Marca Registrada. Bantam Books,
666 Fifth Avenue, New York, New York 10103

PRINTED IN THE UNITED STATES OF AMERICA
OPM 0 9 8 7 6 5 4 3 2 1

PROLOGUE

BEN TOMPKINS WENT FOR A LONG DRIVE THE SUMMER that his wife Anne's drinking began to get out of hand. He didn't tell anyone that he was going to; that would have made the whole situation too pointed and conspicuous. There wasn't any need to explain his absence. There was a three-day recertification seminar down in Huntsville that July, and he fibbed about it and told his wife and son that it ran a week instead of just a few days.

And when the seminar was over Ben rented a car and went driving. Not driving with any destination in mind, just driving on small, smooth rural highways. Letting the countryside roll by him and into him. Trying to be easy enough with himself to make hard decisions, and to decide —to *know*—what it was he needed to decide.

Anne had a temper. A bad temper; sometimes Ben even thought it was dangerously bad. When she drank it got worse, and lately she seemed to drink all the time. Ben and their son, Jimmy, had taken a lot of abuse from Anne the last few months. Not physical abuse—not the sort of thing you called the police about and then went upstairs to pack your bags. Verbal abuse. Nastiness. Mean-heartedness, pure and simple. Not so bad when she was sober, not even in the mornings when she tended to be hung over.

And Ben wasn't sure he wanted to live with it anymore. He wasn't even sure that he *could* live with it. And he sure didn't want his son growing up in an atmosphere like that.

But no matter what she did, Ben knew, Anne was Anne, and she was his wife, and he loved her. Whenever Ben thought about leaving he ran into that love, smacked his head and heart against it as though it was a hard-glass wall and he were a bird trying to fly through a sky that was only reflection. Sometimes at home his mind would go all quiet, and he wouldn't even know that he was thinking or feeling anything, and he'd reach up half-automatically to rub his eyes. And his hands would come away wet with tears he didn't know he was crying.

It wasn't good. It wasn't good for Jimmy. It wasn't just Anne herself that was the problem, either—how good a father could Ben be if he was so shook up that he didn't even know when something was wrong with him?

But hard as Ben looked, he didn't find any answers. Every choice he could think of was as bad as the one he'd just discarded.

When he set out after the conference, Ben made a point of not thinking about the problem, because all his thinking had gotten him nowhere at all. If he could just get his head clear enough, he thought, an answer would come to him. That's the way it'd always worked when he was younger, when he'd known less about the world and every question had seemed a hard one.

In a way, it worked out exactly as Ben had hoped it would. Inspiration came to him out of the blue and unasked for.

But it didn't come from his own heart, even though at the time he was sure that it had. It came at the wrong time in the wrong place, and it came from a source so vile that if Ben had known it he would have run from that inspiration as hard and as fast as he could.

Ben's inspiration came from the Stone.

The Stone that rested underneath the town of Green Hill.

No one ever knew exactly where it came from, nor what it really was. Those who knew of it called it the Stone because that was what it most nearly seemed to be— though it wasn't stone at all. It was something alive. Not alive as creatures of the earth are alive, but alive even still. The Children had once known how it was found—in the eighteen-thirties by a boy playing pirates' treasure in the caves underneath the town's foundations. That boy, Walt Hanson, had come up out of the caves one evening with strange caustic burns half-way up his arms—and with a fiery blackness in his heart that left him nothing but an empty husk by the time he reached his late teens.

But even that much had been forgotten generations ago.

For the Children the evil thing always was and always would be; it was as eternal as the sun or the moon or the earth.

It was black as a moonless night when the clouds cover the stars, and it was evil, and in its own strange way it *was* alive.

And it was growing.

It lived more than anywhere else in the hearts of the children who lived in the town; there was purchase for the evil tendrils of its spirit in the gentle, uncluttered souls of those too innocent to recognize it.

But it was not a thing that could abide complexity, nor the depth of character that comes with understanding others. Each child, as he began to reach the first stirrings of adulthood, would slip from the thing's grasp.

The Stone, rather than be known by a heart it could not possess, would then pull its spirit and all other useful evil away from the child. And with the evil it would take all memory the child had of evil.

Which left behind, by perverse process, a miraculous and wonderful thing: the town's adults were as free and pure of all those senseless and petty evils that characterize mankind as any folk ever were. And even more, they were free of the larger evils as well. There was not a wrongful bone among them.

No adult in Green Hill ever knew of the ceremonies that took place in the fields on moonlit nights, or sometimes in the forest at dusk or dawn. If any had ever seen such a ceremony the memory of it would have washed away in the time it took him to glance away from it.

So it had been for generations—the Stone, slowly growing and becoming more evil in the caves underneath the town, while above darkness and light embraced each other in the love of children and their parents.

A little before noon that Wednesday Ben drove into Green Hill for the first time. At first glance the town didn't strike him as remarkable in any way; the land the town was built on was as pretty to Ben's eyes as all the land in this part of the country. Rich, red soil. Sandstone. Pine trees everywhere, and all around and between them smaller plants thriving in the warm sun.

He didn't realize that there was anything unusual about the town until he pulled into the drive of the café that an out-of-towner named Dan Henderson ran, but as soon as he opened the screen door he could feel it. It was . . . a flavor in the atmosphere, he thought. The people, maybe.

Yes, he realized, walking across the room, passing between the crowded tables. It was the people. *Look at them,* he thought. *There's something strange about them. Not bad, but strange.* Ben was a grade-school teacher. He made his living watching people, paying attention to them. Young people, granted, but people. His eye for character was careful and very fast—and necessarily so. A teacher doesn't survive long if he can't cope well on his feet, and that coping requires either a great deal of sensitivity or a very cold heart.

The old man behind the counter smiled comfortably at him as he took Ben's order, almost as though he were an intimate acquaintance. And that's what made Ben realize what he was seeing.

Sharpness. None of them have any sharpness.

He thanked the man and looked out across the room. The people in the café were all talking animatedly, gossiping about this and that and God knew what, but all the little harshness, all the tiny meannesses Ben always saw when he watched people talking to each other—all of them were *missing.* No one here was trying to prove anything. There wasn't anyone in the room trying to dominate a conversation.

And Ben thought about his wife, who came back from her office every night so full of rage that she had to drink to live with it. Who had so much anger bundled up inside her that it poured out onto Ben, and onto their son. And as he thought about the tiny, growing hell he lived in when she was home, he looked out at a room full of people who were nothing but simple and gentle. And thought he'd somehow wandered into paradise.

He marveled at the idea all through lunch; when his sandwich and his cup of coffee came he put them down without even tasting them.

And he wondered.

There was something here, he was sure, that held the answers he'd come looking for. He sat at the counter, eating, and watching, and not paying any attention at all, waiting for it all to become clear to him.

And the Stone, buried deep in the sandstone caves underneath the town, saw that openness in his heart. And just for spite it sent him inspiration.

A gift, Ben thought, though the truth was that the thought wasn't his at all.

Anne was human, just like anybody else. She was under horrible pressures at her office. She needed love, and gentleness, and kindness; enough of all of them to compensate for the pressures that she worked with. If she was breaking under the strain of all that, then Ben himself had to be at fault as much as anyone could be. After all, Ben thought, who could she depend on to make her whole if she couldn't depend on him? Part of love is a duty, and if Anne was breaking under the pressure of her circumstances, then it was at least partly because he wasn't fulfilling his part of their bargain.

Or, at least, that was the way it seemed to Ben as he sat at the counter of that perfect café, sipping at his thin, lukewarm coffee. Later, much later, he knew he'd been wrong —but only after events had taken his life to extremes.

A gift. A gift, he thought, would make her feel more cared for. By the time he'd been gone for a week there would be a measure of newness, of freshness, between them. Not enough for a fresh start, but enough to give them the possibility of a new direction. If he brought her something special, something extraordinary, it could end up changing everything. Or it could, at least, with patience and faith and a little good luck.

Ben could almost picture the gift he wanted to get her— it was jewelry, but not harsh and glittery like polished metal. And it was beautiful, and strange, and *special*.

Ben paid up his bill and got himself back on the road. Twenty minutes later he was in Tylerville, the next town along the highway. Tylerville was a larger town, with shops and gas stations and even a shopping center. In the middle of the town there was a small antique shop, and Ben found himself turning into its parking lot without even understanding why. Then, as he opened the shop's door, he remembered the café, and the people inside it, and the gift for his wife that his mind's eye couldn't quite see.

The woman at the shop's counter smiled at Ben as he walked in, and she said hello. Ben nodded back at her, and he meant to smile, but later when he thought back about it he wasn't sure that he had.

He didn't say anything to her, though, and he didn't browse the way he usually did in shops like this one. He walked straight to a dusty, cluttered, shadowy shelf in the back of the store where his hand sifted through a deep cardboard box of junk jewelry almost as though it had a will of its own.

He would have questioned his own behavior if he'd stopped to think about it. Inspiration didn't generally take him so forcefully, or with such quiet insistence. And if he had he might have worried about what exactly had come over him. It would have been possible for him to do so, too —the Stone could rule the simple, unwary minds of children easily, and it had great power over those who'd grown up serving it, but a whole and healthy mind like Ben's it could little more than influence. But the way Ben had worked all week at relaxing himself, worked at opening himself to possibilities, had left him vulnerable to just the sort of suggestion that the Stone had planted in his mind.

And Ben didn't even think to question it. He couldn't have, not then.

His hand came up out of the jumbled box, holding something almost like a cameo, but made of some strange stone Ben didn't recognize. It was more like glass than it was like stone—blue-tinted black and faintly translucent, with a powdery finish. Warm to the touch. And instead of a profile portrait, it had the image of a low, grassy hill carved and painted into it.

Ben's heart almost froze as he looked at it. He felt the small hairs on the back of his neck rise up and stand on end. That should have warned him, too, but instead of recognizing the danger he let the feeling reassure him that what he was doing was *right*, just right, and told himself that when he got home everything was going to work out for the best.

And maybe it might have, too. Maybe the charity that was Ben's nature could have salved the things that festered inside his wife's heart. The solutions he'd found aren't ones that work for everyone, but Ben was a sincere man and a gentle and good one, and all those things in combination can work real miracles under the right circumstances.

But the gift he carried home with him was a fragment of the Stone that lived under Green Hill. The Stone itself was evil made real and solid, and that cameo was a seed from the Stone. An evil seed whose roots in due course wrapped themselves around his wife's heart and coaxed her to evil beyond any redemption.

PART
ONE

CHAPTER

ONE

THE STONE *TOUCHED* JIMMY FOR THE FIRST TIME A year later, when he and his father were on the highway, somewhere in the Carolinas (or maybe it was Georgia), hours and hours before they got to the new town. Jimmy Tompkins and his father, Ben, were moving from New Jersey to a town in the Deep South called Green Hill. Most of their furniture and stuff had gone down ahead of them in a big moving van, but there'd been enough that dad'd forgot to pack that at the last minute they'd had to get a U-Haul trailer. Jimmy didn't like being in the car with the trailer behind them—it made it so that he couldn't see anything out the back window, and it did funny things that

made him seasick every time the car went over a bump in
the road.

Jimmy was nine, and moving seemed like a pretty terrible thing to have to do. But staying in New Jersey would
have been lots worse, and he knew it. It'd gotten real bad
in New Jersey since what his mom did last winter.

Jimmy squeezed his eyes shut and shook his head; thinking about his mom made him uncomfortable these days.
He shifted away from the door he was leaning on, half
sleeping, and looked out the windshield at the highway.

It was night out. Black-dark night. The road ahead
looked white and endless underneath the headlights, and
the stars were glorious and brilliant against the blackness
of the sky. They were beautiful, and kind of wonderful,
too; the night wasn't dark enough for very many stars in
the part of New Jersey where they'd always lived.

Jimmy closed his eyes and savored the afterimage of
starlight on the inside of his eyelids. Without even opening
them he bunched up his sweater on the seat beside him
and stretched out so he lay with his head near dad's thigh.
It wasn't very comfortable with the seat belt strapped
across his waist, but it was better than trying to curl up
against the door. Or different, at least; it didn't pull the
same muscles out of shape.

As he started to drift into sleep he fell into something
that must have been a dream . . . but felt nothing like a
dream at all. Jimmy's dreams never seemed that *real* to
him. And when he was dreaming things would happen
because he thought they might, or because he was afraid
they would. But if this was a dream it was as strange and
different and *alien* as the time his dad and mom took him
to an Ethiopian restaurant when he was six. Or even the
hairless dog from China that his Uncle Glenn had, the one
with the big white pimples all over its back.

When the dream first started Jimmy felt as though he
was being watched close and hard by something far away.
With a telescope, maybe. Or maybe the way he'd looked at
the amoebas through the microscope in science class.

In the dream he looked up, trying to see whatever was
watching him. But everything was clouded in bright-
bright light, and it hurt his dream-eyes and made them
blink instead of letting them focus. So he closed his eyes

and curled himself into a ball and tried to pretend he wasn't there to see. That was kind of stupid, he knew. It was like ostriches when they try to hide by burying their heads in the sand. It couldn't work. The world didn't *work* that way.

But after a moment the being-watched feeling went away, and when he opened his eyes the light was gone and his dad was shaking his arm and saying, "Jimmy."

He sat up slowly; his stomach was a little sore from the seat belt. They were pulling into a rest area.

"I've got to stop for a couple of minutes and stretch my legs, Jimmy. Do you want to get up and use the bathroom?"

Jimmy nodded. It always made him feel kind of strange the way dad knew things like that before Jimmy knew them himself. Even though it'd always been that way, even though dad had been that way as long as Jimmy had been alive, it didn't seem *right*. People weren't supposed to know you better than you knew yourself. But he guessed that if it had to be somebody who knew him like that, it was a good thing it was dad.

He really loved his dad.

Dad pulled the car to a stop in one of the long open-ended parking spaces made for trucks, to save them the trouble of backing up. It was trouble if they had to back out of a parking space; the U-Haul trailer didn't want to be steered when it was moving backward. The first morning of the trip, after they'd spent the night in a hotel in Virginia, someone had parked too close in front of them, and it'd taken them most of an hour to get back on the road. Once it'd even looked like the trailer was going to tip over from getting jammed sideways.

Jimmy's father put the car into park and yawned and stretched his arms back against the roof of the car. "You coming, Jim-boy?" he asked. Dad was always making up silly names to call Jimmy. Jimmy didn't much like being called names, but when his dad did it it didn't seem like a bad thing. Jimmy even kind of liked it; it felt, in a strange way, almost like a hug or like when his dad mussed his hair. Comfortable, and kind of warm.

Jimmy shrugged. "I'll be out in a minute, I guess."

Dad smiled and yawned again. "Okay. Give me a holler when you do, all right?"

His father climbed out of the front seat and closed the car door behind him.

When he thought about it for a moment Jimmy realized that he needed to use the bathroom pretty bad, and that he needed to get out of the car and stretch his own legs something awful. But something about the half-dream he'd had was still bothering him, and he needed a moment alone to try to figure out what it was. He fidgeted in the car seat a couple of times and started pulling back and forth on the ashtray under the dash. Dad didn't like him to fidget or play with the car when they were going somewhere. The only times he could really do things like that were moments like this one, when he was alone.

The third time he yanked on the ashtray it came farther out than he meant it to, and a little light came on inside it.

It was empty, and very clean. Cleaner than a car ashtray ever should be. It looked like it hadn't been used in months. Maybe even since last winter, back when his mom had still been with them.

He thought about that for a moment, and he realized that it was probably exactly true. His dad had never smoked, and Jimmy sure didn't, but his mom smoked like a chimney. (That's the way his grandmom always said it: "Anne, you *smoke* like a chimney." Jimmy always thought that was pretty funny.)

Jimmy slammed the ashtray back into the dashboard. He didn't like thinking about his mom. It made him hurt. He gave up on trying to figure out his dream, got out of the car, and closed the door behind him.

He got a better look at the rest area once he was outside. Three streetlights hung over the loop of road that led back to the highway, and the light from them was enough to make it possible to see most of the rest area. Not very well, though. Most of the little park was a big wide swatch of grass that stretched into the woods surrounding the highway. There were a few bushes and a couple of picnic tables and at the far end there was a concrete block building with a porch light where the bathrooms were. At the outside edge the grass faded into trees.

There weren't any other cars in the parking area.

Jimmy didn't see his dad anywhere, which probably meant that he was in the bathroom. But even if dad was that close, Jimmy still felt for just an instant so cut off and alone that he might be the only boy left alive on earth. The parking lot and the rest area, which just a moment ago had been benign and kind of dull, turned sinister and unearthly in just the time it took him to draw a breath. Jimmy shivered. He felt just the way he had when he was younger, when he'd still been afraid of the dark. The muscles along his ribs twisted tight. He felt as though he couldn't breathe; as though some bully were sitting on his chest, pounding on his head.

Out on the highway a car went by, its tires hissing, its engine rumbling. Jimmy wasn't sure why he was afraid. Was it something to do with that dream? He didn't think so. This was the kind of fear he'd always known; it reminded him of the time when he was four when he'd jumped nearly out of his skin from seeing some horrible thing that turned out to be his shadow.

But even if the fears were familiar, they were still real. Maybe they were stupid, maybe there was really nothing to be afraid of, but just thinking that didn't stop him from being scared.

"Dad?" He said it loud enough to make the sound carry across the rest stop. There wasn't any answer.

Dad had to be in the bathroom. Jimmy set off running toward it, as hard and fast as he could. Even though he was running, the distance seemed much longer than it'd looked. He wanted to be wherever his dad was *now*, but the distance seemed to drag on forever, and he still couldn't breathe, and his legs didn't seem to want to move right at all.

When he finally got to the bathroom the door wouldn't open. For a moment he thought it was locked, but it was just that the handle was jammed; when he pressed on it and twisted it to the left the door swung free.

"Dad?" No answer. A roach crawled across the mirror that hung over the sink. "Dad, are you in here?"

An image bloomed in Jimmy's mind: his father, beaten and robbed and left half-dead in one of the stalls. Bleeding, probably, and all broken inside. For a moment the person in the image became his mother, but he drove that thought away. The thought of his father, hurt, turned his fear of the night and the emptiness into panic and anger. He slammed open first the door of one stall and then the other, but his father wasn't in either one, hurt or otherwise. His breath caught and his heart clutched, and suddenly the anger was fear again, pure white terror. It was just his own plain stupid fear of his own shadow, but he really was alone, and his dad was *gone.* He was alone and it was night and not just *alone* but alone for miles and miles, no one anywhere in any direction, and God knew what someone would do when they found him and—

—his *mom*—

—he opened his mouth and screamed *"Dad-dy!"* and when the word was done he just kept screaming, so high and shrill that his throat stung, *burned* from the sound.

"Jimmy?"

His dad. It was his dad, standing in the doorway. His scream stopped with a shudder and his knees collapsed out from under him. He hit his head when he fell on the floor, and dad picked him up and held him in his arms just like he was a baby.

"Jimmy? What's the matter, Jimmy? Are you hurt?" There were tears all over dad's face. He looked pale as a ghost underneath the fluorescent light of the bathroom.

Jimmy shook his head, which made his head feel a little dizzy from where he'd hit it on the floor. "I couldn't find you, and I thought you were gone or that something happened to you, and—and . . ."

His dad looked like something hurt him deep deep down. "It's okay, Jimmy. You don't have to say that. You don't have to think that. You don't ever have to think that."

Dad hugged him so hard and long that it hurt, but Jimmy didn't want it to stop. He didn't want it ever to stop.

After a few minutes dad saw that Jimmy was mostly okay, and he made that face that always made Jimmy giggle. Dad set Jimmy down, and they both went into toilet stalls and used them.

"Where were you, dad? I didn't see you anywhere," Jimmy said loudly, so that his dad could hear him over the partition.

"Over by the trees. You should see them. The pine cones

are huge." Dad flushed his toilet and waited a moment for the sound to finish. "You didn't hear me when I answered you, I guess. When I saw you running I thought you had to go to the bathroom pretty bad. I didn't realize something was wrong."

Jimmy flushed his own toilet, zipped up, opened the stall door. Dad was already waiting for him.

"Silly, huh?"

Dad shook his head. "Being scared isn't silly. After what you've been through it's a miracle you can ever look at your own shadow without being scared out of your wits."

Jimmy frowned and nodded.

Dad reached over and mussed Jimmy's hair and put his arm over his shoulder. "C'mon," he said, "we need to get back on the road."

CHAPTER

TWO

JIMMY LEFT THE SEAT BELT OFF THIS TIME WHEN HE curled up to lie on the seat of the car, and his sleep was deeper and more comfortable.

But even if it was deeper sleep, it wasn't perfect, or deep enough to be impenetrable. A couple of hours before the sun came up he felt the touch of the thing that had watched him before. He felt it probe him, search him with tentacles made out of ghost. As it pried through his memories Jimmy saw images from the memories it touched flash through his mind like too many snapshots all at once.

Then he saw his mother with the wicked-looking carving knife in her hand and her eyes all crazy-wild and bloodshot. Hanging from a chain around her neck was the pendant dad had brought back for her last summer, so black and dark that it seemed to swallow all the light that touched it. She looked as real as she had on that night last winter, and he thought—no, he *knew*, his heart *knew* that he was going to die.

The image faded. Time seemed to run backward, away from the vision of his mother and the knife, until it paused and settled on the evening before.

It was a Thursday, and tomorrow was the start of a long weekend. His father had just left for a three-day conference, some kind of a seminar or something for schoolteachers.

Jimmy tried to force his mind away from the memory. He didn't want to think about that weekend. He didn't want to have to *ever* think about that weekend again.

But it wasn't a memory. Memories were like ghosts of things that had happened; they were real, but they weren't as substantial, and there were always things you forgot. This was real, as real as it'd been when it happened.

And it wasn't anything he could control. He felt as though someone had tied him up and forced his head down into a sink of water, tried to drown him. But instead of hands wrapped around his throat and skull, there were black tentacles made of evil wrapped around his heart and mind, and instead of drowning in water he was suffocating in his own past.

Jimmy was in the backyard, playing with little green plastic army men in the sandbox he didn't use much anymore, when his mom got home. It was January and it was cold, very cold. Jimmy had bundled himself up in a heavy jacket and his long wool scarf before he went out, but even so he felt the chill. It was about seven o'clock; the sun was down three hours ago, but there was a light over the back patio, and that was plenty to see by.

He knew she was home as soon as she got in, just like he always did, because she always slammed the door behind her. Slammed it *loud*. Loud enough to hear half a block away. When he heard the slam he gathered up his army men, put them in their plastic bag, and hurried toward the front door.

Mom didn't like him being outside after dark, but if he went in when she first got home she wouldn't notice; she always made a beeline for the liquor cabinet when she got home. For the fifteen or twenty minutes it took her to put her second drink down she didn't see or hear much of anything else.

Jimmy had to go around to the front door because he lost his key a couple of weeks ago. He could have had another if he'd asked his dad for one. But dad would be disappointed in Jimmy when he found out he'd lost the key. Mom and dad had had a big argument over whether or not to give Jimmy his own key; Mom had told dad that Jimmy would lose it.

Disappointing dad always made Jimmy depressed. Dad never did anything about it, but it still made Jimmy feel awful.

He almost suspected that mom had taken the key out of his pants pocket one night while he was sleeping, just to prove her point. It was possible. In a stupid way kind of likely. But it was crazy. Even considering how crazy mom had been acting lately it was hard to believe she'd do anything *that* weird.

Both of the outside doors to the house had the kind of deadbolts that open with a key from both sides. Jimmy couldn't even get out of the house without a key. But dad kept an emergency key on a hook in the wall not far from the front door, and when dad was home in the daytime he always kept the front door unlocked. Dad always got home from the school where he taught before Jimmy got home from his school, so Jimmy hardly ever really *needed* a key.

After dad left for his convention Jimmy had gone out to the backyard, and he'd taken the wall key with him.

When he opened the door he could smell right away that mom had been drinking all afternoon. That was bad. He closed the front door behind him quietly as he could, hung the key back on the wall, and started to tiptoe toward his room. He didn't like being alone with her in the house. He wanted to stay away from her.

But mom came out of the kitchen while he was still in the living room. He thought for a moment that she was going to watch television, but then she turned, shouldered him aside, and started toward her room.

"Stay out of my way, Jimmy." She said it mean, like he was a bug she'd found in the kitchen.

When mom was drinking it was trouble. She was a mean drunk. A *nasty* one. She always drank when dad went away; she missed him and that made her sad. (That never made sense to Jimmy. After all, being drunk never made her happy. But that's why dad said it was, and dad knew a lot about these things.) Lately mom seemed to drink all the time, too. Not that dad was always gone. Dad was around more than mom was. He taught school for a living, and since the school where he taught was only a few blocks away and Jimmy went to a school three towns away and had to take a bus to get home, dad was almost always home in the afternoon before Jimmy was. When he had a lot of work to do he took it home with him.

Dad said the reason mom was drunk all the time lately was because things were going so badly at work. Mom worked in a big tall building in New York City, and between the bus that took two hours to get home and the way she always had to work late, sometimes it seemed like she was never home. She almost always came home smelling like she'd had too much to drink, and so tired she was asleep before she'd been home half an hour.

Dad said mom had a drinking problem. Lately they'd been fighting about that a lot; dad kept saying that she needed to get help for it, and mom kept saying that he was out of his mind and should mind his own business. Usually she cursed when she said that.

Dad had looked a little worried when he talked to Jimmy before he went out of town. Before mom got home that night he said, "Jimmy, if your mom starts drinking while I'm gone you just stay out of her way. Do you understand me?"

Jimmy bit his lower lip and nodded. Dad had frowned and hugged him and mussed his hair. Dad knew how mean mom was to Jimmy sometimes—especially when she'd been drinking. Once she'd even got so drunk she'd told him she wished he'd never been born. A lot of other times she'd hit him, and the one time dad had seen her do that there'd been a terrible fight—a fight so bad that they were still screaming that night when Jimmy fell asleep.

Jimmy spent the night that his dad left hiding in his

bedroom. Twice during the night he woke up and went out to use the bathroom, and both times his mother was sitting in front of the television smoking cigarettes, with headphones over her ears. The first time there was a half-empty whiskey bottle beside her; she took a drink from it as he passed.

The second time it was long after midnight; there was a sound somewhere, and Jimmy woke up needing to pee. Outside his window there was a full moon, and it was snowing, and the night was full of silver-shining snow-flakes. When he passed the living room his mother was still awake, sitting in front of the television. The ashtray was overflowing. There were two more liquor bottles on the table beside her—one of them was vodka and the other one he couldn't read from across the room. All but the vodka bottle were empty, and even that one looked like it was almost gone.

Jimmy woke up earlier than he should have the next morning. The sun wasn't even close to rising yet; he looked at the glowing clock on his dresser and saw that it was a few minutes after five.

Mom was always her worst in the early morning. Waking up didn't agree with her. If there was any time to stay clear of her, this was it. But he'd been in his room too long already; if he stayed in it any longer, he thought, he'd go crazy himself.

He tiptoed out of his bedroom and down the stairs, heading for the door in the kitchen that led to the basement. His dog, Duke, was in the basement; it was the only place his mom would let Jimmy keep him. Duke was half German shepherd and half poodle, and he was strange-tempered and sometimes a little surly. He didn't usually care much whether or not anyone gave him any attention, except when it was time to eat or go outside. Even then he wasn't gracious. He'd bark—his bark was harsh and mean—until someone did for him what he wanted, and then he'd go on about his business as though no one else existed. He was skittish, too, and he got very upset by loud noises and violence. But he was a dog, and dogs by nature are important to boys. Jimmy spent a lot of time with Duke, especially when there wasn't much else to do.

As Jimmy passed the living room he saw that his mom

was still awake, still watching television. There was another bottle on the end table, and two of the others had fallen on the carpet. The ashtray was spilled all over the rug, too.

The basement door hung a little out of skew, and it always made a loud creaking sound when he opened it. He pulled it open as quietly as he could, but it still screeched horribly, and he was sure his mom would come storming into the kitchen, screaming that she wanted to "know what the hell's going on in here." He closed the door behind him and hurried down the stairs that led into the basement.

He turned on the light switch when he got to the bottom of the stairs. Duke looked up at him; Jimmy knew the dog well enough to recognize the glance even though nothing moved but the dog's eyes.

"Hey ya, Duke," he said. The dog ignored him. Jimmy sat on the bottom step and waited for the dog to wonder what he was up to. When he thought he had Duke's attention, he snapped his fingers and pointed at the ground by his feet. "Come here, boy." He said it sternly, seriously.

It was a trick he'd learned from his dad. It worked more often than it didn't, and this time it did. The dog stood up —slowly, as though it was a terrible burden to lift himself from the cold concrete floor—and padded over to Jimmy. He set himself down not quite out of reach, so that Jimmy had to bend himself into a funny position when he reached down to scratch the dog behind the ears.

After a bit Duke began to pant deep and low. Jimmy was pretty sure that for all that the dog tried to put himself above it all he really enjoyed attention. Maybe he even needed it—after that week when he had to do the book report, when he didn't have any time to spend with the dog, Duke had been real happy to see him, even though dad had filled his food bowl every night.

Jimmy looked over into the corner of the basement and saw that Duke's water bowl was empty. That wasn't too bad; there was a sink down here in the basement. It'd only take a minute to fill. Then he noticed that the food bowl was just about empty, too.

That was trouble. Dad kept the big sack of dry dog chow upstairs in the kitchen pantry, and the wall between the pantry and the living room was so thin that rummaging around in there always made a muffled racket in the living room.

Mom was in the living room, and it was morning and she'd been up all night drinking. Drinking made mom mean, and mornings made her meaner. Not getting any sleep made her meanest of all. The only thing that was worse than that was when she didn't have cigarettes, but that hardly ever happened.

Jimmy didn't want to think about what she would be like this morning. He didn't want to go upstairs, not until mom passed out for the day. He was afraid. He wanted to stay down here until things were all right upstairs, even if that meant being down here all day.

But it wasn't right to leave the dog without food. Jimmy couldn't do that, even if there *was* trouble upstairs. So he tousled Duke's ears one last time, and patted the dog's head. He stood, got the food bowl, and started up the stairs.

He climbed up them as quietly and quickly as he could, then opened the door gently, slowly, watching the kitchen carefully as he did.

But careful as he was, he couldn't have seen his mother on the far side of the door, carrying a big steel platter with the leftover end of Tuesday's baked ham. The carving knife was still tucked into one side of the platter, its steel blade jammed underneath the slab of meat, just as it had been Tuesday night when she'd tossed the ham into the refrigerator with the rest of the leftovers.

She didn't hear Jimmy open the door, and since she was looking backward at the living room and the TV, she didn't see him, either. She turned her head just in time to walk face-first into the door.

The serving platter jammed into her gut; the carving knife flew loose and stabbed her in the breast, though it didn't break the skin and it only barely ripped the housecoat she was wearing.

Jimmy couldn't see through the door—he didn't know exactly what'd happened. But he heard his mother's grunt when the platter forced the air out of her, and he knew he was in some awful kind of trouble.

He backed a step down the stairs, and thought for a

moment about running. There wasn't any use in it, though: the only direction he could go was down into the basement, and there was no way in or out from there unless you were outside and had a key for the padlock.

As his mother righted herself the basement door swung open on its own, and Jimmy saw her fumble with the ham and the platter and the knife, juggling them, trying to make them all fall back into her hands.

It didn't work. The ham went rolling across the kitchen floor, finally wedging itself in the tiny space underneath the kitchen cabinets. The platter fell straight down, and slammed edge-first into the toes of her left foot.

But the knife, the knife she managed to catch, but by the *wrong* end, by the blade with her right hand. She cut her fingers wide open catching it, and when she saw her own blood all over the place she screamed.

That was when she saw Jimmy on the stairway.

"Jackass!" she screamed. "You little *jackass*. This is *your* fault." She flipped the blade so that the handle landed in her palm; blood spattered across the kitchen wall. One tiny red droplet landed on the black-black pendant, and Jimmy could have sworn he saw it melt into the stone and disappear. He realized then that even if she was drunk she had all the coordination she needed, at least if she concentrated. He was in trouble. "Didn't I tell you to stay the *hell* out of my way?"

She raised the knife up over her head, like they do with swords in the movies. For a moment Jimmy couldn't believe that she was really going to do anything with it. Even blind drunk **mom** wouldn't get that crazy. But then he looked in her eye and he knew that she was, she really *was* that crazy, and he knew that he was going to die, knew it as sure as he knew that the sun was about to rise.

He ducked down and back, out of the way, and the impossible carving knife swung down, right across the stairway where his head had been, and jammed itself into the wooden railing.

Jimmy could feel the evil thing that had forced him into the dream gloating, drinking in his fear of his mother—and

Jimmy's fear of itself. Jimmy tried to twist himself away from it, tried to hide himself from it as he had before.

But it wasn't any use. The thing had wrapped itself deep around and into him. It *had* him. It pushed him back down into the memory-dream, and held him there.

CHAPTER

THREE

BEN TOMPKINS WASN'T A MAN WHO APPRECIATED driving, not when it meant *getting* somewhere. It wasn't that he minded a drive through the countryside; there were times—like last summer—when he needed the kind of quiet an aimless drive could bring him. But that was different. It was slow, and easy, and relaxing. What he didn't enjoy was pushing himself to get from one place to another.

It certainly wasn't that he couldn't appreciate strange sights or fresh surroundings—he enjoyed a vacation as much as anyone. But every year around vacation time he'd find his backbrain working on silly schemes for *being* in exotic cities—really *being* there, not just reading about the experience or watching a travelogue—without ever having to *get* there. It was a silly habit, born out of a pointless aversion, and he knew it. Sometimes it even embarrassed him. Ben kept his goofy ideas to himself, and lived every summer day of his life grateful to God that no one could read his mind.

There were times, though, when his dislike of travel got out of hand. Times like when they'd gone to England for a week, and he made reservations for himself and Jimmy and Anne on a plane that left Newark airport at ten in the evening, thinking they could sleep through the flight instead of sitting through it. It hadn't worked out that way. The air was turbulent over the Atlantic that night, and the flight was rough, and the cabin pressure shifted far enough to make his ears ache every few minutes. None of them slept at all that night, and it threw them far enough off their stride that they had spent the week walking like zombies through the streets of London.

This all-night drive was another time his aversion to travel had got him in too deep. They'd been somewhere in North Carolina at seven p.m., and he'd begun looking for a hotel with rooms to let, when he'd done a little math in his head and realized that if he drove through the night he could make it to Green Hill by early morning. It'd seemed like a great idea then, but by two in the morning, when he'd pulled into the rest area where Jimmy had the scare, Ben had deep regrets. He was *tired.* And he found himself really hating the drive, instead of being impatient with it.

He'd even begun to find himself regretting the whole trip. Not that there would have been any practical way to avoid it. It was true, he could have paid someone most of a month's pay to drive the car for him. That was what the car-moving services charged. He couldn't see paying that price. It probably wouldn't have set him back that much if he'd sold the car back in Jersey and bought a new one down South. But even if it was practical and economical, the idea was ridiculous. Besides, the Chevy was reliable and in good repair; it worked. The one thing you always knew about a used car was that there was some good reason that someone didn't want it anymore.

So he drove, and yawned, and did what he could to

appreciate his circumstances. Even if the drive was too long, it was gorgeous. The night was jet black and beautiful, the bright-starred sky so dark and still that there was a certain brilliance about its blackness. Ben smiled, sighed, and settled back into the car seat.

Life was good.

On the seat beside him, Jimmy sobbed once in his sleep, and then he was quiet. It was three a.m., two hours or so before sunrise.

Ben worried about Jimmy a lot. He worried about the way he slept so badly, worried about the way he could scream in stark, raving terror at the sight of his own shadow. But what could Ben do? For a month or two after the weekend Anne went berserk Jimmy had seen a psychologist. The boy hadn't been real happy or comfortable with the doctor the people at the hospital had found for him, and the idea of talking to a stranger about the things that bothered him didn't set well with him. He always came back from his appointments looking haunted, with his skin pale white and his eyes all wild and afraid. Finally he'd asked Ben if he could stop going to therapy, and Ben had told him that it had to be his own decision.

It *was* a thing he had to decide for himself, too: Ben always thought that there were things a person had to be responsible for himself—and some of those things were so fundamental that even the fact that the boy was only nine years old didn't make it anybody else's business. Not even his father's.

Jimmy was a lot of the reason Ben was in so much of a hurry to move. It wasn't prudent to make decisions like this one without stopping to consider them for a week or two—or even more. He certainly should have checked things out more thoroughly. But he'd been thinking about moving himself and Jimmy out of the state for a while, and then he'd seen the ad that the Green Hill school board had placed in one of the journals. And he'd remembered the place, remembered spending half an hour eating and sipping coffee in that perfect café, where no one had anything to prove. A day and a half later he'd been on a plane, heading toward an interview. When he got to the town he'd found the café boarded up, but the people were just as he'd remembered them—gentle and easy and perfect.

And the situation in New Jersey was bad. Worse than bad. What Anne had done had been in all the papers for months. Even now it was a story for them every week or two. The local TV news had spent twenty minutes telling the story one Thursday evening. Jimmy needed to be left *alone;* his heart and spirit needed time to heal over. What he didn't need was the kids—and even the teachers—at school telling tales about him every time his back was turned. He didn't need people gaping at him when Ben took him to the mall to shop for sneakers. He didn't need the neighbors' children asking him questions about his mother every time he went outside to play.

Ben had a good eye for character, and he'd never met people as generous and decent, people as . . . *good* as the ones he'd met in the three days he'd spent in Green Hill. There wasn't, he thought, an evil bone among them.

Sure, the couple of kids he'd met weren't anyone he'd want Jimmy bringing home for dinner. But they'd been summer-school kids, and summer-school kids are a mean bunch.

Ben thought of Anne for a moment, and for just an instant he wanted to cry. Even after what she'd done to Jimmy, he loved her. She was his wife; he'd always love her. He didn't know if he'd ever be able to let himself allow her into his life again—or into Jimmy's life—but that didn't mean he didn't love her. He couldn't stop loving her any more than he could stop being Ben Tompkins. He couldn't stop loving her any more than he could stop loving Jimmy.

Ben *needed* to love Anne. But he knew her. She wasn't a saint. Her heart had never been generous; she was always one who'd look for someone else to blame for her problems. Blaming other people, Ben thought, was the seed that had ultimately grown into her insanity. Her career had been on a fast track before they'd had Jimmy. Then, while she was pregnant, the company had passed her over for a promotion. The company where she worked was the kind of place where you put in ten hours a day just to keep people from prying through your desk—the kind of place where no one survived without conniving, back stabbing, and maliciousness.

Things had moved slowly for her since Jimmy'd been born. She'd never forgiven the boy for that.

But even if she had her faults, Anne was, underneath them, a decent human being. The problem was that her character, her backbone, hadn't been as strong as her circumstances were destructive.

And the drinking, too. Maybe the drinking did more to destroy her than the circumstances. When Anne drank, the alcohol stole away all the good and decent things inside her, and left in their place *mean* things—things that were truly evil. That had been even more true this last year, as the drinking had gotten to its worst.

She'd had a bad temper long before she started drinking. But when she was sober and angry she'd fume and boil quietly for ten or twenty minutes, and then you'd talk to her half an hour later and she wouldn't even remember she was mad.

When she was angry and drunk—and when she was drinking she was almost always in a rage—she'd *do* things. One night she got herself all worked up and furious with him while she was on the bus coming home from work— got herself so angry that by the time she got home she wasn't even speaking to him. She'd walked in the front door, slammed it closed behind her, stomped into the kitchen and poured herself a drink. Ben was in the living room, reading the afternoon paper. He didn't say hello; he could tell already that she was spoiling for a fight, and "Hello," might have been excuse enough for her to start it. Ben rattled the paper a little to let her know he was there, but he didn't say anything.

Anne walked into the living room and set her iced vodka on an end table. She walked up to Ben, and before he knew what she was doing she'd slammed her bony-wiry fist into his face.

Ben's head swam. His nose felt soft and numb inside; a trickle of blood welled up in one of his sinuses. She hauled back her fist to hit him again, but he knew it was coming this time, and he caught her wrist before the punch got near him. He was in good shape, and he was much stronger than she was; her arm stopped as if it had frozen.

"No," he said.

She tried to pull her arm away from him, but he didn't let go. He thought she might try to hit him again if he did. She yanked hard, and started to struggle, but the only result was that she wrenched her shoulder. She hurt the shoulder pretty bad, too. Bad enough that her expression went from furious to scared, and she was suddenly very still.

"You don't hit me, Anne," Ben said. He let go of her arm very gently, careful not to jolt it and twist her shoulder further out of shape.

Anne nodded, and looked down at the floor. She walked back to the end table and picked up her drink and sipped at it. "I'm sorry, Ben," she said.

She'd never laid a hand on him again.

A few weeks later, though, he'd seen her hit Jimmy. Not just slap his hand or swat his rear end, but really *hit* him. They'd had a horrible fight that evening, one that had lasted all night. When it was over he thought that that was the end of it; he'd honestly believed that she meant it when she said she knew she was wrong. And maybe she did. But after the weekend when she'd gone crazy, Ben found out that she'd been beating Jimmy for months. Ben felt a lot of guilt about that. He blamed himself for not knowing about it, for not *doing* something about it.

A year ago, when drinking was becoming something she did all the time, something important inside Anne had broken. It'd turned her bad. Maybe some day it would heal over and she could be with them again and loving her would be good again. But sometimes when Ben was awake in bed at night, staring at the pattern in the ceiling and waiting to fall asleep and feeling cold and mournful and alone, he didn't think that he could ever forgive her.

By half past three the all-night drive had begun to drag on Ben in a serious way, and when he came to a weigh station he pulled in to rest his eyes. He wanted to dream about Anne—the *other* Anne. The decent, human Anne; the one with the heart as complex, beautiful, and flawed as anyone else's. As he drifted into sleep he tried to picture Anne the way she was the day they married, or back in the first few months he'd known her.

But even though he tried he couldn't see that Anne anymore. Her image had melted away from his memory. Ben's sleep was deep, without dreams—warm and dark and silent.

He woke at six, when a truck pulled into the weigh

station, saw the booth unattended, and roared out. The
sleep had helped. He didn't feel refreshed, exactly, but the
rest had left him feeling . . . *alive*. Awake and *alive*. The
colors out on the highway seemed richer and deeper than
by rights they ought to be. The taste of the air in his sinuses
was crisp and clean and clear. The sound of the traffic was
warm and vibrant.

He started the car and pulled out onto the road.

Just before he pulled off the interstate onto a two-lane
feeder highway, Jimmy began to make small, frightened
sounds in his sleep. Ben looked over at his son. The dim
glow from the dashboard caught Jimmy's face at just the
worst possible angle, and Ben saw the scars that covered
the boy's cheeks and forehead like a spiderweb. The doctors had done a good job on Jimmy's face; they didn't show
in his skin tone at all. Under ordinary light you couldn't see
them unless you knew to look for them—sometimes not
even then. But the texture of the scars was ever so slightly
different from the skin around them, and in the dim light
they'd sometimes cast a sheen. Ben thought about waking
him, trying to bring him up and out of whatever nightmare had its claws in him. He didn't think that was really
wise, though. Jimmy had to work his way through it; waking him would probably only make things worse.

But at seven the boy screamed in his sleep, and Ben
didn't have the heart to keep restraining himself. Even if it
was wrong, he put his hand on Jimmy's shoulder and
gently, carefully shook him till he woke.

CHAPTER
FOUR

THE BLACK, ALIEN THING IN HIS MIND PUSHED JIMMY back down into his past. He was lying on the basement stairs, and his mother wanted to kill him. She had a carving knife—a long, wicked carving knife—and if he hadn't ducked a moment ago the knife would be deep into the flesh and veins of his neck, tangled in the wiry nerves and vertebrae of his spine.

He might have had a chance—he could have lived a few moments longer, anyway—if he'd got up, got out of her way, and *moved*. But part of him was paralyzed with fear, and part of him had lost spirit and despaired. What was left believed his mother was right because she was his mother, and the only thing it wanted to do was be still enough to take its punishment and still be proud.

Downstairs Duke growled and barked, fierce and bloody sounding, like he was some feral thing. As Jimmy's mother pulled the knife free from the railing it'd dug into when it missed his neck and raised it over her head, the dog came charging up the wooden stairway. He trampled right over Jimmy, and when he launched himself at mom's neck his hind feet pushed off from Jimmy's back, and the dog's claws cut deep into him.

Mom brought her bloody knife arm down to protect her face and throat, and the dog's jaws clamped down on it like a vice. Mom pounded Duke's head again and again with her free hand, while the dog pulled back and forth on the meat of her arm, pulling and jerking just the way he did when he was ripping a rag to shreds—just the way a cat jerks a mouse when it breaks the thing's neck.

The sixth time mom hit Duke she caught him in the spot where the lower jaw meets the skull. Something in his jaw hinge popped loose, and Duke lost his grip on her.

Mom yanked her arm free and kicked the dog with her good foot, *hard*, right in the breastbone. Duke went tumbling head over heels down the stairs. He landed on the last step with his back all twisted funny and his head cocked too far sideways.

"Goddamn dog," Jimmy's mother said. Downstairs, it hit Duke that his back was broken, and he started screaming. The sound was ear-piercing, shrill with agony. Hearing it, Jimmy almost thought he could see the death that Duke was looking in the eye, and he could feel the dog's fear, his unreadiness to die.

Mom heard the sound, too, and it made her eyes bug out with fear and rage. "God*damn* dog," she said, and she started stomping down the stairs. When she got to Jimmy she kept going as though she didn't see him. Her left foot—the one the platter had smashed—came down hard on his back. She stumbled, but even then she didn't seem to notice him; she caught her balance with her bleeding knife hand and continued down the stairs.

When Duke saw her and the knife his scream turned into a wail, sad and low like Grandma Tompkins crying all

day before grandpa's funeral, or like the dirge they'd
played when they lowered his body into the ground.

The knife came down, through Duke's neck, under his
collarbone, and into his heart. The wail turned into a gur-
gling hiss, and then it stopped, and Duke was dead.

But mom didn't stop. She kept stabbing and hacking
even after Duke looked like nothing but blood and fur and
pulp. Bits of grue spattered on the walls.

Jimmy pictured himself that way: flecks of gore spattered on the stairs and the walls and the railing, and he
wanted to puke but there was nothing in his stomach to
bring up.

Suddenly he found the will to run. He stood up and
hobbled up the top steps. His mother didn't seem to notice; she was too engrossed in mutilating what was left of
Duke to see anything else.

Jimmy headed for the front door. The thing to do was to
get out and get away and call the police or somebody or
*something. Somebody who'd take care of him, take his
mother away.*

But when he got to the front door the deadbolt was
locked and his mother had taken the key from the hook in
the wall by the coat rack where it always hung.

There *was* no way out; there wasn't a key hook screwed
into the wall by the back door—dad kept saying he was
going to put one up, but he never got around to it. The
windows were protected by burglar-alarm tape; if you
wanted to open one you had to go to the control box in the
basement and turn off the alarm. If he set off that alarm
mom would be all over him before he could finish climbing
out the window.

Jimmy wanted to scream, but he knew that he didn't
dare, because if he did she'd hear him and—

"Jimmy?"

A hand on his shoulder, shaking him out of the dream
that wasn't a dream—pulling him back into the car, where
the morning sun was shining in through the rear window,
and the morning news was playing on the radio.

It was dad's hand. Jimmy was lying curled up on the
front seat beside his dad.

Even though it was a cool summer morning and air was

gusting all around from dad's open window, Jimmy was soaked with sweat. Jimmy never sweated in his sleep, no matter how hot it was.

"Jimmy, are you okay?" dad asked. "You were screaming in your sleep."

Jimmy rubbed his eyes. "Bad dream," he said. His voice was heavy and slow, not yet awake.

Dad nodded and frowned. Jimmy didn't have to say what he was dreaming. Dad knew. Dad always knew.

They drove for a long while without talking. They were on a two-lane highway paved with black asphalt; pine woods crowded both shoulders of the road.

Once they passed a field covered with an eerie-looking broad-leafed thick-stemmed vine. When Jimmy asked what it was, dad told him it was kudzu. Jimmy felt a chill. The kudzu had an evil look about it, and it seemed to strangle out every other living thing in the field. Even its name sounded evil.

Five miles or so after they'd passed the kudzu field, dad said, "We should be in Green Hill soon. You all ready for the new town?"

Jimmy smiled and said he was. But the truth was that he was very wary of the place. He had an awful foreboding about Green Hill, even though he'd never seen the place.

Dad had been there. He'd gone down three weeks ago for an interview—there was an opening for a teacher at the school. Dad had read about it in one of his teachers' magazines. While he was in Green Hill for the interview he'd fallen in love with it; the people were wonderful, he said. When they offered him the job he didn't even think twice about it. He'd rented the house and made the arrangements before he'd come home to New Jersey.

They rounded a bend in the highway, and suddenly the trees were so thick on either side of the road that their branches met to form a deep-green canopy overhead. Then the road took another turn, and the trees were gone. In front of them was a low grassy hill. It wasn't large—maybe a mile across—but it was striking. It had presence.

And Jimmy recognized it, too—it was the same hill that had been carved into his mother's pendant. He'd have recognized it anywhere.

Jimmy could see at least two dozen houses scattered

across the hill, and there were probably at least that many on the far side of the hill, too.

"That's Green Hill? Where we're moving?" he asked. Dad had told him a lot about the town; this looked like what he'd described.

Don't you recognize that hill? he wanted to ask dad. But he couldn't. The whole idea was just too crazy, like something his psychologist might have thought up.

Dad looked over at Jimmy and smiled. He made one of his weird faces and put on one of his funny voices, and he said, "It is indeed."

Jimmy couldn't help himself; in spite of his uneasiness, he started laughing. Some of those voices dad did got him every time.

"Don't make me laugh," Jimmy said. "I was asking you a question." He couldn't stop laughing while he said it, mostly because dad was looking at him real funny.

"So ask." The goofy voice again, even thicker. And dad was still staring at him all cross-eyed, and not watching the road at all.

Jimmy screeched.

"Dad! The road—you're going to hit that truck!"

Dad's eyes went wide with panic. He turned his head back toward the road; his hands jerked on the steering wheel—

There wasn't any truck. They were perfectly in their lane, and there wasn't another car for miles.

"Tricked you good that time," Jimmy said.

"Turkey." Dad reached over and mussed his hair and gave him a one-arm hug.

The highway they were on ran right through the town, straight up the hill and over it. Just after the crest of the hill dad turned left onto a road that led past half a dozen houses and finally came to a dead end in front of the house they'd rented.

It was a two-storey house, painted white. The grass in the front yard was well kept up, but the yard wasn't very large. Twenty feet or so from the side of the house the carefully trimmed grass gave way to a thorny tangle of raspberry and blackberry bushes.

When they got inside everything was a mess—there

were moving boxes piled to the ceiling in the living room. Furniture was everywhere, most of it standing on end.

"Looks like the movers got here ahead of us," dad said.

Jimmy found himself staring at the clutter in amazement; the whole place looked like one of those paintings by . . . Escher? He thought it was Escher. Or maybe it was like something from that book of Rube Goldberg stuff dad liked to keep on the coffee table.

Dad's bed stood on end, leaning against the wall in the den. He tipped it, then lowered it till it lay flat on the floor.

"I've got to get some sleep, Jimmy," he said. "Go outside if you want, but don't go too far. Okay?"

"Sure." Jimmy had the book he'd been reading on the trip down. He was tired, too, tired enough to think about curling up beside dad and going back to sleep. But he was still wary of dreaming. Both of the last two times he'd fallen asleep he'd had those weird nightmares.

When dad sat down on the mattress and began to take off his shoes, Jimmy went out to the car to get his book.

He opened the front door and saw a boy holding a big bowl, picking blackberries in the briar to the left of the house. He started to say hello, but something caught in his throat and stopped him.

He looked the boy in the eye, and he saw two things. The first was the shadow of the thing that had forced its way into his dreams last night.

The shadow of the living Stone beneath Green Hill.

The second was evil. Not simple evil—not the evil that ordinary people live with from day to day, not the kind that you suffer or commit or overcome, and put behind you.

No.

What he saw in the boy's eyes was the pure, absorbing kind of evil; the kind so powerful and true that it covers over every other fact about a person. What he saw in the boy's eyes was the same wild evil light that sparkled in his mother's eyes just before she killed Duke.

The boy smiled at Jimmy—smiled exactly the way Jimmy had always imagined a cannibal would smile just before it ate him. A long pause, and then the boy began to say something—

A dog barked somewhere. The boy turned and looked to

see which direction the bark had come from. He almost looked afraid.

Then he turned, started to run.

Jimmy wanted to call out after him. He was angry; the boy had all but threatened him. But the boy was already gone, vanished into the briar.

CHAPTER

FIVE

JIMMY SPENT MOST OF THE MORNING AND THE EARLY part of the afternoon reading his book—a hardback with a shiny cover, part of a series he really liked. The books were about three teenagers who kept getting involved in mysteries, and always ended up figuring things out before the police did. The best thing about the teenagers, though, was the underground hideout they had. The hideout was full of really neat gadgets that the brainy-nerdy one spent a lot of time making.

Jimmy wanted a hideout like that. He really loved the idea of scary caves and underground passages. He'd never seen one, but he loved rocks and dirt and digging in the ground. And he liked exploring.

He'd got dad to buy the book for him at the mall, because they were going on a trip and Jimmy had to have something to read. When he bought books the money came from his own allowance, so usually he either went to the library or bought paperbacks. This series only came out in hardcover, and the library never had it. When dad offered to buy him a book for the trip he knew what he wanted. He'd read the fifth book in the series the week after he got it for Christmas, and the sixth one had reached the bookstore in March.

At two o'clock, just at the scariest part of the book—the three teenagers had just fallen into the clutches of the villain—the doorbell rang. Jimmy nearly jumped out of his skin.

Dad groaned in his sleep.

"Somebody's at the front door, dad. Do you want me to answer it?" Dad always slept very lightly; all you had to do to wake him up was talk to him.

Dad blinked a couple of times. "Door?" he asked. He sat half-way up, leaned on one elbow.

"Yeah, the doorbell rang. Should I get it?"

He rubbed the sleep out of his eyes. "Uh. Yeah. I'll be up in a second."

When Jimmy opened the door he saw three people waiting outside. Two of them were adults; a man and a woman. They stood close enough to each other that Jimmy thought they were married, though he wasn't sure.

The third was a girl, maybe ten years old, maybe eleven. The woman had a hand on the girl's shoulder. Her husband held a big casserole dish.

Jimmy's father came walking up to the door from the living room—limping with both legs, the way he always did when he woke up in the morning.

"Hullo," dad said, "what can I do for you?" His voice was friendly, even curious. That was unusual—dad wasn't generally very happy to see people who came to the door when they woke him up.

The woman smiled. The expression looked *weird* on her. Not nasty or vicious or mean, just . . . *weird.* The smile was even pleasant in a strange, unnatural way.

"I'm Janet Anderson," the woman said, still smiling. "These are my husband, George, and our daughter, Roberta. We heard you were moving to Green Hill, and we wanted to stop by and welcome you to town. George, you've got the tuna casserole, don't you?" She looked back at her husband, took the ceramic dish from his hands, and held it out. Jimmy took it from her. "We thought you might be too tired to cook after your drive, so we brought your supper, too."

For a moment her smile was too much to bear; it made Jimmy feel ill the same way eating too much candy did—the same sick-to-his-stomach feeling he got when he saw Tammy Bakker smile on television.

Finally, Jimmy figured out what it was about the woman: she looked like there was something missing from inside her.

Something *big*.

Jimmy imagined for a moment that he saw the woman through a kaleidoscope. Her image twisted and blurred, coalesced, and realigned. When she came into focus again Jimmy imagined her as a crone, old and pinched and gnarled and wicked. He imagined her as the sort of old maid who took her pleasure from squeezing the life out of people and things, and leaving their husks behind to rot.

Then, just as suddenly as Jimmy's imagination had covered her with evil, the evil evaporated away. What it left behind, to Jimmy's eye, was a person who God put on earth to be nasty and mean, all pinched and dried inside—but from whom all evil had somehow bled away. What was left behind was the goodness of her heart, and emptiness. Big, powerful emptiness.

Once Jimmy understood what his imagination was trying to tell him, looking at Mrs. Anderson was like staring at something hollow and grotesque. Like the molted shell of a june bug, left to decompose for a week in a stagnant puddle.

Jimmy looked back at his dad, but dad's expression said he wasn't seeing anything like that. All dad saw was the goodness, and the absence of evil. He wasn't seeing the emptiness at all.

Mr. Anderson held out his hand, and dad shook it.

"You're Ben Tompkins?" Mr. Anderson asked. "Ralph

Williams told us you'd be renting the house. We saw you pull in this morning, and thought we'd stop by and say hello."

Mr. Anderson was missing a part of himself, too. But it wasn't as large or as vital a part as what was gone from his wife. He just seemed . . . *wrong*. Like chili con carne, maybe, without the spices. Or like air without any smell.

"Glad you stopped by," dad said. "I wish I could invite you in, but there're furniture and boxes piled all over the place. The house isn't safe, much less presentable."

Mrs. Anderson smiled and laughed and blushed a little bit. "Oh, that's all right. Mostly we wanted to pass on an invitation. A few of us get together every month or so at one family's house or another's. This time it's out at the Williams farm, and Betty Williams asked me to make sure you knew you were welcome."

Dad smiled back at her again. "That's very gracious of her," he said. "Ralph and Betty took me out for dinner when I was here for the interview."

Mrs. Anderson beamed. "And, of course, we wanted to introduce Roberta to your son Jimmy, get her to make sure he got to know the other kids here in town."

Jimmy made himself smile in spite of the fact that his stomach felt queasy. He tucked the casserole dish under his left arm and held out his right hand to shake Roberta's.

"Pleased to meet you," he began, automatically. Then he saw the look in Roberta's eye, and he froze up stiff as ice.

She was smiling the same evil smile as the boy in the blackberry briar. No—not the same smile. Hers was worse, much worse. The boy's smile, by comparison, was a bad copy of hers.

He didn't want to see her, be near her, much less touch her hand.

But what could he do? If he turned and ran away he'd just look stupid. Her folks sure didn't see that in her. Their expressions were guileless; sincere, and kind of dumb.

Jimmy looked back at his dad, and when he saw dad's expression he felt a little relief. Dad was worried. Disturbed. Dad saw the same thing Jimmy did. Or, at least, he saw part of it.

Still, Jimmy had manners. It wasn't polite to start to shake someone's hand, then back away like they had lice.

He shook her hand even though he was sure as he did it that the blackness inside her was catching, that if he touched her the evil would start to grow inside him. When their hands touched he felt a hot, stinging burn. He smiled and nodded anyway.

His fear of contagion was groundless, or at least wrong. When Jimmy drew back his hand, his heart felt no different than it ever had. He was still himself; his insides weren't black and twisted.

Roberta stared at him; the look on her face was morbid fascination.

"Roberta, why don't you take Jimmy down the hill to the Hanson place, introduce him to Tim Hanson?" Mrs. Anderson smiled a big, wide smile that made the makeup crack away from around her eyes.

Jimmy's heart lurched toward his throat.

Dad, praise God, was nervous about Roberta, too.

"It's awfully kind of you to offer," dad said, "but Jimmy and I have a lot of straightening up to do. We still have to unload the trailer, too. We'll see you at dinner tomorrow though, won't we?"

Mrs. Anderson smiled, *again*. Jimmy didn't know if he could stand it if she did that even one more time. "We surely will," she said. "We'll stop by tomorrow around six, and we can all walk down to the Williamses' together."

Dad smiled back at her. It was a real smile, but it looked tired, worn out. "That sounds great."

There was a long, awkward moment when no one said anything, so long that Jimmy began to think that they'd all just stand there staring at each other forever. He thought about saying something, anything, just to break the silence, but the only words that would come to mind were things like *help* and *run* and *no.* Anything like that would have sounded stupid and crazy. Rude, too.

Finally, Mrs. Anderson said, "Well! I'm sure you'll be busy all day with your unpacking, so we'd better let you get back to it."

Dad nodded. "It's true. First days of driving, and now more days of settling in. Thanks an awful lot for stopping by, though."

"You're certainly welcome," Mrs. Anderson said. Her

husband was already half turned back toward the street; he waved and said good-bye.

But Roberta kept staring at Jimmy like he was some dead thing on a table in biology class; she didn't even seem to notice that her folks were leaving. Jimmy did his best, *kept* doing his best, not to act like he noticed the stare. Mrs. Anderson still hadn't noticed it, but she finally did notice the fact that Roberta hadn't started away with her.

She took the girl's arm and began to lead her gently. "Come along, Roberta."

Roberta finally turned away. Jimmy wanted to let out a sigh of relief, but he held it until the Andersons were out by the road so they wouldn't hear.

Dad heard it, though.

"Strange girl, huh?" he said.

Jimmy shook his head. "They were all strange, dad."

"I don't know. Except for the little girl, they seemed like pretty nice people to me." Dad turned and started back into the house. Jimmy followed him.

"Yeah, dad. The girl is nasty—all black and mean inside. But her parents . . . there's something *missing*. The mother especially. She looks like she's all empty inside."

Dad frowned. "If she really was empty inside, Jimmy, she wouldn't have anything to say to you. That's what a person's character is: a bunch of reasons for doing things, a lot of them so deep down that you don't even know they're there. If you really took away a person's inside, you'd have to take away his reasons, his . . . want-to and his need-to. He wouldn't have the heart to get up in the morning, much less step out to visit the new neighbors."

Jimmy thought about that for a while as he followed dad toward the kitchen. Dad had said it to him before, or words like it. It was true, too. Jimmy had watched people carefully for a long time after dad first told him that, and he'd seen that it was true.

Still, Jimmy had looked at Mrs. Anderson, and he'd seen her all hollow and empty and grotesque, and that was just as true. Jimmy knew the difference between what he was seeing and what he was imagining.

"She's like foam, dad. Like you had a bottle with only a little bit in it, and then you shook it and the little bit at the bottom foamed up to fill the space. Even though the bottle's full of foam, it's really like the bottle's just about empty."

Dad gave that a minute to sink in before he answered. "Think about it for a minute, Jimmy. It doesn't make much sense: people aren't like soap bottles, and reasons for doing things aren't like sudsy water."

Jimmy put the casserole dish on the kitchen counter and thought for a while. It was true: the analogy was pretty lame. Even so, he knew that there was something real, something true, that he was trying to say—even if he wasn't much good at explaining it.

"But dad, what if someone took away all the mean and nasty and cruel reasons she had for doing things. And what if she was a really nasty person, the kind of person who barely even has a handful of good things inside her? The sort of person who's *supposed* to be all shriveled and small and pinched inside. If you took away the bad, there wouldn't be hardly anything left. What was left would be real, and it would be *good,* but—it wouldn't be a whole person. It might *act* like a person, but there wouldn't be anything underneath it. All the down-inside stuff would be missing."

After a while, dad said, "Hmmm. That's logical, I guess. But I don't see how it could be possible to take away a person's motivation that . . . selectively. And I sure don't see how you could know that much just from looking at her and seeing her talk for a few minutes."

Jimmy shrugged. He didn't know, either. Not really. But he didn't think it was anything magical or anything like that. There were all sorts of things you could tell just from looking at a person, looking at the way he held himself and things like that. Not that Jimmy could exactly tell what it meant when, say, someone's upper lip curled funny when he smiled. It was more like: Jimmy would look at a person, the whole person, all at once, and he'd get a feeling about that person. Then he'd think about the feeling a little bit, think about why he felt that way. What made him feel that way was usually something pretty true about the person he was seeing. It wasn't perfect, it wasn't like reading minds in some weird story, but it was right a lot more often than it was wrong. It worked best with people he'd never met before, because he already had feelings about people he knew, and that could make things confusing. On the other hand, when he knew someone he could see changes and differences, and those could tell him a lot.

Dad lifted the lid on the casserole dish; the smell of dead fish and fermented macaroni drifted out. "This looks disgusting," he said.

Jimmy looked in. He nodded. "Smells bad, too."

"Tell you what," dad said, putting the lid back on the dish and putting the casserole in the refrigerator. "You give me a hand emptying out the trailer, we'll drive into Tylerville to drop it off, and I'll take you out for a bite to eat."

"Sure. What's Tylerville?"

"A bigger town, a few miles south of here."

"Eating would be nice, dad. You know we missed breakfast, and it's after lunchtime?"

"Oh *no.*" Dad slapped his forehead. "I was so tired and so sick of traveling that I didn't even think about food. I feel like a louse. You should have woke me up, reminded me."

"I wasn't all that hungry. I guess I would have if I was. Heck, if I was *that* hungry, I'd eat the tuna casserole."

The trailer was mostly light stuff—clothes and things that dad had meant to bring in the car, until it turned out there was too much of it to cram in. It only took a few minutes to unload.

The drive to Tylerville was nice, which kind of surprised Jimmy, since he'd thought that this last week he'd seen enough of the inside of the car to last a lifetime. Maybe it wasn't even the driving that was nice, but just the fact of getting out of town. He certainly felt as though a weight were lifted off his back by the time they were a few hundred yards past the bottom of the hill.

It didn't make a whole lot of sense. They'd been in Green Hill long enough for Jimmy to get that sick of it—sick enough to feel relief just from getting away.

But senseless or not, when they finished dinner and started the drive back home, Jimmy began to dread returning.

CHAPTER

SIX

THEY STOPPED BY A SUPERMARKET ON THE WAY HOME, and it was early evening by the time they got back to Green Hill. Dad set himself right to work unpacking the kitchen. There were three things, according to dad, that they had to be able to do: eat, sleep, and get dressed in the morning. "For all I care," he said, "the rest of this stuff can wait until the second coming." Jimmy knew that wasn't exactly so; even when they were all three together—dad, mom, and Jimmy—dad had been the one who kept the house straight. The house had been cleaner, in fact, since the police took mom away to the hospital.

Jimmy tried to pitch in and help dad out. He managed to

get the strapping tape off his dresser by himself, and once
that was done it wasn't hard to get his clothes out of their
boxes and put away. But he wasn't much use to dad in the
kitchen; he felt like he was more in the way than he was
any help. After an hour or so Jimmy went outside, just to
look at the stars. Dad was so caught up in organizing the
spice rack that he didn't even see Jimmy leave. He would
have told dad if he was planning to go farther than the
backyard, but under the circumstances it wasn't really
worth the trouble. Dad was hard to interrupt when he was
involved in something.

Outside, the sky was less black than it had been last
night. There was a moon tonight, a bright sliver of a moon
not far from the western horizon. It took a few minutes,
but eventually Jimmy's eyes adjusted to the dim light well
enough for him to see the yard.

Somewhere nearby a dog barked. It sounded like the
same dog that had barked earlier in the day—the dog
whose bark had somehow frightened that strange boy
away. A moment or two after that he heard boys shouting
somewhere in the distance.

From inside the house came the sound of boxes, or
maybe furniture, crashing to the floor. Dad was moving
heavy stuff; when that was happening it really was best to
stay out of the way. *Way* out of the way. Dad tended to bite
off more than he could chew when it came to heavy moving. Things would sometimes go flying in all directions.

Jimmy stepped away from the door, out onto the lawn,
just to be safe. It wasn't likely that anything would hit the
door hard enough to burst it open, but it was just as well to
be cautious. Dad once accidentally split open the wall between his office and Jimmy's bedroom with a fold-away
couch/bed he was trying to move.

There was light enough in the yard to see the blackberry
bushes, enough to see the blackberries themselves on their
stems, though not quite enough to see them clearly. Jimmy
had never even seen berries that fresh before—he wanted
to see what they tasted like. But he was wary, too. They
looked like blackberries. And the boy with the bowl had
been picking them, so they were probably edible. But still
. . . for Jimmy food was something you got from the refrigerator or from the grocery store, or even from a restau-

rant. It wasn't something you found growing wild outside the house. Just the opposite: there'd been an ornamental juniper in the front yard back in New Jersey, and all his life his folks had been telling him not to eat the bright red berries that grew on it.

But when it came to food, at least, Jimmy was more curious than he was careful. He walked to the bush, picked a berry, and carefully—very cautiously—put it in his mouth.

Before he took his hand away, a spider jumped off the berry onto his finger, scurried across his hand, and dropped back down on to the bush.

After that, if the blackberry hadn't already been in his mouth he wouldn't have had the stomach to eat it. But it was in his mouth, and he'd already bit into it, and there was nothing to do but enjoy it. It was delicious, too: mostly pungent, but very sweet, and the texture in his mouth was wonderful. It was good enough to enjoy in spite of the fact that he kept expecting a second spider to crawl out of the pulp and dart down his throat.

The shouting boys were closer now; Jimmy thought he saw a hint of motion thirty yards downhill from the house.

"Got him!" one of the boys shouted.

The dog barked again, then screeched and yowled in pain.

What are they doing, Jimmy wondered, *beating some poor dog to death?* That was crazy. People didn't beat dogs. Not people in their right minds.

For just an instant Jimmy saw poor, crazy, surly Duke, tearing at mom's arm as she tried to beat his head in. He shuddered.

The dog was still yowling, and he was getting closer. Too close. Jimmy didn't want to see whatever they'd done to it; he didn't want to meet the sort of people who'd do it. He turned around and started back toward the house.

Then the dog's yowling stopped, and Jimmy thought that that was the end of it, that the dog was dead. He pictured the boys standing over the dog's carcass, pounding it with stones until the meat of its flesh was soft as pulp—

—*the image of his mom, stabbing Duke's bloody cadaver again and again with the long, jagged carving knife,*

*hacking away at what was left of Duke until the edge of
the knife was smooth and the point was bent and twisted
from pounding through Duke into the concrete floor of the
basement—*

—then, just as suddenly as the dog had stopped yowling,
it burst through the briar three yards from Jimmy's feet,
and leapt out into the yard. It was just a mutt, a dirty white-
and-brown mutt, small and beaten and bloody. How could
a dog like this have frightened that boy this morning? How
could it be *worth* hunting down and beating to death?

It noticed Jimmy, and bared its teeth and snarled. Jimmy
braced himself, held his arms out ready to try to knock the
dog away if it attacked him. But the dog hesitated. It took a
longer look at Jimmy, and suddenly it relaxed and whined
and held its head down.

That didn't make any sense to Jimmy at all. He held out
his hand and let the dog sniff at it. The dog, still holding its
head down, wagged its tail and licked Jimmy's palm.

"What's the matter, boy?" Jimmy asked. "You got something wrong in the head, too?"

There were big scabby-looking welts all over the dog,
and one fresh gash about four inches long that ran from his
shoulder to the base of his ear.

Jimmy walked to the front stoop, sat on the doorstep,
and called the dog over to him. "Come here, boy," he said.
"Let's see how bad that cut is."

The dog walked across the yard, limping slightly with its
left front leg. It sat on the grass by Jimmy's knee and
started panting gently. Its breath was horrible; Jimmy
didn't want to think what it had been eating.

The dog was a stray, maybe even feral. Its fur was mat-
ted and tangled right down to the roots. From the look of
its filthy coat, Jimmy guessed that it'd been a year since the
dog had had a bath or even a brushing, if it'd ever been
groomed at all. It didn't have a collar, but there was a curl
in the fur around its neck to show where a collar might
have been. It might have worn a leather collar until not
long ago, Jimmy thought. Duke always wore leather collars, and every year or so the leather would rot away, and
dad would have to buy him a new one.

The gash on the dog's shoulder was deep, and there
were big splinters of wood jammed in it. The wound

leaked blood steadily; the dog's left foreleg and paw were soaked bloody and caked with dirt. Jimmy put his hand on the dog's shoulder, just above the gash, to get a better look. The dog winced in pain, but when Jimmy said, "Be still, boy," it was still. It looked at him soulfully, like Jimmy was Christ come down from heaven to save a dog. But it was still.

"We've got to stop that bleeding, boy," Jimmy said, "or you're going to bleed yourself to death."

Jimmy didn't know if that was really so; he wasn't sure how much blood a dog could lose and still live. But he knew this was a lot of blood, too much to just let it scab over.

Dad would know what to do. Dad was handy with first aid, and he always took care of problems first and worried about being grossed out later. Jimmy was about to go into the house and get him when the boys showed up.

There were four of them, and they all carried rough pine-branch clubs the size of baseball bats.

The dog began to growl.

One of the boys was the one Jimmy had seen this morning picking berries in the briar. "There it is, Christian," another boy said to the one Jimmy recognized. He pointed at Jimmy and the dog with his club.

Christian turned and answered. "I see it." The nastiness that seethed from him now was almost as intense as Roberta's. He turned back and spoke to Jimmy. "Get out of the way," he said, "That dog is ours."

That was crazy. Jimmy couldn't just let them beat the dog to death, not if there was anything he could do about it. Not even if they looked like they'd be just as happy to split Jimmy's head open as they would the dog's.

"What are you going to do to it?" Jimmy asked. He didn't want to fight four boys, not all at once.

"What do you *think* we're going to do with it? We're going to play *fetch.*" Christian said the word *fetch* in a voice so cruel it raised hairs on the back of Jimmy's neck.

Jimmy looked down at the dog and said, "Stay." He stood up.

"Give us the *dog,*" Christian said. He pulled his pine-branch club back like he was going to hit Jimmy with it.

Jimmy shook his head. "Sorry. The dog hasn't got any

tags, and it looks like a stray to me. It's in my yard, and it's doing what I tell it to, so it's mine. You can't have it."

Jimmy wasn't expecting the club to come flying down at his head, not so soon, not so fast. "Give us the *dog*, fuckbrain." Christian shouted as he swung.

The dog growled and whined, but it stayed just as still as Jimmy had told it to.

Jimmy caught the club, but it was moving so hard and so quick that momentum carried it through anyway. The wood made a sick cracking sound as it came down on the side of his skull, then continued down to nearly rip off his ear.

But Jimmy had hurt bad enough and often enough that he wasn't afraid of pain, and he didn't let it stop him. He pulled the club out of Christian's hands—it wasn't hard; the boy wasn't expecting it—and pushed back again, jamming the spike end of the club into Christian's throat. It broke the skin and blood went gushing all over the place, but not *that* much of it. Jimmy hadn't torn any important veins or broken the boy's windpipe.

Still, Christian wrapped his hands around his throat and screamed in unholy terror.

Another of the boys had somehow got behind Jimmy; Jimmy felt the boy's arm wrap around his throat, pinning him, cutting off his breath. Another boy rushed at him from the front with his club raised over his head.

For the first time since the boys had showed up, Jimmy was really scared. The boy wasn't just going to hit him with the club. The light in his eyes said he meant to bash Jimmy's brains in—and that if hitting Jimmy once didn't kill him, the boy would keep pounding away until Jimmy *was* dead. Jimmy tried to scream, tried to shout to his dad for help, but his wind was blocked, and all that came out was a whisper. A whisper too quiet to hear five yards away, much less loud enough for dad to hear through the door and over the sound of moving furniture.

But it was loud enough for the dog to hear. It leapt at the boy with the club, hit him front-paws-first in the chest, and knocked him over. The dog sunk its teeth into the boy's right forearm—his club arm—and stood on the boy's chest, yanking his arm back and forth. The dog's lower teeth dug deep furrows from the crook of his arm toward his wrist.

Jimmy twisted around so that he faced the boy holding him. He brought his knee up, hard, into the boy's groin; the boy let go of him and doubled over. When Jimmy turned around Christian and the fourth boy had already run away, and the third was trying to get away from the dog.

"Heel!" Jimmy shouted, and the dog let go of the boy's arm. The boy ran, and a moment later the one Jimmy had wracked stumbled after him.

Before they'd got out of the yard, dad turned on the porch light and opened the front door. "What's going on out here?" he asked.

There was blood all over Jimmy from where the club had scraped open his ear, and the dog was even bloodier. The boys' clubs were scattered around the yard.

"All the kids around here are strange, dad."

Dad asked Jimmy what he meant by strange, and Jimmy told him about the boys and the dog. Dad listened, but he didn't look happy at all.

"Come here, closer to the light," he said when Jimmy was done. "Let me get a good look at the side of your head."

"It's not that bad. Just a lump and a long scrape," Jimmy said. But he did as his father said, anyway. "The dog's got a real deep cut on the side of his neck."

"You first. I'll get a look at him in a minute." He poked around Jimmy's ear, gently, for a moment or two. "Hmmm. You're right. It could be a lot worse. Clean it up, put a triple-size Band-Aid on your ear, and you'll be fine. Let's see the dog, there."

The dog had been sitting by Jimmy's feet, panting. "Can I keep him, dad? He's a great dog. I think he likes me a lot."

"Well . . . I don't know. He does look like a stray, though, doesn't he? Huh." Dad crouched down to get a better look at the dog. "Come here, boy."

The dog sidled over to the spot where dad pointed.

"So, can I keep him, dad?"

"Sure, why not. But if you're going to keep him you've got to name him first. Can't have a dog in the house without a name."

Jimmy stooped down to look the dog in the eye. "So

what's your name, boy? Can you tell me, or do I have to make one up for you?"

The dog didn't answer.

"You're a goofy kid, you know that?" dad said. It wasn't hurtful the way dad said it. In fact, it was kind of fun. Like a game, almost.

"Grandma always says that the fruit doesn't fall far from the tree."

"You." Dad stuck his tongue out at Jimmy.

It was a pretty ridiculous sight on a grown-up. Silly enough to make Jimmy giggle. Dad looked back down at the dog.

"This dog's been through hell and come back to tell about it," dad said. His left hand pressed down gently on the dog's good shoulder. "Lie down, boy. Let's get a look at your underside. How about Rex? Rex is a good name."

"Sounds a lot like Duke."

"Why not? I named him, too." Dad pressed a little harder, and Rex finally rolled over. "My God, Jimmy. Someone cut this dog's gut wide open."

Jimmy leaned over to look.

A long, straight cut ran from the dog's diaphragm to his groin. The cut was old looking, and crusted with scab and infection; it looked pretty shallow on either end but deep in the center. In spots it had begun to heal together, but most of it looked as though it'd been torn open again and again.

"We've got to get him to the vet," dad said. He was so angry that his hands shook with rage. "I'd sure like to get my hands on whoever did this. Someone needs to be locked up permanently. Either in jail or the nut house, and maybe both."

Jimmy bit his lip and nodded.

They took Rex inside to the bathtub and washed his wounds and fur carefully with warm soapy water. Dad was a little nervous about cleaning him—he was afraid of opening up one of the dog's scabs—but Rex was just too filthy to keep in the house as he was. Too dirty even for the garage. The dog didn't look too happy about getting wet, but he didn't resist, either. He whined as dad drew the long, heavy splinters out of the raw gash near his neck, but he was still then, too. Dad managed to get him clean without doing any harm.

"I bet he's hungry, dad," Jimmy said, "and we sure don't have any dog food."

Dad grinned deviously. "I think I just figured out what we're going to do with that tuna casserole the Andersons brought over."

Jimmy giggled.

Rex gorged himself on the casserole—ate so much of it, in fact, that he couldn't keep all of it down, and Jimmy had an awful mess to clean up.

"One of things about having a dog," dad said as Rex gagged, "is that when he makes a mess you've got to clean up after him. It's part of being responsible for yourself."

That didn't sound all that fair to Jimmy. "But you're the one who gave him too much to eat. You should clean it up."

Dad shook his head. "Another part of being responsible is making sure other people don't overfeed your dog." Dad grinned and went back to his unpacking. Dad was teasing, and Jimmy knew it. If Jimmy called him on it dad probably would have cleaned up the mess himself. But dad had enough to do with all the unpacking. Jimmy dug an old rag out of one of the boxes and wiped up the dog puke more because he felt like he hadn't been pulling his weight than for any other reason.

When he was done he got himself washed up and ready for bed. Rex followed him the whole way, only a step or two from Jimmy's feet. Probably, Jimmy thought, the dog was starved for attention. When Jimmy got into bed Rex curled up on the floor beside him and went to sleep himself.

Jimmy was asleep a moment later, and for a second night the Stone ruled and directed his dreams. This night was different, though: where before the Stone had seemed to press him from a place a million miles away, now it was so close that Jimmy could hear its warm dark breathing in his dreams.

CHAPTER

SEVEN

JIMMY COULD ALMOST SEE THE STONE WITH HIS MIND'S eye as it held him and pushed him back toward the moment where it had left him: Mom was downstairs in the basement, doing *crazy* things with what was left of Duke.

Jimmy didn't want to remember that morning. He was afraid to even think about it; every time he did he got sweaty and shaky and he felt as though his soul would shatter into a million pieces. But the Stone didn't care about that. Just the opposite, in fact—Jimmy could feel it thirsting to see him broken.

In the dream, Jimmy had finally got it into his head that he could escape from her if he tried. But when he did try he found that there really wasn't any way out: the windows were sealed with burglar-alarm tape, and the doors were locked with the sort of deadbolt that you need a key to open even from the inside. Jimmy didn't have any key.

The only thing left to do was hide.

There wasn't anyplace to hide in the living room, or anywhere else on the first floor—not if you were trying to hide anything larger than a loaf of bread. Jimmy was small and wiry for a nine-year-old, but even the day he was born he was larger than a loaf of bread.

He tiptoed upstairs to the second floor. There were four rooms up here: his bedroom, his folks' room, dad's office, and a bathroom. At the end of the hall was a doorway that led to the attic stairs. Hiding in his bedroom was kind of obvious; it was the first place mom would look. Mom and dad's bedroom was kind of a neat idea. Hiding under mom's nose might work. But Jimmy didn't know his way around in there very well. It wouldn't take much bad luck to hide in a place where she wouldn't even have to look for him to find him—if he hid behind the door, for instance, there'd probably turn out to be a hook on the inside of it where she hung her robe every night before she went to sleep.

There wasn't anywhere to hide in the bathroom. Dad's office? There were lots of great places to hide in dad's office. The trouble was that there were so many weird and badly balanced piles of junk in the room that Jimmy couldn't be sure he'd be able to hide *quietly*. It would be easy to knock something over and give himself away.

That left the attic.

The attic was *cold* this time of year, and in a snowstorm it was bound to be even colder. All Jimmy had on were the pajamas he'd worn to bed last night; they weren't enough for weather like this. They'd have to be enough, though. There wasn't time to get dressed.

Jimmy walked to the end of the hall and opened the door to the attic stairs. He stepped in and closed the door behind him as quickly and quietly as he could; if he left a draft behind it would tell mom where he went.

Jimmy had a good idea where he was going to hide before he even got to the top step: inside the partition.

The attic was a tall, A-shaped room with long walls that

met to form a peak above its center. Maybe they weren't
walls at all—maybe they were the ceiling. It was hard to
say; what they were depended on how you looked at it.
The floor and walls were bare, unfinished plywood. A pair
of storm windows faced away from each other at opposite
sides of the room. The stairs came up by the window that
overlooked the backyard.

One spring dad got it into his head that he'd fix up the
attic and get some use out of it; make a playroom out of it,
maybe. He started by trying to put up a wall that would
separate the storage part of the attic from the new playroom he was planning.

Then summer came, with hot summer weather, and dad
realized why he'd never made use of the attic before: it
wasn't insulated, or ventilated. The attic got *hot* in the
summer, and that summer was especially hot.

Dad left the new wall half-finished. Badly finished, too—
dad's carpentry was awful. On one side, the side that faced
the stairs, the sheet rock hung true against its frame. On
the other side it had fallen away. There was a six-inch gap
on that side where the sheet rock was supposed to meet
the wall. That left ten inches of space inside the unfinished
wall, and that was plenty of room for Jimmy to hide in. Dad
had been telling Jimmy that he was going to spend a weekend fixing up the partition—either that or tearing it down
—ever since Jimmy found a squirrel nesting inside the gap
last fall. It was another of those projects that dad never
seemed to get around to.

Jimmy sidled around the old dresser and under the
wedge of sheet rock. It was dark inside, incredibly dark
and quiet.

The quiet didn't last long.

Somewhere downstairs mom screamed his name. She
screamed it five times, and then furniture and things—
Jimmy didn't want to think what sort of things—went
banging against the walls. All of Jimmy's reflexes made him
want to answer when she called him; he had to fight to
keep from crawling out of his hiding space and going
downstairs to see what she wanted.

Mom kept screaming his name, bellowing in rage, and
throwing things at the walls. He listened to her move from
one part of the house to another—she was incredibly loud.

He could almost follow her as she searched for him by listening to the timbre of her screaming.

Someone telephoned while she searched for him, but mom didn't answer the call. Whoever it was held on for a dozen rings before he finally gave up.

Gradually, mom worked her way toward Jimmy. Half an hour after the first time she called him, she opened the door to the attic stairs.

Her voice was quieter now.

"I know you're here, Jimmy darling. I've searched the whole house, and this is the only place left."

Her voice dripped with a sound that made Jimmy picture himself being murdered long and slow—he saw the skin of his neck and arms peeled back and away from him, then left that way so he could bleed to death slowly.

He held his breath and prayed silently that she was bluffing.

"I know where you are, Jimmy. If you come out now and save me the trouble of prying you out of there, I'll let it be fast for you. You don't want to hurt *forever*, do you?"

Fat beads of sweat welted up on Jimmy's forehead, even though he was freezing cold.

Mom was walking straight toward him, softly, quietly, each step measured and direct.

Jimmy let the breath ease out of his lungs slowly, so it didn't make a sound. It wasn't safe to breathe—in a room so small, so quiet, how could she *not* hear his breathing?—but he had to anyway. If he held his breath too long, the air would burst out of him; either that or he'd pass out and fall over. Either one would make enough sound to give him away.

Mom came around the partition and walked directly to the gap in the sheet rock. Jimmy saw her peer in at him, saw her look him straight in the eye—

"I see you in there, Jimmy. Will you come out now, or shall I rip the wall apart and drag you out?"

She was bluffing. She had to be bluffing. It was too dark inside for her to see him. Jimmy didn't move an eyelash.

Suddenly mom screamed. "Where are you, you little bastard? I'm going to kill you when I get my hands on you!"

She started throwing things again. Three times she threw things at the partition, and one of them hit the sheet rock so hard that one of the nails sticking out of the plaster jammed deep into Jimmy's left foot. He had to leave it that way; he didn't dare move with mom still in the attic. He wanted to cry, but he couldn't for fear of the noise it would make.

After a few minutes mom went back downstairs and started searching the rest of the house all over again. She spent another half hour screaming and ranting in bursts, and then she was quiet. Jimmy worried most of all about the quiet. Quiet meant she might be planning something, really *thinking* instead of just storming around, and that was really frightening.

But the quiet could just as likely mean that she'd finally passed out, that staying up all night drinking had finally caught up with her. Jimmy felt a cool *frisson* of relief just thinking about the possibility. If she was asleep he could open a window, climb out, and get away before she even had a chance to hear the alarm and wake up, before she could figure out what was going on. Or, better yet, he could sneak into her purse, get her keys, and leave through the front door.

Just to be safe, Jimmy waited inside the attic wall for another hour before he crept out. He was freezing cold by then, and his whole foot throbbed horribly from the hole the nail had pierced in the side of his heel.

There was a lot of blood, too. It had caked and dried all along the bottom of the hurt foot, and he had an awful moment when he first tried to move it. The blood there on the underside had dried hard, like glue, and when he lifted the foot to take a step there was a horrible tearing sensation as the skin ripped away from the wooden stud he'd been standing on. The pain was mean and the sound was worse; he imagined how his foot would look with the skin ripped away. It would be all tendons and veins and weird muscles, like the monkey his biology teacher had dissected in class. But where the monkey had been dry and bloodless because it was dead, his foot would be sanguine and alive, bleeding in spurts that matched the rhythm of his heart.

Jimmy slid past the edge of the plasterboard and around the dresser. He bit his lower lip, shuddered, and lifted up his left foot to check the damage. It was bad, but it was a relief, too: he hadn't lost much at all. The foot was tender

and pink and bleeding a little where he'd lost a big strip of
callus from the heel. Most of the callus was still there,
though. Enough to walk on if he had to.

He limped toward the stairway.

Once he was moving he began to feel how deep the cold
had set into his muscles and joints; everything he moved
hurt. His body kept starting to shiver, and his teeth wanted
to clack against each other. He didn't dare relax enough to
let them. He needed to *go*, to get out and get away; if he
shivered his hands might slip, and if his teeth clacked it
might draw mom's attention.

He prayed that she was asleep. If she found him. . . .
He didn't want to hurt. He didn't want to die.

He limped carefully and quietly down the stairs, got to
the last step, and opened the door a crack. And peeked out
and saw nothing but empty hallway.

Stepped out, shut the door fast and silently behind him.
Tiptoed, hobbling, down the hall.

His parents' bedroom was the first door on the left, just
before the bend in the hallway. He peered around the
door, and saw his mom sleeping at an odd angle on the bed,
on top of the blankets.

Sleeping!

Her purse was beside her on the floor by her feet—

That was when Jimmy made the mistake that almost got
him killed. Or maybe, in retrospect, it wasn't a mistake at
all; maybe if he'd just climbed out of one of the downstairs
windows and let the alarm go off she would have got him
sooner.

The purse was too tempting. The keys inside it were too
tempting. Jimmy got down on his hands and knees and
crawled quiet as he could into the bedroom.

She was going to wake up.

He knew that.

She was going to wake up and kill him. The tiny part of
him that wasn't living inside a memory inside a dream
tried to pull himself away, to wake up—

Crawled across the rug, where a wide-bright frame of
sunlight shone down on the rug through the big bay window.

Crawled to mom's purse, at the foot of the bed. Reached
in—gently! carefully!—to get mom's keys. Found them.

No— not mom's keys. These were his own keys. She *had* taken them, stolen them right out of his pocket.

Pulled the keys from mom's purse oh-so-quiet—

—a loud, rattling clatter; the sound of a key chain ticking against itself, amplified a thousand times by tension and adrenal panic. She heard it, she was going to wake up, he *knew*, he *knew*—!

No.

She wasn't going to wake up. He knew that.

His eyes darted up, toward mom on the bed—

—to see her staring down at him, watching him. Sunlight flashed as it caught in one of the facets deep inside her Stone pendant. How could he have woke her up? She'd never been asleep in the first place.

Jimmy screamed, loud and long and hard, every terror, every tension escaping him all at once, welling up out of his lungs.

The sound of his scream made mom lurch in surprise. Her scabrous right fist shot out at him, slammed into the side of his face. Jimmy tumbled head over heels across the room until his head slammed into the wall that faced the bay window.

Mom walked across the room, yanked the keys out of his hand, threw the keys across the room onto the bed. She trembled with rage.

She kicked his head with her left foot, then howled in pain and rage from the impact on her swollen toes.

"You fucking little bastard! You want away from me? You want to get out of here? I'll *give* you out of here!"

She bent over, grabbed his crotch with one hand and the collar of his pajamas with the other.

She screamed.

Lifted him over her head.

And threw him out through the double-thick storm glass of the bay window. The second-floor window.

Into the howling-bright storming snow.

His own scream was loud enough to wake him.

It was late morning; the sun shone bright and warm through the bedroom window. He'd screamed so hard he felt as though the wind had been knocked out of him. It took three long, ragged breaths to bring it back.

Jimmy sat up. Dad's feet were pounding toward him in the hall; Rex had crawled up into bed beside him. The dog looked scared. Worried, even protective. Jimmy scratched the top of the dog's head with his fingertips.

"It's okay, Rex. Just a bad dream." The dog's tail thumped against the blankets by Jimmy's feet.

Dad burst into the room in a terrible panic, saw Jimmy sitting up petting the dog, and heaved out a sigh of relief. "Another nightmare. . . ?"

Jimmy nodded.

Dad walked over to the side of the bed, stooped down and gave Jimmy a bear hug. Rex cocked a wary eye at him, but he didn't growl.

"God, kid. I love you, you know that?"

Jimmy buried his face in his father's chest and said that he did.

"Hey," dad said, "you know what's for breakfast?"

Jimmy sniffed the air. "Pancakes?"

"Huh-uh. Waffles. Chocolate waffles. Real maple syrup, too."

Jimmy *loved* waffles.

"Oh *yeah!*"

There were heaps of them. Enough, even, that there were waffles left over for Rex.

CHAPTER

EIGHT

BEN TOMPKINS HAD BEGUN TO HAVE SERIOUS REGRETS about moving to Green Hill.

Both times he'd visited the place it'd seemed like paradise; green and uncrowded and *friendly*. But the move had kicked off something nasty inside Jimmy's head. The poor kid was having serious nightmares—nightmares serious enough to have him screaming in his sleep two nights in a row.

That wasn't all, either: the people here weren't at all what Ben had thought they were. The children were monsters. *All* the children, as far as he could tell. And they weren't just nasty little brats, but vicious, and violent, too.

Yesterday *four* of them attacked Jimmy with clubs. Ben didn't want Jimmy living in a town with children like those. He didn't want Jimmy living within miles of them.

There was money enough to move back to Jersey if they had to. There was always plenty in the bank; between Anne's salary and his own they'd had quite an income, and neither of them was much of a spender. But going back to New Jersey would mean breaking his commitment to the Green Hill school board. Ben didn't like breaking commitments. Giving a commitment was giving his word, and what good was his word if he didn't honor it?

Besides, it was senseless to run away from the place without giving things a chance to work themselves out. At least a week or two, anyway.

Jimmy put down three waffles, six strips of bacon, two glasses of milk, and an orange juice. Ben was always amazed that a little boy could eat that much. Bad dreams certainly didn't do anything to his appetite. Nor to his mood; Jimmy looked about as happy as he ever had since the weekend Anne went crazy. The dog was sitting on the floor next to Jimmy's chair, looking soulfully up at Jimmy's waffle plate. Jimmy seemed to be having a fine time teasing the dog—tempting him with bites of waffle, but never giving him any.

"Dad," Jimmy said as he poured syrup over his third waffle, "why do I still love mom?"

Ben's heart skipped a beat.

Jimmy hadn't said ten words about Anne since the cleaning woman found them in that hotel room. Not to Ben. Not to the police. Not to the young lawyer from the state's attorney's office. Maybe not even to his psychologist, though Ben didn't know about that for sure. He could have found out if he'd tried, but he didn't think it was any of his business.

"It's tough, Jimmy," Ben said. "Moms and dads are important. In a way, it's like they're a part of you, like ghosts of them live inside you. You've got to love them to feel all right about yourself."

Jimmy took a bite of drippy waffle, chewed it, swallowed it. "Okay. But how come I *do* love her? I can see why I have to. But why *do* I?"

Ben wanted to have an answer to that question. Wanted

to *bad*. He could have thought about it for a while and found one, too. But he didn't think he could trust an answer he had to think about. And if not having an answer was letting his son down when he needed help, then giving him one that was probably wrong was something much worse.

"I don't know, Jimmy. Why do you love her? You probably know why a lot better than I ever could."

Jimmy ate more waffle.

"Because she's my mom, maybe?" he asked. "Do I love her because she's my mom?"

Ben shrugged. "Do you think so?"

Jimmy stirred a pool of syrup with the one last bite of waffle. "I don't know."

Ben didn't honestly know what had happened that weekend when he'd gone away to a conference and Anne had finally lost her mind. Jimmy wouldn't talk about it. Anne hadn't said a word to anyone—not a single word—in the months since. At first the doctors had assumed she'd gone catatonic. But a week after they'd taken her to the psychiatric hospital someone had lost track of her for an hour, and when they'd finally found her she was in the janitor's closet, trying to hang herself with an electric cord, but not succeeding because the cord wasn't long enough. She'd tried to kill herself three more times since. She still wasn't speaking.

Ben hadn't told Jimmy about those suicide attempts. The kid had enough to haunt him without news like that.

Even if neither Jimmy nor Anne would speak about that weekend, Ben—and everyone else, thanks to the newspapers—knew a lot of what had happened. There was evidence all over the house, and other places, too. Jimmy's scars. Duke's bloody carcass, and the bits and pieces of dog meat that covered the floor and walls of the basement. Blood *everywhere;* Jimmy's, Duke's, Anne's. Anne hadn't cleaned any of it up, not even the baked ham Ben found wedged under the sink three weeks later. Ben probably would have noticed it sooner if he hadn't spent most of his time those weeks in the hospital at Jimmy's bedside.

If the boy could still love her after all that, it was amazing and sad, and wonderful in a grotesque way. Ben always thought that love twisted and warped and recrystallized into hate when things like that happened. It was a lot of why he worried for Jimmy: it wasn't good for a boy to hate his mother. Hating someone that close to him could turn even a good little kid like Jimmy into something bitter and cruel and sick in the head.

"You're crying, dad. Don't cry like that. Nothing bad's happening."

Damn. Ben dried his eyes on the sleeve of his flannel shirt. He didn't have any special scruples about crying, but doing it where anyone could see always made him feel like a fraud.

"Sorry 'bout that. Don't worry, I'm okay."

Ben took a sip of his coffee. He felt like an idiot. He wanted to say something, anything—fathers are supposed to *know* about things—but the problem was that he *didn't* know anything. He didn't know about being a boy whose mother went bug-hole crazy and spent three days torturing the kid. He didn't even know about being a boy here and now; what he knew about growing up was a quarter of a century out-of-date.

His own folks had been quiet and well-meaning. Mom still was, for that matter.

All Ben really knew about being a boy was how to enjoy childhood, and maybe even let it stretch on past adolescence. God knew Jimmy needed that. But he needed a lot more, too; he needed someone who understood the things he had to live with. Ben tried. Maybe he even succeeded. But the effort always stretched him out past all the limits he was made of.

Jimmy reached for the serving plate. For a moment Ben thought he was going to eat still *another* waffle. Then he said, "Can I give these to Duke?"

"It's Rex, not Duke." Ben corrected him without even thinking about it. "Sure, go ahead. I've had my fill."

Jimmy took the plate and set it down on the floor where the dog could get at it.

"So," Ben said, "we need to find a vet for Rex today. Any ideas?"

Jimmy thought about it. "Look in the phone book, maybe?"

Ben nodded. "Great idea. But we haven't *got* a phone book yet."

"Then let's go to Tylerville, find a phone, read the phone book, and call the vet. We can take Rex with us. I bet he'd like going for a ride in the car."

Rex did like riding in the car. In fact, he seemed to like it a lot. He insisted on riding with his head out Jimmy's half-open window, staring out into the rushing wind as though he were some sort of bizarre living hood ornament that protruded from the wrong part of the car. When Ben braked for the traffic light in Tylerville, the dog crawled down out of the window and stared indignantly at him until they started moving again.

Rex didn't seem to mind waiting in the car while Ben rifled the phone book, either. When Ben got back in the car (armed with the address of the only vet in Tylerville and the knowledge that there wasn't one in Green Hill) Rex and Jimmy were playing some strange game that involved crawling back and forth from the front seat to the backseat. Ben pretended he didn't notice it; he didn't want to think about what a game like that would do to the car's upholstery.

The vet's name was Robin Smith; when Ben and Jimmy got Rex to the office, they found out that Dr. Robin Smith was a woman. The waiting room was empty; when she stepped out from her office and saw Rex, the veterinarian went pale as dough. Ben thought for a moment she was going to be ill. She told them to come back into the office.

"Who are you? What's happened to this dog?" she asked. "Where did you get him?"

"I'm Ben Tompkins; this is my son, Jimmy. I don't think we got the dog so much as he got us," Ben told her. "As far as we know he's just a stray. Four boys were chasing him with clubs; the dog came running to my son for protection."

She nodded. Her face was grim. "Green Hill?"

"Do you mean, are we living in Green Hill? Yes, we are. We're still settling in—didn't get into town until yesterday morning."

She sighed angrily. "Again! Sometimes I'd really like to get my hands on one of those kids. . . . I'm sorry. I shouldn't be venting myself at you. If you had anything to do with what's happened to this dog, he wouldn't be here now."

"What do you mean?" Jimmy asked. "Have you seen Rex before?"

The woman smiled. "Rex, huh? That's a good name for him. It suits him. Come here, Rex." The dog did; she patted his head and examined the gash on his neck. "This isn't the first time I've seen battered animals come out of Green Hill. Usually they're dead, but a few of them get away. It's the children there. The little ones. Rotten to the core, mean-hearted, and bloodthirsty, every last one of them. The older kids and the adults aren't so bad. A lot of them are pleasant, in fact. But the little ones . . ."

She opened a cabinet, took out a tube of salve, and twisted off the cap.

"The little ones are vicious. Once I found a couple of them who'd tied a kitten to a tree with a thirty-foot length of fishing line they'd looped through the poor thing's collar. One of the girls—identical twins—had a cast-iron fireplace poker, and her sister had a yard-long copper pipe. They'd chase the kitten, batting at it with their rods, until just a few feet before the end of its line. Then they'd back away and let it think it was going to get away—until the kitten reached the end of its tether, and the line snapped tight, and the girls pounced on it and clubbed it and got it running all over again in the opposite direction.

"I grabbed the demented little brats by their ears—honest to God literally grabbed them by their ears—and hauled them down to the sheriff's office here in Tylerville." She shook her head. "The kitten lived, even though the girls had broken all its ribs and one of its legs, and fractured its skull. I found it a good home on the far side of the county."

Jimmy told the woman about the boys who'd attacked him and Rex. She clenched her teeth and nodded as she listened.

"The kids are bullies," she said, "and they're cowards, too. If it'd been just one of them, or even two, they wouldn't have lifted a finger against you. I'm surprised that even four of them had the nerve to go after your dog, here. He's a scrapper. One night he took a nice-size bite out of a burglar; old Mr. Henderson found him the next morning still guarding the open window the thief had left through. The dog was chewing on a big piece of trouser leg he'd torn away."

Jimmy's eyes lit up.

"You really knew Rex before he was a stray? Rex was a hero?"

The veterinarian chuckled. "I guess he was. Dan Henderson used to call him Chicklet. Godawful name for a dog like this. But the dog was devoted to Dan. He howled and moaned for a week after Dan died. Then I quit hearing him, and I wondered for a while what had become of him." She shrugged. "I kind of thought some of Dan's relatives had taken him in. Roll over, boy. Let's get a look at your underside."

She made a little sound like a scream—but quieter— when she saw that someone had cut the dog's gut open.

"Oh my God."

"I wanted to warn you about that," Ben said. "That's the main reason we're here. Most of the other wounds look like they'll heal on their own. But that . . ."

She nodded. "I don't know how this dog is still alive. The cut is infected; even if he'd managed not to bleed to death an infection that big and that deep should have killed him." She recapped the ointment tube and set it on the counter.

"Rex is too brave to let being hurt kill him, Dr. Smith," Jimmy said.

The veterinarian frowned. "You might be right, Jimmy. Any other dog I've ever seen would be curled up in a corner someplace, whimpering in pain." She looked back down at Rex's belly. "I'm going to have to reopen the cut, clean the infection, and stitch him closed again. He'll need antibiotics, too. It's best if you wait outside."

Ben and Jimmy sat in the waiting room for forty-five minutes. When Dr. Smith was done Rex was groggy and not quite asleep. She gave them five packets of pills, antibiotics, and told Jimmy he'd have to make Rex swallow two large capsules twice a day. When she told him exactly how it had to be done—Jimmy would have to force the pills down into Rex's throat with his fingers—Jimmy didn't look especially pleased. He made a face that said the idea made him feel queasy, but he didn't complain.

* * *

Jimmy was pensive during the drive home. Rex curled up on the front seat between them and fell into a deep sleep.

"What's the matter?" Ben asked Jimmy as they started up Green Hill.

"Nothing," Jimmy said. The answer came too fast. It didn't sound to Ben as though he were telling the truth.

"Are you sure?"

Jimmy nodded. He stared out the front window nervously; it almost seemed as though he were looking for something that worried him. Boys with clubs, maybe?

Or maybe it was the town itself. If the kids were the monsters that Dr. Smith said they were, then it was time to get out of here now, before things got out of hand. Before the warped little brats who'd attacked Jimmy came back with more help and finished what they'd started. Besides, if the kids around here were twisted enough to try to disembowel a dog, they weren't anybody Ben wanted Jimmy growing up with.

"Jimmy," Ben asked, "how do you feel about this place? Do you want to stay here? In Green Hill, I mean."

Jimmy hesitated. "I don't know, dad."

It sounded to Ben like he did know, and that he wanted to get away.

"We can pack up and leave tomorrow if you want, kiddo. You just say the word."

Jimmy reached down to touch his tennis shoe, and started toying with the knot in the lace. "Maybe we should."

"Huh. I'll tell you what: let's sleep on it. You tell me tomorrow morning and we'll be packed and out of here by dark." Ben sighed. "Most of everything is still in boxes. We can have a moving company come pick it up after we're gone."

Jimmy nodded absently. His eyes darted first right and then left, still searching.

"Looking for something?"

"What?" Jimmy shook his head, as though he were trying to clear it. "No. Nothing. Nothing to look for, as far as I know."

Ben turned off the two-lane highway, onto the winding little road that led to the rented house. "If you say so."

"What makes people act like those kids do, dad?" Jimmy stared out into the woods through the window on his side of the car. "What makes them do things like beat on dogs?"

Ben turned the car into the driveway. "I don't know, Jim-boy. I wish to God I did." He turned off the engine and opened the car door. Rex still lay deep asleep on the seat. Ben patted his head. "Come on, boy. We've got to get up now, go into the house. You coming, Rex?"

The dog didn't stir. Ben put his hand underneath the dog's nose; he was breathing, gently and steadily. "Wake up, Rex." Ben waited another three beats and then carefully lifted the dog out of the car and began to carry him into the house. When he was clear he pushed the car door closed with his foot. "Jimmy," he said, "run ahead and open up the front door for me, would you?"

"Sure, dad."

Ben set Rex down on the floor beside the couch. "He's a good dog," Ben said softly to Rex. The dog was still asleep. "You sleep well, boy."

Jimmy knelt down beside Ben. "Is Rex okay, dad?"

Ben nodded. "Dr. Smith must have given him something for the pain. Sometimes painkillers will make a dog sleep. Make a person sleep, for that matter."

Rex slept through the afternoon. He was still asleep a few minutes after six, when the Andersons stopped by to collect Ben and Jimmy for dinner at the Williamses'.

As they walked Ben watched the Andersons carefully. They chit-chatted with each other and with Ben and even with Jimmy. It *was* strange: there was something missing in their conversation. All of the little bitternesses, all of the not-quite-meannesses that give wit its edge, were missing from them. Ben had met pleasant, vacantly bland people before. There was nothing unsettling or surreal about them. But it wasn't common. George and Janet Anderson would have been an anomaly if it was only the two of them, but it *wasn't* just them. When Ben thought about it he realized that every person he'd met when he'd been in Green Hill for the interview was as *weird* and edgeless as George and Janet were.

He'd noticed it before, but then it hadn't seemed so . . .

wrong to him. Jimmy was right. The people here weren't just good. They were *empty*. Unnaturally empty. What could make a whole town of people so . . . absent of a basic part of human nature?

Before Ben had a chance to take the thought any farther George Anderson was knocking on the door of the Williams farm, and once they were inside there was no time to drift away in thought. By the time he asked himself the question again, it was too late for the answer to do him any good.

CHAPTER

NINE

DINNER AT THE WILLIAMSES' STARTED OUT AS A NIGHT-mare for Jimmy, but it didn't end that way.

The unpleasant part began with the walk from the rented house. The Andersons were with them, the weird Andersons and their creepy daughter Roberta. Roberta spent the whole walk *watching* Jimmy, staring at him just like she had the last time they'd met.

Jimmy didn't like being stared at. Not even by people he knew were doing it by accident. So, finally, he looked her in the eye and said, "Why are you staring at me?"

She blinked; the corners of her mouth twitched. "I'm not staring at you," she said. "You must be mistaken." It was the first time he'd heard her speak, and her voice was simultaneously saccharine and malevolent. It chilled him. She smiled exactly the way he imagined her smiling when she tore off the wings of flies.

"Well, whatever you're doing, don't do it." Jimmy kicked a fist-sized chunk of sandstone off the path into the weeds.

Roberta just kept smiling.

Dad looked back, raised an eyebrow at him. Jimmy shrugged in response.

The path that led from their house to the Williamses' farm started across the street and led four hundred yards through woods and fields and blackberry brambles before it opened up into the Williamses' backyard, at the edge of one of their cornfields. Mr. Anderson led them around to the front and knocked on the door.

The woman who answered it was middle-aged and plain looking.

"Hello, Betty," Mr. Anderson said. "You already know Ben Tompkins, don't you?" She nodded, and smiled. "This is his son, Jimmy. Jimmy, this is Mrs. Elizabeth Williams."

Jimmy stepped forward and reached out to shake her hand. It was warm and damp, and her grip was weak.

"I'm pleased to make your acquaintance, Jimmy Tompkins," she said with a drawl as thick as honey, but sweeter. Too sweet, even, to be pleasant.

"Thank you," Jimmy said. "I'm glad to meet you, too."

She led them all into the parlor, where a lot of people were already waiting. There were more introductions, too many all at once for Jimmy to remember them at all. He never did get the adults straight; the emptiness was so striking in each of them that it was hard to remember anything else about them, or to tell them apart. But by the end of the evening he had clear impressions of each of the children.

The one he noticed first was Christian—the oldest of the boys who'd attacked Jimmy and Rex with clubs. Jimmy's heart jerked hard in his chest when he saw him. Jimmy tugged on his dad's sleeve to try to tell him that he recognized the boy. But dad didn't even notice that Jimmy was trying to get his attention; he looked too confused from all the introductions to take in anything else.

The children, all of them, looked as nasty as Christian. Or nearly so, and some of them were worse. But none, not even one, had the pure cruelness about him that Roberta did.

There were two tall, muscled brothers named Brady— Sean and Thomas. The meanness was as plain in their eyes as it was in Christian's, but they were polite when they introduced themselves, and Jimmy thought that whatever else there might be about them, they both had a great deal of common sense. Most of the others seemed to take their cues from Sean and Thomas, or sometimes from Roberta Anderson.

There was a pair of identical twin sisters, Jan and Eileen Williams. Jimmy wasn't sure which one was which, and neither one seemed bright enough to remember well anyway. The nastiness in their eyes was like Christian's, too. But where Christian's evil had ambition the two girls seemed to have only pettiness. Jimmy could imagine them as the two girls Dr. Smith had found torturing a kitten; they didn't look as though they had the nerve for anything larger.

But the one who stuck in Jimmy's memory hardest after that first impression was Tim Hanson.

". . . and this is Tim Hanson, Jimmy. You and Tim Hanson have a lot in common. Tim's dad is a single father, too."

Jimmy shook the boy's hand.

"My mama died in a car accident when I was just three years old," Tim said. "What happened to your mama?"

Jimmy flushed, and his tongue turned thick and clumsy in his mouth. He suddenly wanted to duck out of sight, to push out of the crowd and *run* until he never had to see any of them again. But that was crazy, and Jimmy didn't want to act crazy. Thinking he didn't want to act that way didn't change the way he felt at all. He looked up and back to catch dad's eye; dad looked worried and concerned. But what Jimmy thought of when he saw his dad wasn't just the worry and concern—he imagined dad embarrassed for him because Jimmy was acting crazy. That wasn't fair, probably, to dad. Dad always stood up for him, and he never acted like Jimmy was an embarrassment. But Jimmy couldn't bear the thought, the possibility, that he'd shame dad. He couldn't let himself act crazy and stupid, no matter how he felt.

So Jimmy stood still, even though he felt like the world was rushing around him like a whirlwind. "Mom's in the hospital," Jimmy said. "She's very sick, and she's going to be there a long time."

That's when Tim did the thing that surprised him. Instead of grinning maliciously and bathing in Jimmy's discomfort—which is what all the other children were doing —he frowned and apologized.

"Sorry," he said, "I guess that's none of my concern."

Jimmy didn't know how to respond at first. The whole room was quiet. All the adults were watching them, and all of them but dad were staring at Tim like he'd just got off a shuttle from the moon. The kids didn't act like they saw anything at all. When Jimmy finally knew what to say his voice tripped over his tongue and jammed in his throat for a moment before anything intelligible would come out. "It's okay," he said. The scratch in his voice came out more as a tick than as a stutter. "I'm sorry about your mom."

Tim nodded. "Me too, I guess. About your mom, I mean."

The grown-ups kept staring for a moment or two. Then someone—Christian Ross's mother, Jimmy thought; he wasn't sure—shrugged and blinked a couple of times and all the adults from Green Hill started laughing. Someone said, "Why are we all just sitting here?" and they all laughed harder. Jimmy wasn't sure why, but he got the feeling that not a one of them remembered what they'd all watched so intently just a moment ago.

The situation was uncomfortable enough that Jimmy wanted to get away from it; he excused himself and asked Mrs. Williams for directions to the bathroom. She pointed him toward the hallway.

One of the walls in the hall was covered with bloodstains.

As Jimmy got back Mrs. Williams bustled into the kitchen, and then just a moment later she bustled out again and called everyone in to dinner. There were two big tables in the dining room; she pointed Jimmy at a seat at the smaller of the two. He went to it and sat, and one by one the seats around him filled. There were only a couple of chairs left empty before he realized that all the children were at this table, and that the adults would eat at the larger one.

Tim sat down two chairs away from Jimmy, at one of the ends of the table.

Tim had the same mean-spirited light in his eye that the rest of the children did. Jimmy could almost see the same cruel possibilities written on his face. But the other children were mean and purely mean; the strongest thing inside any of them that wasn't nastiness was common sense. In Tim Jimmy could feel a good-heartedness and honesty tempering the blackness of his nature. The other children seemed to treat him like a nerd, but Jimmy didn't think they saw the better part of him. If they'd seen it, Jimmy thought, they'd treat him like something dangerous and alien.

Christian came around the table, popped Tim's ear with the middle finger of his right hand, and sat down between Tim and Jimmy. "I'm going to get you," he whispered into Jimmy's ear as he sat down. "I'm going to make you *hurt.*"

Jimmy'd coped with bullies before. They didn't really frighten him. He smiled like he was meaner and nastier than Christian could ever think about being. "I'd like to see you try," Jimmy whispered back. "Lay a hand on me and I'll peel the skin off your ass and make a wallet out of it."

Thomas sat down across from Jimmy, glared at Christian. Christian got a sullen, angry scowl on his face, but he didn't say anything else. Could Thomas have heard them? Jimmy had thought they were too quiet to hear, but maybe not. He wasn't sure.

Jimmy had a good view of the adults' table, which was behind Thomas—dad sat on the near side of that table, facing away from Jimmy. If something happened, dad wouldn't know about it until it was already too late.

Thomas thought Jimmy wanted his attention; he nodded. He smiled a smile that reminded Jimmy of the bagman who'd lived on the streets of their neighborhood back in New Jersey—when the bagman would smile you'd see his rotting black-and-yellow teeth, and he'd drool a little, and you'd catch wind of his breath, which always reminded Jimmy of the pair of socks he'd once worn three days in a row. Thomas's teeth weren't rotting, and Jimmy couldn't smell his breath, but somehow the essence felt the same to Jimmy, as though something underneath them both was similar. Decay, maybe. . . ? Yes, decay. Maybe it was decay.

"So, Jimmy Tompkins," Thomas said, "tell us about your journey to Green Hill from the state of New Jersey."

"Driving down here, you mean. . . ?" Thomas nodded. "There isn't much to tell, I guess. We drove a lot. We stayed in different hotel rooms in different hotels in different states, but somehow all the hotel rooms seemed the same. It's hard to remember one of them from another. We ate in a lot of coffee shops and hotel restaurants, and all of those are pretty hard to tell apart, too. The only different part of the whole trip was driving all night before we got here." Jimmy didn't know why he was going on so long; he hadn't meant to say any of that. All of them—all the kids at the table—were listening too carefully. He felt kind of stupid, and that made him blush. He meant to stop.

"What's so different about riding in the car all night?" Tim asked.

Jimmy shrugged. "I don't know. Maybe not much. I had a dream, though. A nightmare."

The two twin girls, who were sitting past Roberta on Jimmy's left, giggled. Then Thomas looked at them, and they stopped so abruptly that it almost sounded to Jimmy as though the sound were some sort of a recording that someone had suddenly turned off.

But Thomas was smiling, too, as though he was enjoying something deliciously mean. "What *kind* of nightmare?" He was almost laughing as he said it, and the rest of the children snickered when they heard that.

Almost as though they knew what Jimmy had been dreaming.

Jimmy shook his head. "Just bad dreams. No special kind." He felt like a small animal trapped in a room with wolves. The idea of being trapped by a bunch of mean-hearted kids made him angry. Jimmy didn't like being picked on or pushed around. Once when he was little he'd sat still for two hours and taken it when an older boy decided to pick on him. It had kept getting worse until

Jimmy got mad enough to hit him. Jimmy got hit back, but the boy never teased him again.

Christian was sitting next to him, and Christian was laughing hard.

Jimmy looked him in the eye and said, "Is something funny?"

Christian grinned like an idiot. "There's nothing funnier than the scars on your face. Where'd you get those from—trying to French-kiss a Mack truck?"

No one got to talk like that about Jimmy's scars. He jumped on the boy. He put his hands around Christian's neck and dug his thumb into the bandage that covered the gash Jimmy had given him last night. Christian's right hand pounded at Jimmy's face; his left tried to do the same, but Jimmy had him pushed half under the table, and Christian's fist just slammed into the table's underside. It couldn't get past.

Jimmy bent down and whispered into his ear. "I'm going to smash your *balls,* scumbag," he said. "You'll never use them for *any*thing." Christian started to struggle, and Jimmy brought his knee up into the boy's groin. Christian went limp and quiet, but Jimmy could still hear his hand moving over by the table.

Jimmy looked up and saw that Mrs. Williams was staring at him. For an instant she looked shocked and horrified, and he thought she was going to scream. Maybe she'd even step into the fight and pull him away from Christian. Then he blinked his eyes and she was smiling pleasantly, and she waved to him as though she didn't even see what was happening.

Christian still lay there limp as a rag doll, fumbling around on the table with his left hand. Suddenly Jimmy heard a slapping sound, and somebody grabbed him by the back collar of his shirt and yanked him up.

It was Thomas. He'd pulled Jimmy up off of Christian with his left hand. His other hand held Christian's left arm by the wrist.

That's when Jimmy saw exactly what Christian had been fumbling with at the table as Jimmy held him down: a knife.

A five-inch-long serrated steak knife, with a wicked-sharp point and a wooden handle, exactly the kind they set out at restaurants, so sharp that the meat is easy to cut and seems more tender than it really is.

"You jerk," Thomas said to Christian. His eyes were gleaming; bloodlust fought against self-preservation on his face. "You do this sort of shit, his father's going to see you. You think his father isn't going to remember? Outsiders, dumbfuck. Outsiders remember. It doesn't matter if your old man and your mother think you're a little angel. His old man'll see him dead, and the sheriff'll be here, and we'll all be in reform school, just like on TV." Thomas shoved Jimmy and Christian away from him, and spat on the floor. He looked at Jimmy and gave him an extra shove. "Keep your nose *clean*, new boy. Or I'll take a piece of it off with my pocketknife and clean it for you."

Thomas turned and started back toward his seat, but before he took two steps Roberta put her hand on his arm and stopped him.

"You'd better be careful yourself, Thomas," she said. "Jimmy isn't one of the Children." She said the world *children* as though it ought to start with a capital. "Look at him carefully. He doesn't belong to the Stone yet. And maybe he never will. He'll see things no grown-up ever could."

Thomas went white as a sheet. His head snapped around to look at Jimmy—

—and he *looked* at him, and saw Jimmy hard and deep inside. And *recognized* him. And suddenly Thomas looked as scared as Jimmy ever had been that weekend with his mom.

"Shit," Thomas said, almost whispering. "What *is* he?"

"Any trouble over there, kids? Everybody happy with dinner?" Mrs. Williams called over from the other table. Jimmy's dad managed to free himself from the conversation he was having long enough to steal a glance at Jimmy. Jimmy nodded at him, to let him know not to worry.

"No trouble at all, Mrs. Williams. Just getting to know Jimmy Tompkins, here." He still looked scared and worried, but his fear was under control now. He went back to his seat, and Jimmy and Christian both sat back down.

She passed over a plate of rolls. "Jan and Eileen, why don't you all come into the kitchen with me and help me with the serving plates. The rest of you children can help yourselves to some biscuits."

Tim took the roll platter from Mrs. Williams, grabbed one, and passed the plate to Christian, who passed it to Jimmy. Jimmy took one and passed the plate to Roberta.

Thomas whispered to his brother, but he whispered like they do in the movies, hoarse and scratchy, and loud enough to hear half-way across a room. It was the kind of whisper Jimmy expected from a three-year-old who hadn't learned how to keep something secret yet.

"We're going to be in trouble, Sean. There's something wrong with that boy."

Sean whispered back, just as loud. "Why don't you just ask him what he wants. Ask him why he's here. Maybe he doesn't just want to make trouble."

"If you're going to whisper, you ought to do it so I can't hear," Jimmy said. Thomas flushed; Sean looked furious. "Didn't you ever have to keep anything secret before? You sound like somebody on a television cartoon. The idea is to talk normal, but too softly for anyone to hear. And all I want from you is to be left alone."

Neither of the brothers said a word.

Christian snickered in his ear. "You've got them really mad now. They're going to kill you when they get a chance. They've got awful tempers." He kept snickering as he said it.

"I'm not afraid," Jimmy said, loud enough to be heard across the room. Dad looked back at him again, but Jimmy just shrugged. He looked straight at Thomas and said, "I don't want anything from any of you. I just want to be left alone."

Thomas didn't answer him; it didn't even look as though he'd heard him. Sean had heard, but he wasn't speaking either. He looked too angry to speak.

By the time Jan and Eileen got to the table with their platters, Thomas looked ill.

Jimmy wanted to get up, pull dad out of his chair, and leave. He didn't like bullies. He didn't like being bullied. But most of all he didn't like to have to act like he was a bigger bully than they were, even if it was the only way he knew to cope with them. For a moment he almost started to get up and go—then he realized what he was doing and stopped himself. He wasn't going to act like a fool. He wasn't going to embarrass his dad.

Dinner was roasted chicken; Mrs. Williams had carved it in the kitchen before her girls had brought it out. When Roberta passed him the platter that Eileen had passed her, Jimmy took enough to be polite, even though he wasn't hungry, and passed the platter on.

Thomas's hands began to tremble about the time that Christian took the platter from Jimmy.

Roberta passed a big serving bowl filled with orange-brown mashed squash. Jimmy was only barely able to force himself to take a portion of that; he *hated* mashed squash. Hated the look of it, the taste of it, the feel of it in his mouth. Even the smell by itself was enough to make him feel queasy. He set a tablespoon of it on the far edge of his plate and passed it on.

He looked up from passing the bowl just as the chicken platter reached Thomas. Sean moved the platter from one hand to the other, offering it to Thomas, and Thomas doubled over and started dry-heaving into his plate. For a moment Jimmy thought he was going to puke all over the table. That made Jimmy feel two things at the same time: part of him was disgusted, afraid Thomas would upchuck forcefully enough to spatter Jimmy with vomit. It was Jimmy who'd get it, too, since Thomas's seat faced Jimmy's. The other part of Jimmy was hopeful at the idea, since he'd have to go home if Thomas puked on him, and just then there wasn't anything in the world he wanted more than to get out of that room.

But Thomas didn't puke all over the table; he pushed his chair back and hurried away from the dining room, toward the toilet.

Jimmy heard his dad ask, "Is something wrong?"

Someone over at dad's table said, "Nothing wrong with Thomas but growing pains," and all the adults but Jimmy's dad laughed as though it were a wonderful joke.

When they were all quiet again dad asked if they were sure, and someone else told him that they were. "What's the matter, don't kids up in New Jersey have growing pains?" the second adult asked dad, and they all laughed again.

"Not growing pains like that, they don't," dad said, but he said it pretty quietly, and no one seemed to notice.

Then Thomas was coming back from the bathroom. And maybe whoever said it was right, maybe getting sick to your stomach was growing pains in Green Hill—because Thomas wasn't the same Thomas anymore.

Thomas had lost something. The sharpness was gone out of his eyes; the only things still visible on his face were common sense and good nature and something large and empty. Not so large and empty as the vacuum in the heart of Mrs. Anderson, but still big. Nature had meant Thomas to be a big, good-hearted, bad-tempered man, and it had given him enough horse sense to keep him out of trouble. Jimmy almost thought that maybe he'd used up his anger and didn't have any left anymore. But that couldn't be. Jimmy knew enough about people to be sure that they don't just use parts of themselves up. It was just the opposite. The people Jimmy had seen always grew more and more like the things they did. When a part of a person shriveled up and died it was because he'd never used it, or because he'd ignored it too long.

Still, Thomas sat in front of him, and one of the most important parts of him was gone. The fact that it was missing was written all over his face.

Thomas's brother, Sean, looked murderously angry.

"Sorry I'm late," Thomas said. He reached across the table to shake Jimmy's hand. "You're the new boy dad told me about? Jimmy Tompkins?"

Jimmy blinked, tried to clear his head. He shook Thomas's hand more by reflex than intention. "Uh . . . ? Yeah. Yes, I'm Jimmy Tompkins."

"Well, I'm glad to meet you. You just moved here from New Jersey, dad said. I think that's what he said—sorry, I'm a little foggy. Am I right? New Jersey?" Jimmy blinked again, and nodded. "Something in your eye?"

Jimmy kept wanting to think the boy was putting him on, setting him up for some sort of a nasty trick. But he seemed sincere, and even casual. He looked too relaxed to be planning something strange.

"No," Jimmy said, "just a little confused. Five minutes ago you looked like you wanted to tear my throat out."

Sean still looked like he wanted to kill Jimmy, but now he was snickering, too.

Thomas's eyes opened wide with shock, as though suddenly he remembered what was best forgot, and then, slowly, his face went slack and confused. He rubbed his eyes and frowned. "Sorry, I'm feeling awfully foggy—I can't even remember what I was saying." He coughed. "So, Jimmy Tompkins, how was your trip down here to Green Hill?"

Jimmy felt the bottom falling out from inside him; no matter what was wrong with the children here—no matter how vile or ill-tempered they were—whatever was wrong with Thomas was worse. He'd seen people with stumps for arms and legs once when dad took him to New York. Even one wrinkled old woman who didn't have a nose. But what Thomas didn't have was a part of *him*, not just a part of his body. Was it just the memories of badness that were gone, and maybe the desires and needs that grew out of them?

It was crazy. What Jimmy was thinking was crazy. The psychologist had asked him if he ever imagined things, things just like this. The only thing to do with craziness was to put it behind you and forget about it; Jimmy knew that.

But it *wasn't* just craziness. It couldn't be. Jimmy hadn't imagined the strange scars and oozing scabs on Rex. Dad had seen them too. And he hadn't imagined Thomas and Roberta talking like they were part of some conspiracy, or the way grown-ups around here seemed to just . . . not see whenever something bad happened. No. Even if it was crazy, it was real.

Jimmy tried to imagine himself like Thomas, shucking the memory of the bad things that he did and the bad things that happened to him, as though he were a snake and the memories were a skin he was ready to shed. He pictured himself without any memory of his mother or the psychologist or the hospital or a million other things. They were things that he didn't want to think about anyway, but. . . . Even if he didn't think about his mother, like dad said, she was a part of him. Who she was and what she'd done shaped him. Molded him. Whether she was something horrible or not, Jimmy wouldn't be himself without her.

The idea of losing his mother forever made Jimmy sad, and it made him sad for Thomas.

"Jimmy Tompkins? Are you okay?" Thomas asked.

Jimmy set his teeth and forced himself back into the moment. "Yes, I'm fine. I guess I'm a little foggy too."

Thomas laughed, deep and loud and clear. "I like you, Jimmy Tompkins," he said. "You're all right. So, how was your trip?"

Jimmy suddenly found himself liking Thomas. "The trip was fine," he said. "It wasn't bad at all."

Sean spat on his plate, shoved back his chair, and left the table. All the children at the table but Jimmy and Thomas had finished eating. Tim excused himself; Jan, Eileen, and Roberta just got up. Thomas stuffed a big hunk of chicken into his mouth and started chewing on it as though he didn't even see his brother's sticky phlegm sitting on the place by his elbow. "You going to eat any of that?" he asked Jimmy, talking around his food.

"I ate some. I'm not very hungry."

Thomas swallowed. "Huh. Well. Think I'm done here, too. You want to play some blackjack?"

"Blackjack. . . ? I don't know. I don't like betting very much." Jimmy really didn't, either. He almost always won at cards—unless he bet at them. When he bet he usually lost.

"Aw, come on. You don't have to bet to play blackjack. More fun if you don't. Nothing to worry about if you're not betting."

Jimmy shrugged. "Okay. Sure, I guess." It sounded like a weird idea to Jimmy, but at least it was something to do.

And as it turned out it *was* fun—a lot of fun. That was probably mostly because he found himself enjoying Thomas's company. It was almost like he was a friend, though Jimmy didn't know if it was right to count someone as a friend who he'd only just met that night. Especially since Thomas had looked like he'd wanted to kill Jimmy for a while. But friends were important. Jimmy hadn't really felt like he had any friends since that weekend with his mom. All his friends back in New Jersey had gotten weird on him after that weekend, probably because of the stories in the newspapers.

That was how the evening that had started as a nightmare turned into a dream—something special, something wonderful. Jimmy hadn't realized how much he needed friends. When he and his dad started the walk home, Jimmy was still caught up in the wonder of it; he almost felt as though he'd just begun to come back to life after months of hibernation, or maybe even death.

It wasn't until after they were home and dad had already tucked him in that it occurred to Jimmy that there were things he needed to tell dad. About recognizing Christian, about fighting with him while Mrs. Williams watched but didn't see. About the strange things that Roberta said, and the ones that Thomas said before he suddenly changed. He almost got up and talked to dad right then. But telling dad all that would spoil the warmness of the evening, turn it back into something cold and hard. It would keep till morning, Jimmy thought, and he decided to let it wait.

That was probably the worst decision Jimmy ever made. There weren't many he regretted more.

CHAPTER

TEN

JIMMY LAY AWAKE IN BED FOR A LONG WHILE, WAITING for the touch of the thing that had forced itself into his dreams two nights running. He could hear Rex's slow, steady breathing at the foot of the bed. The dog was asleep; still asleep. He'd been out since early afternoon because of whatever painkiller the veterinarian had given him.

After half an hour Jimmy began to drift into sleep, and as he did he felt the touch of the Stone. He recoiled from it— forced his eyes open and forced himself awake.

Rex, breathing slow and steady as a metronome at the foot of the bed, made Jimmy feel like he had when he was little, when his grandmom would sometimes sing him lullabies that called him down toward sleep. Jimmy resisted the call, and he lay awake in bed for most of another hour. But he couldn't stay awake forever; his body was tired. Even though he was frightened and angry, and his heart beat fast and hard, nothing demanded his attention enough to keep him awake. He fell asleep around midnight without even noticing that it happened.

Jimmy's mother lifted him up over her head with both arms and hurled him through her bedroom window. Glass burst around him, making a thousand cuts along his face and chest, and he sailed out into the swirling, sunlit snow.

He fell two storeys and landed in a snowdrift that had piled high over his sandbox. The snow and the sand broke most of his fall, but his left leg smacked hard on the wooden rim of the sandbox, where the snow was thin. He could feel it begin to swell up right away, in spite of the cold.

Jimmy sat up, trying to ignore the pain in his leg and a million other places. The breaking window had torn his pajamas to rags; cold bit him everywhere. Wind chilled the leaking blood on the skin of his neck until it burned with iciness. Flakes of snow drifted through the gaping holes in his pajama top, and when they landed on his chest they melted and refroze, and the tiny dots of ice stung like needles.

But he was alive; he was breathing and he was free. Or he was free till his mother laid hands on him again—free enough to run, if his leg wasn't broken.

He wasn't sure about the leg. The swelling was horrible, but already the pain in it was ebbing.

That was usually a bad sign. Jimmy hardly ever felt anything when he was seriously hurt—at least not until later, when it began to heal. He rolled up the left leg of his pajamas to get a better look. The leg didn't *look* especially broken. His shin was in the right place on both sides of the swelling, and the skin wasn't broken. That didn't necessarily mean anything; Jimmy broke his arm when he was four, and the arm hadn't looked anything but swollen then.

But whether it was broken or not, he had to run on it if he wanted to live. He stood—using both arms and his right leg so that he didn't put much weight on his left foot—and the only pain he felt was from the snow that ground into his feet. He took a step, and that didn't hurt the leg either, so he hobbled off toward the supermarket five blocks away. There was a hired policeman there who guarded the store—mostly from shoplifters—and there were enough people there even when business was slow that Jimmy didn't think mom would dare act crazy.

He was half a block away—still limping more than walking—when he heard the back door fly open, then slam closed. It was only a moment after that when he heard her scream, "James Tompkins!" and he knew that she'd seen his trail. It would have been hard to miss; the snow was fresh, and his were the only footprints in it. Worse, he was bleeding all over, leaving behind a trail of bright red spatters that stood out brilliantly on the white drifts.

Jimmy *ran*.

He turned off the sidewalk and took a shortcut through the neighbors' backyard, and the backyard of the house behind them. The snow was deep and uneven; a couple of times he stumbled in it and almost fell. He couldn't fall, though—he didn't dare. There wasn't time to fall.

By the time he got to the next street over his feet had quit burning. They were numb to the cold, and maybe they were getting frostbit. He couldn't feel anything in them.

Mom screamed his name again, and a car door slammed. The engine started and roared loud enough to hear a street away. Mom was going to hunt him down with the car.

Jimmy darted across the street, ran across two more back-to-back yards.

Mom's car roared down the street he'd just left behind.

Jimmy wanted to scream for help, but there was no one out walking around in the snowstorm to hear him. Besides, falling snow took in sound and made it soft and quiet. He was too out of breath; there was no way he could scream loud enough for anyone to hear him through the snow and through the walls of houses. He saved his breath and kept running.

Two more blocks and a sprint down the sidewalk to the through street, and Jimmy was standing at a crosswalk catty-corner from the supermarket. The light finished changing, and he crossed the through street, then jaywalked the smaller one. He could have jaywalked both of them; there wasn't a car anywhere in sight.

The supermarket and its parking lot took up two square blocks of land between them. The store lay diagonally at the far end of the parking lot from the corner. Jimmy was a third of the way across it when he heard the engine of his mother's car.

There were four cars parked near the door of the supermarket; Jimmy could see through the big glass front that the lights were on inside and there were people at the registers. But there was no one outside. If he couldn't get to the door before his mother reached him, he was going to die. She was going to kill him. Mom could do anything when she was drunk and angry, and Jimmy had never seen her angrier.

He ran harder than he thought he ever could, even though it meant sliding crazily through the icy snow that covered the parking lot. He screamed for help, but the sound got tangled in the snowstorm and disappeared.

He was only fifty yards from the door when he heard his mother's brakes screech behind him as she tried to stop. It didn't work; Jimmy heard the brakes lock up, heard the car's tires turn into snow skis as the car began to slide across the icy pavement. Jimmy kept running, but he only made it three more yards before the car slammed into him.

Jimmy was lucky: even though the car was moving, it was going slowly enough that it didn't turn him into pulp. Only two of his ribs cracked; most of the muscles that the car twisted out of shape until they ripped were healed by April—or, at least, by April they were as healed as they would ever get.

The car slammed into him, and sent Jimmy sliding twenty yards face-first across the asphalt. He was lucky about that, too—lucky that the snow covering the blacktop was icy. If it had been summer he only would have slid five yards, and the tar would have ripped his face from his skull; it would only have taken a moment for him to bleed to death. As it was he got by with nothing more than a crazed webwork of interlocking ice cuts and abrasions. When they healed all they left behind was a fine lacework of white scars—scars so fine that they were barely even visible except when he had a tan, or when the light caught them just right and their texture made them visible.

The car finally stopped a few inches before its left front tire crushed Jimmy's skull.

Jimmy tried to get up. He tried to get up and make himself run. But his body wouldn't listen. It wouldn't move. He was thirty yards from the store, thirty yards from people who could help him and protect him, and all that happened when he tried to get up for the second time was that his left hand twitched.

There was blood everywhere, even in his eyes. The door to his mother's car opened and slammed shut. She was out of the car, and she was screaming.

"You goddamned fucking little bastard," she said. It sounded as though she were miles and miles away, screaming at him through a narrow tunnel. "You're going to learn. I'm going to pound your bones into pulp, beat you till you *learn* about trying to run away from me."

Part of Jimmy tried to be scared. It really did. It knew that horrible things were going to happen. But his adrenaline was all used up; running had bled it all away from him and he had nothing left to be scared with.

Mom grabbed his left foot and yanked him out from under the car; his body slid across the pavement, gliding on a film of half-frozen blood. When he was clear she turned him over and looked at him. He blinked, and she screamed at him again. "Little *bastard,*" she said, and she smacked his face hard enough to make his whole body slide a few inches through the snow. Her hand came away covered with his blood. Jimmy hardly even felt the pain. His skin and his flesh were numb from shock and from the cold. What he did feel was the impact of the blow; he felt it with his bones.

She grabbed his hair and lifted his head up so that she could look him in the eye. "Do you know how much I regret the day you were born, you ungrateful little asshole? How *dare* you not come when I call you? How *dare* you try to run away from me!" She pushed his head back down into the pavement.

She brought her fist right down into his belly, punched him so hard that Jimmy felt his heart press up into his ribs. Her left fist came down from over her head and pounded into his shoulder. "Answer me, damn it!" she said. Then she was flailing, punching him again and again and again. All Jimmy felt of it was the strange pressing of his muscles against his bones—that and the vibrations of his bones against themselves.

"Lady, take your hands off the little boy. Take your hands off him *now.*" It was a man's voice, deep and firm and quiet.

Someone from the store had seen them!

Jimmy recognized the voice, he thought. He remembered it vaguely, as though he'd heard it often, but without paying much attention. Mom sat up to look at the man, and Jimmy got a glance of him—it was the manager of the supermarket. He was looking at them like he didn't even recognize Jimmy or his mom.

"What do *you* want?" Mom asked. She said the word *you* like she was talking to a worm. "What business is this of yours?"

There were more people standing by the electric doors of the supermarket, watching them.

"I don't care whether or not it's my business, lady. You're about to beat that poor kid to death, and I'm not just going to stand here and let you do it."

Mom stood up. She stepped over toward the man, kept going until her face was only five inches from his.

"Mind—"

—mom put her hands on his shoulders and *pushed.* The man's dress shoes didn't have any traction on the icy-slick pavement; his feet flew out from under him and his back slammed hard into the ground—

"your own—"

—mom took another step, hauled back her good foot and kicked the man in the groin with all the strength she had—

"—fucking—"

—mom stomped hard onto his chest, and stood on it. She hauled her foot back again and slammed his jaw into his skull—

"—business!"

The store manager didn't move again. Mom stooped over, grabbed Jimmy's hand, and dragged him into the car. Jimmy didn't struggle; he still couldn't move.

Mom opened the back door of the car, lifted Jimmy by

his hair and the waist of his pants, and threw him onto the backseat. She slammed the back door, opened her own, slammed it shut. She turned on the ignition and floored the gas, then jerked the car into gear with the engine still roaring. The car's tires spun on the snow, then caught— the car moved wildly, unevenly, accelerating too fast. One of the tires thumped over something solid, as though it had run over something fairly big, like a curb or a rock or a man's leg, Jimmy didn't know what. All he could see was the ceiling of the car. He pictured the store manager's legs crushed by car tires, and suddenly he wanted to cry again, but he just didn't have the strength to cry.

Mom shifted gears; the car accelerated again and swerved even more wildly. Jimmy's head rocked on the seat and bounced against the seat back. He must have hit some lump on his head, because after that he blacked out, and when he woke he was in a place he'd never been before.

When Jimmy came to he was in a hotel room.

Mom was still drunk; ranting drunk. Jimmy heard her before he saw anything. She was screaming about something he'd done when he was three, and Jimmy woke and tried to open his eyes to see her. They didn't want to open at first—the blood on his face had dried while he was unconscious. There was scabrous blood dried on his eyelids, sealing them shut. He tried to wipe it away with his hands, and realized that his hands were tied behind his back. There was something jammed into his mouth, too. Whatever it was was so big and packed so tight that he couldn't move his tongue, and the rear of his tongue was jammed back into his throat. It felt soft and coarse, like nylon mesh, and it tasted like sweat. One of her stockings, maybe. Yes, Jimmy thought, it probably was.

Jimmy pressed his eyes shut and tried to open them again, and managed to work them free enough to raise his eyelids.

The first thing he saw was his mother, glaring at him. She was still furious, trembling with anger. Her eyes were bright red and bloodshot, and she reeked of whiskey and sweat. Behind her on the bureau of the hotel room there were four liter-size bottles of whiskey. One of them was empty; another was open and only half-full.

There was a digital alarm clock on the bureau beside the whiskey bottles. It read 5:27:41 p.m.

"So, you're awake now, huh?" She spat at him. Saliva spattered on his forehead and trickled down into his left eye.

Jimmy nodded. The motion made his head swim.

"Do you know what you've done to me now, you little jackass? You've ruined me. Ruined me." She reached over to her purse, took a cigarette out of it, lit the cigarette. "You're going to pay for that, do you hear me?" She took a deep drag from the cigarette, then let it dangle from one corner of her mouth. "You're going to *pay.*"

She grabbed his hair with her left hand and slapped him across the face with her right. She hit something that was already bruised deeply, or maybe even broken; Jimmy felt himself begin to black out. The slap opened up a few of the scabbed-over scratches on his face, too, and blood began to ooze into his eyes and mouth. Mom must have seen him begin to black out, because she grabbed him by the collar and shook him.

"You're not getting away from me again, do you hear me? Don't even think about going back to sleep."

Jimmy propped his eyelids open with willpower.

"Those people *saw* us as we left the parking lot. Do you understand what that means to me, you shit-eating little pig? I'm ruined. Three of them were taking down our license-plate number as we drove away. The police will be *looking* for me. You run away from home, and the police come looking for *me,* and I'm the one who goes to jail."

She took the cigarette out of her mouth and took a long drink from her whiskey glass. When she was done she screeched. "You goddamn little *bastard*!" She threw the whiskey that was left in her glass into Jimmy's face. Jimmy squeezed his eyes shut, but not fast enough; the whiskey leaked through his eyelids, and it *burned.* Jimmy whined; the whiskey was the first thing that had actually caused pain that he could *feel* since his mother had first thrown him out into the snow.

He blinked the whiskey out of his eyes.

Mom took another pull off her cigarette, then took it out

of her mouth again. "So, that hurt you, huh? Well, see how you like this." Slowly, very slowly, she brought her burning cigarette up toward his face. Smoke drifted up into Jimmy's nostrils when he breathed; it stung his sinuses. "You little bastard," she said.

She yanked the gag out of his mouth.

"I'm sorry, mommy," Jimmy said. "I won't do it again."

"Do you think I believe that for a minute?" She was just inches away from his face; her whiskey breath blew cigarette smoke into his eyes. "You've already ruined me. If I gave you half a chance you'd kill me."

She pulled the cigarette back away from him, and for a moment Jimmy thought she was just going to put it in the ashtray. Then she stuffed the stockings back into his mouth and started pushing the cigarette at him again, pushing it right toward his right eye. Jimmy screamed through the nylon cloth and squeezed his eyes shut again, but it didn't do any good. She pressed the cigarette into his scrunched-up eye and twisted it, ground it into his eye until the ember was dead.

Mom started crying; Jimmy heard her throw herself down on the bed. "You've ruined everything," she said, still crying. "My life, my job, everything I have is gone—and it's all *your* goddamn fault!"

Jimmy worked his eyes back and forth until the cigarette came lose and fell onto his chest. Once it was gone he tried to open his eyes, but the burn had sealed his right eye closed, and it was beginning to swell, too. He didn't try to force it; it didn't seem like a good idea.

Still, he could see through his left eye. The digital clock read five-forty now. Mom lay facedown on the hotel room's king-size bed, crying; her whole body shook from her sobs. Jimmy thought about trying to get away again, but there wasn't any use in it. His hands were tied behind the back of the chair he was sitting in, and his ankles were tied to its legs. Besides, he thought, if she saw him trying to get away again she really would kill him; she wouldn't even hesitate.

So he sat there, not moving, and watched as his mother sobbed herself to sleep. She stopped crying around six, and she lay so still that for a moment Jimmy thought she'd died. Her position was contorted and uncomfortable looking;

the chain that her pendant hung from was snagged on the bedclothes and pulled so tight across the soft part of her neck that Jimmy was ready to believe she'd strangled herself. Or maybe she'd drunk herself to death. He'd read somewhere that that could happen—that people could drink so much that the alcohol became a deadly poison. But then she groaned in her sleep and cursed, and grabbed the chain around her neck, pulled it hard and angrily until it broke. She threw the chain and the pendant across the room without opening her eyes; she didn't even see the tiny fragment of the Stone smack against the wall—didn't see the shards and slivers clatter against the rim of the wastebasket and fall inside. But she groaned again, more miserably, when the pendant broke, and for a moment Jimmy was half-certain that she'd felt it breaking.

Sometime after seven Jimmy fell asleep himself. He drifted in and out of sleep all night. Around two in the morning his body began to feel the pain it had been post-poning since the morning of the day before, and he woke up hurting so bad that he wished he were dead. He heard himself moan into the stockings, felt his eyes full of wet tears that helped rinse away the blood and cigarette ash.

Eventually he fell asleep again in spite of the pain.

At six a.m. some sunlight began to filter in through the curtained windows of the hotel room, and for the first time he noticed that there was a mirror over the headboard of the bed. He turned to look at it and caught sight of himself. His stomach dry-heaved. He looked like something out of a bad horror movie; he was covered with dried blood and bruises and grime. His skin was a sallow yellow color where he wasn't bruised. He turned away.

His stomach dry-heaved again, and then it found something to puke up. Bile and acid pushed up from his stomach and tried to force their way through his mouth. But his mouth was blocked by the stockings, so the vomit kept going up through the fleshy parts inside his nose and out his nostrils. It *burned* inside his nose even after most of it had run out over his mouth and down his chin.

Two and a half hours after that his mother began to stir in her bed. She spent most of twenty minutes tossing and turning in her sleep, and finally waking up.

And when she woke, she was the mom that Jimmy loved, the mom who she was when she was sober and not drinking.

She sat up in bed and rubbed her eyes. She looked deathly ill.

After a long moment she opened her eyes and looked around her. She looked confused at first, as though she didn't quite recognize where she was, or remember how she'd got there. Then she saw Jimmy, and recognition bloomed on her face like some terrible flower coming into blossom all at once. And Jimmy saw her remembering.

"Oh my God," she said. "Oh my God, what have I done?" Her hand clutched absently for the pendant that no longer hung from her neck. She looked around the room, and then she looked back at Jimmy. "My *baby*," she said, "my God, what have I done to my baby?"

Jimmy wouldn't have known what to say to her even if he hadn't been bound and gagged. He was still terrified, and he knew that she could see that in his eyes. But he loved her, too—she was his mother, and he couldn't stop himself from loving her. She looked as though she were going to curl up and die right then and there from guilt and shame and self-disgust.

She stood up, stumbled to the bureau, and grabbed the half-empty whiskey bottle. For a moment Jimmy thought she was going to drink out of it, and start the whole nightmare all over again, but then she hurled it at the door, where it exploded in a hail of glass and whiskey. She threw the two unopened bottles after it, and finally the empty one. Glass and alcohol were everywhere; Jimmy felt wet sharp slivers spatter his skin.

One fat wedge of glass four inches long and an inch and a half wide rebounded from the door and wedged itself in the collar of her dress and drew blood from her neck. It lay there, trapped and digging itself deeper into the skin of her neck, until she pulled it free.

"I shouldn't be alive," she said. "No one who can do this to her child should live." She took the shard of glass and slowly cut a wide deep T in the inner flesh of her left wrist, then shifted the glass from one hand to the other and did the same to her right.

She bent over and kissed Jimmy's scabrous forehead.

"Your mama loves you, Jimmy. You always remember that, do you hear me?"

Then she lay back on the bed with her arms stretched out, so that the blood could flow more freely from her arms.

Jimmy's good eye went wide with horror. *His mother lay on the bed beside him, bleeding herself to death.* He wanted to scream out to her. He wanted to make her stop. She was his mother, and he loved her. If she died in front of him a part of him would die with her. He tried to scream around the stockings gagging his mouth, but it didn't make enough sound for anyone to hear.

And then another part of him was looking at her, seeing the crazy woman who wanted to kill him.

And she was dying.

Her body convulsed as she bled to death.

And she was his mother.

He loved her.

She was dying, and he was glad, he was letting loose a sigh of relief, because she was dying, and she was crazy enough to kill him.

Jimmy felt the Stone that held him down in the dream lose its grip on him and shatter into a million tiny flecks of obsidian sand. He could still feel its touch inside his mind, but he could also feel that it had no power over him. He was free; he could open his eyes and wake up now if he wanted to, and it couldn't stop him. He knew that the moment he woke up it would be gone from inside him, and it would never be able to force its way around inside him again.

If he wanted to he could lift himself out of the dream and never look at this memory again.

But he didn't do that. He set himself back into it, and saw it through.

There wasn't that much of it left; seven minutes after his mother had slit her wrists the hotel maid had knocked on the door.

"Housekeeping," the woman called as she knocked. She didn't even wait for a response before she put her key in the door and opened it.

The first thing she saw was Jimmy, all tied up and bloody. Then she saw his mother, still convulsing, bleeding to death on the bed. She screamed like a banshee and left the door open as she went running down the hallway screaming for help.

The ambulance was there five minutes later, in plenty of time to keep mom from bleeding to death. It took both of them to the hospital, but not before someone at the hotel had called the police, and someone else had called a friend at a newspaper. One of Jimmy's most vivid memories was of the camera's strobe light flashing in his eyes as the attendant lifted his stretcher from the ambulance.

Jimmy was in the hospital for a month before they let dad take him home. Mom was only there for a week and a half before they transferred her to the mental ward.

But the thing that followed Jimmy as he woke was the memory of wishing his mother dead as she lay on the bed beside him, dying.

CHAPTER

ELEVEN

ONCE WHEN JIMMY WAS SEVEN HE BORROWED HIS FA-
ther's razor and made a make-believe out of shaving, even
though he didn't have anything to shave off—just to see
what it was like. He cut his face twice when the razor dug
too deep and scraped away his skin. He'd kind of expected
it, but even so it stung something fierce.

What he hadn't expected was to get done and notice that
his left hand was covered with blood. That didn't make any
sense. He'd used his right hand to lather and shave. His left
hand hadn't been anywhere near the razor since he'd
changed the blade when he first started. . . .

The old blade was still on the counter where he'd left it.

Both edges were bloody. The cuts on his left hand were deep and even. They didn't hurt. Not at first, anyway. Later on that day they started to itch, and by the next morning they stung every time he moved his hand. The razor blade had been so sharp, its edge had been so thin, that he hadn't even felt it when it cut him.

Jimmy woke up feeling sad and haunted and free all at the same time. He woke up thinking about his mom, and for the first time in months thinking about her didn't make him break into a cold sweat, though she was the thing that haunted him. He loved her, he knew that. Not just because she was his mom, but because, in spite of whatever else was true about her, there was a good and decent person living in her heart. He loved her, even if he didn't know if he'd ever be able to let her into his life again.

Jimmy's leg itched.

He was hungry. He sat up, ignoring the itch, and headed toward the kitchen. Dad had bought Pop-Tarts at the grocery. Jimmy loved Pop-Tarts, especially when he had the time to toast and butter them.

Rex wasn't sleeping at the foot of the bed. That was strange; he'd been so deep asleep from the painkillers last night that Jimmy half expected him to still be unconscious this morning.

Dad had plugged in the electric clock and set it on the counter; it read half past eleven. That was late. Jimmy couldn't remember ever having slept that late. His body, he guessed, was still out of sync from the drive down.

Rex wasn't in the living room, the dining room, or the kitchen.

"Rex . . . ?" Jimmy called. The dog didn't come. Dad had probably let him out. He might even be outside with the dog—Jimmy didn't see or hear dad, either.

His leg still itched.

Jimmy resisted the impulse to scratch; scratching an itch only made it more irritated.

He went to the cabinet, took a envelope of Pop-Tarts out of the box, opened the envelope, and put the pastries in the toaster. He turned to the refrigerator to get out the butter and saw the note pinned to the freezer door by a smiley-face magnet.

> *Jimmy—*
> *Gone to Tylerville to run a couple of errands.*
> *Should be back a little after noon. Decided*
> *whether you want to stay here yet?*
> *Keep a close eye on Rex—the darned dog's still*
> *asleep. Maybe that shot the vet gave him was a*
> *little too much. Why don't you try to wake him*
> *up, take him for a walk?*
> *—Dad*

That was especially strange. Rex wasn't with dad, and if he was in the house he wasn't answering when Jimmy called. Jimmy left the Pop-Tarts still toasting and did a quick search of the house. He didn't find the dog; if Rex was anywhere in the house it wasn't anyplace obvious.

Jimmy shrugged and went back to his Pop-Tarts. Maybe dad had let Rex out for a walk after he'd written the note. All sorts of things were possible.

In the kitchen, the pastries were already sticking out of the toaster and beginning to cool. Jimmy plucked them out and dropped them on a plate quickly as he could—even if they were cooling, they were hot enough to burn his fingers. He cut the cold-stiff butter into thin slices and spaced the pats out so they'd melt. By the time he put the last curl of butter down, the first was soft enough to spread.

He poured himself a glass of milk, carried the plate and glass over to the kitchen table, and sat down to eat.

Dad must have spilled something on the kitchen floor; Jimmy felt himself walk through something wet and sticky. He didn't look down to see what it was. He was hungry. He didn't want to think about sticky-wet messes on the kitchen floor.

The itching on his leg was getting worse.

He took a bite of Pop-Tart, and without even thinking about it he reached down to scratch.

Something was wrong.

Something was wrong with his leg. Rex was missing. Dad was gone.

And when Jimmy reached down to scratch his leg, he

felt his flesh part under his fingernails. His stomach clenched; half-chewed Pop-Tart lodged in his throat. He lifted his hand away from his leg and saw that it was covered with blood.

He didn't want to look at his leg. He didn't want to have to see whatever was wrong. He didn't want his world to be a place where he had to see things like that.

He looked around the room, trying to find something to focus on. Something that would capture his attention enough to give him a few more minutes of peace of mind.

What he saw was the door that led from the kitchen to the backyard.

It was the sort of door that has windowpanes built into it; most of it was made of solid wood, but the top half was a big window partitioned into six smaller panes of glass. Jimmy had always liked that sort of door. It brought sunlight into the house where you wouldn't expect it. It brightened things up.

Someone had broken the glass pane nearest the handle of the door. The door was unlocked and ajar.

Somewhere outside Rex screamed a dog-scream of fear and rage.

Jimmy looked down at his leg. His heart pounded, catching the anger and fear in the dog's scream. When he saw what someone had done to his leg his good sense rejected it. It was impossible. How could someone disfigure him that badly without even waking him up? But then he thought of the time last year when he'd snuck into the bathroom while his parents were asleep, and borrowed his dad's razor. Someone could have cut him that way—cut him with something so sharp that he didn't even feel the blade. He could have slept through something like that. He must have.

Jimmy stared down at his leg. It was covered with fresh blood. Someone had carved words into the flesh of his calf with a razor, and the words were still bleeding.

The Children

There was blood all over the carpeting and the tile floor of the kitchen. Jimmy had tracked it behind him as he walked.

Outside, Rex screamed again.

Jimmy ran to his bedroom, threw on blue jeans and a T-shirt. He jammed his feet into his still-tied sneakers without even bothering to wipe away the blood. He ran out the back door without slowing down to shut it behind him.

The Children.

It wasn't hard to see which way they'd gone when they'd left the house; the raspberry bushes were in a parted disarray at one corner of the backyard.

He jumped into the part in the bushes without thinking about the thorns. A dozen paces in there wasn't any sign of a trail, but he kept going anyway, hoping that straight was the right direction. After thirty yards the briar gave way to pine woods.

Jimmy was a hundred and fifty yards from the house before he heard Rex scream a third time, far away and off to his left. That way was uphill, but still Jimmy turned and ran for all he was worth.

All Jimmy could think about as he ran was the question dad had asked in his note—did Jimmy want to stay in Green Hill?

No.

He didn't want to stay in Green Hill. He didn't want to *be* here, much less stay here. Running away from New Jersey was wrong. Even if things were bad there, it was *home.* And even if Green Hill *could* be a good place to live —and Jimmy couldn't imagine how a place this crazy could be good—it couldn't ever be home.

Jimmy began to hear voices ahead of him. In front of him was a small rocky crag that came to a point—not the top of Green Hill, but the top of a minor hillock. Jimmy kept climbing.

Someone spoke, and so many voices replied all at once that Jimmy couldn't have distinguished any of them if he'd tried. The people who'd replied had spoken in unison, and with a single answer; it almost sounded like a responsive reading at church.

"The Stone gives us all we have. In time he takes it all away." Jimmy recognized that voice. It was Sean, Thomas's brother. He said the words as though they were practiced—used so many times that they had no meaning left.

Three feet from the top of the crag Jimmy felt a burning tingle in his arms. It felt almost as though he'd set his hands onto an uninsulated electric wire.

CHAPTER

TWELVE

THE BURNING WAS STRONGER ON HIS LEFT; JIMMY turned to see what caused it . . .

And saw with his eyes the evil thing that had haunted his dreams.

Saw the Stone.

It was black, and smooth, and irregular; if he'd seen a picture of it in a book he might have mistaken it for a strange black rock or maybe the egg of a creature from another planet. But he wasn't seeing a picture; he was standing not five feet away from it, and the Stone wasn't something Jimmy just saw with his eyes.

He could feel it, feel its electric fire on his skin, even though he wasn't touching it.

And there was something else, too—something that wasn't touch or taste or smell or sight, but was almost bits and pieces of all of them. Looking at the thing, Jimmy could *feel* evil seething from it, dripping and oozing and spattering from it, almost as though the Stone was a sponge overfull with every meanness in the world.

The touchable part of it, the part of it that was solid and real enough to be certain of, was black and unearthly and so smooth and slick that it shone in the sunlight. It looked like rock, a boulder the size of a milk crate—but it wasn't rock at all. Jimmy knew that when he saw it. It couldn't be rock. Rock was cold and hard and no more good or evil than the soil it came from. The Stone was none of those things.

It was alive.

It was alive, and it was hot and electric and *evil.* It was every wrong Jimmy had ever seen, distilled and captured in a single spot. It was his mother, drunk and angry and pounding Duke into bits of hamburger with a butcher knife. It was the kids at school, snickering as Jimmy walked into school the day after he got out of the hospital. It was the way the wrinkled old lady in New York City had somehow lost her nose.

On the far side of the crag, forty or fifty voices spoke at once, responding to Sean:

"We are the Children."

Jimmy ignored the electric burning that came from the Stone and kept climbing. The air around him felt so charged with static that it was hard to breathe. He lifted his head above the last rock and saw the Children.

They were dressed in their Sunday best—clean white shirts and black slacks on the boys, white and pastel dresses on the girls. Every child in Green Hill stood in the little hollow below the crag. Directly underneath Jimmy, Sean stood at a stone altar facing the Children. Roberta stood beside him. Rex was tied to the altar, belly up, his legs pointing at the sky. A shiny wood-handled steel hatchet lay on the altar next to the dog.

Sean held a long-bladed rusty skinning knife in his left hand.

"An old priest has left us," Sean said. "A new priest must lead us now."

The bizarreness of the moment froze Jimmy in place. He was much closer to the Stone now; the electricity that burned his skin hummed and buzzed in his ears. He shook his head, trying to clear away the sound.

"We are the Children of Green Hill," the Children responded to Sean.

The Stone was on Jimmy's left, inches from his head. Jimmy could feel it feeding on his revulsion. Feeding on Rex's rage and fear. Feeding on the blind, unquestioning worship it got from the Children.

Again, the call from Sean, and the response—

"Thomas was your leader. He has left you now."

"We are the Children of the Stone."

The Stone lay on a black stone altar that had been cut from the stone of the crag.

"I am Sean, who most of you have always known."

Sean handed the knife to Roberta, who took it in both hands and raised it up over her head, poised to cut Rex open.

"We will follow you, even as we follow the cold will of the black Stone."

The buzzing was getting worse; Jimmy was foggy-headed and dizzy. He was too close to the Stone. The electricity in the rocks, in the air, the buzzing in his skull— every sensation was so intense that he had to force his mind to think.

Roberta spoke. "With this living blood I consecrate your priest!" and she began to bring the knife down, into Rex's belly. The blade glinted in the sunlight.

"*No!*" Jimmy screamed.

All of them, Roberta, Sean, the Children—sixty of them, at least—standing before the Stone, looked up at him.

There were too many of them, and suddenly every one of them was angry. They wanted to kill him.

"Get away from my dog!" Jimmy shouted. He made it sound like a threat, but he knew there was nothing he could do. There were too many of them.

Sean cleared his throat and spat on Rex. He looked up at Jimmy. "Turn around and leave if you want to live. Forget you were ever here." He picked up the hatchet from where it lay on the altar beside Rex, swung it back and then *down*, hammer end first. The blunt steel of the hatchet slammed into Rex's left hind leg so hard that it twisted him under the rope, turned the dog onto his side. The hatchet crushed Rex's leg into the stone of the altar, smashed the flesh and bone and skin of the leg into limp pulp. Rex screamed; blood went flying everywhere. "Forget you ever had a dog," Sean said. "No one wants to have to hide a human body. But we'll kill you if we have to."

Sean brought the hatchet down again; a fleck of Rex's blood spattered in Jimmy's eyes.

"NO!" he cried. But there was still nothing he could do.

All of this came from the Stone. It had to. Half-delirious from the fog inside his head, Jimmy smacked his fist into the slick black rock beside him. Hit it with his fist and felt it —it was hard, but hard like frozen leather, not hard like stone at all.

Jimmy hit the Stone, and when he did, the Stone screamed.

Not a scream that he heard with his ears. Not even some strange telepathic scream, like something from a comic book or a science fiction story.

No.

Jimmy heard the scream in his heart, felt it like a thousand agonizing deaths, or like a lifetime spent in hell that had somehow all focused into a single moment.

He saw the scream on the faces of the Children—confusion, pain, and fear. One of the Children at the far end of the hollow lost his balance and fell.

Roberta lost her grip on the knife; it fell to the ground and clattered on the stones by her feet.

Rex was still screaming in pain.

Jimmy hit the stone again. Pain-burning electric fire shot up his wrist, his forearm, his elbow.

If Jimmy could hurt the Stone by punching it, what would happen if he pushed it off its ledge—let it fall the dozen feet to the ground?

Jimmy climbed up onto the platform, wedged himself behind the Stone. There was pain everywhere, fiery-burning pain so intense it made his vision dim. Jimmy pictured himself afire, burning like a human bonfire, alive but broiling to death underneath an oven. He wanted to collapse

and die, but if he let himself then Rex would be nothing
but blood trickling on a stone altar, and when they were
done with Rex they'd cut Jimmy open, too—

—Sean was crawling up the rocks, toward him.

Jimmy stooped over and pushed on the Stone. It rocked
forward, then rolled back, almost crushing Jimmy's foot
into the smooth rock of the Stone's perch. He didn't feel
the Stone press down onto his foot; he saw it—the fiery
pain that the Stone made him feel everywhere was too
intense for Jimmy to feel anything else. Jimmy pushed on
the Stone again harder, and it rolled forward—

—and it kept going, tumbling off the stone platform,
pounding the rocks just below the ledge. It bounded over
Sean and shattered on the rocks below his feet. Shards of it
went flying yards in every direction.

Sean's grip went slack; he fell to the ground like a limp
rag. The Children collapsed, almost as though they were
marionettes who'd somehow come untangled from their
wires.

It's over, Jimmy thought. It seemed too easy. But they
were all unconscious, every last one of them. Jimmy wasn't
even sure they were breathing.

He scrambled down the almost-sheer rock face of the
crag, toward the dog. Rex's scream turned into a whimper
when he saw Jimmy. Jimmy bent down to pick up the knife
Roberta had dropped, so he could cut the ropes that held
Rex down—

—and saw that the shards of rock that had been the
Stone were *moving*. Moving toward each other. And
slowly but steadily reassembling themselves.

The Children were beginning to wake.

Jimmy cut the ropes, picked Rex up—cradling him in his
arms like the dog was a baby.

And ran.

Jimmy was a fast runner. There probably wasn't a child
in Green Hill fast enough to catch him under ordinary
circumstances. But carrying Rex, he wasn't nearly so fast.
Rex was small for a dog, but not *that* small—he weighed
somewhere around twenty pounds. Even if twenty pounds
isn't much for a dog to weigh, it's a lot for a nine-year-old
boy to carry, at least if he's going to run. Especially if the

twenty-pound dog has a leg so thoroughly broken that it hangs slack at an impossible angle.

Jimmy got to within fifty yards of the rented house before the Children caught up with him. He could hear them just behind him; he looked back and saw that the nearest of them was almost close enough to reach forward and touch him.

Before he turned to look forward again, Jimmy's foot caught on an old root. He tripped, and went flying face-first into a blackberry briar.

Rex was thrown clear; he landed left-side-first on the far side of the briar.

Somebody smashed Jimmy's face farther down into the blackberry thorns. He felt one thorn pierce his nostril. Another only barely missed his eye. Then someone else grabbed the back collar of his T-shirt and yanked him out of the thorns.

Rex was on the other side of the briar, trying to figure out how to get around the thorns. Shattered leg or not, the dog wanted to fight. But even if he'd been whole, he wouldn't have been much use against sixty children.

"Run, Rex. Run and get dad."

The dog stopped pressing at the briar for a moment. He hesitated. But he didn't go. His leg. Could he run with a leg broke that bad? No, that wasn't it. Jimmy had seen three-legged dogs; they were better runners than he was himself.

"Go *on*, Rex!"

Jimmy saw the dog turn and start away before whoever had his collar pushed him back down into the thorns. Someone else grabbed him by the shoulder and *pulled*, raking him across the thorns, then shoved him to the ground. A kick came from the same direction, into his ribs; that rolled Jimmy over. He opened his eyes—the scratches on his eyelids *burned* as he did—and all he could see was the sky.

And the Children. They crowded so close around him that the only thing Jimmy could see besides them was the tiny blot of sky directly above him. They looked . . . changed. And furious, vengefully angry to the point that it covered over every other thing about them. *That* was the change, Jimmy thought. The anger on their faces was so

intense and so identical in every one of them that it was
hard to tell them apart. It wasn't just that they were angry;
it was as though all the anger on each of their faces had
somehow come from a single, shared heart.

For the first time all morning, real fear began to chill
Jimmy's heart. Their faces said that they didn't want *just* to
kill him.

No.

They wanted him to suffer first. Suffer long and slow.

"His face," one of them said, "kick his face."

A heavy shoe slammed into Jimmy's cheekbone, just
below his eye, and everything went black. It stayed that
way, too—even later, when he woke.

Rex *hurt*.

The dog's body, unlike the boy's, didn't hide pain from
him when it became too intense to bear. And the pain was
so intense that the dog's brain had trouble keeping its grip
on what it had been told.

It had to find the man.

That was how the dog thought of Ben Tompkins: he was
a man, and he was good. Rex had heard the man call to
Jimmy, and he had begun to associate the boy with the
name—to a degree, anyway.

Jimmy had looked Rex in the eye and told the dog to get
his father. Jimmy was in some awful kind of trouble. Rex
knew what trouble was; he could see trouble coming a long
way off. If Jimmy was in that much trouble and he was
sending Rex off on an errand, then the errand was powerful important.

Rex had a lot of good sense, in the way that dogs have
sense. He understood what was going on and what was
needed. He didn't understand it with words, and he didn't
understand it especially clearly, but he understood.

The problem was the pain.

The pain screaming up out of the left hindquarter of his
body was loud enough that it very nearly shut away his
mind. It pushed every other thought aside. Or almost did.
And besides the pain, there was fear: three times he'd
looked back at his leg, and he'd seen how it hung from his
groin all bloody and limp as a rag. The sight put the terror
of death in the dog.

Ten yards from the edge of the bramble behind the backyard, the dog blacked out—partly from pain and fear, partly from loss of blood. Half a minute later he caught himself, forced himself back awake. The dog pressed his way through the last few yards of blackberry thorns, onto the low-cut grass of the backyard.

He heard a car pulling into the driveway, and limped toward it.

The man was opening the door of the car when Rex came around the side of the house. He said, "Hello, boy," or words that meant something like that, and then he saw Rex's leg, and he made one of those small sounds that meant that he was shocked.

"Oh my God, dog. Who in hell did that to you?" That didn't mean anything to Rex, but then the man reached down to lift the dog into the car, and Rex understood that.

The dog tried to back away. It was obvious: the man could see that he was hurt, and he was going to take Rex somewhere because of it, like he had the day before. But when the man saw Rex shy away he only became more insistent. Rex wasn't in any shape to resist; the man got his hands around him and lifted him into the passenger seat.

"Don't worry about Jimmy, boy. There isn't time. He's probably in the house watching television. Won't even know we're gone."

The dog didn't know what that meant, either. But he did know that he'd been given something important to do, something powerful important.

And he knew that he'd failed.

Depression and pain and the smell of his own death washed over him. His blood was leaking into the soft fabric of the seat of the car. What blood was still in the dog's veins went cold from lack of pressure, and Rex blacked out.

It was a long time before he opened his eyes again.

PART
TWO

CHAPTER

THIRTEEN

WHEN TIM HANSON WAS FOUR YEARS OLD, HIS DADDY took him aside for a talk.

"Look me in the eye, son," Tim's father said. There was a haunted look in his eyes that Tim had seen at least a dozen times before. It was a look Tim had never understood, an expression on his father's face that frightened and unsettled him. But now, even though he was only four years old, Tim began to understand his father's nightmares.

"Yes, daddy?" Tim said.

"Don't you ever do anything you won't be proud of, boy. Don't you ever do anything you won't want to remember." His daddy's voice got real quiet. "Because whatever you do, it'll follow you the rest of your life."

Tim didn't feel any need to be coy; he knew what his father meant. And he was still young enough to know when there wasn't any sense in lying.

He bit his lower lip and looked back into his father's eyes, and nodded. Daddy stood up.

"There's evil things you do, son." He looked away, and Tim saw a strange mix of shame and love painted on his face. "Evil things. They shame you, but you love them because they're a part of your town and your people, and loving them shames you. And the biggest shame of all is the shame you feel when you betray that love."

He patted Tim on the back and wandered outside through the garage door, to mow the lawn or some such.

Daddy remembered. He remembered everything that every other adult in the town didn't have to. Tim didn't understand why, but the thought made him very sad. And there was something else, too—something that Tim still didn't quite understand. But even if he didn't understand it, it frightened him, and left him frightened of his father.

Tim didn't tell anybody about the talk with his father. Nor did he tell his father about the things that honestly bothered him—things like the time, much later on, he helped Christian sacrifice the dog. He was the one who'd tied the dog down, and he'd been so sick to his stomach about the idea that it made his hands tremble. Trembling hands aren't much use for tying knots, and sure enough the dog got loose while Christian was still cutting him open. Christian liked to cut slow, one layer of skin at a time, and he'd barely got past the skin when the dog twisted free of his rope. After that the dog had haunted all the Children for half a year—until finally that Tompkins boy, the one that the Stone didn't have, had taken the dog in.

No one had trusted Tim with anything since he'd screwed up with the rope.

Tim had nightmares about the dog and the rope. Horrible nightmares. None of the other Children ever had regrets, much less nightmares. Some nights Tim would dream that he was tied down to the altar, instead of the dog, and layer by layer Christian was cutting away the skin over his belly. Tim struggled against the ropes, tried to get himself free, but whoever had tied the knots this time hadn't screwed up the way Tim had. Tim twisted and pressed and tried not to feel the cutting and tried not to look. Then someone said his name from the general direction of his feet, and before Tim could catch himself he looked to see who it was.

The first thing he saw was the skin of his belly pulled back like the gullet of a roasted Thanksgiving turkey.

Then he saw his pulsing veins and arteries, and his live, translucent intestines with the bits and pieces of half-digested food moving through them.

The third thing he saw was the face of his father, who stood near his feet.

"Tim," daddy said, "what are they doing to you?" His voice was concerned, but hesitant.

"They're cutting me open, daddy," Tim said. "I guess I'm going to be a sacrifice for the Stone."

Christian was still standing beside Tim, smiling at Tim's dad just like he was a little angel.

Daddy shook his head, elbowed Christian aside, took the knife from him. "Don't Children today know *anything*?" he asked. "It's the heart. You've got to go for the heart."

And as Tim watched, his daddy took that knife and, ever-so-carefully, set its tip in the center of the boy's abdomen. And pressed the blade—point first, edge upward—through Tim's diaphragm, under his sternum, into the flesh of his heart.

Which was when Tim woke. When he always woke when he had that dream. Gasping for air. Feeling the muscle-flesh of his heart clutch around smooth, ethereal steel.

It was early evening. He was sitting in the two-seat sofa in the den at home, and Tim was covered with sweat from his nightmare. The television was on; he could remember, now that the dream cleared away, that he'd fallen asleep watching it. Watching, more specifically, the dialing-for-dollars movie that came on at three p.m.

It had been a Tyrone Power film. Tim wasn't sure which one—the title had gone by while he was still in the kitchen, pouring himself a Coke. Tim liked Tyrone Power, liked the actor enough to make the movie worth seeing even if it was pretty dull. But even if Tyrone Power could make a bad movie worth seeing, he couldn't make it interesting enough to keep Tim awake.

Daddy would be home soon. Or maybe not that soon; sometimes he liked to stop in Tylerville and have a beer on the way home from the foundry. Daddy was strange that way, too—as far as Tim knew he was the only drinking man in Green Hill.

There was a boy in a wooden cage down in one of the caves. The cave next to the one where they'd all put the fragments of the Stone after they'd gathered them up.

Tim wasn't sure if the boy was still alive. He thought so; Roberta said the Stone needed him to die slowly. But the Children who'd carried the boy down into the cave had had a little fun with his unconscious body. Tim hadn't been watching them. Or, at least, he hadn't made a point of watching them. But once he looked up and saw them slam the boy's head against the wall of the tunnel. And then nearly drop him because the sound of his skull hitting rock was so funny.

Tim didn't like it at all. He knew the Stone; he loved it as much as anyone else. But murder was too much. It wasn't as though they were torturing a dog or splitting open a kitten. Murder was serious. It was policemen and sheriff's deputies and somebody going to jail. Maybe even *everybody* going to jail.

And it was worse things than that, too—it was seeing the look in that boy's eyes when Sean took the hammer end of the hatchet to his dog. Tim didn't ever want to have to think about that again. Not that he had any choice; the image wasn't going away.

Tim got up, turned off the television. Daddy would want dinner ready when he got home. *And it better not be cold, either.* Daddy always said that. He meant it, too—the one time when Tim had tuna sandwiches waiting for him, his father had cuffed Tim a good one. Tim was real careful after that. He'd taken to fixing something out of a can—like stew or chili—that he could leave warming all night if he had to, as long as he set the burner to LO.

There was a can of Sloppy Joe mix on the top shelf of the cupboard; Tim dragged one of the kitchen chairs over and got the can down. Daddy liked Sloppy Joes.

Tim opened the can and poured the slop into the quart-size teflon pan he always used to heat canned dinner.

It occurred to him as he turned on the burner that if the Children knew what he felt—if they knew what he really *thought*— they'd probably use him for a sacrifice instead of the Tompkins boy.

It wasn't the first time the thought had occurred to him. But nearly as Tim could tell, that sort of trouble wasn't ever going to happen. A hundred times, at least, Tim had let his doubts or fears or even misgivings slip out in front of other Children. But they just didn't hear those things, didn't see them any more than any of the grown-ups—besides Tim's father—could see the nasty things the Children did. There was a part of Tim that no one in Green Hill could see besides his father, and daddy wasn't hardly ever around to see it anyway.

His conscience was in the secret part of him, hidden away from everyone.

Tim covered the pot, set the electric burner down to LO, and went to his room.

He lay down on his back in bed without turning on the light, and stared out the window at the stars. The sky was dim but not yet black; he could only see the brightest stars.

That boy was probably dying down in the cave.

Tim thought for a minute: he could hike down and set the boy loose.

That wasn't a very good idea. The other Children might be blind to a lot of what he did, but they weren't *that* blind. There was the time when Roberta wanted him to cut off a dog's foot so that she could set it loose for a couple of days and see if it would bleed to death before they caught it again. Before he'd even heard what he was saying, Tim had told her no. He hadn't had the heart. Sure: she didn't see that the idea made him sick of himself, that if he could make himself do that he wouldn't be able to stand his own reflection. But it wasn't like she didn't notice that he couldn't do it. She thought it was just a matter of Tim not having any nerve. She thought he was a chicken-shit.

That's what Thomas called him when Roberta told him about it. "Tim," Thomas said, *"you* are a chicken-shit."

Still: even if they hadn't seen him for what he was, they'd made things hard on Tim after that. The Children treated him almost as though he weren't one of them; the Stone ignored him now even more thoroughly than it had before.

Sometimes when he lay awake at night he could still hear Thomas say it: "Tim, *you* are a chicken-shit."

There were times when Tim thought that was all it was himself.

They'd probably kill him if he set that boy loose—even if they did just think it was a matter of nerve. The Stone *wanted* that boy. The way Sean talked, he almost seemed to think it had a score to settle. Tim guessed that it did.

Tim pulled himself up out of bed to check on his father's dinner. He had to make sure it wasn't burning; daddy got real upset if Tim wasted food. When he lifted the lid he saw that it was simmering, but only very slowly. Not fast enough to burn.

He went back to the two-seat couch he'd fallen asleep on, and thought some more about the look on the boy's face as Sean smashed the dog's leg.

He was still thinking about it at eight-thirty, when his father came home stinking like a brewery. By then he knew that he had to do something, that he wouldn't want to live with himself if he didn't.

But hard as he thought about it, he didn't know what he *could* do.

CHAPTER

FOURTEEN

BEN TOMPKINS WAS A NERVOUS WRECK.

He could still hear Rex screaming in the veterinarian's office as the drugs she gave him began to settle in. The way the dog screamed almost made it seem as though the poor thing was more terrified of being unconscious than he was of the pain. What was going *on* in that dog's head? There wasn't any way to find out, especially since Dr. Smith had given him enough medication to put him under for days. She was keeping him at her office for the moment, too— she wanted to keep an eye on him. Apparently there was some chance of the dog developing an infection or going into shock.

The car smelled of blood; even with the windows wide open and air rushing in at fifty miles an hour, Ben was sure he could smell it. There'd been enough blood that smelling it shouldn't have surprised him—the passenger side of the front seat was soaked with it. Ben's hands were covered with dried blood, too, from when he'd lifted Rex into the car and from when he'd carried the dog into the vet's office. He glanced away from the road, down at his shirt, and saw that there was a big round welt of it just below his diaphragm. He should have remembered to clean his hands, at least, while he was at the vet's.

He shuddered. What was happening to him? He wasn't thinking at all.

Ben put the car into park, engaged the emergency brake and pressed it home. Jimmy was supposed to decide today whether or not he wanted to stay in Green Hill.

Ben sighed.

There was probably going to be packing to do. Even if Jimmy wanted to stay here, Ben was pretty sure he'd change his mind when he heard about this new business with Rex. Regardless, Ben wasn't sure he'd go along if Jimmy wanted to stay. It was too much; he couldn't have the boy growing up in a place like this.

They'd have to stay another two or three days, anyway, until the dog was well enough to travel. Unless Ben could get the veterinarian to put Rex in an animal carrier and send him up by plane. That was an idea. Ben could call Dr. Smith, and spend the afternoon packing, and they could be out of here by midnight at the latest. Leaving that late would mean finding a hotel before they'd gone two hundred miles, but it would be worth it. Getting out of this place was the important part.

First thing was going to be cleaning the dog's blood off that car seat. Ben didn't think he could handle driving all the way up to New Jersey in a car that smelled like blood.

After that Ben would have to call the realtor up north and have him get the house off the market. It would be bad to move back home and find that home had already been sold out from under them.

Bed opened the front door of the rented house.

"Jimmy," he called. "I think we should start packing,

son. Something's happened to Rex. I really think it's time to get out of this place."

There wasn't any answer. Had the boy stepped out for a walk? If he was any farther than the backyard, Ben thought, he'd have left a note. Unless, maybe, he was still asleep. *This late in the day?* That wasn't likely. But he'd been asleep when Ben had left at ten, and that wasn't likely, either. Ben closed the front door behind him and headed toward Jimmy's bedroom.

Jimmy wasn't in bed, though the bed was still rumpled, the sheets and blankets disarrayed. Which was strange. Jimmy usually went back and made his bed—or straightened out the blankets, at least—after he had his breakfast.

There were dark blotches on the carpet near the bed—they looked like chocolate syrup, or something similar; it was hard to tell exactly what on the army green carpeting.

Ben turned around and started toward the refrigerator in the kitchen. That was where he'd left his note to Jimmy. Chances were that if Jimmy had left a note for him it'd be clipped up with the same magnet.

He was halfway through the living room when he saw the blood pooled and smeared on the kitchen floor.

His heart tried to leap up and out through his throat; he felt his blood press against the backs of his eyes.

"Jimmy!" Ben's voice was shrill—he was almost screaming. *"Jimmy!"*

He turned and saw the broken glass on the back door, saw bloody fingerprints smeared on the knob.

For a moment the blood was just too much for Ben, and he couldn't move and he couldn't think and he couldn't even see. All he could do was remember the weekend he'd gone to the conference, the same weekend Anne had gone out of her mind. He remembered calling Anne and Jimmy just to check in on Saturday morning, and assuming, when no one answered the phone, that his wife and son had gone out for breakfast. Or maybe even gone out shopping.

He remembered the phone call he got from the family doctor that Sunday night, when the doctor finally figured out how to get in touch with Ben by taking an indiscreet look into Anne's purse, where he'd found a brochure about the conference. Ben remembered wanting to think that the doctor was playing some sort of a warped practical joke. Remembered not wanting to believe, and refusing to believe, and then finally realizing that it was real. Driving the two hundred fifty miles home in a little more than three hours, getting to town and going straight to the hospital, without even driving past the house.

And he looked again at his son's blood on the floor and the doorknob.

And he screamed.

When all the air was emptied from his lungs, he filled them and began to scream again. He kept picturing his little boy in the hospital, covered head to toe with bandages, half a dozen IV bottles bleeding their contents into his arm.

Ben caught himself, held himself still. Screaming himself into hypoxia wasn't going to get Jimmy out of whatever trouble had found him. All screaming could do was turn Ben's throat into raw meat, and maybe make him deaf in the bargain.

He looked up into the corner of the room, where the ceiling and two of the walls met, and took a deep breath.

There were two things he could do: run off looking for Jimmy, or call the police and get them looking for the boy.

He had to do both. Anyone who could do something this violent to his son could just as well do the same thing to Ben—and if both of them were gone it might be quite a while before anyone even noticed they were missing.

He lifted the phone receiver from its hook, tapped out 911 with a shaking index finger. Did 911 work in this town? It must—the connection was ringing.

Four beats into his description of the scene, the sheriff's department operator interrupted him and told him to hold. "Let me put you through to a detective, Mr. Tompkins," she said. "I've got two deputies on their way to you already."

The phone went dead for a moment, and then the connection was ringing again. A man answered after the second ring.

"Mike Peterson," the man said.

That was all the man said at first. Ben almost didn't know what to say; he'd already exhausted the words he'd meant to use by trying to say them to the woman who first answered the phone. The words he hadn't got out had somehow lost themselves in his panic. Five seconds of silence—while Ben tried to find his balance—felt like half of all eternity.

"Hello," the man, Peterson, said from the other end of the line. "Can I help you?"

Ben blinked.

"My son," he said. "There's blood. My son is gone, and the house is covered with blood."

"Your son . . . ?" The man's voice was quiet, almost afraid. "God in heaven, sir. I'm sorry." A pause. "I need to know . . . how long it's been since you've seen him. Your name, where you are. Tell me everything you can. I'll get out to you as fast as it takes to drive there."

Ben felt hysterical and angry. "I'm Ben Tompkins. I'm renting the old Henderson place on Crag Road in Green Hill. Jimmy was still asleep when I left the house at ten in the morning, and I'm home now and he's *gone*. And I've got to *go*. You do what you want. I've got to find my boy!"

Ben almost hung up then—he wanted to run screaming off into the woods and fields, looking for his son. But he hesitated, and the hesitation turned into a moment long enough for Peterson to respond.

"Mr. Tompkins, you've got to wait for me to get there. We're going to need you if we're going to find your son. Anyone who'd do God-knows-what to a child won't hesitate to do the same thing to you." The man sucked in a breath. "Give me ten minutes and we'll go out and find your boy together."

Ben was trembling. He leaned against the kitchen table to steady himself, looked down to focus his eyes, and saw that he was standing on a big dried smear of Jimmy's blood. Air forced itself out of his lungs; when it reached his throat it became a small involuntary cry.

"I'll wait," he said. "Okay. But you've got to hurry, God damn it. *Hurry.*"

Someone pounded on the door.

"I will, Mr. Tompkins. I'll be there before you know it." And the line went dead.

"Come in," Ben shouted. He set the telephone back into its cradle and started toward the door. The two deputies were in the living room before he'd taken three steps.

The taller of the two men looked at Ben and began to ask, "You're the one who called—" then he caught sight of the blood on the kitchen floor behind Ben; he grunted with surprise, interrupting himself "—called about his son?"

Ben nodded; the motion wasn't quite enough to start him shaking again.

The man asked Ben to tell him what he could about the circumstances, and Ben repeated the information he'd given the detective over the phone. When he was done he told the deputy about the detective who was on his way, and asked him to wait for the man while Ben took a look out back for Jimmy.

The deputy—his badge said that his name was Myron White—stood by the back door examining the bloody doorknob. Ben noticed that the man was careful not to touch it.

"It's better if you don't, Mr. Tompkins," White said. "There'll be a trail—we can get dogs out here to track it. If you go tearing around out there your scent may throw them off."

Ben forced himself to take a deep, slow breath. The man was right; what he said made sense. Even if Ben was half out of his mind with the need to *do* something, he wouldn't let himself make matters worse.

"Get on the radio, huh, Seymore? Tell them what we got up here—have them send up some dogs and a search party?"

The man nodded and left the house through the front door. Five minutes later he came back, shaking his head. By then White was crouched in the kitchen, staring into the bloodstains on the tile floor.

"Peterson already did it. He should be here in a minute or three. The dogs and the searchers are probably twenty minutes behind him."

White nodded. He looked up at Ben. "Mr. Tompkins, these are a child's footprints. Your son's, most likely. It doesn't look as though he even knew he was bleeding—the pace of his steps is casual. Does he have some sort of a problem feeling pain? Can you think of any reason he'd track his own blood around and not even notice it?"

Ben rubbed his eyes, tried to think. Pain. . . ? Jimmy? "A problem? I don't think so. He takes it well enough—he never was the sort of kid to have a tantrum because he'd stubbed his toe. But he knows well enough when he's hurt."

White shook his head.

"Somebody broke in here, all right. That window above the doorknob was broken from the outside. But your boy looks like he left on his own steam."

Ben shuddered. He forced himself to take three deep breaths. His body was calming down—a little, at least. His heartbeat was slower. But his blood was still thick with adrenaline he wasn't using. He wiped away the sweat beading up on his eyebrows.

If Jimmy had left the house on his own, then maybe he was all right.

God. Please.

Maybe if Ben just stepped out the door and shouted his son's name—*Jimmy!*— the boy would answer him. Maybe there was nothing wrong at all.

"Hello? Anyone in?" From the direction of the front door. White's partner, the man he called Seymore, must have left it open. Ben recognized the voice from the telephone; it was Detective Peterson.

"We're back here," Ben said. "Come on in."

Mike Peterson wasn't a tall man—he was inches shorter than Ben, and Ben was only five-foot-eight. But the man was so burly and heavy-boned that he seemed large and intimidating. His shoulders and chest were broad enough to suit a man well over six feet. His hair was brown, and his light, freckled skin had a bad sunburn.

White told Peterson what he'd figured out so far by looking at the kitchen floor and the doorknob. Peterson examined both as White spoke. When White was done, Peterson was looking at the kitchen table.

"You noticed this, didn't you?" Peterson asked. He pointed at the plate with Jimmy's Pop-Tarts still on it. One of them had fallen half off the plate. There was one bite gone from that one. The other hadn't been touched. "The boy left here on his own, all right. But he left in one hell of a rush."

CHAPTER

FIFTEEN

JIMMY WOKE IN A DARK PLACE THAT SMELLED OF SOIL and stone.

And woke confused. For long moments as he drifted up away from sleep, the boy imagined that he was back in New Jersey, and that it was winter. He thought that somehow time had turned against him, and drawn him back into that weekend when his dad had gone away.

The weekend that his mother had lost her mind, and done her best to kill him.

And thinking that he wanted to scream and scream for help, help from anyone who might be nearby to stop her, to make her set him free—

No. He wasn't in New Jersey. Even if the place he was was cold, it wasn't winter-cold. He was in Green Hill, and, and—

And backed away from wakefulness, because where he was wasn't anyplace he wanted to be.

He tried to imagine that he was in the hospital, that Rex had found dad and dad had got Jimmy away from the Children. Hospitals smelled strange, and they were dark sometimes. They smelled at least as strange as dirt and stone. And sometimes when he was half-awake one strange smell could twist around in Jimmy's mind and become another.

But even as he wished that it were so, Jimmy knew that it wasn't.

He could feel his face covered with a mask of scabbed-over blood. He was only breathing through half his nose; one of his nostrils—the one the thorn had pierced—was clogged solid with a wedge of half-dried bloody mucus.

His head pounded, too. When he reached up to touch it he discovered that the whole left side of it was a big puffy-swollen lump. It wasn't a concussion—not quite—but he was bruised deep into the bone of his skull. Bruised and scraped and bloody, and there was already an infection thriving in the half-clotted blood beneath his skin.

Gently—*gently!*— he lifted his hands and rubbed away the scabrous blood that sealed his eyes shut. Twice he tried to open them, only to find that he'd missed bits of stiffened scab that twisted and scratched his eyelids.

He was in a cave. Some sort of dim red light came from one end of it. Light enough to give Jimmy hints of the uneven rock walls, and of the wooden bars a few inches from his face.

Jimmy patted around him and discovered that the bars closed him in from above and from all four sides. Beneath him was packed dirt; the vertical bars were sunk into it too deep to pry loose. Too deep to work loose right now, any-way—Jimmy felt too weak to even try.

He closed his eyes again, tried to let himself relax and drift off to sleep. Wherever he was was bad, and there wasn't any getting loose from it. Not now, anyway. Jimmy felt too weak to sit up, much less batter down a wooden cage. Keeping awake and fretting would only make him weaker.

Jimmy was halfway between sleep and wakefulness when he heard the footsteps.

(It was his mom, his mom out there in a dark hallway somewhere coming to get him he knew it he knew it—)

He opened his eyes. A moment later he saw vague flickers of yellow candlelight reflect against the same corner of the cave that the dim red glow came from.

Jimmy forced himself to sit up and wait. Forced his head and his heart to clear enough to know where and when he was. The cave. Green Hill. Summer.

Were they coming to beat him again? Jimmy's heart lurched; he felt his blood push and press and throb in his lumps and bruises. There was something seriously wrong with the side of his head—sitting up made him feel nauseated and woozy. But still, the pain and the blood woke him up. For the first time since he'd come to, his brain was alive enough to think. Dimly, at least.

Rex must not have made it back to the house. The Children had probably caught up with him, just as they'd caught up with Jimmy.

Most likely the dog was dead, gutted and bled dry. Most likely Jimmy would be soon, too—for that matter, why was he still alive? They couldn't be planning to turn him free when they were done with him. Kidnapping was serious business; if Jimmy got free to tell of it there'd be hell to pay.

No.

If he was awake, and he was here, then the Children had something *special* planned for him. The fact that he was alive at this point only meant that what they were planning was elaborate enough to take time.

Jimmy's stomach clenched when he took the thought to its logical conclusion: the truth was that just now he'd probably be better off dead than alive.

But even if he wanted to die, there was no way to kill himself. His belt was gone. And his pockets were empty, even though there had been nothing in them more dangerous than his comb.

The light was closer now—it was likely just a single candle, not much light at all, but Jimmy's eyes were adjusted to the darkness, and looking at the reflection of the light on the stone of the cave made them ache.

"Jimmy Tompkins?"

Jimmy started to answer, but all that came out was a cough. He recognized the voice from dinner at the Williamses'; it was the strange boy, Tim Hanson.

Jimmy cleared his throat. Doing it made his whole neck hurt.

"Yes?"

Tim Hanson came around the last bend in the tunnel. In one hand he held a candle. In the other he held a brown paper sack. The light was too bright; Jimmy squeezed his eyes shut and looked away.

"Got your dinner," Tim said. He sounded nervous, which struck Jimmy as almost funny: Jimmy was the one who was going to die, and one of the people who was going to kill him was nervous.

Jimmy nodded. He opened his eyes a slit, trying to get used to the brightness of the candle, but he kept his head turned away.

"Something wrong? You can look at me when you answer. I'm not going to kick your head in."

"The light—your candle is too much light. My eyes are used to the dark."

"Oh," Tim said. "Sorry. Think you can get used to it?"

Jimmy nodded again. "Yeah," he said. He turned toward Tim, opened his eyes a touch wider, blinked a couple of times. "Give me a minute."

"Sure," Tim said. He sat down in front of Jimmy's cage. He dropped the paper sack in front of him, then twisted around to put the candle behind him, so that it didn't shine directly on Jimmy. Jimmy rubbed his eyes again, rubbed away some of the loose scab on his cheeks and eyebrows. His eyes were almost used to the light; they hurt a little when he opened them, but they didn't hurt too much to ignore.

"You okay now?"

"I guess so. My eyes are, anyway."

Tim brought the candle around and set it in front of him. He picked up the brown paper bag, held it out to Jimmy. "This is your dinner. But don't start eating it right away. I want to talk to you first."

Jimmy took the bag and opened it. Inside were two carrots and a mushed sandwich. Tuna fish on white bread? It was hard to be sure. The light was bright enough to hurt Jimmy's eyes, but it wasn't really bright enough to see clearly. The smell was rotten and wonderful at the same time—rotten because it smelled tainted, wonderful because Jimmy hadn't really had anything to eat since last night. Hungry as he was, Jimmy wasn't sure that he could eat it. His stomach felt like it was made of broken glass.

Jimmy didn't remember getting hit in the stomach. What had they done to him while he was unconscious? He shuddered. God knew what they'd done. Jimmy didn't want to.

"Give me a minute," Tim said. "We shouldn't say anything now."

"Huh," Jimmy said. "Okay. Sure, I'll wait."

Tim sat there, quiet as the dirt and rock around them, for the longest time. Jimmy watched as the candle burned down to a nub, began to sputter; before it went out Tim took another—they were plain white plumbers' candles—out of his pocket and lit it from the first. Jimmy expected him to put out the first, then set the second down. But instead Tim held it in hands and stared hard into the flame.

The sight of him staring into the fire that way—it reminded Jimmy of something. Something . . . What?

His mom. Mom used to look exactly like that. When she was upset, or angry. But sober enough to hold her tongue. She'd look just like that, staring into the glowy ember of her cigarette.

Jimmy almost fell asleep again twice while he waited for Tim to say whatever it was he wanted to tell him. The ache in his head was even worse than he'd thought, he realized. He shouldn't be sleepy. He'd barely been awake at all today. He should have been stir-crazy, ready to get out and *do* something.

What it probably meant was that he ought to be in a hospital. Jimmy didn't know a whole lot about sickness, but he had a good sense of what he could sleep off and what he needed to see a doctor about.

The first candle finally finished burning itself out; Tim planted the second candle in the pool of wax it left behind.

"I think it's asleep now," Tim said. "I'm pretty sure, anyway."

Jimmy looked up at him. "What?" he asked. "I don't understand that."

"The Stone. I think it's gone back to sleep. I don't think it can hear us anymore."

"How can you tell?"

Tim shrugged. "I don't know. You get used to it enough to tell the difference, I guess. Maybe it's like it's always there in your head, but sometimes you can tell it's just not paying attention." Tim bit his lip and looked down at the dirt floor of the cave. "It's tired now. From getting broken and putting itself back together. And from making all the smells go away so the dogs from the sheriff's department wouldn't find you. It woke up when I walked past it, bringing you your dinner. But it's too tired to stay awake if nothing's going on."

Jimmy just nodded. He didn't know what the strange boy was talking about, or why he was saying it to him.

"Sean says the Stone wants to watch you die. He says it wants to watch you hurt as long and hard and deep as you can before you go. I talked to Sean tonight, so that I could be the one who fed you and watched you, and he told me. The Stone *hates* you."

Why *was* he saying these things? They were all kind of obvious, Jimmy thought. Still: it didn't *sound* like the boy was trying to needle him. Unless maybe he was really bad at it.

Jimmy's stomach gave another little lurch. His head, too. He felt sick—not from what the boy was saying so much as from the swelling in his head and stomach. He needed to go back to sleep, to rest long enough to let his body recover from the things that'd been done to it. He wished the boy would go away. To be polite he smiled as best he could and nodded again.

"So," Tim said. He didn't say anything else. He was sweating nervously; Jimmy could see a trickle of it on his forehead glitter in the candlelight. Jimmy waited five minutes for him to finish the sentence he'd started, but he never did.

Jimmy finally broke the silence himself.

"Is it all right if I eat this now?" He looked down into the paper bag.

Tim choked on something—it almost had to be his own spit, since he wasn't eating anything—and coughed it loose. When his breath was free again he looked at Jimmy, and for a moment Jimmy thought he was going to cry.

"Don't eat that. Please?" The boy *was* sobbing. Jimmy was kidnapped, and they were going to kill him, and his keeper was crying. The idea was weird enough to laugh about. Jimmy forced himself to be still.

"Okay," Jimmy said. "Sure. I won't eat if you don't want. But how come? What's the matter with eating?"

Jimmy saw something shatter on Tim's face; suddenly the boy was crying and talking at the same time.

"The sandwich is *poisoned,*" Tim said, sobbing. He buried his head in his arms and cried until he ran out of steam. When he was still, he said, "They're going to kill me. I told you and they're going to know and Sean's going to split me open with the skinning knife, just like he was going to do to your dog."

That didn't make any sense at all to Jimmy. If Tim was going to help him, why didn't he just cut the ropes that held the cage closed? And if he wanted to kill him, why the warning? "Why would they want to poison me? They could kill me any way they wanted. If you've got to die, poison isn't even all that mean a way to be killed."

Tim shook his head. "It's not poison to kill you. They don't want you to die yet." He wiped his eyes. "Sean pounded a glass soda bottle with a rock until the glass was powder, and he made me put the glass powder in the tuna fish. If you eat it the glass will tear a million tiny holes in your stomach, and you'll bleed to death a little bit at a time from the inside out. The Stone wants you to die *slowly.* It *needs* you to die that way. It needs to feed on your suffering."

Jimmy reached down into the bag and took out the sandwich. He turned it over and over in his hand, looking at it. "Shit. Where did you hear about that ground-glass trick? Did somebody get it off the television?"

Tim looked mystified. "How did you know?"

"Because it doesn't work, that's how." He took a bite out of the sandwich and chewed on it. The powdered glass made gritty sounds between his teeth, but there weren't any splinters. "You think they'd put something like that on TV if it really worked?"

Tim didn't answer; he looked dumbstruck.

"You know what they make glass out of?"

Tim rubbed the top of his head unconsciously. "They make it out of sand, don't they?"

"Uh-huh. And if you grind glass up, it goes back to being sand. Sand can't kill you. Not from eating a little bit of it, anyway."

"Maybe not," Tim said. "I still wouldn't eat it if I was you."

Jimmy shrugged. "You bring anything to drink? I need to wash this down. It's kind of dry. And what time is it, anyway?"

"After midnight. Not sure how long. Meant to bring you a soda—sorry, I forgot. Why don't you chew on one of those carrots for a while? Carrots are wet. Sort of."

The idea didn't appeal much to Jimmy—as far as he was concerned, carrots weren't *that* wet—but he didn't have any alternatives. He lifted one of the carrots out of the bag and tried to get a good look at in the candlelight. It was kind of soft and rubbery, like it had sat in the refrigerator a little too long, and it hadn't been peeled or rinsed, either. Tiny bits of dirt stuck to it in places. He brushed off as much of it as he could with the sleeve of his T-shirt, which maybe wasn't such a great idea, since the T-shirt was dirtier than the carrot.

He took a bite of the carrot and chewed and chewed; it did help him get the sandwich down, at least some. When he'd swallowed the carrot he took another bite of the sandwich. It still tasted funny.

"I'm not worried about the glass," Jimmy said, "but you should be careful about mayonnaise. If you leave it out for an hour it can get tainted. Give you food poisoning."

Tim nodded absently. "I didn't plan on you eating it."

Jimmy took a third bite of the sandwich and set it back in the bag. He still didn't think there was anything *that* wrong with the tuna fish. But his stomach was tender from whatever beating he'd gotten while he was unconscious. If he ate too much he wouldn't be able to hold any of it down.

He crumpled the top of the bag so it would stay closed and set it in the back corner of the cage.

He looked up at Tim. "Are you going to let me out of here?"

Tim's eyes went wide with panic and fear.

The pale red glow by the tunnel end of the cave grew bright enough to see, brighter than the light that came from the candle.

And then, suddenly, Tim was furious.

"You woke it up," he hissed, under his breath. Then, louder, "And that's not all, either. Tomorrow Sean's going to take you out of there and tie you to the wall in front of the Stone. And he's going to beat you. He's going to beat you until every bone in your body wants to die. But he won't kill you. Not then. Not even if you beg."

Tim was standing now. He took a running start and kicked the wooden bar in front of Jimmy's face so hard that the whole cage rattled. One of Jimmy's fingers, too close to the bar, got caught up in the kick, jamming his knuckle and the bone behind it back into his wrist.

"Not even if you beg," Tim said.

He left without looking back.

And as Jimmy watched him walk away in the receding glow of candlelight, something strange happened inside him. Shifted, in a way that was weird and painful and almost wonderful all at once. It started with resentment coupled to confusion: where did Tim get off hurting him like that, when Jimmy hadn't done a thing to him!—And why?

And then something deep inside him rose to meet the situation.

It doesn't matter, a quiet, bell-clear voice inside him said. *No matter how they hurt me. Not even if they kill me.* The voice was his own, and no one else's; and even if he didn't understand it he didn't doubt it for a moment. He thought of his mother—thought of loving her in spite of all she'd done to him—and knew his body from his spirit, and knew that there was nothing that anyone could do to his heart that he couldn't undo himself.

Jimmy sat caged and battered deep inside a cave he'd

never seen from the outside, and breathed in the calm of his own conviction, and felt the pain in his head and his hand recede as his heart grew big enough to carry him through hell.

CHAPTER

SIXTEEN

WHEN THE SHERIFF'S DEPUTIES FINALLY LEFT—WHEN
they'd given up trying to fill their sampling pouches, when
they'd covered the house with fingerprint dust, led the
German shepherds back into the vans that had brought
them—when the sheriff's department finally gave up and
went home for the evening, Ben Tompkins screamed.

It was after midnight. If the nearest house had been five
yards less far away, someone might have heard him. And
the ones who would have heard him would have sat up in
their beds and worried for him, even if it was so clear and
true a scream of frustration that no one could have thought
it a scream of terror.

The blood itched in Ben Tompkins's veins. For nine hours he'd forced himself to be and act calm, even though his heart demanded that he run to the hills and tear the earth apart—stone by stone, root by branch—until the world coughed loose his son.

His rational mind knew that tearing the world to shreds was absurd, useless, and even self-destructive. That didn't make the need a bit less powerful or true.

He'd stood at the front door of the house to watch as the sheriff's deputies left, and he waited until the last of their lights disappeared before he let himself scream. When the scream was done he closed the door behind him and went back to the kitchen.

He had to *do* something. Either that or find a hospital with its emergency room open, and get the doctor to give him a sedative. Ben didn't think much of people who used sedatives to solve their problems; making yourself blind and numb to trouble, he thought, wasn't any solution at all.

What he needed to do first of all was eat. He'd had neither the time nor the presence of mind to think of eating since he got home and found Jimmy missing. His only meal before that had been breakfast—light coffee and buttered toast.

Ben took a couple of slices of white bread out of the bag above the freezer, opened the refrigerator door, and rummaged around on the shelves until he found the plastic package of sliced bologna he'd picked up at the grocery. He took out five slices and put them between the bread. The sandwich really needed mayonnaise, but he was too hungry to spend the extra time it'd take to spread it onto the bread.

He carried the sandwich with him as he left through the back door. After a couple of bites he began to wish he'd taken the extra time for the mayonnaise—the bread was on the stale side, and very dry—but he didn't want it bad enough to go back to the kitchen and do something about it.

The moon was bright and not quite full. After a moment his eyes adjusted to its light, and he could see well enough to get around.

The men from the sheriff's department had found Jimmy's trail easily enough, even if their dogs hadn't been

able to smell it. The poor kid had been bleeding something
fierce; there were spatters of blood everywhere his left
foot had touched the ground. Jimmy's path led through
one corner of the backyard, past the bramble and way out
into the woods, over toward a dry sandstone ravine, and
then back in the direction of the rented house. It ended
with a few extra traces of blood, thirty yards before it came
full circle.

There were signs here and there that someone had followed Jimmy through the last leg of the trail—more than
likely several people. But, again, the dogs found no scent of
him.

Walking slowly—carefully, since his eyes were still adjusting to the darkness and the ground underneath his feet
was uneven—Ben started into the bramble, following the
trail of blood spots the deputies had found. He'd already
forgotten about the sandwich. A few yards after the blackberry bushes gave way to pine trees the sandwich fell out
of his hand and wedged itself between two melon-sized
sandstone rocks; he didn't even notice that he'd lost it.

"Jimmy . . . ?" he shouted. After a long while he heard
the question echo back to him, vague and distorted. There
should have been no echo; from this side of Green Hill all
the land in eyesight—except Green Hill itself—was
smooth and almost level. What little slope it did have was a
gentle descent toward a river that lay five miles to the
south. There should have been no echo; there was nothing
to reflect the sound. But Ben had never understood echoes
well enough to be certain how they worked, so the obser-
vation wasn't one that struck him hard enough to catch in
his craw. It might have if he hadn't been sick and half out
of his mind with worry about his son.

If he'd actually thought about that echo, if he'd given
any mind to it at all, he likely would have thought to look
for the sort of strange geologic artifact that could have
produced it. Eventually he would have thought to look for
a cave.

And when he'd looked for caves, he would have found
them. Green Hill is a hollow labyrinth of caves. The en-
trances are hidden, but not all that well; the Children had
never needed to fear that anyone would look for them.

Ben reached the place on the trail where Jimmy had

turned to follow the sound of Rex's scream. It was too dark under the pine trees to see the traces of blood his son had left behind. But Ben didn't really need to see them anymore. He'd followed Jimmy's path back and forth at least a dozen times today, one of them—the first one—stooped so far over that he was almost on his hands and knees, picking out the blood spots on the rocky ground with a pair of deputies. He didn't need much light to follow Jimmy's trail. He probably could have walked it with his eyes closed if he'd had to.

When he got to the ravine where the trail turned back toward its beginnings he climbed up into the rocky crag. There was a place near the top where Jimmy must have paused and rested several minutes, to judge from the amount of blood that had dried on the rocks.

This is my fault, Ben thought. *If I'd been there for my son, none of this would have happened. It's just like it was last winter, when I left him alone with Anne.* Right then it didn't occur to Ben that he couldn't be with Jimmy every waking moment of the boy's life. It didn't occur to him that he owed Jimmy a measure of independence; that watching the boy like a hawk would do more harm than help.

Not far from the bloody rocks was a stone shelf—it looked as though it might have been carved into the rock, but it was hard to be certain. It was smooth and weathered; if it was man-made, and not just some peculiar accident of lightning or geologic wear, then it was at least a hundred years old. Ben crawled up onto the ledge and sat on it with his legs dangling over the edge.

He stared down at the bloodstains and let his mind go blank. Why had Jimmy paused here? What would the boy have been thinking? Ben tried to picture himself as Jimmy, lying half-upright on these rocks. Seeing—what would be in front of him, the ravine?—seeing the ravine. Had something been in the ravine, something that now was gone? There was nothing in it now but rocks, big sharp-edged chunks of sandstone. Jimmy would have been thinking . . . what?

Ben didn't know. He couldn't imagine.

The dog.

Rex—Rex had to be the key to this. Ben had got to the house and the dog had been a bloody, hobbling mess. Was

the trail of blood that led here a trail of the dog's blood?
Ben didn't think so. The trail started in the house, and the
marks on the carpets and on the kitchen tile were all from
Jimmy's feet. A dog's three-toed paw prints would have
been distinct. Ben wouldn't have missed them, not as
many times as he'd pored over the floor of that house,
trying to puzzle out what had happened.

Jimmy and the dog had both been involved in something. It was just too unlikely that they'd both been
maimed at more or less the same time in incidents that had
nothing to do with each other.

But they'd left separately.

And Jimmy had walked around the house calmly bleeding on the floor as he made his breakfast. A breakfast that
the boy had suddenly left behind, all but untouched.

It didn't make any sense at all to Ben. Every series of
events he could think of that would explain all the bits of
evidence seemed too unlikely, too . . . *weird.*

A few hundred yards uphill, where the crest of Green
Hill made a near horizon against the starry black sky,
something was moving.

Someone?

Yes, someone—a child most likely. A boy, Ben thought,
judging by the dim silhouette he could see in the moonlight. Whoever it was was moving up and over the hill,
away from Ben.

Something clicked together in Ben's head.

Jimmy.

The dog.

Jimmy recounting how the dog had stumbled into the
yard, running from—

Children.

Four boys.

Now Jimmy was missing and the dog was mangled and
there were children wandering the fields after midnight.

Ben jumped down off the ledge, into the ravine, and ran
clumsily on the dark unfamiliar ground. Ran uphill, after
the boy.

By the time he got to the top his lungs felt as though
they'd been pierced half a dozen times by something sharp
and smooth. His breath tasted like cool metal in his throat.
Ben was years beyond being out of shape; he did enough

walking to have some muscle tone, but he hadn't run two hundred yards uphill since he was a boy.

He pushed himself up the last few yards to the crest of Green Hill and paused there to get his bearings. The boy's silhouette had disappeared over the top of the hill while Ben was still a hundred fifty yards away. But the boy had been walking, and much as it hurt, Ben had run. The boy would still be close enough to pick out in the moonlight, or Ben hoped he would. . . .

There! Off to the left, fifty yards downhill, something moving near the head-high wild shrubs—they looked like holly bushes, but the light and the distance made it hard to be sure.

"You there!" Ben called out. "Hold up. Stay where you are!"

That was the wrong thing to say. The boy—and it was a boy, Ben was close enough to see that now—took off, running like a frightened rabbit.

Ben ran after him.

Tall grass and trees shadowed out most of the moonlight on this side of the crest; the ground underneath his feet was almost impossible to see. Twice Ben nearly lost his footing as he ran after the boy. Ben was winded; even when he wasn't stumbling he was losing ground. The boy was young, and surefooted, and even in the dark he knew where he was going. Ben could tell he knew the trail, even seeing him run from this distance. The boy didn't hesitate an instant when his way led into shadows. He had to *know* the path to run like that in the dark, had to remember every rock, every rut, every rain-bared root.

Ben didn't know the path at all, much less know it intimately. Where it turned off to the right near the wild holly there was a shadow so wide and black that Ben knew he'd break his neck getting through it if he wasn't careful. But there wasn't *time* to be careful. The boy had something to do with the fact that Jimmy was missing. Ben was certain of it. So he ran headlong into the shadow, and to hell with the fact that he couldn't see where he was going.

Three paces in his right foot came down on a loose chunk of sandstone. The rock rolled a little to one side under his weight. Ben's balance shifted, went out of kilter, and suddenly his ankle was twisting out from under him, and his stride, instead of carrying him forward, became a breast-first dive into the rocky ground.

Automatically he stretched his arms out to break his fall, and an instant after it was too late to fall any other way he remembered how a friend of his in college had shattered his arm trying to ease a fall with exactly that maneuver. For a moment, as he felt the impact of the fall slam up through his left forearm, into his elbow, he thought his arm *was* going to break. In that instant he relived the image of his friend's arm, curled impossibly inward—a four-inch shard of bone spiking out through the skin, all white and red and bloody. But then the sandy gravel under his palm slid loose. His whole body stretched forward and longwise, and his breastbone smashed into a large flat rock and took most of the weight of the fall.

Ben shook the dirt off his face and looked up. The boy had glanced back to see him fall, but he was still running. Ben pulled himself out of the dirt and started after the boy again. He'd hurt himself in the fall—maybe even hurt himself badly—but there wasn't time to stop and see how badly. His left arm felt wet—up near the palm and wrist—which probably meant that he was bleeding. The center of his chest stung every time he moved his arms.

Up ahead, way ahead now, the boy skipped twice over something big in the darkness and bolted off into the thick woods to the right.

A moment later Ben saw that the boy had needed to skip because there were two fallen trees blocking the path. Ben had to slow down almost to a walk to get over them. When he was past them and looked to his right he saw that the woods the boy had run into were made up of broadleaf hardwood trees. They were too thick for any moonlight to penetrate at all.

Christ, Ben thought. *He can't run in that, even if he does know his way through it.*

There certainly wasn't any way for Ben to run through that kind of darkness. His only hope was that the boy was hiding—up in a tree, maybe, or in the thickness of a bush.

He stepped slowly, carefully, and quietly into the dark. He held his breath and listened: yes, he heard something, yards ahead and off to the left.

"I don't want to hurt you," Ben said. "It's my son—my son is missing."

No answer. And the noise was gone now.

"My boy," Ben said. "His name is Jimmy. He disappeared this afternoon. Not too far from where I first saw you."

Still no more sound of the boy. But Ben had a fix on where the noise had come from. He walked in that direction gently, one step at a time, letting each foot feel the ground, letting it find purchase before putting his weight on it.

"You can't imagine how worried I am. God I love that kid. Look, if you'll look me in the eye and tell me you don't know anything about my son, I'll turn around and pretend I never saw you. It's none of my business if you're running around in the dark after midnight. Nobody's business but yours and your folks'. And I won't make it my business to tell them."

A tree, directly in front of him; his bleeding hand felt it before he saw it. He stepped aside, forward, and around the tree, and kept walking. But now he was less certain of the direction—it was too hard to keep his bearings in the darkness.

"Please. Just talk to me. I don't even have to see who you are."

Over there—on his right. The sound of breathing. Ten feet away? Fifteen? Ben turned toward it.

Stepped forward.

Another step; another.

A gap in the foliage above that let through a beam of moonlight the size of a dinner plate. It lit the ground directly at his feet now. If he didn't go around it, the moonlight would shine for a moment directly in his eyes. He'd have to start adjusting to the darkness all over again.

But what did it matter? He'd been here five minutes and he still couldn't see anything farther away than his nose.

Another step forward.

Light! So bright in contrast to what his eyes expected that it was blinding.

Then, suddenly, the sound of motion not even six feet away. The sound of the boy throwing something. There was just time for Ben to tense his body for impact before—

—not what Ben expected at all. A flash-glimpse of a spray of sand and gravel in the moonlight that lit his face, and then his eyes were burning, stinging, trying to blink out the handful of dirt and rock the boy had thrown at them.

The boy was running now. Ben could hear him. Blinded, still blinking (and each blink ground the coarse sand deeper into his eyes), Ben tried to follow.

It was useless.

Ben forced his eyes to stay open. He needed them to run even if it was too dark to see anything; trying to run with them closed made him feel off balance. But even with them he was off balance and all but blind; three times he ran into trees hard enough to send him reeling off in the wrong direction. There wasn't enough light to see the boy —and even if there had been Ben wouldn't have been able to see him anyway. There was too much dirt in his eyes, and on top of the dirt tears kept welling up to rinse the dirt away, and that blurred things further.

"God *damn* you," Ben shouted. He wanted to scream again, out of frustration, but he couldn't spare the breath he'd have needed to scream, not if he wanted to keep running.

He followed the boy by sound, the sound of his footsteps crashing through the leaves and twigs and pine straw on the floor of the woods. And he could hear that the boy was getting away from him, getting ahead of him. The sound of his footsteps grew more dim as Ben listened to them.

Ben kept following, anyway, and forest—it was a forest now, not just a woods—grew deeper and darker around him. His eyes hurt less and less; the tears gradually washed them free of sand. But there was still nothing to see, nothing but pure, lightless darkness. Something small and fearful in the back of Ben's mind wondered if he were truly blinded, wondered if he'd ever be able to see again. He tried not to listen to it. He tried to think about nothing but his son. Even so, he was afraid—afraid for himself.

He ran for five more minutes before he realized that he wasn't hearing the boy anymore, and hadn't heard him for a long time. By then he was lost beyond any hope of guessing where he was. He kept running; running was the only thing he could think of.

That was a mistake. When the wind finally sagged out of him the situation was bad. Jimmy was gone and Ben was lost and everywhere he looked was black and dark and hopeless. The only sound he could hear was a cricket somewhere close in the darkness.

He wasn't running anymore. It wasn't that he'd meant to stop; he was still pressing himself as hard as he could. The motion of his body was still the motion of running, but it was slow; there were times when he'd gone faster and still been walking. He bumped into another tree, and it stopped him cold. He would have slid to the ground if he hadn't stopped himself.

Ben put his hands on the trunk of the tree, braced himself, pushed away, and made himself stand. His body was trembling with exhaustion—he wanted to collapse. But God knew what would happen to him if he let himself collapse this deep in the woods. He had to keep going, walking at least. Sooner or later he'd come to a road, or a cultivated farm, or something. He had to. This part of the country wasn't that wild.

A hundred yards later the ground cover became dense for a few steps, and then suddenly it gave way altogether. There was light again—not moonlight; the moon had set—starlight. Ben had never been accustomed enough to the dark for his eyes to see by starlight. But the starlight was plenty bright enough now. He'd somehow ended up on the two-lane highway that ran through Green Hill. But this part of the highway was miles away—halfway between Green Hill and Tylerville, if Ben remembered right.

At least, Ben thought, he knew where he was. It was something. He turned and began to follow the shoulder of the road back toward Green Hill.

The sun was rising by the time he got back to the rented house.

CHAPTER
SEVENTEEN

MIKE PETERSON HAD NEVER FELT EXACTLY RIGHT about being a detective for the county sheriff's department. He'd grown up with television, just like everyone else. A sheriff was someone from a western who shot it out with the bad guys at high noon. His deputy was someone who hung back and made sure that the guns were full. Maybe if he was brave he'd make it his business to make sure there weren't any townsfolk on the street when the bullets started flying.

A detective was somebody else altogether. Somebody from another century, who worked in a big-city police department with lots of other detectives and a few score patrolmen. The archetypal detective, in Mike Peterson's mind, lived a strange and dangerous life, a life so full of intrigue and adventure that sometime in his late thirties he'd write a book about it and retire on the royalties. Later there'd be a couple of movies, and eventually the Fox network would pick up the rights and produce a weekly TV series.

Being a deputy sheriff with the rank of detective made him feel out of kilter; the concept, he thought, was just too off balance to make a good book proposal, much less net him a movie deal.

Not that he had a whole lot of choice. Tylerville was home. It always had been and always would be. And the county needed law enforcement as much as any other place did, even if there wasn't a town inside its borders big enough to support a police department. So the sheriff's department, instead of being something from a movie with one man and his deputy, functioned as a police department for the entire county. Like any other police department, it needed people who functioned as patrolmen and others who didn't.

Because Peterson had lived in the county all his life, he'd known sheriff's deputies all his life, knew who was what in the department from knowing them at church. It still seemed wrong. But he liked the work anyway; he'd been with the department ten years because he felt like he made a difference in it—felt like he was doing something good for the world, and not just for himself.

There was plenty to make for himself, too, if he wanted it. The whole county was booming—factories had been moving down to this part of the country from the North-east steadily for the last ten years. There were five new plants in the county; because of the money they brought in, real estate had gone crazy. There was construction everywhere. Four of Peterson's five best friends from high school could retire today if they wanted to. Each of them had offered to hire Peterson away from the sheriff at one point or another, but he'd always turned them down. The only times he ever regretted it were when he sat down to write out the bills.

And, sometimes, moments like this. The Tompkins man, Ben Tompkins, had called at seven-thirty this morning.

He'd been hysterical and raving, full of crackbrained ideas about what had happened to his son. The man actually thought his son had been cut up and kidnapped by a bunch of children.

Christ on a crutch, Peterson thought, *save me from hysterical parents.*

The man's ideas were just plain stupid. Green Hill kids were mean-hearted little sons of bitches. Peterson would admit that any day you cared to ask. But God never made a kid mean enough to commit kidnapping and torture. Not in the world Peterson lived in. Not even Green Hill kids were that bad. Not if you asked Mike Peterson about it, anyway. Sure, Green Hill kids got into trouble—sometimes *bad* trouble—but not like this. Not like maiming little boys and carrying them off.

Still, the Tompkins man had called in and told Peterson his crazy ideas, and even if it had been so early that the sun had still looked tired on a morning after Peterson hadn't got home until two in the a.m. the night before—even still the ideas had to be checked out. It was Peterson's case; it had been his call, too. So here he was, driving to the vet's office to take a look at the Tompkinses' dog.

Peterson felt pretty stupid about it. He would have been a lot happier with the search party in Green Hill. That was how they were going to find that boy, if he was anywhere to be found at all. There were deputies from six counties wandering around Green Hill today. That boy was going to be *found,* even if the dogs couldn't track him.

He still couldn't figure that one out. The boy had left scent all over the house. He'd bled enough for a dog to smell half a mile away. The dogs had no trouble following his spoor out the back door. Through the backyard. Then, two yards into the blackberry briar, the dogs couldn't find anything, even though there was a blood trail plain as day for the eye to see. Peterson made sure that the lab people down in the state capital checked that blood out, too—he had a couple of deputies run samples down in a car last night.

The lab people said it was the same blood that was on the kitchen floor.

Human blood. Same type as the Tompkins boy's.

It wasn't natural—blood on the ground and dogs

couldn't smell it. Peterson didn't like that at all. What the hell kind of case was this, anyway?

He turned the cruiser into the vet's parking lot. Three years ago there hadn't *been* a veterinarian in this county—not a pet doctor, anyway. Old Dr. Simpson, just the other side of the county line, did a circuit twice a year for the cattle farmers, and he wasn't all that far away if you needed him other times. Then a couple of years back this Smith woman comes down from Michigan and sets up shop in the building Stop 'n' Shop outgrew the year before. She did a good business, too, from the look of things. The place was all finished over with two-tone brick and wooden shingles. If Peterson hadn't *known* the place used to be a Stop 'n' Shop, he never would have thought it.

He knocked at the door before he remembered that the office had a waiting room with no one sitting at the desk. If Dr. Smith was working she'd never hear him, and anyway there wasn't any need to knock before you went into a waiting room. A harsh electric bell started ringing when he opened the door, and didn't stop until it was closed behind him.

"Dr. Smith. . . ?" She wasn't anywhere Peterson could see.

When she answered her voice sounded muffled, as though she were two or three rooms away. "Just a minute."

It was less than a minute, actually, before she came through the door in back of the desk.

"Mike Peterson," she said. "Good to see you. How is the sheriff's department these days? What can I do for you?"

Peterson frowned to himself—He hoped it didn't show in his face. But the woman talked too much and too fast for him to be comfortable with. "Things are pretty grim just now, to tell the truth," he said. "There's a boy missing in Green Hill. His father called me this morning with a wild story." Peterson let out a tense breath. "He said you could confirm part of it."

Dr. Smith looked confused, and a little distressed, too. But not nearly as upset, Peterson thought, as she'd look when she heard what had happened.

"Anything I can do to help," she said. "What sort of story would I know anything about?"

Peterson didn't feel any need to conceal his frown this

time; this frown didn't have anything to do with the veterinarian. It had to do with what he had to say. To tell her what had happened he had to think through the sequence of events again. He couldn't do that without having the acid in his stomach get all churned up.

"Jimmy Tompkins disappeared yesterday morning, while his father was running a few errands here in Tylerville," Peterson said. He let out a sigh, and what came out of his throat sounded to his ears almost like a groan. "When his father got back to the house there was blood all over everything, and the boy was nowhere in sight. We're looking for him. We'll find him, I think. But we haven't found him yet."

The veterinarian looked agitated, almost frantic. "The dog—"

"Yeah, the dog. That's the first thing I need to ask you about. Ben Tompkins called me early this morning, all frantic with facts and theories—some of which look kind of dubious, and other parts of which are just plain weird. Something about children, and a dog, and a boy running around in the woods after midnight." Peterson cleared his throat. "He said that the dog had been hurt, and that it was here with you now. He also said that you were the one who first told him about these children."

She looked furious now. She was a tall, fair-skinned, black-haired woman, and the anger did something almost beautiful to her eyes.

"The dog isn't just 'hurt,'" she said. Her jaw was clenched; her words hissed out between her teeth. "Someone took a hammer to it. The ham bone of its left hind leg is broken in five places. Its knee joint is so badly smashed that I'm not sure that the dog will ever be able to use it again, even if the bone *does* heal properly."

Peterson blinked and swallowed. He hadn't meant to upset the woman. Bad will was the last thing he needed from anybody. Life was just too short for that kind of hostility in a town this small. "I'm sorry, ma'am. I didn't mean any offense. If you say that someone mangled the dog, I'm sure they did."

She pursed her lips and hissed. For a moment Peterson thought she was going to start screaming at him. But then her anger seemed to recede a little. "Come back to my office," she said. "I need to show you the dog. I want to show you the x-rays I had to make before I could open its leg up and pin the bone back together."

She didn't wait for a response before she turned around and started back toward the examination room. Peterson followed her; it was the only thing he could do.

When he got there she was already digging through a file drawer of photographic transparencies.

"There," she said. "This is the one." She lifted out a sheet of film, snapped it into the light box that was mounted on the wall, then switched on the box's fluorescent light. "Look at it," she said. "Do you see what you're dealing with? Do you understand the sort of people we're talking about?"

Peterson didn't know a thing about x-rays. He didn't know how to read them, and, in fact, had not been able to identify anything at all in either of the other two x-ray photographs he'd seen in his life.

"Um . . . Actually, ma'am, that doesn't make any sense to me at all. Can you show me what I'm supposed to be looking at?"

She looked at him. For half a breath she seemed puzzled. She took a pencil from a canister on the counter and pointed at the x-ray with it. "Here," she said, "these white fragments. You see how they're more or less in a line?"

Peterson nodded.

"They're supposed to be one bone. The thigh bone of the dog's left hind leg. Do you know how much force it takes to break a dog's thigh?" She paused, waiting for him to answer, but Peterson just looked at her blankly. He didn't know; he didn't have any idea at all. "A lot. A dog's hind legs are where most of his strength is—except for his jaw, of course. The bones have to be sturdy to take the stress and wear.

"But the worst thing about it is *how* the leg was broken. The hammer marks are on the *inside* of the dog's thigh. The dog had to be lying still and on his side for that to be possible. Someone tied the dog down to keep it that way—I found marks that look like rope burns on his underside. Come on. I'll show you the dog."

She dropped the pencil on the counter and started for the back door without hesitating a beat. She had the door open and was halfway through it before it finally sunk through to Peterson that he had to follow her.

"Are you coming?" she asked.

Peterson felt himself flush. "Oh. Yes, I am." He was thinking about that idea: tying a dog down and mutilating it with a hammer. It was pretty damned sick. You heard stories like that about Green Hill kids if you grew up in Tylerville the way Peterson had. But you kind of assumed they were folktales, like ghosts in the woods or wild-eyed bogeymen in the cellars of old buildings.

But kids everywhere had a sick streak in them—or at least some of them did. Even growing up in Tylerville Peterson knew kids who did mean things to animals. Tying up a dog and pounding on it with a hammer, though. . . . Peterson had to admit that *was* worse than tying tin cans to a dog's tail, or setting a cat afire. It was more intimate. But it wasn't *that* much worse.

And setting into another child with a knife—or whatever it was that had the Tompkins boy bleeding all over hell and creation—that was another matter entirely. Peterson just couldn't see kids doing anything that . . . *evil.*

Or maybe he didn't *want* to.

Maybe he just didn't *want* to believe kids could be that bad. Peterson felt the muscles at the back of his neck bunch up and begin to ache. There was at least a measure of truth there: he really *didn't* want to have to believe children could be that bad.

By the time Robin Smith opened the door to the ten-cage kennel where she kept animals she had to treat overnight, Peterson had begun to have doubts. When he saw the dog, the doubts began to harden into something more real.

Rex was asleep, and he was the only dog in the whole room just then. When Peterson saw him he almost wanted to cry.

"My God," he said, "that used to be old Dan Henderson's dog, didn't he? What in the hell happened to that thing?"

She shrugged. "Ben and Jimmy Tompkins brought him in the first time a few days ago. Jimmy had found four Green Hill boys chasing him with clubs. When he made them stop, they went after him, instead of the dog. Luckily for Jimmy he's pretty handy in a fight—God knows how, but he managed to chase all four of them off. Ben and Jimmy brought the dog in to me the next day."

Peterson shook his head. "You're sure about this?"

She shrugged again. "How sure can I be? I didn't see it myself. Jimmy was the one who told me the story."

Peterson nodded, and turned back toward Rex. The dog was a mess of scabs and bandages and loose fur from one end to the other. His left hind leg was strapped to a wooden splint with white adhesive tape.

"Most of the wounds are old," she said. "The shattered leg happened yesterday; Ben Tompkins didn't know his son was missing when he brought the dog in. All but a couple of the rest were scabbed over when they brought the dog in the first time." She opened the dog's cage, reached in, and gently rolled him half-way over, so Peterson could see his underside. A careful line of stitches ran from the dog's groin to his breastbone.

"Somebody tried to gut him alive?" Peterson asked. He was beginning to feel sick to his stomach.

"Started to," she answered. "It's not actually one cut. When I went in to clean away the infection and sew him up I found out that the cut only went halfway through the skin. Then I looked a little closer and saw that it wasn't one incision at all, but ten or fifteen of them, not always following exactly the same line. It looked to me as though someone wanted to cut the dog's stomach open one layer of skin at a time, and only got the job halfway done. What kind of warped mind would do that I can't imagine. But I caught the Williams twins, Jan and Eileen, doing something damn near as bad six months ago. Ask Myron White about it. He was the one at the desk when I hauled them down to your office."

Peterson was going to say that he would, but then he saw the dog begin to wake. He reached down to pat its head before he even stopped to consider whether it was a good idea.

"Hey ya, Chicklet," he said. "How ya doin'?"

The veterinarian smiled. "Ben and Jimmy Tompkins are calling him Rex, now," she said.

"Rex, huh? It's a better name for a dog than Chicklet." She was still smiling.

The dog opened his eyes, then, and what Peterson saw in those eyes stayed with him the rest of his life.

Part of what he saw was need. And desperation. And failure. But there was something fiery in them, too—fiery and hard like a powerful determination.

Later, when he thought back about it, Peterson wondered how he could have seen those things in a dog's eyes. What was there in a dog's face that could show that much expression? Fur? He didn't know; he didn't think he ever would. Perhaps it was a trick of his own imagination. But even if it was, the thought and image of those eyes still haunted him for years.

Rex stood up on three legs, slowly and laboriously. Then his eyelids slowly fell shut and his legs fell out from under him.

The veterinarian made a small startled noise.

"Is he all right?" Peterson asked.

"He should be. He didn't fall on his splinted leg. Even if he had, that's exactly the sort of thing the splint's there for." She closed the cage. "I'm surprised he even woke. I've got him pretty heavily sedated. I had to—the pain from that leg has to be tremendous."

Peterson felt shaken. *I need to get out of here. I need to get out in the sun and sit there drinking it in until my head clears.* "I appreciate your help," he said. "But I've got to get back on the road. There are a few other things I need to check on this morning."

"Sure. Anything I can do to help, let me know, okay?"

Peterson hesitated. He had an idea, but it felt too stupid to say out loud. "Give me a call when that dog's all right enough to do a little walking, would you? I feel kind of stupid saying it, but I've got a feeling that dog knows something about all of this."

Myron White was in Green Hill, along with everyone else who could be spared, searching the woods and fields for Jimmy Tompkins. It took Peterson most of an hour to find him.

White told him the story about Jan and Eileen Williams and the kitten they'd tortured and beaten until it was all but dead. White had gone out to the tree Robin Smith had told him about before he'd taken the girls home to their folks.

It was real, all right. White had been amazed a kitten could leave behind that much blood.

There was a big piece of Peterson that still didn't want to believe that children were capable of anything that bad. But even so he told White to take a couple of other deputies and keep a casual eye on the children hereabouts— especially the Williams girls.

Then he went back to his work and did his best to forget the whole idea. Not that it did any good.

CHAPTER

EIGHTEEN

NOT LONG AFTER TIM LEFT, JIMMY HEARD HIS FA-
ther's voice calling his name.

The shout came from far away—or it sounded far away,
at least, and it echoed half a dozen times against the walls
and passages of the cave. Jimmy had already fallen half-
way back to sleep; he opened his eyes and sat up.

His heart was pounding. *Oh God.* Please *God.*

"Dad!" he shouted. *"Dad!* I'm here!"

The red glow at the far wall of the cave flared to a
brilliant crimson. And dimmed after a moment.

His shout didn't echo at all, and even though he could

feel himself almost screaming his voice sounded like a whisper. Was there something wrong with his throat?

No. His throat felt fine. It was just about the only part of him that did.

A normal tone of voice: "Dad . . . ?"

He heard it fine. There wasn't anything wrong with his throat.

"Dad!" he shouted again, *"I'm down here in the cave!"*

Again the red glow momentarily flickered bright as daylight, and again all he heard of his own voice was a whisper.

Maybe, he thought, it was some strange acoustic trick of the rock. Maybe dad could hear him even if he couldn't hear himself.

But even as he hoped it was so Jimmy knew that it wasn't. The red glow was something magical . . . magical and evil. It soaked in the sound the way a sponge soaks water.

Still: Jimmy shouted for his father a dozen more times before the force of his screaming shook something loose in the swollen part of his head. Then he blacked out all at once, still sitting up; he didn't even realize it was happening.

He slept without dreams until late the next morning.

Jimmy was still unconscious late the next morning when Tim brought him breakfast. He didn't wake until Tim reached into the cage and shook him gently.

"Are you okay?" Tim asked as Jimmy opened his eyes. "You don't look so good. Are you sure it's okay to eat that stuff with glass in it?"

Jimmy squeezed his eyes open and shut a few times, trying to steady himself. Tim had his candle with him, but it wasn't lit—there wasn't any need to light it. The red glow coming from the far end of the cave was at least as bright as dusk.

"No," he said, "my head—dizzy and sick. Something's wrong, I think."

"You want me to bring some aspirin or something next time I come?"

Jimmy sat up. "Aspirin? I don't know. It's supposed to be bad when you're bleeding. Doesn't this kind of swelling—"

he pointed at the side of his head "—come from bleeding under the skin?"

"I don't know. I guess it does. How come you know all this stuff? Are you smart or something?"

Jimmy shrugged. "What's smart? Don't you ever see those commercials on TV about dangerous things? I always remember the ookey parts. Doesn't everybody?"

"I guess. Just never get any use out of them. How come you do if you aren't smart?" Tim rubbed his nose and lifted the paper sack that was by his knee. "Hungry?"

"I ought to eat. What did you bring? Anything to drink?"

"Two cans of Coke. I brought you a ham sandwich and some Fritos, too. Sean had me put the glass underneath the top slice of ham. Wipe it off before you eat, okay? Even if it doesn't make your stomach bleed, it makes me want to get sick to watch you eat it."

Tim held the bag out; Jimmy took it. "Sure, if you want." The ache in Jimmy's stomach felt a lot less bad than it had yesterday. Everything felt better, except for his head. He was hungry, and he was thirstier than he was hungry. He opened one of the cans of soda—they were still wonderfully cold—and drank half the can in one long swallow.

"How come the light over there is so bright?" he asked Tim as he opened the sandwich and began to wipe away the glass. "What exactly is the light, anyway?"

"From the Stone," Tim said. "It glows like that, at least a little, any time it isn't in the sunlight. Or maybe you just can't see it when the sun's out. It's so bright like that right now because it's working hard. There are people outside all over everywhere looking for you. It has to make sure none of them see the ways into the caves, even though they're looking straight at them sometimes. It's going to be real tired tonight. Hungry, too. Going to need another sacrifice soon."

Jimmy choked on the bite of sandwich he'd just taken. "Sacrifice?" he asked. "That's me, you mean. They're going to sacrifice me. They are, aren't they? Tonight? Or soon, anyway."

Tim shook his head. "No. They're going to have to find something else. Or somebody. Sean says the Stone has plans for you. But they're going to have to find the sacrifice soon. The Stone is hungry. Magic always makes it hungry.

It's never had to use this much magic before. Not that I ever seen."

Jimmy thought about that as he finished the sandwich. Were they going to sacrifice Rex? It was beginning to seem like they didn't even have the dog. Tim would have said something about it by now if they did. It didn't even seem like they were thinking about Rex. Jimmy started to ask Tim about the dog, but then it occurred to him: if they'd forgotten about Rex, then it was better not to remind them. Not even when Tim seemed genuinely friendly. Tim had a conscience, that was obvious. Even if he was tied to the Stone, the same way all the other Children were, Tim didn't like hurting people, probably didn't like hurting animals. But it seemed to Jimmy that if Tim thought that killing the dog would help him save Jimmy, then Tim would kill Rex himself.

Jimmy wanted to live. He wanted to live so bad he could taste it. But he didn't want to live bad enough to have people or things he loved dying to save him. Jimmy didn't want that hanging over his head the rest of his life.

Besides, Jimmy wasn't completely sure about Tim anyway. Why had he suddenly started acting so crazy-mean last night, just before he'd left? And how come he was even friendlier now than he had been before? Jimmy could guess—he thought it had to do with the red light from the Stone that had got so bright just before Tim had gone crazy. But he wasn't sure enough to be comfortable.

"What was the matter with you last night? Just before you left, I mean. When you were talking about killing me."

Tim looked down, away from Jimmy's eyes. When he spoke he sounded guilty. "I'm sorry. I don't really want to kill you. But you woke the Stone up when you asked about that. I had to talk like that—it was listening to me. Listening to you, too, even though Sean says it can't hear inside your head anymore. It can still hear what you say out loud. Hear what anybody says out loud, if it wants to or if something catches its ear like that. When it gets bright and starts paying attention like that, you got to be quiet."

"It's bright now. Why're you saying things like that if it's awake?"

Tim shook his head. "It's too busy to pay any attention to

either one of us. Might not even hear me if I talked right to it."

Jimmy pulled open the bag of Fritos and started to pick at the chips. After a moment Tim's expression turned first confused and then furious. Then the red glow from the end of the cave began to dim. It kept growing dimmer until it was only barely possible to see by its light.

"Eat it all," Tim said. "We don't want you starving to death before we're ready to kill you." His voice was cruel and icy.

What's going on? Jimmy wondered. *What's changed now? Why is he acting like this?* He felt confused and off balance and betrayed all at the same time, in spite of the fact that Tim had as much as warned him that he'd have to act that way.

"That was a good idea you had last night, Tim." Sean's voice, coming from the same passage that the red glow came from. "The Stone told me all about it this morning. It *wants* to see this Jimmy boy hurt so much he begs to die. Stone *likes* that idea. But we got to be careful exactly what we do. Stone says it's seen a lot of people die from being hurt too much. It says we shouldn't go much deeper than the skin."

Sean was in the cave with them now.

"Should I open the cage and take him out? Where are we going to cut him?"

"Hold up a minute. We're going to need both of us—we wouldn't want him to try escaping, would we? Then we'll drag him into the next cave and string him up on the wall so the Stone can watch."

The ends of the rope that held the cage shut stretched to the wall of the cave, where they were tied to a jagged spike of rock. Sean walked over to the spike and untied the knot, then went to the cage and unraveled the rope from the bars of the door. When it was gone the cage door swung open like a gate.

Sean looked at Jimmy. "Get out of there," he said. "Get out of there and do like you're told, or this is going to be even worse than you know."

Jimmy shook his head, to clear it, and started to lift himself up off the hard-packed dirt on the floor of the cage. Everything was stiff; it hurt when he even thought about moving. He didn't want any more trouble than he could avoid getting; he would have got up faster if his legs had let him.

"That's a good boy now," Sean said as Jimmy hobbled past the cage door. He put his hand on Jimmy's shoulder, almost as though he were going to pat him on the back. "Make sure you do like I say when I tell you, you hear?"

Jimmy nodded—or started to. Then Sean pushed him from behind so he went flying face-first into the dirt. Pushed him so hard that he slid a few inches on his face after he hit the ground. It didn't do as much harm as it might have; the dirt wasn't soft, but it was worn smooth, so it only scraped him up a little.

But it hurt his pride something serious, and that was a real injury. *No matter what they do,* he told himself. *No matter what.* And forced himself to think of his mother damping out the ember of her cigarette in his squeezed-shut eye. And forced himself to remember that he loved her.

And when he did it seemed to Jimmy that there was nothing Sean or Tim could do that would *really* hurt him.

"Get up," Sean said, "Get up *now.*"

Jimmy stood up as best he could. He was dizzy and unsteady; he could feel himself sway on his feet.

"That's better," Sean said. He turned and spoke to Tim. "Kind of fun to watch him dance, ain't it?"

Tim smiled like a cartoon snake who'd just found a sleeping cartoon mouse. "Sure is. Why don't you really make him dance? Put on a show, just for us?"

"Nah. We got to get down to business. The Stone's in a hurry to see him. And I bet Jimmy Tompkins is just as anxious to see the Stone. Ain't you, Jimmy Tompkins?"

Jimmy wasn't sure how he was supposed to answer, or whether he was supposed to answer at all. "Sure I am," he said. "If you want me to be, I am."

Tim and Sean both broke up laughing.

"You hear that, Tim? Jimmy Tompkins just *can't wait* to meet the Stone. Best thing I ever did hear." Sean shoved Jimmy's shoulder again, but not hard enough to knock him over this time. "Go ahead. Move. Toward the light in the passage."

Jimmy did as he was told.

When Jimmy had first noticed the light he'd assumed that it came from something inside the passageway. But as he walked toward the passage he saw that it wasn't so—the light reflected into the passage from another cave, fifteen feet away.

"Keep going," Sean said. "You can follow the light. You've got enough sense in your head for that, don't you?"

Jimmy nodded, and nodding made him feel as though the whole world were shaking. He turned into the passage. Walked through it, and into the other cave. The light inside it was red and bright enough that Jimmy's eyes had trouble adjusting, and he stumbled on something near the entrance—he fell, and landed chest-first on the dirt.

"Going to have to teach that boy to walk before we kill him if we want to get any use out of him," Sean said. "He don't seem to know whether he's supposed to get around on his feet or on his belly. What's the matter, Jimmy Tompkins, you some kind of a worm or something?"

Sean and Tim laughed even longer at that. After a moment Sean walked over and kicked Jimmy in the side, just above his belly.

"You're supposed to *answer* me when I ask you a question, Jimmy Tompkins. Are you a worm or what?"

Jimmy still lay on the ground, looking into the dirt. "No," he said. "Not a worm."

. . . . *doesn't matter doesn't matter doesn't matter.* . . .

The two Children laughed even harder. When they'd rung the last bit of nastiness out of the joke, Sean kicked Jimmy again. The pain and the force of the blow shot through him, hard; much as he tried to push it away it dug into him. Dug right into his heart.

"Time for you to get up, Jimmy Tompkins. You've got to meet the Stone."

Jimmy saw it as soon as he began to lift himself off the ground. It was magical and powerful and evil, and the strange red light that danced above it—

Jimmy had seen light like that once. The summer he was five his mother and father took him up to Canada for vacation, out to a cabin on a lake. The lake had been surrounded by mountains—tall, sharp-peaked mountains that almost seemed to watch him from above when he was alone. Their third evening in the cabin Jimmy had gone

wading in the lake-edge while his dad had made supper—
very late supper; dad liked to eat at dusk if he had a choice,
and this far north in July dusk meant nine-thirty. Mom sat
in the sofa with the arms made out of polished wood, reading. Neither one of them paid much attention when Jimmy
went outside. It wasn't as though there were muggers or
bagmen up here. Or even streets for them to lurk on: after
they turned off the highway they'd had to follow a winding
mud-and-gravel road three miles before they got to the
cabin.

Jimmy had waded barefoot out into the water, watching
minnows and tadpoles dart around his toes and ankles.
He'd waded fifteen yards along the edge of the water
when the world seemed to hush, as though every living
thing for a hundred miles in every direction were holding
its breath all at once.

He looked up, and saw the darkening grey-blue sky begin to shiver everywhere with impossible light, curtains
and waves and waterfalls of light.

It's the end of the world, Jimmy thought. *It's the end of
the world and mom and dad don't know and I've got to tell
them.*

He ran back toward the cabin to warn his parents, but by
the time he was even half-way there the shimmering light
had stopped.

All that night and through the next day he'd waited on
edge for the rest of the apocalypse. It never came. But
early the next evening, while he was out on the lake in a
rowboat, fishing with dad, dad said, "Look up," and Jimmy
had.

Again the sky had been filled with wild light.

"The sky is on fire," Jimmy had said. "The world is going
to blow up, huh, dad?"

Dad had laughed, not a whole lot and not mean at all.
"No, Jimmy. The world isn't going to blow up. That's the
aurora borealis—it's kind of like lightning, but it happens
everywhere in the whole sky all at the same time. Only
happens way up north like this."

"Oh." Jimmy felt kind of dumb, but not *that* dumb.
"That's good."

Dad had mussed his hair and gone back to fishing.

* * *

The Stone was like that, here in the dark.

It was black as a thousand nighttimes condensed into a single moment, and all around it an aurora the color of fresh blood crackled and shimmered. Looking at that aurora, Jimmy thought he could see the Stone's heart. He could taste it, almost—taste the richness of its hate with his eyes. More hate than Jimmy could imagine, so thick and strong that it coalesced into electric fire just the color of an open vein—so thick that Jimmy wondered if it would turn solid if there was any more of it.

But if the sparkling-black stone and its dancing blood-fire were hatefully evil, they were magical, too—wondrous and sorcerous and secret. Like a special treasure no one else could see and still remember. He wanted to reach out and touch its electric fire, to let it dance between his fingers so he could remember it forever. But he knew from when he'd been too close to it before that it would burn him. And here in the dark, Jimmy was sure, it was more powerful than it had been under the sun.

Besides, God only knew what Sean would do if he tried. Jimmy didn't want to find out.

"The rope is over there, Tim," Sean said. "Tie it to the rock over there on the wall. Hang Jimmy Tompkins up there by his wrists, so the Stone can watch while I cut him."

CHAPTER

NINETEEN

THEY WERE WATCHING HER NOW, TOO.

It made Roberta Anderson furious; angrier, she thought, than she'd ever been before. And Roberta had felt very little in her eleven years besides anger and a thirst for meanness.

The twins were idiots. This morning one of them noticed that a couple of those sheriff's deputies were watching them. The men were trying to be casual about it, but they weren't casual enough not to be obvious.

So what had the fools done? They'd started skulking around, trying to sneak away without being noticed. Which, of course, made it obvious to the deputies that they

knew about them, especially since they couldn't sneak
well enough to fool their own mother, much less two deputy sheriffs. And then the idiots led the sheriff's department straight to Roberta's house.

It had only taken Roberta a moment to figure out what
was going on, and as soon as she did she lit into the twins
mercilessly. She'd screamed at them, and slapped them
around more than a little. That, Roberta realized now, had
been a pretty serious mistake. She'd been loud enough to
hear three houses away—loud enough, easily, to be heard
by the deputies, who were in the field next to Roberta's
yard, pretending to search for Jimmy Tompkins. When the
twins had left, one of the two deputies had stayed behind
to watch Roberta.

Roberta sat in the den, not even watching the television
show that was on. The more she thought about it, the
angrier she got. But even though the anger gave her a
certain satisfaction—the nearest thing to pleasure that she
knew—she had to calm down. She couldn't think when her
blood throbbed in her ears this way. She had to *think*—
clearly and quietly and carefully.

Sean needed to know what was going on. The Stone
needed to know. But she didn't dare go near either one of
them, not if she didn't want to make everything fall apart
even faster than it was falling apart now. No matter how
important it was for Sean to know, it was more important
not to do anything suspicious.

But what was suspicious? What did sheriff's deputies *expect* children to act like? Everything Roberta knew about
ordinary kids came from television. The kids on TV
weren't anything like the ones in Green Hill . . . and
Roberta had never known any children besides the ones in
Green Hill. All TV kids were stupid, stupid as the twins.
Watching them always made Roberta anxious; she couldn't
see them without wanting to hunt them the way she always hunted baby rabbits in the spring the week after
their mothers gave birth. It always got Roberta excited,
and she didn't like to act that way in front of her parents,
even if they weren't apt to notice.

What did kids like that act like? Roberta honestly didn't
know. She could picture them doing things like jumping
rope. Or playing hopscotch. Cards, maybe? Yes—games

like Old Maid or Go Fish. Roberta didn't know a thing about any of that.

Or they played in swing sets, or jungle gyms. There wasn't a single swing set in Green Hill—not even at the school.

When they were at the beach they built sand castles. That was in a movie once. She could see building sand castles, and especially she could see wrecking them afterward. But it didn't matter; Green Hill wasn't anywhere near the shore.

She couldn't just stay home. That would make the deputy outside suspicious. She had to act like she didn't even know anyone was following her, like she was a normal kid doing what a normal kid did on a summer day.

But what was *that*?

Roberta was beginning to grow uncomfortable when inspiration finally struck her: the library. Television kids were always going to the library. Or reading things like comic books. Mom would take her to the library in Tylerville if she asked. Today was mom's day for grocery shopping; she had to go up to Tylerville anyway.

Roberta thought about Jimmy Tompkins as she sat in the front seat of the car, watching her mother drive to Tylerville. This was all his fault—all of it.

There was a sheriff's car following quietly behind them, so far back that you almost had to know it was there to see it.

Roberta wanted to lay her hands on Jimmy Tompkins . . . sink her fingers into his flesh and show that boy what she thought of him. The thought of it made her smile.

Jan and Eileen Williams were having fun.

Life was always fun for Jan and Eileen. The world was full of things that begged to hurt, or break, or be defaced. And nothing under the sun, if you were to ask the twins, could ever be as full of wonder and delight as destruction, or the suffering of others.

Just now the twins were at home. A few moments ago Jan had found a fly buzzing and buzzing at the living room window, trying to get out of the house. Pulling the wings off flies was old stuff for Jan and Eileen—it hadn't quite lost its charm, but it had gotten homey and familiar. And this last week had been so full of hurtfulness—so rich and so fresh and so *new*— that homey pleasures had begun to lose their luster.

But then Eileen had come up with a new idea, one that changed all the parameters of the fly's suffering.

What if, she'd said, instead of pulling its wings off, we pin it down and cover them with honey? Or even Kayro syrup. . . ?

It was a wonderful idea. How the fly would suffer, with its wings too sticky to fly, too weighted down by its heart's desire to ever be of any use again! There was a richness about it, an irony that neither girl could have put a label to, but one that delighted them both.

It was a task, capturing the fly without doing harm to its wings. Finally, though, Jan had been able to do it. Of the two of them, her eyes were far the sharper, and her hands much quicker. Neither one of them was especially bright, but what quickness of wit they had between them rested mostly with Eileen. Eileen's real gift, though, wasn't her intelligence—it was her vivid and demented imagination. She used that imagination for all it was worth; there weren't many of the Children who had more fun than Jan and Eileen.

The fly was buzzing now, buzzing unevenly as it battered itself against the windowpane. Here and again it would brush a wing or the top of its abdomen against the glass, and it would stick there for a moment, smacking its wings back and forth. The sight of it was comical, at least to the twins. Each time it happened they broke out into giggles, fits of laughter that went on long after the fly managed to shake its way free.

"Let me kill it now," Jan said when she finally caught her breath. "Time to *die,* fly." She brought her hand up toward the window. "The bug is getting *boring.* I want to kill it."

Before her sister could even respond, her hand darted out toward the glass, and she thumped the fly in midair with her index finger. The fly's body bounded off the glass, smacked into the wood of the window frame, and stuck there.

Eileen punched her sister in the chest, so hard that Jan almost lost her balance. *"Stupid!"* Eileen said. "It didn't

even hardly have a chance to get tired. I wanted to see
what would happen when it finally wore itself out."

Jan braced her feet against the floor and turned to face
Eileen. For a moment she looked as though she were going
to lunge, but then she had a chance to see the look on her
sister's face. Eileen was mad enough to fight, mad enough
to fight *hard*. Eileen was dangerous when she really
wanted to hurt you . . . sometimes she got excited and
didn't know when to stop. Jan knew that better than anybody.

"Sorry," she said. Jan didn't like backing down. But she
hadn't liked it the time Eileen yanked three fistfuls of her
hair out by the roots, either. It hurt having that much hair
pulled out, and it made you bleed all over the place, too.
There was still blood all over the walls to remind Jan of that
fight. Mom would have cleaned up the blood by now, but
every time she saw it she got this blank look on her face
and forgot whatever she was doing.

"He's still watching us over there," Eileen said. "That
deputy sheriff."

"What? He is? You'd think a sheriff would know that
grown-ups aren't supposed to stare into people's windows.
I seen on that TV movie. They go to jail for it when they
do."

Eileen snickered. "Why don't you tell that to him? I bet
he'd like to hear." She shifted her voice into a falsetto. *"Mr.
Sheriff, they going to put you in jail if you don't stop
looking in our window. Why don't you just run along and
pretend you can't see us, like you was a real grown-up?"*

Jan ignored the dig. "Think I'd rather give him something to look at," she said. She let her eyes get all wild and
blood-hungry, and she stared right at the man, who still
looked like he was pretending not to watch. After a moment of that the man began to look very uncomfortable, as
though what he really wanted to do was to look away, to be
anywhere else in the world at all. But it was his job to look,
and he was going to watch because he was a man who did
his job—all of that was written on his face, plain as day.
When Jan had him looking so uncomfortable that she
thought he couldn't take any more, she picked the mostly
dead fly (a couple of its legs were still twitching) off the
window frame and popped it in her mouth. She chewed

and swallowed the bug with an exaggerated flourish, and then, before her sister could stop her, she lifted the window open and hollered out at the man.

"It's kind of sweet from the Kayro syrup," she shouted. "And it's real crunchy!"

Eileen waited until her sister was done before she said anything. "That was really dumb," she said. "Didn't you hear Roberta tell us not to act suspicious? Don't try to tell me that wasn't something weird. You ever see anybody eat a fly on television?"

"Don't make no difference. You ever see anybody kill a fly with sugar? He already seen us do that. That sheriff already knows whatever he's going to know. You want to have fun or what?"

Eileen shrugged. If Jan had pressed her she would have admitted it was a good point. "Why don't we put on the television and act quiet for a while? I don't want Roberta any madder at us than she already is."

Christian Ross was thinking of murder.

Sean had seen that yesterday afternoon when he'd looked Christian in the eye. That was why he'd told him to "stay the hell out of the caves"; the Stone wanted Jimmy Tompkins alive for a long while yet. And Sean knew that if Christian got anywhere near that boy, Jimmy Tompkins would die.

It was frustrating, and Christian wasn't used to being frustrated. All his life, when he wanted something, he took it. When he wanted to do something, he did it. Or tried to, anyway. But Sean had said *don't*, and there was a reason why Sean was in charge and Christian wasn't, and Christian knew it. Sean was bigger and stronger and smarter and meaner than Christian ever would be. Christian had gotten into fights with Sean and with his brother Thomas while he was still one of the Children, and with Roberta, too. Christian had come out of each of those fights a bloody mess; there were times, remembering those fights, when Christian was amazed he was still alive.

No matter how much he wanted to, he wasn't about to go near that Jimmy Tompkins boy. And since that was what all the Children had been busy with the last couple of days, there wasn't anybody to do anything with. That was depressing—and it was another thing he owed to Jimmy Tompkins. If he didn't get an opportunity to settle up with that boy while he was still alive, Christian decided, he was going to take it out on his carcass. The idea of stretching Jimmy Tompkins's bloody innards across half a mile of woods made Christian feel warm and comfortable inside.

He had to get out of the house. Christian was going to go out of his mind if he didn't. But meanness was never much fun when you had to do it alone. And sometimes the thing you were beating on would turn on you, and that was dangerous when you were alone. Christian didn't much care for getting himself hurt—the truth was, though he wouldn't have admitted it to anyone, not even the Stone, that pain was a thing that frightened him. That left out having fun with anything bigger than a small kitten. But there were plenty of things that small around if you looked for them. Christian put on his hiking shoes and went outside.

He walked into the pine woods that began in his backyard without even really giving much thought to where he was going. Usually when he went through the woods he took the path that led mostly uphill and off to the left; this time he didn't pay any attention to the path at all. It wasn't really that necessary to follow the path, anyway. In the fields you almost *had* to follow them—the brambles and the tall grass were just about too tall to force your way through. But the pine woods here were so thick overhead that there wasn't much to talk about on the ground. Pine straw. Old branches. A few mossy rocks. Pine cones, and every now and then a little scrub or a seedling pine tree.

Christian had gone half a mile before he gave any thought to where he'd gone. When he did look up to see where he was, he found himself in a part of Green Hill he didn't recognize.

That was a strange idea: lost in Green Hill. Christian had lived here every day of his life. It was almost like somehow getting lost in the middle of the night between your bed and the toilet, in your own home. Sure, it was something you could imagine. It could happen, especially if you were still half asleep. But whether it was possible or not, the fact that it *had* happened was annoying.

Christian stooped over and picked up a handful of small

stones, planning to throw them at the trunk of a broad-trunked ancient pine. But then he saw the squirrel, and once he'd seen it he couldn't resist it.

The squirrel had paused, hiding, in the rotted stump of a tree that looked as though lightning had split it. Then it saw Christian looking at it, and its eyes lit up with beautiful fear. The squirrel panicked; it bolted across the pine straw toward the trunk of the wide old pine. Christian took a guess at its speed and which way it would go, and he threw one of his rocks. He put all of his anger, all of his rage and frustration and hate for Jimmy Tompkins into throwing the rock, and it left his hand moving faster than a pellet would have if he'd used his slingshot.

It hit the squirrel square on the head, just below the ear. The impact shattered the squirrel's skull—the skin that covered its head ripped and burst. Blood and brain and eye-flesh spattered in every direction, painting a bright red Rorschach blot on the pine straw for two feet around the squirrel.

Christian felt a thrill of satisfaction. Of relief, almost. He *needed* the sight of blood. But it wasn't enough, not by a lot. He felt his frustration like it was a hunger, or a thirst.

Bloodthirsty.

Christian had heard that word on television. He'd even read it a couple of times in comic books. He'd never really understood what it was about. When they said it they almost made it sound as horrible and exotic as leprosy. If what the word meant was just the need to see suffering, then why did they say it that way? The need to hurt others was something as ordinary as eating breakfast in the morning—even ordinary people felt it, though they didn't like to admit it.

He wondered if what bloodthirsty meant was a real, literal thirst for blood, some kind of an instinct for vampirism that everyone had, or could have, but no one really admitted. It was possible. Or it seemed possible to Christian. Ordinary people were full of things like that that they always felt but didn't admit.

The only way to find out, he decided, was to taste the blood. He didn't think it would hurt to experiment. Wild meat sometimes wasn't good for you if you ate it raw, he knew, but it wasn't usually a problem as long as it was fresh.

Christian lifted the squirrel's limp corpse off the pine straw. Blood oozed in throbs from the limp pulpy shreds of flesh that had been its head. Christian opened his mouth and held the squirrel over his head to let its blood drip onto his tongue.

It *was* satisfying, and exhilarating, and a million other wonderful things. After a few moments the squirrel's heart began to realize that it was already dead, and the flow of blood began to damp. Christian scowled and wrapped his hands around the squirrel's torso and *squeezed*, trying to force out more blood. It worked, too, but along with the sweet blood was bile and gut and sweetbread and other bitter things Christian couldn't have named if he'd had to. The *mélange* was disgusting; Christian spat it out against the rough bark of the pine.

"Goddamn squirrel isn't good for nothing," he said, and he took the squirrel by the tail and smashed it against the tree again and again until finally its pulpy carcass slid free from its skin and went skittering across the pine straw.

Christian didn't bother to retrieve it. He went deeper into the woods, looking for another squirrel—one that was still alive.

He never noticed the two sheriff's deputies   men who'd been out all day, searching this part of the woods for some sign of Jimmy Tompkins—who'd watched, amazed, as he'd killed and mutilated the squirrel. Christian never had been one to pay much mind to grown-ups.

CHAPTER
TWENTY

TIM WRAPPED THE ROPE TWICE AROUND EACH OF JIM-
my's wrists, and tied the loose end to the longer part of the
cord. When he was done he dragged Jimmy to the part of
the wall where Sean had pointed, looped the rope around
the protruding rock as though it were a pulley, and hoisted
Jimmy off his feet.

Hung him from his wrists.

Jimmy pictured himself as a side of beef, hanging in a
meat locker somewhere. That image made him feel as cold
and dead inside as though he *were* a side of beef.

But that was what they wanted. Jimmy knew that, if only
because they'd said it. They wanted him to suffer. Sean

hadn't said it, but all the same Jimmy knew that they wanted to kill his heart, to break his spirit so thoroughly that when they killed him he'd be dying for a second time.

Not that they were ready to kill him yet. Soon, maybe, but not right now. And he knew that if he hung there feeling like the end of the world it would really be the end of him—he'd kill himself in a way that none of the Children or even the Stone itself could ever hope to.

So Jimmy did the only thing he could: he gritted his teeth and tried not to let it hurt him.

That was easy enough until he saw the knife. He recognized it as soon as he saw it; it was the blade Roberta had almost used to cut Rex open. Jimmy had used it himself when he'd cut the ropes that bound the dog to the altar.

"Are you going to scream when I cut you, Jimmy Tompkins?" Sean asked. "Screams are kind of neat if you pay attention to them. You know that every animal I ever cut open had its own special scream? Dogs always scream in short little bleats, almost like they was sheep. Cats scream long and shrill, so high-pitched that almost you can't hear them sometimes. But not very loud. A cat could scream the last scream of its life, and you might not even hear it six houses away. You know that a squirrel will scream when you cut into it? That surprised me, I'll tell you. Never heard a squirrel make a sound from its throat till I killed one. Screams even quieter than a cat does. And screams are different even from one dog to the next, from one cat to another. I bet you never cut anything open in your life—not while it was still alive. You don't know what you're missing, not hearing those screams." He tugged at the denim cuff of Jimmy's jeans. "I never heard a boy scream from being cut open before, Jimmy Tompkins. You going to put on a good show for me? You can scream as loud as you want. The Stone will make sure that none of the sheriff people outside can hear you."

Jimmy blinked; he wasn't sure whether or not he was supposed to answer any of those questions. The thing to do, he thought, was to ignore them. They were meant to frighten him. To break him. But he knew that if he did ignore them, it would only make Sean angrier. And God only knew what that boy would do if he got angry enough to lose what little self-control he had.

"Jimmy *Tom*pkins. Didn't I *tell* you to answer when I talk to you—not just hang there thinking about it?" He brought the heel of his palm up into Jimmy's groin. The pain made Jimmy curl up like a baby, even though he was hanging from his wrists. "What you got in that head of yours instead of brains? Sawdust? I'm going to have to crack that skull of yours open when we're done with you, so I can take a look. I never seen sawdust making believe it was brains before. Pretty neat trick. If I can get a chance to see how they did it when they made you, maybe I can make a few more like you. Might be handy to have around . . . long as I can get 'em to do like I say."

Jimmy heard himself make a sound half-way between a groan and a whimper. He couldn't really hear Sean anymore; all he could think about was the throbbing pain between his legs. He was losing himself, he knew. Hard as he tried to be calm and still inside, he was slipping away. The pain and the abuse were sinking through and turning his heart toward fear. *It doesn't matter,* he told himself. *Doesn't, doesn't, doesn't.* But they were only words inside his head; they had no effect at all.

Sean chuckled. "You know, you're all right, Jimmy Tompkins. You ain't bad at all for a piece of meat."

One throb at a time, the pain eased. Jimmy uncurled himself, forced his legs and stomach to relax.

"That's a good boy, Jimmy Tompkins. You did that before I even had to tell you to. You keep it up like that and this'll be a lot easier for both of us."

He took the right cuff of Jimmy's jeans and pulled on it, hard. For a moment Jimmy thought he was trying to pull his pants off. But then Sean lifted the knife up and started cutting away the denim, pulling the knife straight down. Twice as he was cutting Jimmy felt the blade's razor-sharp edge whisper into his flesh, cut him with a sensation that almost wasn't a sensation at all—barely even a tickle. The denim cut as easily as Jimmy's skin; even as tough as the cloth was, the knife still never caught or tugged or hesitated. Not until Sean got down to the triple-thick hem of the cuff, and even there the blade only paused for the time it takes to blink.

"Shit," Sean said. "I can't use this leg. Forgot all about this. Here, Tim, take a look." He stepped away, and Tim came closer. Jimmy looked down, too, though he was more than a little afraid to see.

THE CHILDREN

With everything that had happened since, Jimmy had almost forgotten the words that he'd found carved into his leg yesterday morning. The inside of the leg of his jeans was stiff and soaked through with dried blood. The letters were hard to read, now; his blood had run together as it scabbed, made them indistinct.

"You see that when I did it, Tim?"

"Huh-uh. I didn't. What's it say?"

Sean raised the knife and pulled its edge carefully back and forth over the leg, scraping away the scab. At first it didn't hurt too much, as the looser parts flaked away. But when they were gone the words were still blurred and indistinct, so Sean started scraping harder, pulling away the parts of the scab that were rooted in the cuts. The scraping hurt, but the pain was a pretty small thing beside the aching in his head and groin.

By the time Sean was done, Jimmy's leg was bleeding freely again, and the fresh blood made it hard to see. Sean took the blade and pulled the edge down along Jimmy's calf like a squeegee.

THE CHILDREN

Blood started welling up from the words again right away, but for a moment they were clear and crisp.

"Not bad, huh, Tim?" Sean asked.

Tim whistled. "You did that without waking him up? How'd you do it?"

"Keep the knife sharp. Sharp enough you can't hardly feel it when it cuts you. You want to see?" His tone was eager, as though he were showing off instead of threatening. But he moved the blade over toward Tim's palm, and almost began to cut him.

Tim jerked his hand away. "That's okay," he said, "I believe you."

Sean shrugged. "Suit yourself." He took a tissue and a ceramic bar out of his left pocket; cleaned the blood from the blade, freshened the edge. "Bitch of it is that now we can't use that leg for what I had planned. Make the skin tear—make a godawful mess."

He grabbed the bottom of Jimmy's left cuff, and pulled the knife down through the pants leg fast and hard. He wasn't careful at all; Jimmy felt the point of the knife part open a slit that stretched from his knee to the top of his foot. Twice as Sean cut Jimmy felt the knife dig deeply into him and snag for an instant on the bone of his shin.

When Sean finished cutting through the cuff he said, "Let's get all this stuff out of the way, so we can get some real work done." He gathered up the loose denim and cut away the leg of Jimmy's pants just above his knee. "That's better, ain't it, Tim? Get a good look at what we're doing, now."

Tim grunted.

Sean looked up at Jimmy. "You ready for a little pain, Jimmy Tompkins?"

Jimmy shook his head. Inside his chest his heart was pounding wildly, pressing blood too hard and fast through his veins.

"That's too bad. You going to hurt more than just a little."

Jimmy nodded. Maybe that was so—there certainly wasn't any way for Jimmy to get loose. But Sean didn't seem to realize that Jimmy's legs were free. The truth was, of course, that it had not occurred to Jimmy until that very moment that it made any difference. All the same, Jimmy didn't see any reason to remind him. If he was going to make any use of the fact, he had to bide his time, wait for a chance to hurt Sean as badly as Sean was hurting him. The building fear inside him turned to anger: *You just put your face a little closer to my leg while you've got that knife in me, crazy fucker,* Jimmy thought, *and you'll get to see what a little pain is like, too.*

Sean fingered the cut that ran down Jimmy's leg. "What you know about that, Tim? Looks like I already got my work started for me." He lifted the blade up to Jimmy's shin, just under the soft part of his knee, and pressed it into the cut that was already there. He pulled the knife down, parting Jimmy's skin open. It was just like Sean had said to Tim—the blade was still sharp enough, even after cutting up both legs of Jimmy's jeans, that the sensation of being cut felt as soft and gentle as a kiss. Sean stopped cutting half-way down Jimmy's shin. "God damn it," he said. "Will you look at this?" He didn't wait for Tim to answer. "Looks like I cut right down into his shinbone while I was cutting away his pants."

Sean turned the knife in his hand and used the back edge to hold the cut open. He stooped over and bent close to get a good look at it. "This could make it tricky skinning him," Sean said. "Don't want the meat pulling off the bone when we peel away the skin."

Now, Jimmy thought.

He kicked his knee up into Sean's face; his bloody shin forced the razor edge of the knife straight at Sean's eye. Jimmy followed the kick through, bringing his knee up as far and as hard as it would go. His knee smashed into Sean's nose, jammed the knife flat into the bone of the older boy's cheek and forehead. When his knee was as far up as it would go Jimmy kicked with his foot; he caught Sean square in the chest with the ball of his foot. Sean went flying backward, and fell onto the Stone. The knife clattered across the floor of the cave.

Sean covered his eye with his hand and cursed half a dozen times. There was blood all over him, some of it from the cuts on his eyebrow and cheek, some of it from Jimmy's leg.

"You fucking asshole," he said. "I'm going to kill you now, Jimmy Tompkins."

And Jimmy thought: Good. Kill me now, and I'll only die once, at least.

He started toward Jimmy's throat with his hands stretched out like he was going to strangle him. He was going to do it, Jimmy thought. He was really going to kill him. Then suddenly the Stone was glowing bright as the sun, and Tim was putting himself between Sean and Jimmy.

"Sean," Tim said, "the Stone. If you do. . . ." His voice sounded frightened, as though he almost expected Sean to try to kill him instead. "Look at it before you kill him, okay? I don't want it mad at me, too."

Sean grabbed Tim's shirt and threw him into Jimmy. But he did stop—stopped in his tracks and turned around.

He stood there staring at the Stone and mumbling for three minutes that seemed to Jimmy to last most of an hour. And as he talked to it, Jimmy's fear began to come back to him. Tim glared up at Jimmy and shook his head. He looked mad enough, Jimmy thought, to kill Jimmy himself.

Which meant that he thought Jimmy had done something pretty damn stupid. Maybe it was so. But Jimmy didn't see how it could make things worse; either way Sean was going to do horrible things to him with that knife, and either way he was going to leave him alive and hurting when he was done. The worst thing that could happen was that Sean would go a little too far, and kill him. And that was the one thing that didn't scare Jimmy anymore.

Sean stopped mumbling, cleared his throat, and spat angrily on the floor of the cave. He walked past the Stone, to where the knife had fallen, and picked it up. The blade was covered with dirt and blood. Sean took off his shirt and wiped the blade with it, then used the shirt's clean side to wipe most of the blood off his face. It helped some, but not much; the cuts on his forehead and his cheek both gaped wide open. Both of them bled like tiny rivers. There was a hairline cut along Sean's eyelid, too, a cut so thin and slight that Jimmy would have thought it was a scratch if he hadn't known it had come from the knife.

"Hold his legs down, Tim," Sean said. "If he kicks me again I'm going to cut *you* open, too."

Tim nodded. He grabbed Jimmy's legs at the ankles, crouched, and pulled down on them with all his weight. Jimmy felt the rope holding his wrists tighten and stretch, cutting off the little bit of blood that had still been circulating to his hands. He closed his eyes and tried not to think about what was happening, or about what was going to happen. It wasn't much use.

"I can't kill you yet, Jimmy Tompkins. But I'm going to hurt you. I'm going to hurt you something special."

Jimmy didn't answer. He couldn't have answered, not without giving any more of himself away to fear. He felt the tip of the knife probe into his shin, just where it had been when he'd kicked Sean. He felt it press and draw, felt the whisper of its edge as it cut down along his shin. Then it stopped and pulled away for an instant. A moment later

Sean cut a horizontal semicircle around the front of Jimmy's leg, just below his knee. Then another horizontal cut, a couple down.

As Jimmy saw with his mind's eye the crosshatch pattern Sean had cut in him, he began to realize exactly what Sean had in mind for him. *No!* he thought, *No!* But he wasn't certain whether the words were meant for Sean or for himself.

Because he was losing himself. He was afraid and more than afraid, terrified, and his heart was beginning to crumble under the weight of his fear.

"That was the gentle part, Jimmy Tompkins. Now comes the part where I get to have fun."

Jimmy felt Sean's fingers gouging into the open cut, felt his fingernails digging under his skin. And then he stopped, still grasping his skin between thumb and fingers like a strip of animal hide. Jimmy felt those fingers like they were the center of the world, dug under his skin and just . . . *waiting* there.

Jimmy's stomach was tying itself over and over in knots. Hard as he tried not to feel what Sean was doing, tried to detach himself from what was going on, he couldn't; the sensation of Sean's fingers inside his skin was too intimate to ignore.

"You *ready*, Jimmy Tompkins? I don't think you've ever felt like what you're about to feel right now." Sean let out a long, contented sigh. "You hold his leg real tight, Tim. This is going to make Jimmy Tompkins move something fierce."

Then Sean tightened his grip on the strip of skin, and he *pulled*, and Jimmy felt the strip of skin tearing away from the muscle of his leg. And he heard the sound of it tearing, like the sound of ripping Velcro, but wetter and more intimate, and his eyes bugged open and he looked down and *saw*. . . . And Jimmy lost himself. Lost himself completely and absolutely in the inner night of his pain and his fear.

He woke a long moment later, when Sean threw a bucket of water at his face.

"Jimmy *Tom*pkins," Sean said. "You really think you can get away from me by going to sleep? Hard to believe that even you can be *that* stupid." Sean took the knife where it lay, near the Stone. "Get his legs again, Tim."

Jimmy squeezed his eyes shut as he felt Tim bear-hug his legs. The pain in his legs was beyond anything he'd ever felt or imagined, and it scared him and it hurt him—but there was something else, too. Something that he'd known all along but somehow forgot.

He tried to reach for it, but before he could find it Sean's fingers were in him again, tearing.

Water again, washing over the lids of Jimmy's eyes.

"You got to *learn*, Jimmy Tompkins. You think I'm not going to notice when you fall asleep right in the middle of me playing with you? If you do, you're wrong. You ain't going to get to sleep through this."

Tim's voice, clear and distinct even though everything was a blur to Jimmy's eyes: "Sean. . . ? You remember what you said before, about too much pain being enough to kill him?"

"Yeah—what about it?"

"Look up at him, hanging there. He don't look so good. He don't look good at all."

It was quiet for a long time before Sean answered.

"Maybe you're right. He is looking pretty bad. Stone wouldn't be happy if we killed him . . . besides, what use is it to hurt him if he's going to keep falling asleep like that?"

Jimmy felt himself fade away again. And as he faded he saw the thing he'd tried to reach for before—and it was his mother, holding him close in her warm soft arms years ago when he was very small. And he loved her and she scared him and he hated her all at the same time.

But most of all, as the shrill blanket of pain enveloped him more thoroughly than her arms ever could, most of all he loved her.

When Jimmy woke again he was deep in shock, and what he could see outside himself he watched through the pain that his body had begun to hide from him again . . . it was like a curtain, now, grey-red and shimmering. The physical damage to his body—even counting everything that had been done before—wasn't so great that he couldn't survive it. But the pain was another matter altogether; there was so much pain that his body was hiding it from him. Intuitively, he knew that no matter how he felt about it—no matter whether he let it break him or not—that much pain was a real danger to his body. And the infection in his head was bad enough that in another few days it would be enough to kill him—if he lived that long.

But now, at least, he was alive. No matter how he hurt he was alive. *No matter.* He was alive and he was himself and no matter what anybody did to him they couldn't take his heart and they couldn't take his mind unless they killed him, and they could only kill him once. And knowing that they couldn't gave him the strength to press the pain away, to damp it.

It gave him strength enough to live, even if his body wanted nothing more than to curl up and die.

He lay on the ground with his hands still trussed above his head. He couldn't feel his leg at all. He couldn't feel anything at all below his waist. Sean and Tim were kneeling above him, talking. Tim looked sick with himself and half out of his mind from fear. Sean looked angry and almost . . . *satisfied.*

Sean pulled a roll of wide brown-plastic packing tape out of his pocket and handed it to Tim.

"You tape him up, Tim, so he don't bleed to death before the Stone is ready for us to kill him. I got to go to the cave with the creek running through it and get this blood washed off of me."

Tim nodded; he still looked anxious and afraid, but Sean didn't seem to see that at all. "What about cleaning his leg, here? Aren't you supposed to clean a wound before you bandage it up? 'Cause of infections and stuff like that?"

"Shit," Sean said. He cleared his throat and spat a half-dollar-size clam into the exposed meat of Jimmy's leg. "I don't give a good goddamn if he gets infected. Sure as shit won't kill him before we're ready to." He left through the passage without waiting for Tim to respond.

When Sean was gone Tim shook his head. "Christ All Mighty, Jimmy Tompkins. I'm sorry. God I'm sorry. But if I'd tried to stop them they would have killed me and you too. No matter why they thought I was helping you, they would have killed me. I've never seen the Stone this hungry—and the only thing it's hungry for is you. You shouldn't even have gone and pushed it off that ledge. It ain't used to being on the receiving end of pain." He took off his shirt and used it to do what he could to clean Jimmy's leg. "Even if we managed to get away from him now, sooner or later he would have caught up with me. My dad ain't moving anywhere. I'm probably going to be here the rest of my life. If they want to find me, they're going to find me."

Jimmy grunted; he didn't have it in him for any more of an answer. He managed to lift his head enough to see how badly Sean had mangled his leg. In places the thin muscle that covered his shin had pulled loose, and the bone was visible. Tim was carefully pushing the strips of skin back into place, now, and taping them together.

Jimmy let himself relax, let his head fall back onto the rock and packed-dirt floor of the cave. If he kept looking he was going to feel nauseated, no matter how weak he was. The last thing Jimmy needed was to feel even worse than he already did.

After a while Jimmy heard Tim pulling loose a long strip of tape, and a moment later he felt the tape rolling around and around his leg, wrapping the wound closed.

"You done there yet, Tim?" Sean's voice, here in the cave. Jimmy hadn't even heard him come in.

"Just about. Give me a second." Jimmy heard him cut the tape away from the roll, felt him press the tape end against the skin on top of his foot. "There."

"Good." Sean walked across the cave, and stood looking over Jimmy. His face was even more of a mess now; the skin on one side of it was scraped bloody on his eyebrow and his cheek.

Tim must have seen it about the same time Jimmy did. "What'd you do to your face?" he asked. "You fall or something?"

Sean smiled. "Nuh-uh. Scraped it back and forth on the sand a few times while I was down at the creek, so it would look like I did. Can't go walking around with a knife cut on my face with all these sheriff people all over the place." He spat on the floor of the cave. "And you can't walk around all bloody, either. Go get yourself cleaned up in the creek. I'll carry Jimmy Tompkins here back to his cage."

Jimmy heard Tim take his shirt off the ground and leave. Sean bent over and lifted Jimmy over his shoulder. Getting lifted was painful in the parts of Jimmy that could still hurt; Sean's shoulder jammed into one of the bruises in his ribs, and the motion was so fast that the swelling in his head made the whole world spin around him.

"How you like that for hurting, Jimmy Tompkins?" Sean asked. "Pretty good, huh? We'll see what we can do for you tomorrow. Maybe get part of that other leg, or start in on one of your thighs." He chuckled. "I'm sure we can think of something good for you. Don't you worry about that for a minute."

They were in the cave with the cage now, and there was hardly any light at all. Jimmy heard Sean open the cage with his free hand, and then his body started shifting as Sean threw him in.

Jimmy's head and back slammed against the bars opposite the door. Mostly that made a whole new lump on the top of his skull, but the impact opened up the skin on the swollen part of Jimmy's head, and blood started leaking all down the back of his neck.

Sean must have seen that, because he started laughing as he tied the cage closed. He was still laughing when he left.

When he was gone Jimmy almost started laughing himself, for different reasons. He wasn't happy about his bleeding head, or being prisoner in a cave, or the pain in his leg that his body wouldn't let him feel.

No.

He had a real reason to be happy, besides the strength he found deep inside himself. He'd felt something when his back and head smashed into the back of the cage—felt something happen to the bars.

He'd felt the bars tear loose of their moorings in the floor of the cave. If they were that loose, they could be worked until they came free. And Jimmy could get out of the cage.

Out of the cave.

Out of this town.

The last thing he thought of before he passed out was his warm, clean bed, back in the house they had run from in New Jersey.

CHAPTER

TWENTY-ONE

Ben said more than he'd meant to when he called the sheriff's department. He was exhausted, and maybe a little bit feverish. He should have stopped and thought before he'd called, but it didn't even occur to him. He sat in one of the kitchen chairs and dialed the number Peterson had left for him. He told the man exactly what he was thinking—told him about chasing the boy through half-lit woods and fields, told him about the four boys who'd attacked Jimmy and the dog, told him about coming back to the house and finding Rex mutilated. Told the deputy other things, too. When he was done he wound it

all together into a conspiracy that sounded ridiculous even
to his own ears, even then.

Peterson listened patiently to all of it. Less patiently
toward the end. But he was never rude, even if he did
think Ben was a crank. Or maybe he just thought Ben was a
father, half out of his mind with fear and guilt and stress.
When Ben was done the deputy told Ben to get some
sleep, and that he'd be back in touch in the late afternoon
or early evening.

The man's patience and politeness just made it worse for
Ben. When he got off the phone he wanted to start screaming again: he felt stupid and crazy and *useless*.

Even worse than that was the nagging, lurking guilt.
Every sensible bone in Ben's body knew that he had done
his best—and that he was still doing it. But he was Jimmy's
father; if something was wrong, the guilt said, then Ben
was to blame.

Just as he was to blame for not leaving Anne the first
time he'd seen her lay hands on his son. . . . Just as he was
to blame for loving his wife too much to leave her.

His son was missing, kidnapped most likely, and the only
thing Ben could do to help find him was wallow in guilt and
imagine conspiracies that belonged in comic books.

He was going to get up in a moment, he decided, and do
something practical. Something sensible. Something that
would make a difference. He was going to calm down and
calmly and rationally figure out what he ought to be doing.
He wasn't going to be frantic anymore.

He took a deep breath and closed his eyes, waiting for his
heart to slow down enough to let him think. Waiting for his
blood to cool. You had to *be* calm to think calmly. Ben
knew that; it was obvious.

Ben fell asleep that way, sitting upright at the kitchen
table. Around one in the afternoon he shifted in his sleep
and fell headfirst onto the carpeted floor. That didn't wake
him, though his head had a knot from the fall when he
woke. The smell of Jimmy's blood on the floor filled Ben's
dreams with nightmares.

He woke around four in the afternoon, when Mike Peterson called, just as he'd promised. He was dreaming
deeply when the phone rang—dreaming of the smell of
blood—and at first the sound of the phone bell blended

into his dream. And it kept blending; when he finally woke
enough to reach up, take the phone from its cradle, and
answer it, that seemed to be part of the dream, too. Or
maybe it was that the dream didn't seem to be a dream at
all, but rather something more real than awakeness.

When Peterson heard Ben answer he said something
about Jimmy, or looking for Jimmy, or whoever had taken
Jimmy. Whatever he said, it disappeared into the dream
completely—and without a trace. Ben thanked the man
and said good-bye and fell back to sleep with the phone
still in his hand. Much later, when he really woke, Ben had
trouble remembering the phone call. He might not have
remembered it at all if the first thing he'd seen hadn't been
the uncradled receiver buzzing a loud on-and-off buzz on
the floor not far from his head.

Seeing the phone on the floor forced him to try to remember the phone call. After a few moments he did,
dimly, at least. But he never did remember exactly what
Peterson had said. If the man had said anything important,
he thought—he tried to be sure—it would have woke him
up, no matter how deeply he'd been dreaming.

Ben sat up. With one hand he kneaded his forehead and
rubbed the sleep from his eyes; with the other he reached
for the phone and set it back into its cradle. When he'd
done that he turned his wrist and looked at his watch. It
was after midnight again. Almost one in the morning. He'd
slept away an entire day, a day he didn't have to spare. A
day *Jimmy* didn't have to spare.

He stood up, stumbled toward the kitchen counter,
groped until he found the kettle, and put on water for
instant coffee. What in the name of God was he going to
do? If he just sat here, waiting for the sheriff's department
to find his son, he was going to go out of his mind. And what
if they never found him? Ben shivered at the thought. It
was possible that they never would. The sick tension in his
gut told him that it was even likely. He had to do something. If he didn't he wouldn't be able to live with himself
—even if the sheriff's people *did* find his son.

But again: what?

It was a mean question. None of the obvious answers
made any sense at all. None of the answers in his gut were
even practical. Ben *knew* that the children around here—

some of them, at least—had something to do with the fact that his son was missing. But which ones? Even if it was all of them, you couldn't just find a kid at random playing in his yard, grab him by his ear, and shake him until he talked. You couldn't *do* that to a kid, no matter how bad he was. Not unless you wanted to go to jail yourself. And what if he was wrong? Bad enough manhandling a child who'd kidnapped your son, or one who knew something about that kidnapping. But Ben wouldn't be able to live with himself if he knew he'd laid hands on an innocent child, not any more than he'd be able to live with himself if he didn't do anything at all.

He could bluff, though. He could tell them he knew exactly what they'd done, and that they knew, if they just thought about it for a moment, what he'd do if Jimmy didn't turn up. If he said that to a kid who didn't have anything to do with Jimmy's disappearance, he'd sound like a lunatic. But so what? Ben could live with sounding like a lunatic. The sheriff's department might lock him up if they heard he was wandering around the town saying things like that to kids, but they probably couldn't keep him locked up for it. It was the sort of half-baked thing you'd almost *expect* a distraught father to say; the worst that would happen was that he'd have to tell a judge that he was sorry and that he realized he was wrong. And it was *something*, anyway—if Ben was right it might help. It might help a lot.

The kettle began whistling hoarsely. Ben turned off the electric burner. He took a large cup and a spoon from the dish rack and opened the jar of "freeze-dried coffee crystals" that was already on the counter. He put one more spoon of the instant coffee than he should have into the cup; when he poured the water, stirred, and tasted what he'd made, the flavor was too sour and too bitter. Strong and unpleasant. But strong enough to wake him up, and that was good.

There was a bad side to bluffing, too, when Ben thought about it. If he was right, and for some reason too bizarre to think about the children here in Green Hill were the ones who'd kidnapped Jimmy, then making them think he knew what they'd done, and why they'd done it, might panic them. And that might mean a lot of trouble for Jimmy, wherever he was.

It could be very bad indeed.

But if they'd kidnapped Jimmy they hadn't done it for money, or Ben would have heard about it by now. And that probably meant that they weren't planning to turn Jimmy loose at all, and that they ultimately planned to kill him. It might even mean that they'd killed him already.

No. They hadn't killed his son. Not yet. They couldn't have killed him; Ben would know if they had. He'd just *know*. Ben was sure of that.

He also knew that no matter how dangerous it was to panic the ones who'd kidnapped his son, he had to do it—it was far more dangerous to do nothing at all. In the morning, he decided, he'd find one of the kids who lived in this town, and tell him that he knew what had been done. Then he'd find another and say the same thing. And another, and another, until Ben was certain that the message would get to the ears that needed to hear it.

He spent the rest of the night packing away the parts of the house that had been unpacked. He was going to get Jimmy away from whatever sort of trouble had found him. And once Jimmy was free the two of them were going to get out of Green Hill so fast that heads would spin watching them drive away.

CHAPTER

TWENTY-TWO

WHEN THE VETERINARIAN, ROBIN SMITH, CALLED PE-terson a little after nine-thirty that morning, he was already out at Green Hill, talking to Myron White. There was no way to patch the call through to the cruiser's radio, but he got the message to call her only a minute or two after she'd left it, and it only took him a moment or two after that to find a phone. The phone he found was the phone in the Tompkins house—the one that idiot from the phone company had insisted on servicing the day Jimmy Tompkins had disappeared, while every deputy in the county had business inside the Tompkins house. Peterson and White had been talking in Peterson's cruiser, and the cruiser had been parked in the Tompkins driveway.

Ben Tompkins was still packing. Peterson had thought that was a little suspicious when he'd first seen it—earlier this morning—and he'd asked Tompkins about it. Tompkins had explained how he was planning to get out of Green Hill, as far and as fast as he could, the moment he had his son back. Ordinarily that explanation wouldn't have done much to ease Peterson's suspicion—he had a very suspecting nature, at least partly because it was his job to have one.

But there'd been a *look* in Ben Tompkins's eye as he explained, a look that somehow mixed together terror, concern, and good sense. Seeing a grown man looking like that had gotten right down into a little wormhole in Peterson's gut, and it had stayed there. Peterson found it hard to be suspicious with something like that nestling in his insides.

Tompkins barely seemed to hear him when he asked to use the phone. The grunt he made seemed to Peterson to sound more like yes than it did like no, though, so he went ahead and called the veterinarian.

She didn't answer until the fifth ring. Peterson was just about to hang up, check the number, and redial when he heard her lift the receiver on her end of the line.

"Robin Smith," she said. "Can I help you?"

"This is Mike Peterson, from the sheriff's department," he said, "returning your call."

"Mike—good. Glad you could get back to me so quickly. I wanted to talk to you about Ben and Jimmy Tompkins's dog, Rex—you asked me to get back to you when the dog was well enough to walk." She paused a moment, drew in a breath. "I wouldn't say he's recovered yet. But he's certainly awake enough. The poor dog came to sometime during the night, and he's been trying to dig his way through the metal floor of his cage—well, for hours, at least. If he keeps at it much longer he's going to rub the skin of his front feet bloody. He's already worn his claws flat. Which is quite a task when you consider that the sheet-metal floor of the cage is too smooth to cause much wear to a dog's claws."

Peterson thought about that for a while—thought about

what he'd seen in the dog's face when Rex woke for a moment while Peterson was in the kennel. Maybe, Peterson thought, there *was* something to the crazy hunch he'd had. Maybe the dog *did* know something about Jimmy Tompkins's disappearance. Maybe what was burning in the dog's eyes was the need to do something about what he knew.

The idea was goofy enough that Peterson didn't feel too comfortable even thinking it. He didn't think he'd ever be ready to say it out loud. He needed to try it, anyway—even if it meant that the rest of the department would think he was out of his mind. *If I'm lucky,* he thought, *no one else will see me do it.*

"Huh," Peterson said. "He's up to a walk? You're sure?" He waited a breath or two for the veterinarian to respond, to reassure him that he wouldn't be dragging around some poor mangled animal and causing it even more harm. She didn't say anything. "I can be there in an hour or so. That won't be too soon?"

She hesitated a long while again before she answered. "No," she said finally. "This dog is going to do himself more harm trying to get out of the kennel than going for a walk would cause him. Even if it ends up being a long walk. Maybe he's just feeling a burning need to get back home. But I don't think so. I've seen dogs pining away for their homes before. They don't act like this. This is something else altogether."

"What do you think it is?" Peterson almost didn't ask that question; there was a part of him that didn't want to hear the answer. The momentum of the conversation made it almost impossible *not* to ask, though. Besides, it was his job to ask, and Peterson wasn't a man who could be comfortable with himself when he ignored his obligations.

The veterinarian sighed, not quite angrily. "What do *you* think? Why are you taking this dog 'for a walk'? The dog saw whatever happened to Jimmy Tompkins, that's what *I* think. The dog saw something and it needs to do something about it. Just for God's sake don't get him near whoever it was who took a hammer to him the first time. I don't honestly think my heart could take having to patch this dog together another time."

Peterson winced. "I'll do my very best, ma'am." How

could he be sure of that? He didn't *know* who'd maimed
the dog. If he'd known he wouldn't have been running off
on a half-baked goose chase like this one. But he wasn't
going to let the dog out of his sight, either. With a little luck
that would be plenty safe enough. Even without much
luck; the sort of people who'd maim a small dog or kidnap a
little boy didn't seem to Peterson to be the sort of people
who'd have the courage to threaten a grown man.

"An hour then?" the veterinarian asked. "I'll be here."

"Yes, ma'am. I'll see you then."

Robin Smith didn't say good-bye before she hung up the
phone.

On his way out the door Peterson told Ben Tompkins
he'd be back in a couple of hours, but the man only barely
seemed to notice that he'd spoken. Peterson sighed and
shook his head. That man was going off the deep end.
Peterson was going to have to have someone keep an eye
on him, too—not so much because Tompkins was a danger
to anyone else as because he was a danger to himself. A
man half out of his mind with grief, Peterson thought,
would make as inviting a victim as a little boy. Or a small
dog. Nearly as inviting, at least.

Myron White was still waiting for him in the cruiser.
There was a certain relief for Peterson in seeing White
again. White, at least, still knew how to hold a conversation
—unlike Tompkins, who was definitely beginning to come
unhinged, or the veterinarian, who was ornery even when
things were going well.

"I got to chase down a wild goose, Myron," Peterson
said. "I better let you get back to business."

White shrugged. "You sure? There were a couple other
things I wanted to let you know about. Nothing all that
urgent, but—well, things you ought to know."

"Huh—tell you what. I'll get back with you about four
o'clock, buy you a cup of coffee. You can finish filling me in
then, okay?"

"Sure." White opened the door on his side of the car.

"Nothing I'm likely to step in in the next couple of hours,
is there?"

"Nah." He climbed out, closed the door, and spoke
through the open window. "You got the worst of it already."

What White had told him already this morning was pretty bad, too—even worse than what Peterson had expected.

He started up the cruiser and backed out of the driveway. Two minutes later he was on the road to Tylerville.

The kids in Green Hill were as bad as Peterson had always heard. Every bit as bad.

No—that wasn't true. They weren't that bad. They were worse.

Much worse.

White hadn't just told a couple of deputies to keep an eye on the Williams twins. He'd gone a little farther and put the word out to most of the deputies searching Green Hill, told them to let him know if they saw children acting strangely.

All of the children in Green Hill were strange. Every child anyone had bothered to watch for more than a couple of minutes turned out to be . . . *sick*. Sick was the only word for it.

The Williams twins had stood in their living room window, torturing flies that buzzed against the glass—and eating them.

The twins had seen White and the other deputy watching them, and they'd made a big to-do of sneaking away to tell Roberta Anderson that they were being watched. She screamed at them, and roughed them up a little, White thought. But after that she'd acted at least fairly unremarkably, or so it had seemed. She spent the rest of the morning at home, watching television as far as White could tell. In the early afternoon she'd gone to Tylerville with her mother. Mrs. Anderson had dropped Roberta off at the library and gone on across the street to do her grocery shopping.

Roberta hadn't done anything especially unusual in the library. After a while White had gone in and begun quietly chatting with the librarian, more to help pass the time than because there was any need to—Roberta had taken a seat and started reading in the plush couch by the big front window of the library, and White could have watched her from his car without any trouble.

Eventually, White's conversation with the librarian had drifted toward the subject of Green Hill, and segued from there to Roberta. That was when, half-amused and half-appalled, the librarian had told White what Roberta Anderson was reading.

The girl had taken two books off the library's shelves, and White could see her leafing through them with great delight. Once he knew what to look for, he could even read the titles on their jackets:

Gray's Anatomy.

The Rise and Fall of the Third Reich.

Peculiar reading, to say the least, for a nine-year-old.

Peterson didn't even want to *begin* to think about what kind of nine-year-old could find *Gray's Anatomy* that fascinating. Or why. But then he'd always been on the squeamish side himself. When he was ten his uncle had bought him a plastic model kit called the Visible Man—the outer shell, shaped like a man, was clear plastic, and there were little plastic organs you were supposed to paint the right color and put in the right place inside him. Peterson had only barely had the stomach to open the box. He'd never had the stomach to put the model together.

About that same time of day a couple of deputies—men that the next county over had lent to the department—had noticed a boy stomping through the woods where they were searching for Jimmy Tompkins. White had thought, from the deputies' description, that the boy was Christian Ross. Whether it was Christian Ross or not, he'd looked mad enough to kill. The deputies had just stood quietly in their tracks, not trying to hide, but not making themselves obvious.

The boy hadn't noticed them. He'd walked right past the deputies, passing within yards of them, so caught up in whatever rage he was full of that he didn't see them at all. The boy stopped a few yards after he'd passed them, sighted a squirrel, and picked up a handful of stones. He threw one of the rocks at the squirrel, so hard that the rock had taken the squirrel's head off. That was bad enough, but it wasn't the worst of the story—not by a lot. The boy had stood staring at the tiny grey corpse for a moment or two . . . and then he picked it up and drank the animal's blood from its headless neck.

Peterson had felt sick to his stomach as he'd listened to

White telling him that story. There was one other, and that one, thank God, wasn't anywhere near as grisly.

White had come back to Green Hill in the early evening, and left another deputy watching Roberta Anderson. The girl had seen White watching her more than once, and he'd decided it was time to be a little less obvious. He'd taken a walk, to try to clear his head before he checked around to see if any other deputies had noticed anything peculiar.

White had wandered generally downhill, through a couple of blackberry fields and another field overgrown with tall grass. He hadn't put a whole lot of attention into where he was going; he didn't want to get *to* anyplace so much as he wanted to get far enough away from Roberta Anderson to not have to think about her anymore.

White hadn't been quite sure where he was when he saw the two boys—Sean Brady and Tim Hanson. The Brady boy had a nasty scrape that covered the left half of his face. That, naturally enough, had caught White's attention.

"Hey, there," White had called as soon as he was in earshot. "You boys. I want to talk to you a minute."

The boys both had an air of forced casualness about them. To White's eye they'd looked guilty as sin. But they'd done as he'd said. How could they not come when he called? It was broad daylight. White had seen them, and he knew who they were. He knew where to find them.

White had waited for them where he stood, in the middle of a small briar patch in a field that was otherwise nothing but tall grass.

"You there—Sean Brady," he'd said when the boys got to the briar. "What's the matter with your eye?" Now that the boys were close enough to get a better look at, White could see that their clothes and hair were damp, as though they'd gone swimming fully dressed a few hours back. "And how come the both of you are half-wet like that, like you're still drying off from a rainstorm the rest of us never saw any sign of?"

Sean Brady was the one who'd answered. "We were hunting for tadpoles down by the creek," he'd said. "I scratched my eye when I fell in. Tripped over a rock I didn't see—went headfirst into the water and busted up my face on the sand."

White didn't believe the boy, not for a minute. But what could he do? It wasn't a story he could disprove, or even dispute. It would have taken a long-bladed knife to make a cut like that one above and below Sean Brady's eye. Neither of the boys had anything in his pockets big enough to be a knife like that. White didn't make them empty their pockets out, but he was sure he would have seen the bulge of a knife that big in the pocket of a small boy. Peterson was inclined to agree with him.

White had to let the boys go on about their business, but he'd spent a good half hour afterward poking around the spot where he'd first seen them. He hadn't found anything all that unusual.

Peterson stopped by the five-and-dime on his way to the veterinarian's. Inside, he bought a leash and a dog collar. He'd lived with and around dogs long enough to know that a dog could outrun him even if it *was* hobbled; the last thing he needed today was for this dog to go running off ahead of him. Peterson wanted the dog to lead him to whatever it was he felt such a burning need to get at, not to get himself into some kind of trouble where Peterson couldn't even catch up with him.

The lady at the store's cash register was a friend of his mother's from church. She'd known Peterson since the day he was baptized.

"You get yourself a dog again, Mikey Peterson?"

Peterson *hated* being called Mikey. The last time someone his own age had called him that—back in high school —the guy had damn near got a broken nose.

But things like that you just had to *take* from sweet little old ladies; it wasn't like they meant any harm. Peterson smiled and shook his head. "Sheriff's business, Mrs. Hawkins. Grim stuff. I don't think you'd really want to know."

Mrs. Hawkins sighed and sort of glowed at him with motherly affection. "You sheriff boys, Mikey Peterson. I'll tell you." But she didn't tell him. She set his change on the counter, glowed at him for another instant, and turned to ring up the woman in line behind him.

When he got out to the cruiser, Peterson threw the bag with the steel-chain collar and leash onto the front passenger seat, sat behind the steering wheel, and started the engine. He drove the car diagonally across the parking lot; there wasn't enough traffic around to bother with the lines and arrows painted on the asphalt.

Robin Smith's veterinary office was only three blocks from the five-and-dime. Peterson found himself pulling up in front of her door before he even got used to being in the car. He took the leash and collar out of the bag and left the empty bag on the front seat when he got out of the car. As he walked into the office he realized that taking them out of the package was kind of pointless—he felt just as silly carrying the chain and collar as he would have carrying a rattling paper sack.

Smith peeked out of her examination room as soon as he opened the door.

"It's you," she said. "Good. I think this dog is going to go out of his mind if he doesn't get out of the kennel soon." She laughed. "Out of his mind? I think the poor thing already *is* out of his mind."

Peterson felt his lips tighten into an involuntary frown. He nodded. "If you're ready to let that dog out of here, I'm ready to take him," he said.

"Good," she said, "good." She sounded distracted. "You've got a leash and collar with you. That means you're thinking a step ahead of me—I hadn't even stopped to realize you'd need one." She started into the examination room, heading toward the kennel. "Come on back."

He followed her. "I figured I'd need them," he said. "You made it sound as if he was eager enough that he might want to get ahead of me. I didn't know that I'd be able to keep up with him without a leash."

The veterinarian opened the door to the kennel. As she opened it Peterson could hear the sound of the dog's claws scratching at the metal floor of his cage. The sound stopped an instant after the door was open.

The dog *looked* at Peterson as he came through the door —looked at him all full of pain and desperation and deep, powerful sadness. Seeing that look again made his gut twist up around itself until it hurt. He looked away, down toward the floor. He had to; he really couldn't stand to see some poor dog looking at him like that.

"It's okay, Rex," Robin Smith said. "Mike Peterson here is going to take you to find your Jimmy. It's all going to be

okay. All right, boy?" She lifted the latch that held the cage
door closed. The dog crouched, as though he were about to
jump out; she put her hand on his shoulder and made him
stop. "No, Rex." She turned toward Peterson. "We'd better
put that collar on him now, or we may not be able to put it
on him at all. How are you with dogs? Would you like to do
it, or would you like me to . . . ?"

"I'll get it," Peterson said. "Lived with a dog half my life.
No problem at all."

She stepped a little to one side, so that Peterson could
get to the dog, but she stayed close enough to keep her
hand on Rex's shoulder.

"Okay, boy. You ready for this? Don't look at me like
that. I know how you feel—I hate collars, too. Think about
it this way: you're lucky. You won't have to button this one.
I have to button mine every morning, and it isn't any fun at
all." He threaded the chain of the choke collar and slid it
past the dog's face, over his ears, around his neck. "That's
not so bad now, is it, Rex? You look a whole lot more
dressed with that on." He looked back at the veterinarian.
"Think I should snap the leash on there while I'm at it?"

She nodded. "Go ahead. I'll lift him out of there when
you're done."

He had the leash clipped on before she finished speaking.

She leaned over and reached in with both hands. Carefully—it was hard to find a spot on the dog that wasn't
scabbed or bandaged over—she lifted Rex out of the cage,
one hand on either side of his chest. She set him on the
floor of the kennel so softly that it took the dog a moment
to realize he had to stand.

"You should probably take him back to Ben Tompkins
when you're done with him," Robin Smith said. "The dog
ought to be resting, and I've got a feeling he isn't going to
get any rest here—he may do better if he's back at home."

The dog was straining at the leash already, pulling hard.
Peterson wasn't expecting a dog in that kind of shape to be
so strong; when Rex first reached the end of the leash he
almost pulled Peterson off his feet. Peterson gave a small,
sharp tug on the chain—not enough to hurt the dog, but
enough to tell him that Peterson meant to be in charge. It
was necessary. If the dog spent this whole excursion yank-

ing that hard against his collar, he probably *would* do himself some harm. Still, even if it was necessary to make the dog know who was boss, Peterson felt guilty about it. He didn't *like* seeing things hurt—people *or* animals. His own dog had been spoiled rotten.

Robin Smith wished him luck before he left. Not that it did any good.

Peterson parked the cruiser in the Tompkins driveway, right behind Ben's own car, but he didn't go inside. He got out from behind the wheel, went around to the back door of the car, and had to scramble to grab hold of Rex's leash before the dog could finish bolting out the door.

"Come *on*, boy," he said. "We've got to cooperate here. How are we ever going to find your Jimmy if we don't cooperate? From what I've seen of your leg, you didn't do too well last time you tried to cope with these people on your own."

The dog looked up at Peterson over his shoulder and whined at him. But he strained a little less at the leash.

The dog, hobbling on three legs, lead Peterson toward the backyard. When they got around the house Rex turned to follow the now-worn path through the blackberry bramble, the path where they'd found a trail of Jimmy Tompkins's spattered blood. Rex didn't hesitate or sniff at the ground the way dogs do when they track; he went quickly and directly, walking steadily as he could, as though it was a trail he'd always known. A trail with a destination he was certain of.

Half a dozen yards into the thicket, Rex veered away from the blood trail and pointed himself directly at the spot where Jimmy Tompkins's trail had ended.

Peterson smiled to himself. That much of his hunch, at least, had been right.

When they reached the end of the trail, the dog paused —he almost seemed confused. He looked down at the ground, and then back up at Peterson, and growled at him.

"What do you want from me, Rex? I sure as hell don't know any more about this than you do."

The dog kept staring at him for a while after that. But eventually he seemed to realize that Peterson wasn't going to do anything until he did. He sniffed a little at the

ground, and it looked to Peterson as though the dog had
actually managed to scent some kind of a trail. But just
when Peterson thought the dog was going to start track-
ing, Rex snorted impatiently and growled again.

Then, for a long while, Rex . . . *looked* out at the woods
and fields around him. To Peterson, watching the dog stare
out at Green Hill, it almost seemed that the dog was study-
ing a puzzle before sitting down to solve it.

Finally the dog started walking again, more slowly, but
just as deliberately. He led Peterson uphill, not following
any trail or path at all, making a line as straight as he could
through the briars and fields. The way led past but not
through the rocky culvert where Peterson knew Jimmy
had paused.

The dog finally came to a stop not far from the top of
Green Hill, in front of a great slab of sandstone so sheer
that it was almost perpendicular to the ground. The enor-
mous rock was half-buried in the hill; only the one face of it
was showing. That face was mostly obscured by bushes and
vines run riot.

Twice Rex tried to scramble up the rock, and then a
couple more times he tried to jump up and into it.

It wasn't much use. Even if the dog could climb a sheer
rock—which didn't seem especially likely to Peterson,
even if the vines were tangled and thick enough to give his
legs a certain amount of purchase—Rex couldn't make a
climb like that with one of his hind legs all splinted up.

"What are you trying to do, huh, Rex? Jump right
through that rock or something?"

The dog was still trying to climb up through the vines.
But he was weaker now, and he was having even less luck.
One of his front paws got tangled up in a vine; when he
finally managed to work it free he lost his footing and fell
rump-first onto the ground.

Peterson looked up at the slab of rock, away from the
dog. What was Rex seeing? The rock was nothing but rock.
The vines and bushes were nothing but stems and leaves.
Peterson stepped around the dog so that he could examine
the sandstone more carefully. Were there faults in the rock
he wasn't seeing?

No.

He reached up with his free hand and patted the slab

from one end to the other. All he felt was coarse, sandy rock.

Something above the rock, maybe? That had to be it. Peterson couldn't climb twelve feet of sheer sandstone any more than the dog could. But he could walk around the slab and uphill for a few yards, and get to the top without a whole lot of trouble.

The dog wouldn't follow him, even when Peterson tried to use the leash to drag him away from the base of the slab. Peterson shrugged and let go of the leash—Rex wasn't going anywhere. Unless he'd somehow developed an ability to jump through solid rock.

It only took Peterson half a minute to climb up and around the rock. But it was a wasted half minute, even so; whatever the dog was seeing, it wasn't any more revealed from above than it had been from the bottom of the slab. As Peterson stood on the sandy grass that grew over the stone, all he saw was what he'd seen before—bushes, vines, sandstone. Saw the dog, mooning at the sheer dead rock as though it were his long-lost love.

Just then Rex leaped at the rock one last time, leaped with all the strength and heart he had. It carried him a little higher, but it was just as useless as every other thing the dog had done since they'd got here. Rex smacked snout-first into the sandstone, and fell to the ground unconscious

Peterson hurried down to the base of the rock. The dog wasn't dead; he was still breathing. He half considered taking the dog back to the veterinarian's, but as he carried the dog back toward his car, Rex began howling softly, low and sad—almost moaning.

It almost broke Peterson's heart to hear it. But, for reasons he didn't entirely understand, it made him certain that whatever damage the dog had done to himself would heal on its own, and instead of taking Rex back to Tylerville with him, Peterson left Rex in the Tompkins house.

CHAPTER

TWENTY-THREE

BEN LEFT THE HOUSE A LITTLE WHILE AFTER PETER-
son—the deputy sheriff who seemed to be in charge—a
little while after Peterson got done with the telephone.

He was already having regrets about what he was going
to do. Even if the children in this town were as warped as
he was sure they were, there was something sick in the
head about walking up to children and saying strange and
intimidating words.

Was he coming unhinged? Was he getting to be as sick as
they were? He wasn't sure. It was a possibility, he knew
that.

But he didn't have another plan, and his heart was certain that if he didn't do something his son would die.

If Jimmy wasn't already dead.

So he went for a walk, following a path that started a dozen yards down the street and led up and over Green Hill. He didn't have any special direction in mind. He didn't really even pay attention to where he was going—if it hadn't been broad daylight, if he hadn't had big landmarks like Green Hill itself to navigate by, he might have got himself lost completely.

The first of the Children Ben came across were the Williams twins—Jan and Eileen, he thought their names were, or maybe Judith and Elaine. He wasn't sure. He'd seen them at the big dinner over at their parents' house, and whoever it was who'd introduced them had said the girls' names so quickly that it was hard to remember.

Ben didn't see them until he was only a few yards away; he rounded a bend on the trail and suddenly the holly bushes on the left gave out, and there the little girls were, glaring at him. They were in the woods not too far off the path, lifting rocks and poking at the grubs and insects that lived underneath. A hundred yards uphill was one of the deputy sheriffs who seemed to be all over everywhere.

The way they looked at him was so hostile and predatory that it threw him off balance. He should have expected it, he guessed. If the children in Green Hill were as bad as he'd convinced himself they were, then it made sense that they'd be hostile. He left the path and walked toward them, in spite of the uneasiness they made him feel.

"What do *you* want?" one of them asked. Her voice was a shrill, hissing stage whisper. The other glanced back and uphill, at the deputy sheriff. Ben turned to see what she was looking at. It hadn't really occurred to him before then that the man was watching the girls. Watching him now, too.

But he couldn't let that stop him—*couldn't*.

"I want to talk to you," Ben said, "to tell you something." He knelt, so that he could look both of them right in the eye, and he spoke very softly. "I know what you've done to my son," he said, "and you know what I'm going to do about it. Oh, you do know. You know if you think about it for just a moment."

The eyes of both girls went wide with panic. The one nearest Ben turned to her sister, looking for direction, but that girl was looking uphill again, at the deputy.

Ben stood up and walked away before either twin had a chance to respond.

It was half an hour before he saw another child. By then Ben was all but lost, in spite of the fact that it was broad daylight. All he knew about his whereabouts was that he was on a sandy path in a pine woods where the trees were almost too thin to really be a woods. It was low on Green Hill, and on the far side of the hill from the rented house. Parallel to the path and a few yards away was a deep ravine; a stream about half a foot deep ran along the bottom of it.

He caught sight of a boy, walking uphill about thirty yards or so on the far side of the ravine. Ben recognized him, and remembered the boy's name, too. It was Tim Hanson—the boy who'd said those strange things to Jimmy while they were being introduced at the Williamses'. Strange things, but not things that were unkind or badly meant. Even if he hadn't said a few peculiar things, Ben probably would have remembered him—he'd been the only child in the room, bar Jimmy, without a malicious gleam in his eye.

"Tim Hanson!" Ben shouted, louder than he really needed to. "I want to talk to you!"

The boy turned to look back at Ben for the first time. He looked scared; for a moment Ben thought he was going to run.

"Are you going to talk to me, Tim Hanson, or am I going to have to speak to your father about you?"

The boy's shoulders slumped; his arms went limp. All of the spirit seemed to drain out of his eyes. He looked, Ben thought, weak and terrified. Like a field mouse who's finally realized that he can't avoid becoming a meal for an owl.

Was this the sort of child who'd kidnapped his son? And if he wasn't, why in the hell did he look so damn guilty?

The boy waded across the stream toward him.

"Yes, sir," Tim said. When Ben didn't respond to that, he said, "What did you want to tell me, Mr. Tompkins?"

The words he'd meant to say seemed to clot up in Ben's

throat. *How can I go around doing things like this? Grown men don't go around trying to intimidate small children. I feel like a child molester. And I'm a schoolteacher, damn it, not a pervert.*

But when he tried to say "Never mind," and let the boy be on his way, his heart ran into a brick wall as big and hard and cold as the moon. This boy had something to do with Jimmy—that much was plain and clear and obvious as the sunlight all around them. And if Ben just let Tim Hanson walk away, his heart told him, there was no telling what might happen to Jimmy.

"My son," he said. His voice was almost sobbing. "I know what's happened to my Jimmy. Don't you know what I'm going to have to do if I don't get him back?"

Tim gasped and made a small sound that almost turned into a scream. Suddenly the boy was running, uphill and away from Ben. In a moment he was gone, disappeared on the far side of a tall knot of holly.

Ben lost himself then. His knees buckled out from under him, and he fell to the ground, and the half-sobbing sound that had been in his voice became wracking, crying hysterics.

Ben wanted to curl up and die; if someone had come to him just then and offered to murder him, he would have thanked that person. He didn't want to be a person who said hurtful things to children, and if he had to be that sort of person he didn't want to be alive. He didn't ever want to have to see that kind of fear in a child's eyes again, especially not if he'd caused it himself.

After a while his mind went cold and blank and numb, and his sobs grew quieter and quieter until they were just the sound of his breathing. A long time after that a small voice in the back of his head spoke to him.

You're being selfish, the voice said. Can you honestly call yourself a father when it's more important for you to be able to live with yourself than it is for your son to live at all?

Ben made himself get up, then, and made himself keep walking. But his heart was dead and cold, buried in some black, icy place a million miles away. He wasn't aware of time at all, nor aware of anything around him besides the ground under his feet. Maybe he passed children a dozen times while he was walking. Maybe he never passed any at all. When he finally began to come back to his senses, around four o'clock, he honestly didn't know.

He knew where he was, at least; he recognized the area. How could he *not* have recognized it? He was back on the side of Green Hill that faced Tylerville, only a couple hundred yards from the blood trail Jimmy had left behind. Another hundred yards or so beyond that was the rented house.

And there, sitting on a sandstone boulder not a dozen feet from Ben, was Thomas Brady. He had an innocuous-looking Boy Scout knife in one hand and a weathered-grey hunk of pine wood in the other, and he was carving. It was hard to say, just yet, exactly what he was carving from the wood. At the moment it looked like an uneven model of a dugout canoe, but probably it wouldn't stay that way.

Ben remembered Thomas Brady very clearly; he was the one Jimmy had hit it off with so well after they'd finished dinner at the Williamses'.

Because he had to, because his son's life depended on it, Ben looked the boy in the eye and kept walking toward him until he was close enough to touch.

Thomas's eyes were guileless. They were innocent.

But how could Ben be *sure* of that, just looking into a boy's eyes? The best liars always seemed innocent—Ben had taught grade school long enough to know that. He gritted his teeth and forced himself to speak, even though he was trembling and so flushed that his skin was sweating from its own heat.

"I know—" he said. That was as far as he got before he saw Thomas's expression shift from puzzled to concerned. Concerned for Ben, not worried for himself, or threatened. For a long moment, as pieces of his mind rebelled against each other, Ben could feel the rest of his words trapped in his throat. Felt them—slowly, one millisecond at a time—dissipating like tiny clouds of fog.

Then the tension and the hurt inside him grew great enough to pinch nearly closed one of the arteries that fed his brain, and Ben fainted.

When Ben came to, Thomas Brady was running across the briar field toward him. A dozen yards behind Thomas was a deputy sheriff—Myron White, Ben thought it was.

Both of them looked concerned to the point where concern becomes frightenedness.

"Mr. Tompkins!" White called, "are you all right?"

Ben heard the words, and in some small part of his mind he understood them. But the part of him that needed to respond was cold and lost and out of phase with the world around him. He didn't answer Myron White; he couldn't have, even if he'd had the sense about him to try.

Then White and Thomas Brady were standing over him. White knelt down and looked into his eyes. Ben felt his eyelids blink, but that was all he felt. "Ben Tompkins . . . ?" White asked, softly. "Damn. Thomas, I think we're going to have to get him to the hospital."

The next hour Ben only half remembered. What he did remember seemed like a motion picture projected through an out-of-focus lens—White calling for help over the radio he carried at his hip; more deputies, and then ambulance attendants; staring at the white ceiling of the ambulance as it drove him to the hospital. The emergency room where what seemed like a hundred people scurried in every direction, doing every imaginable thing. Then, finally, the emergency room's doctor, who gave him a shot in the crook of his arm—a shot that drew a thread of coldness through the artery that led toward his hand, and from there back into the veins that flowed into his heart.

And sent him down into dreamless merciful unconsciousness.

When Ben woke again, everything was different.

Not to say better.

No.

Things were much, much worse.

CHAPTER
TWENTY-FOUR

TIM HANSON WAS HIKING AROUND ALL THE WAY DOWN by the creek—still trying to wear out the deputy sheriff who was so determined to follow him—when he heard Jimmy's father calling him. The sound of the man's voice turned his heart to ice. Or it felt that way—cold and hard, dead and stiff with frosty crystals.

He'll kill me, Tim thought. *If he knows what Sean did to Jimmy, while I just stood by and watched—even* helped *him!—he'll kill me.*

Run.

I've got to run.

He turned back and looked at Mr. Tompkins. There was

no way to outrun him; Tim couldn't even outrun his daddy, and Jimmy's father was in a lot better shape than daddy was. Besides, what would that deputy think if he saw Tim suddenly haul off and start running from Mr. Tompkins? There was too much trouble flying around looking for a place to light already, without Tim calling more on himself.

He can't kill me with that sheriff watching. No matter if he knows or not, he can't kill me now.

Mr. Tompkins called out, "Are you going to speak with me, Tim Hanson, or am I going to have to speak to your father about you?"

No. Not daddy. Daddy was trouble. *Please not daddy.*

So Tim swallowed his cold, half-frozen heart, and turned to face Jimmy's father. There was something wild in the man's eyes, crazy-wild like grief and desperation boiled slowly for hours in his son's blood.

Maybe if he kills me it'll be the right thing, Tim thought. That idea made him sad, but there wasn't a voice in him that wanted to deny it. *Maybe I* should *die if I can stand there and watch Sean do things like that.*

Tim waded across the creek and walked the last few yards to get to Mr. Tompkins.

But once Tim had got to him it almost seemed that Jimmy's father couldn't talk anymore. The man looked so miserable that Tim almost began to feel sorry for him, even if Mr. Tompkins was going to kill him.

"Yes, sir," Tim said, trying to prompt the man. When it didn't work, he said, "What did you want to tell me, Mr. Tompkins?" That didn't seem to get through for a long while, either, so Tim just waited.

By the time he finally spoke, Jimmy's father was crying. "My son," he said. "I know what's happened to my Jimmy. Don't you know what I'm going to have to do if I don't get him back?"

He knows! He does *know! He's going to catch me and tie me to the altar and kill me—slice me open and take out my guts one piece at a time.*

And when he's done, he'll take out my heart and eat it. Just like Sean's going to do to Jimmy.

In the time it took to suck in a breath—a time that for Tim seemed endless—Tim imagined his own evisceration.

Watched himself consumed and devoured, uncooked but steaming with the boiling heat of his own blood.

No!

Tim didn't think about the sheriff, about daddy, about Mr. Tompkins. He *ran.* Ran for his life without saying a word.

Without even paying attention to where he was going; he was at the vine-tangled mouth of the cave before he even realized it.

That was bad. If the deputy was still behind him . . . ! But no, he wasn't, Tim saw as he looked back. There was no one anywhere in sight; the deputy sheriff must not have been able to keep up with him.

Tim reached up into the vines that didn't quite cover the mouth of the cave and climbed the five feet of flat sandstone between the ground and the cave floor. It only took a moment, and then he was inside, stumbling along the rock entrance. No one could see him here, no one but the Children. No one but the Children could even see the entrance he'd climbed in through; the Stone made sure of that.

Jimmy Tompkins was in his cage, still unconscious. When Tim looked at him the boy was so still that he wasn't sure he was alive, so Tim walked to the cage and held his fingers up to Jimmy's nose, to feel his breath. He was breathing—too slow and shallow to see, but enough for Tim to feel with the fine hair on the back of his fingers. Tim checked the bag he'd brought Jimmy's food in yesterday and found that Jimmy hadn't eaten any more of it since Sean had showed up yesterday afternoon.

Had Jimmy been asleep all day?

I've got to do something soon.

He left Jimmy's cave and kept going, toward the Stone— it was asleep, too, as deep asleep as Jimmy—until he got to the tiny cave that the larger creek ran through. The water made a soft noise in that cave, a noise that somehow made it quieter than in the other caves and tunnels, even though there wasn't any noise in them at all. Tim sat down on the sandy cave floor, wrapped his arms around his shins, and rested his face against his knees.

He sat that way, just thinking and worrying, for a long time—an hour, at least, maybe two or even three hours.

It felt as though the world was closing in on him—closing in on him from every direction. Sean and the Stone were going to kill Jimmy Tompkins soon. Tim could feel the moment growing closer and closer. When he closed his eyes he could almost *see* that moment, made solid and wearing a cloak as black as Death itself, walking slowly toward him.

That sheriff's deputy had followed him everywhere today. That scared Tim more, almost, than the murder in Sean's eyes. Tim didn't want to go to jail for ever and ever. That was what they did to you when they found out you were a kidnapper and a torturer's assistant, even if in your heart of hearts you really were just trying to keep things from getting worse. Even if the main reason you were there was to try to figure out a way to help Jimmy Tompkins get *out* of there.

And now daddy, Tim's daddy, was beginning to figure out that something *serious* was up—beginning to realize that the Stone had gone off the deep end. Tim didn't want to think what that was going to mean; it was just too much to cope with.

After a while he drifted off to sleep. He woke a long time later, when he heard Sean's voice speaking softly to the Stone. When Sean was quiet Tim got up and went to see what was going on.

Sean looked worried—even more worried than Tim felt. He looked up when he heard Tim.

"Didn't know you were here," Sean said. His voice was angry.

"Sorry. Been here a while—fell asleep." Tim nodded over at the Stone. "What did it say? What are we supposed to do?"

Sean didn't answer right away. "It said that we shouldn't worry. It said that if we have to we'll just kill all of them."

That didn't make an awful lot of sense to Tim. "Won't they just send more? If we kill enough of them they'll send the National Guard, I bet. I saw the National Guard on TV. They don't look that easy to kill."

"Kill them anyway, I guess. What else we going to do with them?"

Tim shrugged. After a while he said, "Was one of those sheriff people following me all day today."

Sean had been staring vacantly at the Stone, but when he heard that he looked up at Tim. His eyes half lit up with something that wasn't quite excitement and wasn't quite fear—uneasiness, maybe, or even resignation, though exactly how resignation could be a light in someone's eyes Tim wasn't sure.

"You too?" Sean asked. "They've been following Jan and Eileen for two days. The twins called me this morning and told me about it. Someone started following me, too, when I left the house. The same guy who was asking us questions yesterday afternoon. He'd still be following me if Thomas hadn't come running over the hill and called him away. Still don't know what was going on, but I thought it was best to get away while I could."

"Uh-huh. I kind of ended up running for a while. When I was done I saw that sheriff person just hadn't kept up. They don't run that good, I guess."

Sean spat. *"Stupid!* What you trying to do, running from the law like that? Just going to make them suspicious. You ought to know that. Besides, ain't you ever heard you can't beat that radio? You say he lost track of you, he must have, cause there ain't fifteen of them outside the cave here looking for you. But don't do that again. They going to be watching you twice as careful once they set eyes on you again."

Tim shook his head. "Sorry. What you mean about the radio? I didn't ever hear anything about beating up on any radio."

"Not beating up the radio—beating it. Like in those cop shows where they're racing around in cars. One of them cops gets behind and loses sight of the guys he's chasing, and he gets on his radio and tells the next cop down the road just exactly where the bad guy's heading. And then those cops have got you, just exactly like you were somebody's dog trapped in a snare."

Tim thought about that a bit, and the more he thought about it the more it scared him. How was he going to get out here to feed Jimmy Tompkins with sheriff people watching him like that? Maybe if he got out of the house real early, before the sheriffs were awake enough to be watching him proper, maybe that would work. Or maybe someone else was going to have to feed Jimmy. The idea made him want to shudder, but he didn't dare. If it was anybody else feeding him, Jimmy would be dead already—Tim was pretty sure of that. Most of the Children just didn't know when to *stop*.

"I wasn't really meaning to go running away from the sheriff. I was sort of walking around, trying to act like I wasn't anybody special, when Jimmy Tompkins's father called me over. He said something that scared me something awful."

Sean spat again. He was looking real angry now—angry enough that maybe he was going to do something dangerous. "Like what? He say something about knowing what was going on? And like maybe he was getting ready to do something about it?"

Tim felt as though the whole world had fallen on him all at once. *Is Sean following me around, too? Or one of the other Children?* "How did you know?" There was more of his fear in his voice than he wanted to let on, but there was no way he could have hid it completely.

"Twins. He said something like that to them, too. That's what got them riled up enough to call me."

No. He isn't *following me. Thank God for that.* Tim leaned against the wall of the cave and forced himself to calm down. If he didn't calm down, he was sure, he'd give himself away.

"You think he really means it? Even if he doesn't, somebody's going to find out what's going on. There's too many of them. They're getting too close to us."

Sean glanced at the Stone, then looked back at Tim. "Don't let that worry you none. They get too close, we kill them. That Tompkins man tries anything funny, we kill him. May have to kill him pretty damn soon, when you think about it. It don't make no difference." He smiled hungrily. "You look in on Jimmy Tompkins yet? He awake?" Tim shook his head. "Well, then, let's go wake him up and have us some fun."

Sean lit a candle as they walked toward Jimmy's cave. "Hey, Jimmy Tompkins," he called, "you ready for some more fun? You pass out on us this time, we just going to wake you up."

Jimmy didn't answer; when they got close to his cage Tim saw that that was because he was still unconscious.

Now, in the candlelight, Tim could see that Jimmy was soaked with sweat. His skin was pink and feverish looking, and there were deep blue-black circles under his eyes.

Sean set his candle so that it stood upright on the floor of the cave, shook the cage, and shouted Jimmy's name. It didn't wake him. When Sean realized that it wasn't going to work, he said, *"Shit,"* and untied the rope that held the cage closed. When he was done—it took him a while to untie the knot, because he was angry enough that his hands were shaking a little, probably angry enough that he couldn't see straight—when he was done he yanked the cage door open and dragged Jimmy out by his shoelaces.

"Hey, Jimmy Tompkins," Sean said, "what use are you if you're out cold as frozen leftovers?" He grabbed Jimmy's shirt and shook him up and down against the floor of the cave. "Tell me that, huh? What the fuck good are you?"

Jimmy still didn't answer; as far as Tim could tell he was still unconscious.

Sean looked up; the expression on his face was disgust. "Tim, do me a favor, huh? Fetch that bucket from the next cave down and get me some water from the big creek?"

"Yeah," Tim said. "Be a minute."

"Take your time."

Tim didn't hurry. The last thing in the world he wanted to do right then was help Sean get started torturing Jimmy again. But what could he do? If he didn't do like Sean said, Sean would beat him to a pulp. When Sean was done and Tim was too bloody to move, Sean would get up and take care of what he wanted himself; it wasn't like he wasn't capable. If Tim tried to stop Sean from doing what he wanted with Jimmy, Tim would get beat up even worse. And then, when Sean was done, he would start wanting to know *why* Tim didn't want to see Jimmy Tompkins getting beaten. And if Tim didn't answer him, and answer quickly, Sean would start beating him again, and keep on beating him until he got the answers.

And once Sean had the answers to those questions, he'd probably kill Tim. If he could actually hear the answers when Tim said them. Tim wasn't sure he'd be able to.

When Tim got back with the water, Sean was bent over Jimmy and whispering in his ear and chuckling. He looked up as Tim walked into the cave and grinned that wild grin he always had when he was about to get blood on his hands. "Can't wake this boy up for nothing," he said. "By the look of him—all feverish like this—maybe he's already got an infection. Bad enough to kill him, I bet—maybe bad enough that he won't even wake up before he dies." Sean's grin went away. "*Shit.* Stone's going to be pissed if Jimmy Tompkins is too close to being dead to be woke up when we're ready to kill him. Give me that water. *Now.*"

Sean was suddenly very angry. Tim was half afraid that he'd take off and start beating on him just for the spite of it. He handed Sean the bucket in such a hurry that half the water in it spilled out onto the floor of the cave.

"*Careful,* stupid. I bet this is *your* fault—you were the one who bandaged him up. You put dirt in his leg or something while you were at it?" Tim shook his head. "*Hell.* Maybe I shouldn't have spit into him. *God*damn stupid fucking Jimmy *Tom*pkins." He poured all the water in the bucket onto Jimmy's face. "*That* ain't going to wake you up either, huh? Well, let's see how this works!" Sean pulled his right foot way back, just exactly as though he was about to punt a football. But the kick wasn't aimed at a football—it was meant for Jimmy's head, and all Tim could think was *Oh-my-God-Sean's-going-to-kill-him, oh-my-God-Sean's-going-to-kill-him.*

Just exactly then, with Sean's leg hauled back for the kick and Tim panicking out of his mind, was when they heard Rex barking outside the cave. Both of them recognized the bark instantly; Rex had harassed all of the Children for months—not really doing any genuine harm, but making a real annoyance of himself.

Sean fell back onto the leg he'd been about to kick with, and turned to run in the direction the bark had come from. Tim's reflexes were slower and more deliberate. He blinked twice when he heard the bark, and hesitated, and—

—and that was why he, and not Sean, saw Jimmy's eye twitch open for the briefest split of an instant.

He's faking, Tim thought. *Jimmy Tompkins is awake and faking like he's unconscious. And, Christ in heaven, Sean left him out of his cage and not tied up at all.*

Tim bent down and whispered into Jimmy's ear: "Left. Right. Down. Swim out." That would take Jimmy out by way of the little creek, and Tim didn't think anyone would notice him going that way. The rock was so thick and heavy that way that sometimes the Stone couldn't hear what you were saying there, even if you were trying to talk to him. Tim ran off to join Sean without waiting for Jimmy to respond; there wasn't time to wait. Sean would be suspicious if Tim was more than a moment behind him.

The dog was outside the main entrance to the cave, and the deputy who seemed to be in charge was with him. Both the dog and the man were staring straight into the cave, but the man couldn't see anything but plain, flat, vine-covered rock, and the dog couldn't jump high enough to get in. Not with his hind leg all splinted up like that—probably not even if his leg had been fine. Tim wondered how much strain was on the Stone right now, hiding the entrance to the cave from a man who was staring straight at it. As he watched, the man pulled his hand across the air at the entrance to the cave, then shook his head as though he'd felt nothing but rock. For a moment the deputy was staring straight into Tim's eyes, and Tim felt an instant of panic, afraid that the illusion had evaporated.

The illusion didn't fool the dog at all. Most dogs were immune to the Stone's magic to one degree or another. It had cost the Stone a lot to burn away the scent of all those trails—Jimmy's, the dog's, the trails that the Children had left behind—back when they'd first captured Jimmy. But there was something special about this dog, even more special than other dogs; it was, as far as Tim could tell, immune to the Stone completely.

Sean hawked up a big clam and spat it on the lip of the cave. "That dog has got to die," he said. It wasn't the first time he'd said it. He'd been saying it for months, ever since the dog had first escaped. Whenever Tim thought about it he was amazed that the dog wasn't dead yet—sometimes he even wondered if the dog wasn't somehow just as magical as the Stone. Tim couldn't see any other way it could still be alive, not after all this time.

Tim grunted. "You think they're going to get in here?"

"Hell if I know. But I know what I'm going to do if they do." He held up the sacrifice knife, the one they always kept beside the Stone. The razor-sharp knife Sean had used yesterday to skin Jimmy's leg. "That sheriff gets any closer, him and the dog are both going to die."

Tim felt his stomach shrivel up around itself. He didn't know what he'd do if Sean tried to kill that man in front of him. He didn't even know if there was anything he *could* do.

But as it turned out he didn't even have to find out. After a few minutes the sheriff stepped away from the front of the cave—probably to look around and see if another perspective would throw any light on the dog's barking, which must have looked senseless to him—and a moment after that the dog took one last leap at the mouth of the cave.

The leap would have carried him in, too, but as soon as the dog managed to poke his snout into the cave, Sean kicked it right in the teeth with the toe of his shoe. The kick knocked the poor dog senseless, and sent it tumbling back to the ground. The deputy sheriff showed up real quick after that. But he must not have seen what actually happened, because he just picked the dog up off the dirt and carried it back toward the house Jimmy Tompkins's father had rented.

When Sean and Tim went back to Jimmy's cave, Jimmy had already escaped. A few minutes after that the Stone found out, and it was so angry that it burned Sean's mind away, and left him dead inside forever.

CHAPTER

TWENTY-FIVE

WHAT WOKE JIMMY, FINALLY, WAS THE SOUND OF SEAN whispering in his ear.

"C'mon, Jimmy Tompkins. Don't you want to come out and play?" A drop of Sean's spittle fell on Jimmy's cheek, ran down the side of his face, and pooled in the crook of his ear. "You know, you remind me of those kids in the books we have to read in school. Like Dick and Jane, back in first grade. Did you have to read about Dick and Jane, Jimmy Tompkins? Are you a dick?"

Sean waited five beats for a response before he went on. Jimmy was more awake now, but he still felt dazed. He tried to open his eyes, but it just wasn't in them to move.

Something was *wrong* with him, some kind of sickness that might kill him if it didn't stop soon. Moving even as much as an eyebrow would have taken everything he had in him.

"Dick and Jane and you, Jimmy Tompkins—*you*— you all are always being so *nice* to everybody all the time. Nice to *every*thing. Don't any of you ever like to *break* things? How come you never hurt people unless you have to? Don't you know how much fun it is to hear something small and hairy screaming because it knows it's going to die?"

Jimmy's eyes were still closed, but he could feel the world coming into focus around him. He could move now, he thought, if he really had to. But why was Sean trying to wake him up? It sure wasn't because he wanted to feed Jimmy breakfast. No, Sean wanted to wake Jimmy up so he could take that knife to him again. The best thing Jimmy could do was pull back into himself and sleep. Sean didn't just want to mutilate him, he wanted Jimmy to feel it. And that meant that Jimmy had to be awake to be tortured.

"It ain't right, Jimmy Tompkins. It ain't right not to have fun. What kind of life can you have without fun? Boys were made for breaking things, and girls are meant for making things suffer." More of Sean's drool was falling on Jimmy's face; the pool in his ear had begun to overflow and leak into his hair.

Jimmy heard the sound of footsteps coming into the cave—another of the Children was here. Jimmy felt Sean pull up, away from him, to speak to the other one. "Can't wake this boy up," Sean said, "for nothing. By the look of him—all feverish like this—maybe he's already got an infection. Bad enough infection to kill him, I bet—maybe bad enough that he won't even wake up again before he dies." Sean made a snarling noise. "*Shit.* Stone's going to be pissed if Jimmy Tompkins doesn't wake up enough for us to kill him. Give me that water. *Now.*"

Water?

Sean stood up, and there was the sound of water sloshing in and spilling from a bucket.

He's going to pour water on me. To wake me up. I've got to relax, to pretend that I'm already dead. If I jerk around he'll know I've been pretending, and then I'm really in trouble.

"Careful, stupid," Sean said. Jimmy wasn't quite sure what he meant, but he thought it might have something to do with the water he'd heard spilling. "I bet this is *your* fault—you were the one who bandaged him up. You put dirt in his leg or something while you were at it?"

It's Tim he's talking to. It's got to be Tim. Jimmy remembered Tim bandaging up his leg. The memory was dim and pretty uncertain, but it had to be Tim who'd taped up the wound—Tim was the only one besides Sean who'd been there, and Jimmy would have remembered being bandaged by Sean. But even if it was Tim, was that good news or bad? Tim acted like a friend any time they were alone together, but when Sean was around he was . . . dangerous. Almost as dangerous as the rest of the Children.

"Hell," Sean was saying now. "Maybe I shouldn't have spit into him. *God*damn stupid fucking Jimmy *Tom*pkins." Jimmy felt a lot of water spattering hard into his face—at least a gallon of it, maybe more. It splashed up into his nose, into his sinuses; it was all he could do not to choke and sneeze it up. "That ain't going to wake you up either, huh? Well, let's see how this works!"

Sean stepped back, away from Jimmy, and kept scrambling a few more paces backward. When he started forward again the sound reminded Jimmy of playing little-league football last year, back in New Jersey. It was exactly the sound of the kicker's running as he builds up momentum to kick a field goal.

He's going to kick me. He thinks my head is a football, and he's going to kick me. If he kicks me from there, he'll hit the banged-up side of my head.

Well, at least then I will be blacked out again.

Either that or dead, if my skull caves in.

But then, the instant before he expected to feel the toe of Sean's sneaker slam into his head, there was a sound, the sound of a dog barking, and suddenly Sean had no interest in kicking Jimmy's head at all. His footsteps were off and running down the tunnel before Jimmy even realized whose bark it was.

Rex! Rex is here, somewhere in the cave—the dog found me!

Jimmy was so excited, so ecstatic at the possibility of getting away that for a moment he forgot his ruse, and his left eye twitched open involuntarily, trying to see what was going on. Not that there could have been anything to see; the bark came from a long distance away.

And Jimmy saw Tim, staring straight at him.

Jimmy panicked; he closed his eye, hoping Tim hadn't noticed—trying to pretend he was still unconscious. But it was too late. Tim hadn't missed anything. He was bending down close to Jimmy's ear, and whispering: "Left. Right. Down. Swim out," he said.

And then he was gone, running away from Jimmy's cave as quickly as Sean had.

Jimmy felt adrenaline flood his veins. The words were instructions. They had to be. *He wants me to escape. Maybe he really doesn't want to see them kill me. He must not want that. . . .* Unless it was some sort of a mean trick, something meant to get Jimmy's spirits up, to make him a better victim. That was a crazy thought, Jimmy knew. He even knew the word for it—paranoia—but given his situation he didn't think it was all *that* crazy.

But he didn't have that much to lose by trying, and if he didn't try things sure weren't going to get any better. He opened his eyes and tried to get a look at what was around him.

He was most of the way out of his cage. There was a candle set into the dirt a couple of yards away, burning unevenly. He tried to sit up, and, in spite of the adrenaline that made him feel nearly alive, the cave spun wildly all around him. He tried to find his balance, to stop the spinning, but he couldn't. So he ignored it, and forced himself to sit up anyway. His body knew the right motions well enough to get up, walk across the cave, and get the candle, even if he only knew which way was up because he recognized the floor.

Left. Right. Down. Swim out.

By the time he got to the place where his cave met the tunnel, his head was only spinning a little—or maybe it was just that he was getting used to the vertigo. It didn't really matter. Either way, it meant that he could walk if he made himself. Before he went out into the tunnel he looked down at the candle. Was it safe to carry it with him? Sean might notice the extra light from wherever he was in the cave. But even if he was less dizzy, he was too dizzy to walk very far without light—unless he wanted to be falling all over his feet and making a racket. Noise, he decided, was probably more likely to attract Sean's notice than light was.

So he picked up the candle and stepped into the tunnel and turned to his left.

The fact that Jimmy didn't have an absolute sense of up or down made the unevenness of the tunnel floor seem like a series of wild dips and unpredictable slopes. Even with the candlelight, his feet kept trying to trip over themselves, and more than once he lost his footing and stumbled into the tunnel wall. The third time he hit the wall the puffy part of his head smacked into one of the jagged rocks that protruded from the tunnel, and the pain was so bad that Jimmy had to bite his tongue to keep from screaming.

Why am I trying to run? he thought when the pain finally eased enough to let him move again. *Rex is here. If he's here and he's alive and Sean's worried, then he must have brought help.*

He pictured himself as someone from a bad movie, running into the clutches of the villains just as the cavalry came over the hill. That would be just exactly the sort of luck he'd have these last three days—awful, or even worse.

Maybe I should head back to the cage and go back to playing dead.

But when he thought about it Jimmy realized that counting on anyone else to get him out of trouble wasn't a great idea. The Stone was magical, and the best magic it had was the kind of magic that hides things—like the way it made Jimmy's screams sound like whispers even to his own ears. It didn't matter if Rex was at the entrance to the cave with every sheriff in the county. All of them could search for hours and not see what they were looking at.

Left. Right. Down. Swim out.

Right was a smaller tunnel, only barely big enough for Jimmy to stand up in. That tunnel seemed, by the time Jimmy was done, to have stretched, twisted, and wandered up and down for at least a quarter of a mile. The distance was probably less than that; dizzy as Jimmy was, walking from his bed at home to the toilet down the hall would have felt like a hundred yards.

The narrow tunnel eventually opened out into a wide,

deep cave—too big to see across with just the light of a candle. To the right and back behind him the cave ran upward; straight ahead it ran down. A stream ran along the floor of the cave, too far away to see but close enough to hear. Jimmy climbed up and over the lip of the small tunnel, toward the stream.

It turned out to be so small that Jimmy almost walked right over it. It would have been easy not to notice it at all if it weren't for the sound of running water. It wasn't so much a stream as it was a rivulet no wider than his hand.

How am I supposed to swim out through that?

Jimmy couldn't imagine. But Tim's instructions had been good so far. They *seemed* to be good, anyway. All Jimmy was likely to do by heading off in some other direction was get himself hopelessly lost.

He followed the trickle of water down, deeper and deeper into the inside of Green Hill. The stream did grow wider and deeper as he went; everywhere along the bottom of the cave there was water seeping from the rock to join the flow. Two hundred yards past the winding tunnel he'd left, a much heavier stream joined the flow, and suddenly the water was half a foot deep and four feet across.

After another hundred yards the water formed a pool—and in the bottom corner of that pool there was daylight.

At first that seemed incongruous to Jimmy. How could there be daylight under the water? Incongruous or not, it was daylight, and the only way to get to it was to swim.

Jimmy waded into the pool. When the water was knee-deep, he doused the candle, but he kept it with him—the last thing he needed to do right now was leave behind a trail. The water was cold, powerfully cold, like ice water, or like the ocean in winter. He gritted his teeth, braced himself, and kept going. The water got its deepest near the wedge of light—when Jimmy stood on tiptoe the water came to just above his navel. The water was painfully cold, especially around his groin and down on his leg where it pressed against the taped-down skin. He took three deep breaths, let his legs go slack underneath him, and started to swim down into the light. But the shock of the cold at his neck and under his arms startled him, forcing the air out of his lungs.

That made him gasp before he could even get his head

back to the surface, and he ended up coughing out what felt like half a gallon of icy water. When he finally stopped coughing he could feel the coldness of the water already trying to seep down into the insides of his bones. He had to hurry; his body was already enough of a mess. It wouldn't do him any good to give the infection in his head more room to grow.

Again, three deep breaths, and a dive into the light. The water was still bitter cold, but his body was ready for it now, or at least not surprised by it.

The passage at the pool bottom was only barely big enough for Jimmy to squeeze through. He was extra careful not to bump his head—the consequences of knocking himself senseless underwater weren't something he wanted to think about. He ended up being so careful of his head that he smacked his taped-up shin on the sandy bottom twice. That was excruciating, even with the numbing coldness of the water.

Then, finally, he was through, and there was so much sunlight—sunlight that he hadn't seen in *days*—that it hurt his eyes to see it. He had to close them before he got to the surface, and even the red, veiny light that glowed through his eyelids was too much.

His head rose above the water, and Jimmy sucked air in through his mouth. His balance, he realized, must be recovering—otherwise how would he have found the surface with his eyes shut?

I'm going to make it. I'm going to get away from here alive, *and me and dad can move back home, and everything's going to be all right.*

He felt his shoulders relax for the first time since he woke up and found Rex missing. He was free, and everything was really going to be just fine.

Just fine.

He slitted open his eyes, enough to see but not enough to hurt. The water here was about as deep as it had been on the other side . . . which meant, it seemed to Jimmy, that it was really one pool with a lot of rock in the middle. Another stream led out and away from the pool, down the side of Green Hill.

I need to go home. I need to get dad and Rex and we need to pack up and get away *from here.*

But which way is home?

It was a good question; Jimmy wasn't anywhere he recognized at all.

The Children would be following him soon enough. It wouldn't do to stand here right out in the open, trying to figure out which way to go. Rushing off half-cocked wouldn't do either—if he just wandered out into the woods they'd find him sooner or later.

There was a knot of tall bushes a few yards from the pool; he climbed out of the water and headed toward it. It would make him a little less obvious, anyway, and give him a moment to think.

By the time he sat down in the middle of them he already knew what he had to do—head uphill. With just a little luck he would be able to see the rented house from the top. He sat still for another moment, trying to spot any landmark he might recognize . . . there was no sense going all the way up to the top of the hill if it wasn't necessary.

But if he was anywhere near home, he couldn't see it. The only thing to do was head on. Jimmy stood up—

—and as he did a stray, withered branch poked into one of the scabs on the soft part of Jimmy's head. The scab tore, and broke, and the trapped clotty-pussy gunk that filled the infected gap between skin and skull burst. And it drained, so quick and hard and fast that the suddenness of it blacked Jimmy out. It might have hurt if he'd had a chance to feel it before he faded away.

Jimmy lay unconscious for most of two hours on the dirt at the center of the bushes.

CHAPTER

TWENTY-SIX

ROBERTA WAS AT HOME, WATCHING TELEVISION, WHEN
the Stone called her. The old electric clock over the TV set
read quarter till four. She heard its angry voice in her head
as clearly as if it were only five feet from her.

The cave. Come to the cave. Come now.

Hearing its voice in her head surprised her. *It must be
angry,* she thought. Even with the force of Jimmy
Tompkins's suffering to feed it, the Stone had been tired
and stretched thin for days. Speaking from a distance was a
strain to it. For it to speak that clearly meant that it was too
furious to worry over waste.

Yes, she thought back toward it. *I'm coming.* Roberta was very close to the Stone; it could always hear her if it wanted to.

She got up out of the couch and turned the television off. "Mommy," she shouted, "I'm going out for a little while."

Her mother's voice came from the kitchen. "Okay, Roberta. You make sure you get back here in time for dinner. I'm making hamburgers. Should be ready about six-thirty."

Roberta was grinning to herself as she left. There weren't many things that gave Roberta more of a kick than watching her mother get mad enough to forget who she was. She had a feeling there was no way she was going to be back home by half past six. If Roberta was late coming home for dinner her mother would be hurt and upset enough that she'd forget about it. Mommy put a lot of pride in her cooking, really *cared* about Roberta showing up late for dinner, and she was just like every other grown-up in Green Hill—worse than most of them, even. If she got upset about something it'd slip right out of her mind, like eggs sliding out of a brand-new teflon pan. When she got upset enough she'd start forgetting all sorts of things, sometimes even lose track of herself right in the middle of a sentence.

When Roberta got out to the yard the first thing she did was look around to try to find the deputy sheriff who'd been watching her house all day. She wasn't sure yet how she was going to get away from him, but she knew that she had to. There was no way she could go to the cave with that man following her.

It took her a lot longer than she expected to spot him; for a moment she was almost afraid that the man had somehow developed enough sense not to be so obvious. Then, finally, she saw him—fifty yards down the road, standing by a patrol car, talking to another deputy.

Of course, she thought. *They're changing shifts. They did the same thing yesterday afternoon, right around four o'clock.*

But the best part about it was that neither one of them was watching her. She started walking out toward the cave, as slowly and casually as she could. She was tempted to start running, but if she did it might just catch one of their eyes. It wasn't worth the risk. Besides, there was no telling how many more of them there were between here and the cave. None of them would likely pay any attention to her, but they just might if they saw her running.

But if there were any other deputies along the way, Roberta didn't see them. All of them, she guessed, were changing shifts. Still, she didn't go directly at all; she spent most of half an hour on a walk that shouldn't have taken much more than ten minutes—certainly less than fifteen. Before she went in she waited an extra five minutes by the entrance, just to make sure there was no one else around.

It was quiet and dark inside the cave. She rummaged around in the little niche that was a few feet past the left side of the entrance, dug out a candle, lit it. She didn't hear any sound until she was a few feet from the Stone's cave, and then all she heard was Tim Hanson mumbling to himself.

"Don't hurt me," he whispered. "Please don't hurt me."

The Stone wasn't paying any attention to him. It hardly ever paid any mind to Tim; sometimes Roberta thought it had even more contempt for him than she did.

You have to hurry, the Stone said to her as she walked into its cave. *The Tompkins has escaped. Sean Brady let it escape. Sean Brady will never let anything escape again.*

"Sean's dead?" Her voice sounded frightened when she asked the question. That was bad; it wasn't good for you to act scared in front of the Stone. Sometimes when the Stone saw you afraid it got excited, and then maybe it'd start hurting you before it remembered you were one of its own.

All the Sean inside him is gone.

That was when, finally, she saw Sean. He was lying limp on the floor of the cave, as slack as though he were dead. But he wasn't dead, exactly—if you looked close enough you could see that he was breathing. And his eyes were open. Open, but slack and dead and empty, as though he was nothing inside but a machine made out of meat. Roberta shuddered, not because she was sympathetic—she didn't have the capacity for sympathy—but because she could picture the same thing happening to her if she screwed up.

"Make him go away," she said. "What's left of him is distracting."

You're afraid. She could feel the Stone laughing at her—not laughing exactly, but doing that thing it sometimes did that made her think of laughing. Mean-hearted laughing.

But it did as she asked, anyway; suddenly dead-eyed Sean was standing up, walking past her, walking out of the cave.

The Stone *must need me,* she thought, before she realized that it couldn't help but hear her if she thought in words that distinct while she was this close.

Yes. You are needed. You must get the Tompkins. It must *not escape.* The Stone sounded more hungry for Jimmy Tompkins than worried about trouble. It never worried much about trouble.

"Yes," she said. "I'll get him." Roberta was getting pretty sick of trouble, and sheriff's deputies, and Jimmy Tompkins. It was hard to have any fun when you had to spend all your time being careful. Worse, if the trouble from Jimmy Tompkins ever caught up with them, there might not ever be any fun ever again.

She was going to need help; she couldn't search all of Green Hill by herself. Tim was lying on the floor on the far side of the cave where Sean had been. But what good was he? Even when he wasn't scared out of his wits he didn't have any nerve.

Useless.

"Yes," she said. "He's no use at all. I need to get Christian. The twins. The rest of them, too."

They're coming now.

Roberta nodded. A moment later she went to the main entrance to the cave to wait. When she got there she could see the twins only a few yards outside, hiking up the last stretch of the hill before the entrance. She didn't wait for them to get inside; there wasn't time. She took a fast look to make sure there were no sheriff's deputies in sight and climbed down to meet them. They didn't seem especially surprised to see her.

"I need you two," she said, "right now."

"Sean—" Jan didn't quite interrupt her; but her interjection was annoying enough that Roberta would have cuffed her if she'd had the time.

"I know about Sean. Sean's dead. The Stone killed him. It's just his body that's alive."

Neither one of them had the nerve to say anything after they'd heard that.

"Jimmy Tompkins got loose somehow. We need to find him. Jan, you wait in the cave. When the others show up, send them out again looking for the boy. And make sure they go out in pairs, in case he's got enough left in him to fight back. And make sure they don't all end up going in the same direction, huh?"

Jan nodded.

"Eileen, you come with me. I want to go check his house. That's where he's got to be going, I figure. Maybe he's already got there somehow. Don't even know for sure exactly when he got out of here, much less which way he went."

The twins didn't say a word, which was probably pretty smart of them, given the way Roberta was feeling. But they did as she said—Jan climbed up into the cave, and when Roberta started down the hill Eileen followed her.

The walk to the house that the Tompkinses had rented only took a few minutes. They were lucky enough not to see anyone along the way; better still, when they got there the doors were open. Not that Roberta would have let it stop them if the whole damned sheriff's department had stood between them and the house. Roberta would have found a way past them, or around them, or even through them if she'd had to.

Roberta was going to find Jimmy Tompkins, and she was going to bring him back. She didn't have any doubts about that.

She knew she was going to find him because she knew that if she didn't the Stone was going to do to her what it had done to Sean. And she wasn't going to let that happen.

The bad news was that when they got to the Tompkins house, it was empty.

Roberta tried the back door, and it opened with barely even a tug. She turned back to Eileen before she started in.

"Quietly," she said. "If he's in here, he'll be a lot easier to cope with if he doesn't hear us coming."

Eileen nodded. "Yeah," she said. She said it quietly, but not so quietly that Roberta didn't get an urge to slap her upside the head. But there wasn't time for that, and it would make too much noise, anyway. Roberta promised herself that as soon as she had the time, as soon as all the trouble with Jimmy Tompkins got itself ironed out, she was going to give both of the twins the sort of beating they deserved. She smiled to herself, thinking of their blood; the image made her feel warm and good inside.

The lamps were out inside the living room, and what little of the afternoon sun got through the curtained windows wasn't really enough to search by. Not as much as Roberta wanted, anyway. And it was quiet, too—so quiet that it was hard to believe that there was anyone in the house. At least not anyone awake. She considered turning on one of the lamps, and finally decided not to. If there was anyone sleeping in the house, Roberta didn't want to wake them up. Not yet.

The master bedroom, off to the right of the kitchen, was just as dark and empty as the living room.

There was no one in the smaller bedroom, back on the far side of the living room. But there was a small noise in that room—the sound of breathing, maybe, though it was so quiet in that room that it was hard to tell. Roberta looked around the room, trying to see where the sound came from—

—but the noise was the dog, Rex, and it found her before she found it.

Rex bounded out of the closet, fangs bared, snarling, dusklight catching and reflecting in its eyes and turning them into eerie red lanterns.

My throat, she thought, *the dog wants to tear open my throat.*

Then, almost as though it had heard her and meant to prove her right, the dog somehow managed a leap that would carry it right into her neck—in spite of the fact that its left hind leg was splinted and bandaged and useless.

But Roberta was too feral and carnivorous to blink just because she'd been attacked. Instead of cowering or even ducking aside she stepped toward the dog and kicked it— caught Rex still low in his leap with the sharp toe of her hard black shoe.

The dog screamed in reflex agony and fell back-first onto the floor. It lay there on the carpeting, senseless, and for a moment Roberta was tempted to keep going forward, to kick the dog again square in the skull, and kill it once and for all.

But then she *did* hesitate. This goddamn dog had been a royal pain in the ass for too long. Killing it now—while it was all but unconscious—would be too kind. The dog deserved worse, much worse.

And it had been too long since Roberta had had something to . . . *play* with. Something all to herself. Something to *hurt* that she didn't have to share with the Stone or with the other Children.

And now that she was priestess, she could have this dog all to herself if she wanted it. She could have it to herself even if he was something that all the Children wanted.

And, by damn, she was going to have it.

"Eileen," she said, "get a pillowcase and use it to carry the dog back to the cave. Put it in Jimmy Tompkins's cage. And don't do *anything* to him, you hear me? He's mine. If he doesn't have as much left in him when I see him again as he does now, I'm going to take the difference out of your ass. You understand?"

Eileen went to get the pillowcase from Jimmy Tompkins's bed.

Roberta grabbed her by the hair on the back of her head, all but yanking her off her feet. When she had Eileen all the way back against her shoulder Roberta reached up with her free hand and squeezed a little on the veins at the front of her throat. Then just for good measure she yanked a little more on Eileen's hair, even though all it did was wrench some of it out by the roots.

"When I ask you a question, you answer me. Any trouble understanding *that*?"

Eileen's eyes were wide and frightened, even cowed. Her voice quavered. "Yes, Roberta. I understand."

Roberta eased her grip on Eileen's hair and neck, and the younger girl pulled away from her cautiously, slowly, looking like a small animal with its tail tucked between its legs. Roberta smiled to herself. *Now,* she thought, *I can be pretty damn sure that dog'll still be in one piece when I'm ready to play with it.*

"Don't take too much longer here. Like I said, take the dog back to the cave—and don't let any of those sheriff people see you either. When you're done you and your sister can go out looking with the rest of them. Hear?"

Roberta left the room without waiting for an answer. A moment later she was out of the Tompkins house; twenty-five minutes after that she was on the far side of the hill, looking for Jimmy Tompkins near the creek. She had a feeling that none of the other Children would have the good sense to look around the creek, even though one of the best ways to sneak out of the cave led right to it.

She was right, too—none of the other Children came anywhere near Jimmy. Roberta walked right past him three times. If she'd had the sense herself to consider that he might have blacked out, she would have found him, lying unconscious among the bushes.

But she didn't. When Jimmy woke, half an hour after the last time she passed him, Roberta was half a mile away.

CHAPTER

TWENTY-SEVEN

WHEN JIMMY WOKE, AROUND SIX O'CLOCK, THE SUN was glowing orange-red on the western horizon, and the air was warm and clean and the dusky twilight had shifted the colors of the trees and grass and soil so beautifully that it took him almost five minutes to remember that he was living in the middle of a nightmare.

But once he remembered, it took him only a moment to realize what had happened to him. He could feel fresh, sticky blood all over the side of his head and all over the dirt where he'd fallen. When he looked up he saw more of it on the stick that had poked the soft part of his head. And he felt better, too—draining the pus away had cleared his head, even if it had blocked him out first.

I've got to get home. I've got to get home and find dad.
But how? He *still* didn't know where he was.

Then it began to come back to him—what he'd been planning before he'd blacked out. There was definitely something very wrong with his head; his memory had never been that bad.

I was going to go to the top of the hill and try to spot the house from there.

He took a deep breath, rubbed his eyes, and stood up—more carefully this time. Before he stepped out of the bushes he looked around to make sure there were none of the Children close enough to see him. But there was no one anywhere in sight, Child, adult, or otherwise.

That was a good thing, too—if Jimmy had needed to move carefully and quickly, he probably couldn't have. It wasn't just his head that was infected; the corruption had spread everywhere. He was feverish, and everything ached, even the few parts of him that hadn't been beaten or abused. Even walking slowly he felt as though he was going to trip over his own feet, and as he walked up Green Hill he almost did stumble at least half a dozen times. The ground on this side of the hill was even and smooth and covered with short grass; Jimmy didn't want to imagine what kind of trouble he'd have had walking if the ground had been rocky, like it was near the rented house.

He was twenty yards from the top of the hill when he saw the black flower. It was black and glassy and stiff—not just the petals but the stem and the leaves at its base were glassy black, too. It looked like a sculpture cut from onyx or obsidian, or maybe like some strange casting of a flower, poured from black molten glass. Almost as though it were a flower carved from the Stone. It wasn't a real flower—Jimmy was old enough to know that real live, growing plants were green or brown or even yellow or red, not jet black. And they weren't glassy, either. Coarse, usually, or soft-slick or velvety or waxy. Glass and plant were as alien to each other as air and water.

But if it wasn't a real flower, what was it doing out in the middle of a grassy field, here near the top of Green Hill? Jimmy stopped walking when he got close to the flower and bent down to get a better look at it. Before he even realized what he was doing he was touching it, reaching down underneath the leaves at its base and lifting it out of the soil. It was as hard and glassy to the touch as it was to the eye, and for a moment Jimmy thought it was incredibly heavy, because he couldn't lift it. Then he felt something snap, and his hand shot away from the ground as the flower lifted up all at once.

That's when he saw that there were roots—fine, dense, hairy roots—growing underneath the leaves. In two or three places there were clots of red-brown dirt tangled up in them. The ground where it had grown was tumbled loose and broken from where he'd pulled the roots free.

It is a plant. But how. . . ?

Up close Jimmy could see that the stem was cracked and dangling by a thread half an inch above the leafy base. The break wasn't his doing; when he pulled it from the ground something had snapped *below* the base, not above it. On an impulse he tried to tear the thread that held the stem together, but it was tougher than he expected—it didn't tear at all. To break it almost clear through someone must have trampled it, stepped right on it, hard.

He ran his finger carefully along the stem, then up along the petals of the flower itself. It was like a rose, almost, with petals nested inside petals inside petals. Down inside, at the very center, there were tiny black-glass pistils. It wasn't a rose, though, not even some strange alien version of a rose; there were no thorns along its stem, and the leaves at its base were shaped like dandelion leaves.

Jimmy took both halves of the stem in his hands, twisted, and pulled with all his strength; after an instant the thread that held the stem together broke with a twang like the sound of snapping metal. He tucked the flower into the front pocket of his jeans and pressed the base and roots back into the soil where it had been. Maybe that was silly. It was worth trying, though; Jimmy knew some weeds were hardy enough to take again if you just set them back into the dirt.

Jimmy took a deep breath, and suddenly realized that he'd been wasting time that he didn't have. *I've got to get moving again. If one of them has seen me. . . !*

The flower was like the Stone, Jimmy thought, or like his

mother's pendant, and somehow not like either one of them at all. It was as though the pendant had been a cutting from the Stone that had taken root and bloomed on his mother's breast, and the flower . . . the flower almost seemed a true seedling. Not yet as evil as the Stone—and perhaps it never would be—but every bit as strange and unearthly. If he had any sense, Jimmy thought, he'd pry it from his pocket and leave it behind. But he couldn't bring himself to do that.

He looked around, but he still didn't see anyone. He didn't see anyone at all until after he'd already got to the top of the hill and spotted the rented house. And then he didn't see the Children until they'd already seen him.

He heard a faint noise, far away and off in another direction completely, and when he looked that way he saw two of the Children—the Williams twins, maybe, but it was hard to be sure at this distance—running toward him.

The house was at least three hundred yards away, but the twins were even farther. Still, they were close enough to catch up to him before he got there if he didn't run. Jimmy wasn't in any shape for running. He was sick, and he was tired and battered and beaten and bruised. But he had to run because his life depended on it.

He reached into the quiet place inside him that had given him the strength to survive Sean's abuse, and he *ran*, even though his body was in no shape for it, took off as fast as his legs would carry him. And tried not to think about the hurt and the dizziness. More than once his feet caught on rocks or weeds, but mostly he managed to recover his balance without falling or even losing steam.

Twice he fell, and maybe he hurt himself, but he was too afraid to feel it if he was, and he didn't have time to look himself over and find out. Both times he got up and started running again without even looking back.

When he was a hundred yards from the house he finally did look back, to see how close the Children were. His lungs and throat were burning, and even though he was still running it had taken so much out of him that his run wasn't much faster than a walk.

The twins were still a hundred yards back, but there were more Children following him now, at least a dozen of them. The closest of them was only fifty yards behind him.

Jimmy thought of his mother, thought about how much
he wanted to see her again because it wasn't right to die
without telling her he loved her, and he forced his legs to
move faster again. And suddenly he was really running
again. But the effort made him even dizzier than he was
already, and it made the whole world look dim and grey.

I'm going to black out again.

He forced his eyes open as wide as they would go,
gasped in as much air as his lungs would take. Everything
still looked dim, but it didn't get worse. Not much worse,
anyway. But once he'd started gasping he couldn't stop,
and the gasping became wheezy and ragged. By the time
he'd gone another twenty yards his throat felt as though
someone with long, sharp fingernails had reached down
into it and tried to peel away the skin. His vocal cords felt
torn and loose, and he wanted to cough and cough and
cough, but he knew that if he did he'd lose his stride and
never get it back. Maybe he'd even collapse.

But he didn't collapse. He kept running, even though by
the time he reached the door of the house he was half-
convinced that he was already dead, and what was left of
him was just imagining that it was trying to get away. Dead
or not, it didn't matter, he told himself. He had to keep
trying. If he stopped trying he really would die.

The door to the house, thank God, was wide open—not
even closed, much less locked. He stepped through the
doorway and slammed the door closed behind him, without taking the time to turn around or even to break his
stride. It was a good thing that he didn't. The closest of the
Children was so close that he didn't have time to stop;
Christian ran into the door that suddenly materialized six
inches from his face.

Jimmy heard the impact, realized what had happened,
and turned around to lock the door before the other boy
could recover.

"Dad!" he screamed.

Suddenly Christian's fist was punching through the cardboard that covered the door's broken window, and his
hand reached in to twist open the lock.

"Dad!" he shouted again. But Dad wasn't answering.
Dad wasn't home. Jimmy was home, but he was all alone
and there were Children everywhere outside, breaking

into the house. Breaking into the house, planning to kidnap him again.

He grabbed Christian's hand while it was still trying to find the lock, yanked it *up* and *down* and *in*, raking it across the shards of window glass still wedged in the window frame. The glass bit deep into Christian's arm and dug a furrow through his flesh that ran from his wrist to his elbow. It must have torn open an artery or a major vein, because suddenly there was blood *everywhere*, not just bleeding but gushing and shooting all over the door, the carpeting underneath it, all across the front of Jimmy's already bloodstained shirt.

Christian screamed and yanked his arm back. As he did he caught it on the glass again, cutting it again, and even deeper this time. Jimmy let go, and he heard the boy go tumbling into the yard, still screaming.

The front door, Jimmy thought, *if this one's not locked, I bet it isn't either.* He ran fast as he could across the living room and through the foyer. He was right: the door was hanging half-open. If there were Children on the other side of it Jimmy didn't even want to know; he slammed it closed and twisted home the deadbolt without bothering to look outside.

The front door, thank God, was heavy, solid wood—it would take, Jimmy thought, a battering ram to get through it with the deadbolt locked. It was one thing, at least, that he wouldn't have to worry about again.

Which was good, because there were by Jimmy's count at least two dozen ways to get into a house like this if you didn't mind being obvious or making a little noise. Like, for instance, the noise that was coming from the master bedroom on the far side of the house.

A window opening. In dad's bedroom.

Jimmy didn't hurry to dad's bedroom as much as maybe he should have. But he'd climbed through windows before himself—in his own house back in New Jersey—and he knew that it always took longer than you'd expect, and it left you real vulnerable for most of that time.

Jimmy walked to the master bedroom. He stopped along the way to get the broom out of the kitchen cabinet.

When he got there Jan Williams had already climbed about a third of the way through the window. He took the broom in both hands, as though it were a pike, and braced himself to pound and poke her with it. But Jimmy found himself freezing up when he went to charge her. He almost laughed at himself when he realized why.

You don't hit girls. Especially not with heavy things like sticks that might hurt them. His dad had taught Jimmy not to hit other kids when he was so young that now he could only barely remember it. And dad had always disapproved especially of hitting girls.

Jimmy knew right from wrong, and he knew even now, even under these circumstances, that it wasn't right to hurt other people. But he also had enough common sense to know that there were times when you did things that were wrong because you had to. Either that or you just rolled over and died.

So even though it made him feel bad about himself, Jimmy ran straight at Jan Williams, using the handle end of the broom like it was a lance. He caught her square in the chest, and the end of the broom slid hard up along her ribs, over her throat, and then jammed itself into the soft underpart of her chin. The impact slammed her mouth closed, and her tongue or her lip or maybe the inside of her cheek must have got caught between her teeth, because bright red-thick blood spilled out between her lips and started running all down along her chin and neck. Jimmy thought she probably would have screamed, but he kept pressing back and forth with the broom handle, and Jan couldn't get her mouth open wide enough to make a noise like a scream. What she did do was grunt through her nose, long and loud and coarse.

But she kept going, kept climbing in over the sill and in through the window. Or kept trying to, at least. When Jimmy saw that she wasn't going to back off on her own he pulled the broom handle back for a moment and then shoved forward again, this time right into Jan's diaphragm. She gasped involuntarily when he did that, and an instant later she lost her balance and fell back out the window.

When she was gone Jimmy dropped the broom, stepped up to the window, closed and locked it. That wouldn't stop them from breaking through the glass, he thought, but he was pretty sure they wouldn't want to climb through a window with broken glass all around it.

Jimmy took a deep breath. *I'm going to make it. If I can keep them out of here long enough someone will show up and chase them away. Dad's got to come home sooner or later.*

He left the master bedroom and went around the rest of the house closing and locking the windows.

It was quiet outside as he locked them. Unsettlingly quiet.

Then, finally, it occurred to him: *The phone! All I have to do is call the police, and they'll come here, and then this'll all be over.*

He crossed the living room and lifted the receiver from the wall-mounted cradle that it hung from. Even with all the racket outside, the phone's dial tone was loud enough to hear before Jimmy even raised it to his ear to listen.

Soon, he thought. *Soon now, it'll all be done.*

Jimmy tapped out 911 on the phone's keypad. He listened as the phone rang twice, and then a woman answered.

"Hello. Can I help you?"

It was a strange way for the police to answer a telephone, Jimmy thought. And her voice didn't sound exactly right, either—it just sounded like somebody answering a telephone. But at least she was answering it, and that was good. Jimmy had heard how sometimes when you dialed 911 it was busy and busy and busy.

He calmed himself, forced himself to think clearly as he could, to speak as clearly as possible.

"I'm Jimmy Tompkins," he said. "I'm at home in Green Hill, and they're all outside, trying to *get* me again." He didn't know the street address of the house, yet—didn't even know the name of the street the house was on. But he'd been missing for days; by now half the state probably knew him by name.

"We'll be there just as soon as we can, Jimmy Tompkins. You just sit tight," the woman said, friendly and familiar as though she'd known him all her life.

"Okay. But hurry, please. I'm scared."

"We sure will," she said, and then she hung up, and the line was just a crackly electronic hum.

Now, he thought, *all I have to do is wait.* He went to the living room sofa and sat down. It was almost hard to do; his

body was so keyed up and full of adrenaline that even
standing still would have been a chore. Sitting was almost
impossible. But what else was there to do?

The way it turned out, of course, wasn't as simple as just
sitting in the house and waiting. How could it be?

Twenty-five minutes after Jimmy sat down to wait, he
was still waiting, and then he began to smell the smoke. He
knew what had happened before he even went to check.

*Oh my God. They've set the house on fire. Why aren't the
police here yet?*

Jimmy got up off the sofa and tried to dial the police
again, but now the line was dead. *They've cut the line.*

He tried to figure out where the smoke was coming
from. It only took a moment to find it; the Children had
built a bonfire in front of the back door, and the smoke
he'd smelled was coming in through the door's broken
window.

I've got to put it out, he thought. *I've got to get some
water and put the fire out.*

He went to the cabinet under the kitchen sink, got out
the brown plastic tub that dad used to do the dishes, and
filled it from the tap. That seemed to take forever; by the
time it was half-full Jimmy was impatient enough that he
left the tap running, took the tub, and carried it to the
door.

*The window. I've got to pour it through the broken win-
dow. If I open the door the fire will come right in.*

There were already flames licking in through that window. Jimmy held the tub up to one corner of it and poured
the water out.

It did some good at least; the fire quit trying to tongue its
way through the broken window, and Jimmy heard the
sound of water sizzling and steaming as it tried to quench
the fire. Jimmy ran back to the sink and filled the tub again;
by the time he got back to the door, the flames were just as
high as they had been to begin with.

The fire is getting ahead of me.

It was, too: the paint at the bottom of his side of the door
was beginning to singe, just from the heat outside.

*I've got to keep trying. If I can even slow it down a little,
maybe I can hold out long enough for the police to get*

here. They'll have to let me go if there are grown-ups around.

So he poured the tub of water out the window and went back to the sink to get more. But it was even more a losing battle than he realized; when he tried to take the third tub of water to the door, the fire had taken hold inside the house, and he couldn't get anywhere near it. There were flames bulging everywhere along the door and on the walls around it, and the smoke was getting thick—thicker the higher up it was, because of the way heat made it rise. *In a minute or two it'll be too thick to breathe unless I'm crawling around on the floor.*

He threw the water at the part of the door where the flames were brightest, hoping it would help at least a little. But it didn't help at all. It made the flames flicker a little, and it turned the smoke steamy and even thicker. It burned his eyes and made them tear up; when he blinked it got even worse.

I'd better get as far from this as I can. And maybe get a T-shirt or something to breathe through.

He got down on his hands and knees and crawled toward the dresser in his bedroom. But the bedroom was even hotter afire than the back door; he only got as far as the bedroom door before he had to stop.

Someone must have thrown something burning through the bedroom window. I bet the bed and blankets would catch fire fast. They'd burn fast, too.

If they were throwing fire in through the windows then no place was safe. Except, maybe, for the front door—there weren't any windows anywhere near it. And he could hold out there until the fire was almost right next to him and still get out when he had to.

But the fire was everywhere in the house, and it burned hot and fast. Three minutes after Jimmy scrunched himself against the thick wood of the front door, the flames in the bedroom had begun to eat their way through the wall beside him.

That was when it finally sunk through to Jimmy that the police weren't going to get to him in time—not soon enough and maybe not even at all. And there were Children outside, who wanted to do lots worse to Jimmy than kill him.

I could let myself die here—burn to death in the fire. It might be better than whatever they'll do to me if they get ahold of me.

He thought about that for a moment, and finally decided that it was the best thing. But instinct took hold of him as the fire began to sear the skin of his leg; he threw the door open and crawled out away from the fire. Fresh air made the fire behind him roar to life, singeing his clothes and the hair on the back of his head.

By the time he got five feet out the door two of the Children had their hands on him. They grabbed him by the arms and dragged him across the lawn to Roberta.

The look on her face was bloodthirsty, murderous. For a moment he thought she was going to kill him, right then and there. But she didn't; she just spat into his eyes and smiled at him.

"You should have stayed in the fire and let yourself burn to death," she said. "It would have been a lot more pleasant for you." Her smile grew even more dementedly gleeful. "But I'm glad you didn't."

She laughed, and turned around and started to walk away from him.

Before she'd gone three steps Jimmy said, "Wait," and she turned back around and looked at him. She seemed surprised and a little appalled that he'd had the nerve to say anything. "If you kill me, it'll be a lot of trouble for you. Sooner or later the police will come looking for you, and they'll keep looking until they find you. You don't really want that, do you? If you let me go, dad and me will get out of here so fast it'll make your head spin. We won't tell anybody, and we won't ever come back, I can promise you that. Wouldn't it be a lot better for everybody?"

Jimmy had expected her to look at him thoughtfully and at least consider it. But that wasn't what happened at all; suddenly she seemed threatened and enraged, and then she went wild. He'd only just finished talking when her kicking foot slammed into his groin for the first time. She punched him, again and again and again. He was still conscious when the force of her blows knocked him out of the arms of the two Children who held him, but he didn't stay conscious long after that.

Roberta beat Jimmy to within an inch of his life. But for all the damage that she did, she never killed his heart.

Roberta saw Jimmy black out. She knew when he was already too hurt to feel any of what she was doing to him. But she was too angry to care; she kept pounding and pounding on him for another ten minutes, until her temper was completely spent.

When she was done, Jimmy wasn't just hurt. He was *damaged*. Important things inside him were crushed and bruised and broken. He was bleeding internally—bleeding slowly, but steadily, from parts of his body that would not be able to stem the flow of blood without the help of a surgeon.

Roberta was dimly aware of the fact that Jimmy was bleeding to death. If she'd bothered to guess how long he could live with that kind of internal bleeding, she'd have guessed that he had about another twelve hours. But she would have been wrong.

At the rate he was bleeding, only a miracle could have kept Jimmy alive more than another six hours. A miracle, or a hospital's operating room.

But she didn't guess, because she didn't care. He'd be alive long enough to make it to the sacrifice tonight, she was sure of that. And as far as Roberta was concerned, it was all that really mattered.

Sadie Johnson set down the telephone and let out a soft, high-pitched sigh. She really wasn't cut out for this sort of work, and she knew it. She wasn't happy about missing *General Hospital* and the other soaps; if she'd given it a little more thought she wouldn't have let her cousin Madeline talk her into temping for the sheriff's department. There was some kind of a hubbub going on, and everyone who worked for the sheriff was busy out someplace in the boondocks—Green Hill, Sadie thought, but she wasn't sure.

When Madeline had first collared her, working for the sheriff for a few days had sounded like a great idea. Sadie could always use a little pin money. But Sadie missed her routine, and the work was dull. The phone almost never rang. And when it did it was some old lady with a cat up a tree, or somebody complaining that the good old boys were getting a little too rowdy down at Pete's Tavern, or just some kid, pulling a prank.

Like this one, just now. This boy gets on the phone and calls up the sheriff from his home, lets on like the bogeyman is outside, trying to get in. If there was anything at all outside his house, Sadie thought, it was his mom. Probably the little brat had locked her out of the house and she was ready to give him a licking. She probably *did* look like the bogeyman, if the kid had done that to her. *Yeah,* Sadie thought, *that's probably what it is.*

Even so, she dutifully wrote the call up and took the paper to the radio desk. She put it in the stack with the stranded cats and the good old boys and the pranks. There were half a dozen others ahead of it.

Forty minutes later the man at the front finally got to Jimmy's call, and when he read it his eyes bugged out. But by then it was already too late.

CHAPTER

TWENTY-EIGHT

THOMAS WAS STILL SITTING ON THE ROCK, CARVING A
shape he wasn't yet sure of, when he saw Jimmy Tompkins
running across the briar field. He'd gone back to the rock
and his carving after they'd finally got Mr. Tompkins
packed away and put into the ambulance.

If anyone had asked him why he was carving, he
wouldn't have had an answer to give. He'd never been
much for carving—he'd done so little of it, in fact, that he
barely even knew how to go about it. But early this morning he'd come across an old hunk of weathered pine
branch, shaped almost like a club, and as soon as he'd seen

it he knew he had to carve it. He'd been wrapped up in carving the branch ever since.

Thomas was clearer of mind and stronger of will than most Children were after they'd left childhood and the Stone behind. He could see Ben Tompkins fall ill right in front of him and not have it vanish from his mind as soon as he saw it. Illness, after all, is a natural part of life—certainly unfortunate, and often very sad, but not inherently evil. But not even Thomas was clear enough of mind to recognize as an adult the favorite club he used to beat small animals as a Child.

He actually heard Jimmy Tompkins before he saw him, heard the sound of him running somewhere not far at all behind him, panting and gasping for air.

Isn't Jimmy supposed to be missing or something? Thomas thought so, but he wasn't all that sure. The fact that Jimmy had disappeared was bad enough news that it wouldn't really stay with Thomas. When he thought about it at all he thought in terms of Jimmy's maybe having hiked out to the lake in the hills for a little camping and fishing . . . and so maybe Jimmy forgot to tell his dad, it wasn't that big a sin, was it? Well, maybe it was, but getting grown-ups worried, if you asked Thomas, was just a part of being a boy. Grown-ups were going to worry about you anyway, so why fret over it? Never *really* did anybody any harm . . .

That was the way Thomas thought about it, anyway. While it was true that he hadn't always felt that way, as far as he remembered he always had.

Thomas was tempted to call out to Jimmy, to ask him how the fishing had been—the boy had gone past only a few yards away, but what with the tree behind Thomas, Jimmy couldn't possibly have seen him until he was already gone by, and only then if he'd looked back. Thomas didn't think it was especially neighborly of Jimmy to be in such a hurry, but then people always said that not being neighborly was the sort of thing you had to expect from Northerners. You had to make allowances for them, and you had to be extra friendly to them to get them used to the idea of friendliness.

Thomas was about to holler Jimmy's name, even though by this point the boy was at least sixty yards away, when he heard a whole stampede of people running toward him from behind. He turned and peered around the tree and saw twenty or thirty of the Children—he still thought of them capitalized, though if you'd asked him why point-blank he wouldn't even have heard the question—thundering in his direction over the rocky-dusty ground.

If that don't beat all, Thomas thought. *What are they doing, playing tag in reverse or something? With the whole bunch of them supposed to tag just the one?*

In the time it took to wonder what was going on the Children had passed him. Thomas kept watching them as they ran downhill and across the briar, and finally to the house the Tompkinses had rented.

It was right about then that it began to get through to him that something was wrong. There wasn't anything friendly or playful about the way Jimmy ran into his house and slammed the door behind him, or the way Christian couldn't stop in time to keep from running into it. Then Christian was standing real close to that door, fumbling around and looking like he was trying to break into it. A moment later he screamed, and jerked back and forth like someone inside the house was yanking and pushing on his arm. When Christian finally got himself free he went rolling head-over-heels across the grass, his arm *bleeding*—bleeding so much and so red that even from here Thomas could see a bright crimson line across the grass, and Christian himself looked as though he'd taken a bath in blood.

And Thomas, Thomas whose heart was now his own, whose soul was now the clean pure soul that God had made it to be, remembered.

Oh my God.

His life—all of his life, not just the shadow of it the Stone hadn't stolen away—played by before his eyes. Something surfaced in his mind about people seeing their lives play through in the moment of their death, and for just a second he wondered if he was going to die now.

No. Not dying. I'm being born all over again.

His mind paid no attention as his eyes watched Jan try to break into Jimmy's house. He saw but didn't see her get beaten back, almost as bloody as Christian. It didn't even register when he saw them begin to build the bonfire at the Tompkinses' back door.

Thomas was remembering, remembering every horrible thing he'd done in his life. And he was ashamed.

It took twenty minutes for the shock of regaining his past to wear thin. When his head was finally clear the Tompkins house was hard afire.

They must have kidnapped the poor kid, and he must have somehow got free and got back to his house. And now they're trying to burn him to death. Either that or smoke him out of there.

I've got to get help fast. That house is burning fast.

For days there had been sheriffs everywhere, doing no good at all to judge from their results. And now, when there was actually something they needed to do, where the hell were they?

They'd have to be on the other side of town not to see that fire. The way the wind is blowing, they wouldn't even be able to see the smoke from there.

There was an awful lot of wind, now that Thomas thought about it. More than you could reasonably expect on a clear day like this. *The Stone.* It had to be what was making all this wind. But the Stone wasn't much good at moving real things, things that had weight. Even things like wind, with almost no weight at all. *But it could if it had to. If that was the only thing in the world that it was trying to do. And maybe that's why it lost track of me long enough for me to remember myself.*

That thought hit Thomas hard, burned into him with a great and terrible sadness. *When it finds me again,* he thought, *it'll take all of it away from me again.*

The hurry was even worse than he'd thought. How much longer would the Stone need to make that wind? It was covering for the Children—it had to, or there'd be sheriff's deputies all over them—but how much longer would it be necessary?

And how long after that, Thomas wondered, would it be before the Stone noticed that he'd slipped away from its spell, and set about digging its hooks back into him? Not long at all. Five minutes. Maybe ten. Twenty at the outside. The Stone wasn't omnipotent; it couldn't see everyone in town in a single glance. But everyone in Green Hill had his own place in the Stone's heart. There was no way it would be long before it noticed him.

Thomas had, at most, about half an hour more of life as a real and whole human being, and he knew it. It is to his credit that he didn't spend that time on himself. Instead, he spent it trying to save someone else's life.

Jimmy Tompkins's.

Thomas turned away from the Children and the burning house, and took off running up and over Green Hill with everything he had. But even though he ran as fast as he could it took him twenty minutes to find the deputies. It took him that long because all of them were in one place, and that was the last place on earth he would have expected them.

Gathered outside his own house.

Still, it would have been selfish of him to wonder just then why the law had come calling on his family, and there wasn't room for selfishness in Thomas's heart. Not when someone's life was at stake.

A dozen of the deputies stood in a knot in Thomas's backyard; their backs were to him as he approached them.

"Jimmy Tompkins!" he shouted as he grew almost near enough to touch the closest deputy. "He's—You've got to—"

And then the deputies, who hadn't even seemed to notice he was coming until he'd shouted, stepped aside. And Thomas saw the worst two things that he ever saw as long as he lived.

The first was his mother, his mommy who'd never had a sad moment as long as Thomas had been alive. Her face was warped and twisted with grief; her eyes red with veiny bloodshot and smeared with tears.

The second was his brother Sean, empty-eyed and drooling on himself. His dead brother, breathing.

The blood roared in Thomas's ears. The quick wind blowing all around him went still and dead all at once, and he felt the world spinning unknowably all around him.

He felt the Stone touch inside his mind, and, just before it changed him back to something he was never meant to be, he smelled smoke from a house afire.

Then all that Thomas knew was that there were an awful lot of people around acting strangely, and that his brother Sean had an awfully funny look about him.

* * *

Something was wrong, and Peterson knew it. Something besides just the obvious disasters—like this boy, Sean Brady, suddenly showing up a drooling idiot. Or his brother Thomas running at them out of nowhere, screaming at the top of his lungs like the sky was falling, and then acting like he didn't even know he'd done anything peculiar.

He could cope with people acting strange. It gave you something to be suspicious about, at least. Something almost concrete. But Peterson had been watching the boy's face as he saw his brother. And he'd seen something that looked almost like a transformation of the spirit. That was the only way he could think of it, even if it did sound kind of silly to be thinking in the same terms that the pastor used on those Sundays when he was especially ornery.

The strangest part of it was the way that freak wind had died just as Thomas had seen his brother. Peterson wasn't inclined to be superstitious. Even so, just thinking about that wind made the thin hair on his back bristle.

"How come you're all looking at me like that?" Thomas asked. Peterson had heard the boy ask that question at least half a dozen times now. It was beginning to annoy him.

So was the fact that every deputy on the evening shift had used the excitement here with Sean and Thomas as an excuse not to get down to business. All of them goofing off here like this was just the sort of thing that made it likely that something important was going on someplace else. Luck always did that to you when you screwed around.

He growled at the nearest of them. "Get that grin off your face, huh, Seymore? Why the hell aren't you out there keeping an eye on this town, like you're supposed to be? Quit messing around and get to work, how about it?" He waved at the crowd, most of whom seemed to enjoy seeing Seymore get put to work. "The rest of you, too—get to it. Ain't any call for you here."

They grumbled almost in unison, but all of them began to head off, all but Myron White, who, like Peterson, was still hanging on from the day shift.

Peterson squatted, so that he could get a good look into Thomas's eyes as he spoke to him. "Now then, son. What's this you came up here screaming about Jimmy Tompkins?"

Thomas blinked, shrugged. "I was saying something about Jimmy Tompkins? You sure about that, sir? I haven't heard from Jimmy since we had dinner with him a few days back."

Peterson sighed and rubbed his eyes with his fingertips. "Of course I'm sure, Thomas. Don't be silly with me. Ask your mama over there. Ask Deputy White here. You came running in here like a bolt of lightning, screaming Jimmy's name at the top of your lungs. I know you did it. You know you did it. So why you handing me this bull hooey?"

Thomas smiled tolerantly, easily, as though he was thinking that grown-ups were a class of people you just had to humor sometimes. "If you say I did, sir, then I certainly must have. But I surely don't recall any such thing."

Peterson almost wanted to cry. *God* he was tired. And here this kid was, sweetly and pleasantly letting him know that he had to be out of his mind. He turned to White. "Myron, I'm not going out of my mind, am I? Tell me I'm not going out of my mind, please?"

White groaned and shook his head.

"Excuse me, Deputy Peterson," Mrs. Brady said, "but I can't say as I recall anything like you're talking about."

Peterson grunted and looked up at White. "I can't cope with this, Myron. I've been up since I-don't-know-when this morning, and I just don't think I can handle it anymore. I don't think this is going to go anywhere at all, but we've got to do it anyway. Do me a favor, would you? Get somebody to take these folks down to the department and ask 'em some questions?"

White nodded. "Sure," he said. He looked at least as tired as Peterson felt; Peterson felt guilty about dropping more work on the man's lap. But Peterson could feel himself getting frustrated, and he was tired and ornery enough that he might lose his temper if he didn't get himself away from this nonsense.

"Thanks, Myron." White nodded again; he was already on the radio. Peterson nodded at the two Bradys who still had something of their wits about them and headed back toward his cruiser. *God* he wanted this business to be over and done with. He felt completely out of his element—

confused and a little frightened and completely unsure he was doing the right thing. Maybe part of that was just the fact that he was so tired; he wasn't sleeping well at all. But at least some of it was that he really *was* out of his depth. He didn't know anything about kidnapping or sick-hearted children. Being a deputy in a county like this one meant coping with the good old boys when they got carried away or got a little too drunk. Sometimes there was violence when the boys got out of hand—most often when one of them got it into his head that he could lay hands on a wife or a girlfriend—but Peterson knew how it cope with that sort of bad. He didn't like it, but he knew how to deal with it.

When one of the boys wouldn't calm down, you took out the nightstick and reminded him how he was supposed to behave. It wasn't something you liked doing, but you did it. The worst that came of it was that maybe you weren't careful enough and you had to haul the guy down to the emergency room for a few stitches before you took him in and locked him up.

But this situation . . . ? What could you do about circumstances like these? The closest thing he had to a suspect was this gentle-looking kid, Thomas Brady. Maybe he *did* know something he wasn't letting on. But how were you supposed to get it out of him—with a nightstick? The idea made Peterson sick to his stomach. If that was what it was going to take to get the Tompkins boy back, then as far as Peterson was concerned, Jimmy was going to have to stay wherever he was. There was no way he was going to start beating on children. Not for any reason, not for any cause, no matter how needful it was.

Peterson was still trying to figure out what he was supposed to do about it when he turned on the two-way radio, mostly out of habit, and heard the call go out that Jimmy Tompkins was at his house and screaming for help—forty-five minutes ago.

"God*damn,*" he said. Peterson floored the accelerator; a minute and a half later he was pulling into the Tompkins driveway.

The driveway—and Ben's car, which was parked in it—were the only things on the lot that were still intact. There were already a couple of deputies in the front yard, trying to get ahold of the fire department. If Peterson had turned on the radio in the cruiser he would have heard about the fire before he saw it.

Peterson felt his gorge rising. He clenched his teeth and forced it back down.

It was dusk already, too dark to see much of anything but the light from the fire. He got out of the car and walked over toward the deputies.

"Any idea how it got started?"

One of the two shrugged; the other shook his head.

If it had been just a little lighter they would have seen streaks of fresh blood in the grass. But no one noticed those bloodstains until the next morning, and by then it was too late for them to make any difference at all.

Peterson spent twenty more minutes in Green Hill, watching the fire burn, and finally headed home again. When he got there he fell asleep deeply and almost at once. But even though he slept, he slept badly, and his dreams were nightmares.

CHAPTER
TWENTY-NINE

TIM WAS STILL SITTING ON THE FLOOR OF THE STONE'S cave, trembling, when they threw what was left of Jimmy back into the cage. Except for the trembling, he hadn't moved at all since the Stone had killed Sean. The Children ignored him as they went by; they ignored him again, a few minutes later, when four of them came in and lifted the Stone from the pedestal. They didn't have to tell Tim where they were taking the Stone; he knew exactly the same way they did, without even being told. The four Children were carrying it out to the field, the one with the sacrifice pit. There was going to be a ceremony tonight. A ceremony and a sacrifice.

He managed to stop trembling a few minutes after they'd taken the Stone. A little while after that he managed to stand up and leave the cave.

There's nothing I can do. I did what I could to help Jimmy escape, and they caught him again anyway.

It was true. Tim was lucky to be alive as it was, and he knew it.

I can't do anything more by myself. I probably shouldn't even have tried to do this much by myself.

But he couldn't just go to the sheriffs, either. If they listened to him—and he couldn't really depend on them to do that; grown-ups didn't always have as much sense as you needed them to have—if they listened to him, they'd probably end up throwing him in jail along with everyone else. Tim didn't want to go to jail, not now, not ever. He'd seen jail on TV, and it scared him something powerful.

Daddy. Daddy already knows *that something's going on. And daddy knows about the Children. Daddy can help somehow. He* has *to.*

Tim felt his hands trembling as he walked downhill, toward home. Daddy was almost as scary as the Children were. It was dangerous when daddy was drinking, and daddy almost always went drinking after work.

Please God, let daddy be sober. Please.

But, of course, daddy wasn't sober.

There were two things in Bob Hanson's heart that dictated every other fact about him, and neither of those two things could abide the other.

First and foremost was his love for his people and the place he lived in. Bob Hanson had known and loved Green Hill all his life, and nothing could change that love. And, loving, his heart strove hard to be proud of the town and of its people.

The other thing that ruled him was shame. Bob Hanson *remembered* his Childhood. Remembered cruelty, and the lust for blood, and doing things so horrible that just knowing that the memory was there could make him ache. And he was ashamed of what he'd done.

There was no reconciling the two factions of his heart; wasn't even the possibility of reconciliation. The only peace he ever had came out of a bottle of liquor, and even drunk sometimes Bob found himself in pain. He'd spent years trying to be at ease with himself, but lately he'd come to realize that nothing could change his past, and nothing could make it right to be ashamed of the things he loved, or ease away the love he had for the people he'd known and lived with all his life.

And the only thing to do was to see life through to its conclusion and hope that whatever came after was better.

Since he'd resigned himself, Bob had begun drinking even more than ever. And when Tim came in the door that final night, Bob Hanson was already drunk half out of his senses.

Tim smelled whiskey as soon as he opened the front door. Whiskey was trouble, bad trouble. Daddy liked hard liquor, but it always did bad things to his stomach, and sometimes it gave him headaches, too. Daddy was always a gruff drunk, but when he was drunk and hurting he could be cruel.

"Daddy. . . ?"

Daddy grunted back at him from the living room. Tim bit his lip and closed the door behind him. The TV was on, its sound so soft and low that at first he hadn't noticed it. Daddy was sitting in his favorite chair, watching his whiskey glass, really, more than the television. Daddy looked up from it when Tim came in. The expression on his face wasn't anything like Tim had expected—not angry or mean or even bad-tempered. Daddy looked concerned, in fact.

Downright worried.

"What's going on, Tim-boy? Are you okay? What's going on with that Tompkins boy?" Daddy slurred his words. He was as drunk as Tim had thought he was, but not bad-drunk. Tim always thought of it as silly-drunk when dad was like this. But daddy wasn't being silly at all. Things were too serious to be silly about them.

"I'm okay, daddy. Kind of scared, I guess." Tim's heart was racing; the words were trying to jam up in his throat. He'd never spoken about the Stone to anyone, not in his whole life. Not even to daddy, though daddy had spoken to him about it.

Daddy coughed and took a deep drink from his whiskey

glass. "You want to tell me what's going on? You think I can help? It's up to you. You don't have to, not if you don't want."

"I got to, I guess. Got to talk to somebody. Nobody's better to talk to than you."

His father frowned. "There's nobody else you *could* talk to. Nobody else in this town remembers. I *know.* No one in this town over the age of thirteen could even hear you. Ask them about the Children and they blink at you and suddenly they don't even remember the last four hours. What good's it going to do you to talk to someone like that? No good at all, I'll tell you that."

Tim was unconsciously biting his lower lip again. As his father spoke Tim's teeth clenched harder and harder, until suddenly the flavor of blood made Tim aware of what he was doing. He forced his teeth to let go of his lip. The bloody taste was sickening; it made him want to spit. But there wasn't anywhere to spit in the living room, and this wasn't a good time to just get up and leave.

Don't, Tim heard a small voice say from a corner of his mind. *Don't tell him.* The voice wasn't the Stone, and it wasn't himself, exactly. It was . . . a part of him. His fear, maybe. Or maybe something wiser than that. *It'll be bad if you tell him.* But this wasn't a time for getting too scared to talk, any more than it was a time for spitting on the rug.

"Jimmy Tompkins hurt the Stone," Tim said.

No!

"And when the Stone came to it made us get him. We would have done it if the Stone had just told us to, but it was so mad that it didn't bother. It just picked us up and moved us, like we were puppets or something."

Daddy was beginning to look real grim, but he wasn't saying anything.

"They're going to kill him tonight, out in the sacrifice field. I tried to help him get loose, but they just caught him again. And now they're—"

Daddy blanched, and his eyes bugged out like someone on TV having a heart attack. "You did *what?*"

No!

Daddy was turning red and angry already. Tim felt scared, scared for his life. "I tried to *help* him, daddy. You just can't let people go around *killing* people. You said—you said I shouldn't ever do anything that—that—"

That set daddy off, like a spark touching gasoline. "I told you to watch out for your conscience, *boy,*" he shouted. "I didn't *ever* tell you to betray your own. What kind of a lowlife are you trying to grow up to be?"

No!

Tim couldn't say anything. Fear had him paralyzed, and he was beginning to want to cry.

"Answer me, damn it!"

Tim had seen his father have fits like this one before. The only thing that had ever helped at all was apologizing. Even that didn't help all the time. "I'm sorry, daddy. I try to do right. Honest I do. Please don't hit me."

Daddy's eyes were dark, shrunken beads now, pulled tight with angriness. *"Shit."* He gulped down the rest of his whiskey. "You've got accounts to settle, boy. I'm going to haul you down to that field and make sure you settle them." He banged his empty glass down on the end table. Stood up and growled at Tim.

Tim could hear the sound of his own heart pounding in his ears. *He's going to tell the Children. He's going to tell them.* "No, daddy. Please don't. I'll do what you want. Please let me tell them myself." *They'll kill me if he tells. He'll tell them, and they'll hear him, and they'll kill me.* "They'll kill me, daddy—don't make them kill me. Please—"

Tim never got to finish the sentence. Daddy slapped him backhanded right across the mouth, only it was almost more like a punch than a slap, since the part of daddy's hand that hit him was the knuckles. It left a lot of blood inside Tim's mouth, and made a couple of teeth feel itchy-numb and loose.

"Maybe they will kill you," daddy said. "If you ask me, I say that if they kill you then you deserve to be dead."

There was only one thing left for Tim to do—run. Run as fast and as far as he could, and never come back. It took him two seconds to realize it, and it only took him another second to decide to do it, even though he knew it was a decision that would change his life forever.

A second and a half more, and he was half-way across the room, already running for his life.

But another second after that daddy had his hands on him, before he could even reach the front door.

"Don't try it, you little cocksucker. You think you can get away from me? Who the fuck you think you are?—Answer me, damn it."

But Tim couldn't answer; he was too busy screaming and screaming in stark, raving terror, screaming until Daddy got tired of hearing the sound of it and belted him under the jaw to shut him up.

Tim tried to struggle, but when he did daddy cuffed him again and grabbed him by the ear and pulled up on it so hard that Tim had to stand on tiptoe to keep it from feeling like it was going to rip loose from his skull.

"You're coming with me now," daddy said, "and don't try any more shit, huh? Unless you want a hole in your head where this ear used to be."

Tim tried to say that he'd do like he was told, but the only sounds he could get his throat to make were small grunting noises.

Daddy grabbed his whiskey bottle and opened the door, dragging Tim with him by the ear. He led Tim over Green Hill and through the woods on the other side of it. Led him to the sacrifice field. He used Tim's ear like it was a leash; he didn't let go of it even for a moment. Maybe that was sensible, even if it was cruel—Tim would have run for his life again if he'd even been free for an instant.

When they got to the field, it wasn't like Tim expected at all, and daddy had even more surprises.

Roberta went bug-eyed when she saw daddy come out of the woods dragging Tim. Daddy didn't even seem to notice the way she looked so frightened. That was bad for daddy. It wasn't safe or smart to get Roberta feeling threatened.

"You all ought to be more careful," daddy said. He let go of Tim's ear and shoved him to the ground at the center of the clearing. Tim only barely managed to stop himself from sliding into the pit. "Ain't too smart of you, letting my boy be a knife in your back."

The Stone shone bright, furious red behind Roberta. *It's seeing through Roberta's eyes,* Tim thought. *And it's upset. Threatened, maybe worse than Roberta is.* Tim was always

real careful around Roberta; she was nasty and vile and
mean, but that didn't hurt her insight at all. Roberta had as
sharp an eye as anyone Tim knew. Tim didn't think the
Stone would have been able to see what daddy was doing
without Roberta there. If it could have it would have seen
him long ago, and then everything would have been different.

But daddy wasn't seeing that at all. Maybe he was just
too drunk. Maybe he just didn't have any sense at all. "My
son, here—watch out for him. He's the one who let that
Tompkins boy loose on you. You don't keep an eye on him,
there's no telling what he might do to you next."

Roberta hissed through her teeth and looked daddy
right in the eye. "What are you? How much do you know?"

*The Stone doesn't like surprises. I bet it's real unhappy
finding out that an adult has known about it all along.*

"How much do you think I know? I'm here, ain't I? You
see me looking dumb-faced like I can't remember my
name?" Daddy took a long slug out of his whiskey bottle
and turned to leave.

But daddy wasn't going anywhere, even if he hadn't
noticed it yet. There were Children all around him, close
enough to touch on every side. The first of them had tried
to tackle him before he realized what was happening.
Once he did realize, though, he gave them a good fight—
he managed to beat a couple of them away with the whiskey bottle, and then the bottle shattered when it hit Eileen
Williams's head. After that he managed to cut up at least a
dozen of the Children before five of them, jumping at him
all at the same time, managed to pull him down from
behind.

Tim tried to slip away while everyone was concentrating
on daddy, but he only got as far as the edge of the woods
before Roberta stepped out of nowhere and sunk her
hands into the soft parts of his throat.

"Don't be so quick to leave," she whispered to him,
smiling. "The sacrifice is starting earlier tonight than I'd
expected. Your father's first, but you'll be our guest tonight, too. An honored guest."

Over in the center of the clearing, Tim's father
screamed as they strung him up over the pit.

CHAPTER

THIRTY

THE SEDATIVE WORE OFF AROUND EIGHT O'CLOCK.

Or didn't wear off, exactly; a few minutes after eight the
effects of the injection the doctor had given Ben, to help
him sleep, wore thin enough to let him wake.

Jimmy! he thought as he opened his eyes and saw the
harsh fluorescent light of the emergency room cubicle
where they'd parked his stretcher.

Maybe a part of him knew without having to be told, just
as you'd expect a father to know, that horrible things were
happening to his son. And maybe not. Maybe the truth was
that Ben was frazzled and wrecked, compulsive and ob-
sessed from his son's kidnapping. It wouldn't be possible to

say for certain; both effects feel pretty much the same, no matter whose shoes you're standing in.

Jimmy's in trouble. I know it. Wherever the hell I am, I've got to get out of here. He could remember almost clearly talking to Thomas, and he had some dim recollection of the events after that—the sheriffs, the ambulance attendants, the ride to the hospital. The shot the doctor had given him, and then, a moment or two after that, nothing at all. *I'm in a hospital—probably in Tylerville. There certainly isn't a hospital in Green Hill, and Tylerville's the county seat. How in the hell am I going to get back there without a car?*

A nurse—a heavyset woman with short dark hair—was passing by.

"Pardon me, ma'am," Ben said to her. "But can you tell me how I go about checking out of here? I really do need to get back to my son."

The woman paused and raised an eyebrow at him. "The doctor who was working with you stepped away to get his dinner," she said. "I'm not sure he's done with you, and he'll certainly want to look you over before he signs you out. He may want to keep you in the hospital overnight."

Ben frowned and shook his head. His ears were roaring —most likely, he thought, from the sedative. "I'm sorry, ma'am, but it's urgent that I get back. I really can't wait that long. And I don't have time to stay here all night. Is there anything you can do to help me?"

"I'll see," the nurse said, "but I wouldn't hold my breath if I were you." Ben didn't have a chance to respond before she turned and started toward the front desk.

He almost didn't have the patience to wait for her at all. He did manage to make himself wait five minutes before he got up off the cot, and those five minutes felt as long to Ben as all the time since Jimmy had disappeared. Finally, he stood up and poked his head out of the cubicle, and saw that the nurse was chatting lazily with two people who looked like orderlies.

I'm going to scream. If I don't get up and do something now I'm going to scream. But what was there to do? Get up and walk out? How *was* he going to get back to Green Hill? *One problem at a time. It could be worse. At least I'm dressed.*

Ben didn't know what he would have done if they'd already transferred him into a room in the hospital and put him into one of those backless gowns. He couldn't imagine himself as anything but helpless dressed like that. But as it was he did what was simple and obvious: walked out into the corridor, turned away from the nurses, and found his way out of the hospital by dead reckoning. He walked with as much of an air of confidence as he could muster, and it must have helped, because neither of the two people he passed along the way questioned him.

Then he was outside in the warm, damp night, wondering what he was supposed to do next. It was dark here; he was thirty yards away from the brightly lit entrance to the emergency room. He'd just about decided to hitchhike when he saw the sheriff's car. He looked up, and noticed that the deputy who'd driven it was just going into the emergency room entrance. *He's here for me, I bet. I don't like that at all.* That was paranoia more likely than not, and Ben knew it. But he didn't think it was wise to ignore it.

He peeked into the patrol car, to see if there was anything inside that concerned him. The dash was bare; so were the seats.

But the door was unlocked, and the keys were in the ignition.

Oh God, now I'm thinking like a car thief. He opened the car door and thought about it long and hard for the space of two long, deep breaths. Then he got in the car and started the engine. *God help me, I am a thief.*

He backed the car out of the parking space, and a moment later he had it roaring out of the lot, onto the highway. It took him two minutes to find a street he recognized, and only ten minutes after that to get back to Green Hill.

The deputies and the firemen had already left when he pulled into the driveway of what had been the rented house. But the heat of the fire had been so great that after they'd left, the embers had managed to rekindle themselves, and where they met the damp char the ruins were smoking.

* * *

Rex didn't come to until hours after they tossed Jimmy into the cage with him. But even unconscious the scent of Jimmy had got through to him, and he'd dreamed warm dreams from the closeness of that smell.

But when he woke the other scent, the scent his dreams had ignored, came into focus.

The smell of Jimmy's blood.

Rex nuzzled Jimmy, pressed his snout against the boy's neck, measuring Jimmy's life through the touch of his warmth on his nose.

Jimmy was alive. Breathing too softly to see or hear, his heart beating almost too faintly to be certain of. But alive, and Rex knew that.

Knew it.

Knew it with a certainty because there was a measure of magic in the dog. The greatest magic, perhaps, that there is or can be.

The sort of magic that lets a body see into the hearts and souls of others. Commonplace magic, true; so common that most people don't even recognize it when they see or use it, but great and powerful magic nevertheless. And in Rex that magic ran strong and deep and powerful.

His sight told Rex another thing, too. It told him that though Jimmy was alive, the boy was dying. Bleeding to death inside. By morning, the dog saw, Jimmy would be dead.

And there wasn't a thing, not a single thing, that the dog could do about it.

Nothing but mourn.

Rex reared back his head and howled and howled and howled out his grief to a moon he could not see.

From the bloody field where the sacrifice hung dying, the Stone had laid a quiet on the cave, against the possibility that Jimmy might wake and scream for help.

But that hush had no hold over Rex, any more than any other of the Stone's magic could touch him.

And Rex's grieving howl rung out over Green Hill.

The deputy who heard it didn't pay it any mind.

But Ben Tompkins, who was digging through the steaming-smoking ruins of the house he'd rented, searching for some sign of his son, heard the sound. And recognized it. And knew without thinking what it meant.

When Ben heard Rex howling he took off running with everything he had, following the sound. It took him five minutes to reach the sheer rock slab entrance that was the mouth of the cave, but—praise God!—the howl went on that long, and *kept* on. The slab looked no different to Ben than it had to Peterson earlier in the afternoon. But Ben could hear Rex howling somewhere in the rock, and he was strung out and delirious enough from the last few days that it didn't matter.

At a saner moment, Ben wouldn't have tried jumping through a slab of sandstone. Maybe he would have thought the sound an echo, and searched for its source. But now Ben was reduced to nothing but faith and persistence; faith that he could find his son, in the sound and meaning of the howl.

He didn't pause or hesitate before he leapt at the stone, but ran straight up and into it at a full run. The tactile illusion of the rock was still as strong for Ben as it had been for Peterson earlier—Ben felt his head slam into the rock, felt his hands and arms twist and break, but when that was done he was inside the cave and the harm he'd felt was gone.

And Rex was still howling, not far away at all. Ben reached into his pocket and took out the lighter he'd carried since he'd first started dating Anne—he'd never been a smoker himself, but it always pleased her to have her cigarettes lit, and even though he hadn't seen her in months he hadn't been able to bring himself to pack the lighter away.

Ben stood up, holding the lighter high, and walked deeper into the cave. Twice there were places where tunnels branched off the one he was in, but the sound the dog made was clear enough that he had no question which way to go.

"Rex . . . ?"

When the dog heard that his howl became sad enough to make the hairs on Ben's back stand on end.

"It's okay, boy. I'm almost there."

Ben was more right than he knew; a step later he was

close enough for the light from the butane to show the tiny cave where Jimmy and the dog were penned.

Ben started crying when he saw his son, partly for the joy of having him back, partly with the pain of seeing how he'd been hurt.

"My God, Jimmy. What have they done to you?" His voice was hoarse and creaky with the sound of trying not to sob. He fumbled with the ropes that held the cage closed for as long as he could bear to, then dropped the lighter and set his hands on the cage and tore into the bars with all the strength he had. Instead of breaking, as he'd expected it to, the wood tore right out of the ground. He lifted the cage over his head and threw it as far across the cave as he could manage. Then he fumbled on the floor until he found the lighter again and took a closer look at his son.

There was blood—fresh, red blood—trickling steadily out of Jimmy's nose; everywhere that Ben could see the boy was cut or scabbed or black-and-blue. *I've got to get him to a hospital. Now.*

A hospital as far from this town as I can manage.

He lifted Jimmy up with one arm and carried him like a baby, holding the lighter up to see by with the other. Any other time it would have taken more strength than Ben had, but just now he had enough adrenaline in his blood to lift four times Jimmy's weight.

He started out of the small cave. He was half-way into the tunnel before he remembered Rex. He turned around. "C'mon, Rex," he called, but it wasn't necessary; the dog was already hobbling along behind him.

I want to get as far from this place as I can imagine, as fast as I can go. And I'm not ever going to look back.

But he knew he couldn't just walk away from it that easily. He couldn't go that far before he got Jimmy to a doctor. He'd have to call the police department to let them know he'd found his son. He'd have to get in touch with the school board and let them know that he wouldn't be teaching for them this year.

When he got to the mouth of the cave he jumped out, still carrying Jimmy. His knees crunched as he landed, but they didn't buckle. He set Jimmy down, so he could lift Rex out of the cave, but before he could get his arms up to the dog Rex was already in midair, leaping down at the ground. Ben managed to half catch the dog as he fell, and kept him from hurting his splinted leg by landing on it too forcefully.

At eight-thirty, when the phone rang, Peterson was deep asleep and having nightmares.

By the third ring he managed to wake himself enough to open his eyes and lift the receiver.

"Hello?"

"Mike? It's Charlie, down at the office." Charlie worked the desk on the evening shift down at the sheriff's department. "The Tompkins man walked out of the hospital without checking out. On his way he borrowed Seymore's cruiser. No telling how long he's been gone; Seymore went to the hospital to tell Tompkins about the house, but he didn't actually get around to trying to find Tompkins until he'd been there a quarter of an hour, and he didn't notice the car was gone for another ten minutes after that."

"Hell. Ben Tompkins hot-wired a patrol car?"

"Nuh-uh. Old Seymore left his keys in the ignition."

Peterson rubbed his eyes. "Seymore ought to find himself a new job." He propped the phone between his ear and his shoulder and started getting dressed. "Do me a favor, would you, Charlie? Don't put this one on the radio. I want to take care of it myself. Ben Tompkins isn't any car thief—he's just a father going out of his mind. He probably just drove the damn thing back to his house. What the man needs is a lecture, not an arrest record."

"You got it, Mike. Had a feeling you might feel that way. That's why I called you first."

"Thanks. I'll give you a call when I've got this settled, get you to send someone out to pick up the car."

When Ben was a dozen yards from his car he noticed four children running toward him, shrieking. The largest of them carried a knife over his head like it was a javelin.

They weren't close enough to be a threat, but even so they gave Ben a chill. He hurried the last few steps to the car, opened the back door and set Jimmy on the back seat as quickly and carefully as he could. He had Rex get in the front seat with him; he was pretty sure that if he'd put the dog in the back, Rex would have been careful of Jimmy's wounds, but there wasn't any sense in taking the chance.

The car's engine cranked over three times before it finally started. But when it caught it roared smooth and clean to life. A moment later he was popping the car into gear and tearing across the lawn so that he could get past the stolen cruiser. Thirty seconds after that he was pulling out onto the highway, turning toward Tylerville. His body shuddered with relief, and he felt all of the fear and tension bleed out of him in one long, involuntary sigh.

He hadn't planned, at first, to go to Tylerville. But Jimmy was in serious need of a doctor, and Ben didn't *know* of any hospitals that were close enough besides the one in Tylerville.

He should have been less cautious; driving in that direction turned out to be a serious mistake.

There were headlights on the highway, coming toward him from a mile or so away. Ben didn't pay them any mind. He was taking Jimmy to the hospital. There was nothing, he thought, that could go wrong now. It was just like he'd suspected, he was sure: it was the children of the town who'd kidnapped his son. Children too young to drive. What could they do to him, chase him down with bicycles?

His mistake was in thinking that they had to catch up to him.

Ben didn't even see the first of the Children until it was too late to turn around. By then there was barely even time to stop.

They stood in the middle of the highway, blocking both lanes and the shoulders of the road as well. If he'd been driving any slower he might have been able to do a three-point turn and head in the other direction. But he wasn't driving any slower; he was nursing every bit of speed from the car's engine that he could manage—he needed to get his son to a hospital, damn it.

I'm going to run them over. These aren't kids. They're murderers. Look what they've done to Jimmy.

Ben pressed the gas pedal to the floor and kept his eye on the road.

I'm going to kill them.

The other car, the one he'd seen from a distance, was

coming at the Children from the other direction. They weren't letting it through, either. Suddenly electric blue emergency lights started strobing over the car's roof.

A sheriff's car. None of the Children even so much as flinched.

In a flash Ben pictured what the grill of the car would do to the ones directly in front of it. Pictured their small bodies pulped and bloody and pressed by the car's tires.

And looked up again to see the sheriff's car screech to a halt in the far lane, and told himself, *It'll be okay, there's a sheriff here and the man's got a gun for God's sake. There's no reason for me to kill those children—no matter how bad they are.*

And slammed on the brakes.

But the truth was, he realized as the car screeched to a stop four feet from the closest of the children, that he should have gone ahead and killed them. The sheriff over there—Ben recognized him; it was Mike Peterson—couldn't even bring himself to fire his gun at first. The children were all over him like feral dogs. Ben pushed the transmission into reverse and started a three-point turn, but before he got half-way through it they were swarming all over the car, pounding on the windshield and reaching in through Ben's open window. One of them climbed in right on top of Ben from up on the roof; before Ben even had time to react he'd turned off the ignition.

It was over pretty quickly after that. Ben tried to fight back, but there were too many of them. It took Ben a moment to get over his reluctance to hit children, and by the time that moment was past ten of them had him out of the car and all but pinned to the ground. Then they were carrying him and his son and the dog and Mike Peterson out into the woods, through the darkness toward a clearing where a bonfire burned.

PART
THREE

CHAPTER

THIRTY-ONE

JIMMY HAD A DREAM AS HIS FATHER CARRIED HIM FROM the cave.

When dad lifted him from the packed-dirt floor of his cage, it almost woke Jimmy. But by then too much blood had already seeped away into his abdomen and out through his nose, and no ordinary circumstance could have woken him. Instead, he slipped upward from the dreamless sleep of those who are about to die.

And he began to dream.

He dreamed, at first, about the black, roselike flower he'd found that afternoon near the top of Green Hill—the flower that he'd plucked and secreted in his pocket. The flower that was like the Stone and somehow not like it at all. In the dream he grasped the stem of the flower with both hands, and because it had no thorns it didn't hurt him.

As he held the flower, it began to bloom; bloom so rich and full that Jimmy realized that the flower it had been when he'd first seen it was nothing but a bud.

Then the rich full-bloomed flower began another, stranger transformation: the pistils and the stamen at the center of its petals began to wither away, and in a moment they were reabsorbed. The petals drew back like a cowl unmasking, and the smooth green surface that covered the flower's ovaries took on texture. The translucent black tissue of the plant transformed itself into the skin of a woman, and the texturing of the ovary-surface deepened and deepened until they became . . .

Until they became his mother's face. His mother's face, sculpted from powdery black glass.

For the time it took to blink, Jimmy let go of the flower and drew back from her image in white-cold terror. The first memories his mother brought to mind were ones that frightened him—memories of the weekend she lost her mind.

The flower didn't fall, but remained impossibly suspended in midair.

He saw that she was crying, crying tears made out of blood from ebony-glass eyes. And the look on her face was regret, and loss, and shame. Looking at her, Jimmy felt bad for her, because it looked like she wanted to die, but couldn't, because no one would let her.

Jimmy remembered being relieved and even glad when she'd tried to kill herself. The memory made him look away from her, because he was ashamed of it. Now, as Jimmy lay dying in his father's arms, he knew that in a way he'd been right to want that, to want her death. But just as much as he'd been right he'd been wrong. And every bit that he'd been right had been for the wrong reasons; maybe it was right that she be dead, because no one with any kind of decency could live with herself after she'd done things like mom had done . . . but Jimmy had wanted her dead because he'd been afraid of her.

That was wrong, Jimmy knew. Selfish in the worst possible way. Maybe it was right to close somebody out of your life when they'd done things like mom had. But no way was it ever right to wish your mother dead, no matter how much bad she'd done to you. Even young as he was, Jimmy knew that in a way his mother was a part of him.

And wishing her dead was an evil not just to her but to himself.

When he managed to make himself look up at her again, his flower/mother had changed again—she was metamorphosing into his mother, whole and real, but still made of buff ebony.

"I love you, Jimmy," she said. "I love you, Jimmy, and I'm sorry, and I hope that you can forgive me well enough to grow up to be a decent human being." And then she turned and walked away from him, before he could press his heart back down out of his throat and say anything, anything at all, because he had to respond to her, *had* to. But even though it was his dream and his dreams always bent to his direction when he needed them to, she didn't stop, she didn't wait to hear from him.

And a part of him was certain, even as he knew that he was dreaming, that something very real and unstoppable and unchangeable had happened, and he wasn't certain, not certain at all, that the way it had happened was for the best.

"Mom!" he shouted. "Mom! Come back, mom!" But already she was gone, disappeared into the distant haze of his dream.

And the flower was drifting in the vagueness at his feet— not his mother at all, but the flower, just as it had been before the metamorphosis began.

Jimmy stooped and reached into the dream mist to retrieve it; he touched it, picked it up—

Then something powerful, magical, and evil reached down into his mind and dragged him up into the waking world.

CHAPTER

THIRTY-TWO

DADDY SCREAMED UNHOLY HELL ALL THE WHILE THEY
were skinning him. The Stone didn't even bother to suck
up the sound of his screaming; it was too far, out here, for
anyone in Green Hill to hear him. There was an irony in
this that Tim couldn't bring himself to appreciate, not
even as gallows humor; daddy had been so full of bluster
and mean righteousness as he'd dragged Tim out to the
clearing, so full of blind self-confidence, that it didn't really
sink through to him what was happening, even when they
trussed him to one of the ropes that hung over the pit. Not
even when they roped his legs and stretched him out to
the pit's edge, so that they could get at him without him

struggling too much to work with. He finally began to figure out what was going on about the time Roberta had her skinning knife peeling away half the skin of his arm.

Roberta was especially fond of skinning.

She went extra hard on daddy, cutting and peeling real slow, and being real careful to lard-over the flesh she left exposed, so that daddy wouldn't bleed to death too fast. Daddy had screamed and screamed and after a while he began to beg Roberta to let him die. Roberta didn't pay him any mind at all. She just smiled and sort of basked in the warmth of daddy's screaming, like a cat warming herself in the afternoon sun.

Daddy bled an awful lot, even with all the lard Roberta used. And he screamed horribly and painfully; listening and watching made Tim cry for his father, even though he knew that he was next and that he ought to be crying for himself.

When daddy finally stopped screaming and died, the Children started on Tim. They'd only got as far as cutting the outlines they'd use to skin him when Ben Tompkins screamed from somewhere in the woods. A moment after that there were more Children in the clearing, and they had the Tompkinses and the dog and a deputy sheriff, and getting started with them was more important than skinning Tim, so they strung Tim up high over the pit, next to his skinless daddy, and left him hanging there for later on.

Mike Peterson's world, and everything he knew about it, dissolved in front of him in less time than he would have spent drinking his morning coffee.

Trouble started as something crazy and impossible—children blocking the road. Peterson was on his way to Green Hill to deal with the fact that Ben Tompkins had stolen a police cruiser. He wasn't expecting any *real* nastiness from that. Ben Tompkins was a decent man; Peterson had seen enough of him not to have any doubt about that. Ben was maybe getting a little unhinged, but given the circumstances that wasn't surprising at all. Peterson would have been suspicious, in fact, if the man *hadn't* been acting a little crazy.

Ben Tompkins needed a good talking to, that was all. And after the talk, Peterson was going to have to find the

man a place to stay for the night. Peterson wasn't sure
what he was going to do about that, but God knew he had
to do something; you just couldn't ignore it when someone
you knew had nowhere to stay, not if you had any decency
at all.

Peterson sighed, and then he saw the children blocking
the road. Blocking him, and blocking the car that was
coming at him from the other direction.

What the. . . ?

He hit the switch on the dash and turned on his overhead lights. It didn't make any difference. None of the
children moved, not an inch.

Then he saw the light of the car's headlamps glint off
clean steel.

Knives. My God, two or three of those kids have knives.
Once he was looking for it he saw that most of the ones
who didn't have knives were carrying sticks or clubs.

Holy Christ.

Peterson slammed on the brakes; the cruiser's tires
screeched and skidded; the car fishtailed so bad that by the
time it came to a stop it was at a right angle to the road.

Across the way the children had the other car stopped
and pried open; they swarmed over the driver—Ben
Tompkins!—like ants. Others were hauling a small boy—
Jimmy?—and the dog Rex out of the backseat.

There were times over the last few days when he'd have
bet his life that the children of Green Hill had something
to do with Jimmy Tompkins's disappearance. Others when
he'd been a lot less sure than that. But even if he'd had his
suspicions, there was something unnerving and unreal
about seeing children act like . . . like . . . Peterson
didn't know what. An army of psychotics? Peterson didn't
consider himself an innocent, but he'd never seen so many
people act so violently. Not even when the good old boys
decided they'd take apart a bar.

By the time he got out of the car the children were
already coming at him. There were too many of them with
too many knives and clubs for the nightstick to be any use.
It wouldn't even have made a good threat. So he took out
his gun and cocked back the hammer, and aimed at the
largest of the children.

Peterson considered getting on the radio and calling for

help. But these were just children, damn it. Maybe they *did* have knives and clubs—what did it matter, when Peterson had a gun?

"All of you," he said, "stop exactly where you are. Put down the knives and sticks, and stop where you are."

But they didn't stop; they didn't even slow down. To look at them Peterson wouldn't even think he'd spoken.

I'm going to have to use this damn thing if I want them to stop.

He fired a shot just over the head of the boy in his sights. When that didn't have any effect he fired another shot that sunk a bullet into the tar a few inches from the boy's feet.

The children just kept coming, fearless as machines.

Peterson took aim at the boy's chest, and tried to force himself to squeeze the trigger. But he couldn't. Crazy and violent or not, the boy was just a boy, a *boy,* and how do you shoot a ten-year-old boy?

A ten-year-old boy with a butcher knife. A boy who looked like he was going to kill him.

Then they were all over him, and one of them yanked the gun from his hands, and Peterson didn't have the decision to make anymore anyway. Before he had time for regret they were carrying him away, into the woods.

A couple of the older children stayed behind to move the cars off the road. Older or not, they weren't old enough to be driving; there wasn't a one of these kids who was more than twelve. It amazed Peterson that he could worry about underage drivers at a time like this—but kids going for joyrides in their parents' cars was a problem he knew how to deal with, and just now his mind was desperate to find something familiar enough to hold onto . . . anything at all.

The children carrying the Tompkinses were a good dozen yards ahead of him. Peterson couldn't see anything beyond that but a bonfire. It was hard to say for all the trees exactly what was around the fire, but he figured that it must be in some kind of a clearing, because the flames weren't spreading.

Ben Tompkins was closer, and he saw into the clearing two minutes before Peterson did. And when he saw, he screamed.

Screamed a scream so rich and deep and terrified that hearing it Peterson felt his heart shrink inside his chest.

It put some of the fight back into Peterson; he started to struggle again against the dozen or so children who carried him. He didn't manage to get free, but struggling got him all twisted around, and he didn't see anything but the ground as they carried him into the clearing. He kept trying to get loose until they threw him into the pit.

He hit the steep earth wall of the pit twice on the way down, and landed on his stomach. It knocked the wind out of him, but not far enough out to keep him from getting back on his feet right away. A few feet from him Ben lay on his back, staring wide-eyed with terror into the sky—his mouth frozen open in a scream that no longer made any sound. Jimmy and the dog, both of them unconscious, lay on the ground not far from Ben.

Peterson took a look around, trying to figure out if he was going to be able to get himself and everyone else out of here. The walls of the pit were a dozen feet high, and smooth, and just about sheer. He probably wouldn't be able to get himself out if he didn't spend an hour or two digging handholds in the packed dirt. The walls were a little less steep over at the other end, but there was a fire burning at the top of that wall, so close that burning embers dribbled out of the ashes and down along the wall. . . .

There was something inside that fire. Something black and—and—*alive.* Alive, and sentient, and not human at all.

Whatever it was was shaped like an irregular stone boulder, and if you looked too quickly you might think it was nothing but a strange black rock.

But Peterson didn't think it was a rock, not for an instant. There was a wrongness in Green Hill, a wrongness that Peterson had felt almost from the moment this case had started. And the Stone inside the fire was all the wrongness in Green Hill made tangible and real and recognizable.

Something warm dripped onto Peterson's cheek.

There was a halo of bright red static around the Stone, static so brilliant that it all but eclipsed the flames around it. For a moment Peterson thought he saw a face coalescing from the static. It smiled at him hungrily, the way he'd once seen a cat smile at a mouse it had already caught but hadn't yet killed. But then the pattern in the static shifted, mimicking the flames, and the face was gone.

Another warm, wet droplet glanced across Peterson's cheek and fell to the ground. It made a tiny splashing noise when it landed by his feet. He looked down and saw that he'd wandered a few steps without realizing it, and now he was standing in the middle of a puddle—

A puddle of something much too rich and smooth to be water, or mud. He stooped to look more closely. . . .

A puddle of blood. Warm, fresh blood. Another droplet fell into the puddle from above.

I'm not going to look. I'm not. Whatever it is that's been bleeding on me for the last five minutes, I don't want to know. I don't. Honest to God I don't.

But if there was going to be any hope at all, Peterson knew, he had to keep his head on his shoulders and keep his wits about him; if he started ignoring the situation he'd be as lost as Ben Tompkins, lying on the ground in shock, or his half-dead son.

Peterson looked up.

And saw a man, or what had been a man, once, hanging by his wrists from a rope anchored to the high branches of a tree. There was no way to say just who it had been. Not anymore. Not even the most artful mortician would be able to make that man recognizable again.

A man who'd been skinned alive.

It was still possible to see that the carcass had been a man; there was very little besides his skin missing. Great loops of intestine hung loose from his abdomen, and a few other organs dangled out of place. But whoever had skinned him had been careful to leave in place the things that distinguish a man's body from a woman's.

Blood had begun to crust and dry on the man's exposed flesh; flies and gnats picked at his remains. The man's cheekless, lipless mouth hung open in a dead-quiet scream that wouldn't ever end.

A few yards from the man, suspended from another rope, was Tim Hanson. There were long, bloody gashes along the boy's arms and legs; he was bleeding steadily, but he was still alive. It didn't look as though he'd live much longer.

That was when the world collapsed for Mike Peterson. He felt his spirit and his will slipping away from him, and he tried to keep hold of them; but it just wasn't any use. The sight of the flayed man and the dying boy made his heart as weak as it made his knees.

And he knew that because he'd lost heart he was going to die, and so were the people who depended on him.

Once he'd resigned himself, a tiny measure of his spirit came back—not enough to help him escape, or even struggle against the people and the thing who were going to kill him.

But spirit enough to curse them.

He turned to the Stone whose red aurora burned brighter than the flames that tried to consume it, and spoke to it.

"What are you, some kind of a disease? Or are you a parasite, like a leech or a bloodworm? A worm too weak to infect anyone but little children." He waved at Tim Hanson and the skinless man. "Who are these people?" Peterson asked the Stone. "Are these the ones, like Jimmy and Ben here, who you couldn't infect? What's the matter—do Jimmy here, and Tim, have too much backbone for you?" The red halo around the Stone shone furiously; Peterson could see the face resolving again out of the light. "You aren't shit. It doesn't make you anything special just because you can screw around with the head of a little kid. And skinning a man alive when you got sixty little kids to do it for you doesn't make you anything more than a coward."

A woman made of red electric fire coalesced around the face, and stepped out of the flames and embers. She looked at Peterson with eyes so angry, fiery, and cruel that for a moment he felt as though he'd been skinned alive himself. But he stood his ground, and stared right back at her.

"You're nothing," he said. "Playing games with kids' heads doesn't make you anything at all."

The fire-woman said his name, then, and she started walking toward him. When she reached the edge of the pit she just kept going, walking gently downward as though gravity didn't even exist.

"Nothing at all."

It seemed to Peterson that the woman looked vaguely like Jimmy.

You're wrong, the woman said. Her lips moved, but Peterson didn't hear her words with his ears. He heard them in his head almost as though he thought them himself. *You're wrong, and because of what you've said you'll die as horribly as the one whose blood is on your face.*

Ben Tompkins, still lying on the ground, caught sight of the woman, and seeing her somehow put some of the fight back into him. Ben rolled over, sat up—

She was close now, almost near enough for Peterson to touch. When she set foot in the blood-soaked dirt the blood caught fire, and the flames she was made of burned so brightly that Peterson had to shield his eyes.

But first you'll see. I am a part of everything, everywhere in this world. Every hate, every fear. Every malignant thought that waits to grow to evil is a part of me. Every half-forgotten horror in every soul belongs to me. Every weakness in every heart is mine. *No one is immune.*

Even a boy like this one has enough evil in him . . . to kill his own mother.

Then Peterson heard Jimmy Tompkins stir and groan and sit up dizzily, and somehow Peterson's gun, the gun the children had taken from him, was in the boy's hands, and—

When he looked up again the woman made of fire had a carving knife in her hands, and she was running at the boy and screaming his name.

Ben Tompkins managed to get himself off the ground and charge the woman, trying to put himself between his son and the carving knife. But before Ben got anywhere near her he smacked headfirst into some sort of invisible wall; the man fell to the ground, senseless.

CHAPTER
THIRTY-THREE

JIMMY WOKE IN A PLACE TOO STRANGE TO UNDER-stand, in a moment too loud and hurried to absorb.

Mom was a few feet from him, screaming his name. She was made of fire, now, where a moment ago, a moment before she'd disappeared forever, she'd been made of something that was almost stone—onyx, maybe, or obsidian.

She had the carving knife in her hand. It was the same carving knife she'd had when she'd butchered Duke, but now its stainless steel blade was clean and pure as though it had never tasted blood.

The look in her eyes was murder.

She was going to kill him.

To Jimmy that idea was almost funny. How could she murder him? Roberta had already taken care of that, and Jimmy knew it. Even if his conscious mind had faded away as the girl beat him, his backbrain had watched the beating, and it knew that he wouldn't survive it. His heart, neither conscious nor unconscious, had made its peace with the world, and resigned itself to die. It wasn't a happy death, but it was an ending; in its own way it was welcome.

"Mom. . . ?"

In Jimmy's daze the world seemed all but frozen. Mom was running at him, but because time had slowed for him she seemed to be running under water, or even some thicker substance, each step so slow that it looked unreal.

Jimmy blinked in confusion. But he wasn't afraid. He was already dead—he was sure of that—and what sense was there being afraid when you were already dead? At least part of fear, Jimmy knew, was when your glands pumped things into your blood.

But the dead have no glands, nor blood. If they fear, that fear is a spiritual thing. It may be grim, but there is no terror in it. Terror is reserved for the living.

It was that absence of fear that ultimately convinced the logical part of Jimmy's brain that he'd died. He had no way of knowing that he was wrong; there wasn't time, no matter how much time had slowed, for his mind to wander. If there had been time, the truth might have occurred to him: his body had been so battered and so bled that the glands that would have let him fear were long since drained. Those glands were as bruised and battered and overstrained as any other part of Jimmy was; if at that moment they'd had all the blood and rest and oxygen they'd needed, it would still have been days before they were whole enough to give his blood emotion.

But there wasn't the time or peace of mind for Jimmy to realize that he was alive. All he knew was that he was dead and resurrected in hell, where his mother meant to murder him again and again and again.

She was a step closer now.

That was when Jimmy realized that he had a gun in his hands.

Did that mean he wasn't in hell at all? Was this some

perverse heaven, where the hells you lived in life were remade, only here you had license to revenge yourself? Or protect yourself, at least? Was this a place where his mother would suffer, just the way she made him hurt?

Maybe it was. But if it was, Jimmy wasn't sure he wanted any part of it.

All the same, he raised the gun and sighted with it.

What he saw as he stared over the barrel of the gun were his mother's crazy-angry eyes.

She wants to kill me. She wants to kill me, and I can kill her if I want to.

He sat there thinking about that, looking into his own heart as he watched his mother's eyes, for the time it took her to take another step. He realized, as he thought about it, that whether she was going to kill him or not, he really didn't want to see her die. And if she was going to die, he wasn't going to be the one who killed her. Not even if he had to die in hell a thousand times.

Even if she was a bad woman, even if she was so crazy and violent that it was better never to see her again, she was his mother, and he loved her.

Jimmy lowered the gun and set it on the ground beside him. As he did his hand brushed against the glass-hard flower in his pocket.

He took the flower out, and he looked at it; when he looked up at his mother again she was inches away from him, and the carving knife was coming down toward his neck.

Still, Jimmy wasn't afraid, even though he probably should have been. He held the flower out to her, to give it to her.

"I love you, mom," he said. And as her hands and the knife swung toward him, the flower brushed across her wrist.

When the flower touched her, the thing made out of flames that Jimmy thought was his mother burst into a hundred thousand filaments of light.

And the Stone, roiling in the crackling bonfire above him, screamed. And shattered, and died, and its shards stopped drinking in the flames, and began to burn.

To burn as bright as the sun.

As it died and burned, the fiery shock of its death seared

the brains of the Children who served it. More than one of them blacked out. Roberta and Christian, who stood closest to the Stone, were too numb to move or even notice when the bonfire went wild. Its flames consumed them.

As the sorcery that kept Jimmy conscious dissipated into the air, his mind slowly faded back toward black sleep. He was in the hospital ten days before he woke again.

CHAPTER

THIRTY-FOUR

THERE ARE OTHER PIECES OF THE STORY LEFT TO TELL:
small pieces.

As the woods south of Green Hill began to burn, Mike
Peterson managed to get the Tompkinses, Rex, and Tim
Hanson out to the road. Once he had them safe he went
back again to save as many of the Children as he could . . .
but he didn't manage to save many.

The Stone's death left the Children in shock, and as the
stone burned hot and hard it set fire to the trees around it.
The ones who survived the forest fire that night spent
numb weeks recovering their senses, but they did recover
them eventually. Some day they will grow up to be the

people that their hearts and deeds make them to be—not good, necessarily, but not bad, either.

The adults of Green Hill remembered themselves, and many of them have heavy consciences to this day. But not all of them; there are those who are bad-hearted enough to miss the Stone. One or two may try to resurrect it, but they won't succeed—the Stone's essence is gone from Green Hill.

Mike Peterson through long and hard about leaving the sheriff's department and going into real estate, but he never did. Early in the fall he and Robin Smith, the veterinarian, started dating. They're still seeing each other.

When Tim Hanson got out of the hospital, a state agency found him a home with foster parents in a part of the state far away from Green Hill. He's happy there, and doing well in school.

Sean is growing up all over again—his mind was stripped bare, but his soul was still alive underneath it. Thomas and his mother spend long hours nursing and teaching him, and changing the boy's diapers several times a day. Some day Sean will begin to come back into focus, but it isn't likely he'll ever remember what he used to be.

When Jimmy finally left the hospital he and his father and Rex the dog began the drive back to New Jersey. And as they drove, Jimmy came to a decision: he was going to visit his mother in the hospital. And when he saw her, he would give her a flower—a very special flower, that wasn't like any other flower in the world.

ALAN RODGERS has been active in the fields of horror and science fiction for the last several years, serving as one of the first editors on *Rod Serling's THE TWILIGHT ZONE Magazine* then later as the co-creator and editor of *Twilight Zone's* all-horror spinoff sister magazine *Night Cry*. In recent years he has turned his attention to writing full time and his stories have appeared in *Weird Tales* Magazine, the Doubleday Foundation hardcover *Full Spectrum 2*, Graham Masterton's *Scare Case* anthology, and *Masques 2*, which published his 1988 Bram Stoker Award-winning and World Fantasy Award-nominated short story "The Boy Who Came Back From The Dead." He currently lives in New York, where he is at work on his next novel, *The Voice of Armageddon*.

ALAN RODGERS

THE VOICE OF ARMAGEDDON

Two countries on the brink of nuclear war. A dangerous religious organization vying to control the fate of the Earth. A mysterious virus leading to the resurrection of dead all over the planet. These are the elements at play in a terrifying epic novel of the world in what might be its final days.

Here is a preview of this powerful reading experience, which will be on sale this summer wherever Bantam Books are sold.

Ron Hawkins checked his watch. It read eight forty-five in the evening, which meant that it was time to make one final pass of the waste baskets in the wing. It wouldn't take that long; he'd only have to check the offices where he knew the researchers kept late hours. Six, seven offices, the same number of labs, so spread out that Ron knew it would take more time to cover the distance between them than it would to empty the baskets.

Most of the offices and labs produced little enough trash that Ron could empty their wastebaskets into the garbage bag on his cleaning cart. But Dr. Bonner's office (stress on the *Dr.*; Bonner was a European with strong ideas about the pecking order) was one of those on the late run, and the man somehow managed all by himself to produce enough trash to fill a plastic garbage bag three times over.

Ron didn't look forward to visiting Bonner's office.

It wasn't just that the man was unfriendly. Bonner wasn't the problem; it was his . . . project.

Ron wasn't quite sure what Bonner was trying to do, or why, but there was a *thing* in Bonner's laboratory, a bestial nightmare of a creature with extra heads and limbs. And there was a light in its eye, a light that said to Ron that the thing maybe had more brains in his head than Ron had in his own. Bonner kept the poor thing in a tiny cage right there in his laboratory, a cage not even big enough for the pathetic thing to stand up in, just like it *was* nothing but some poor, dumb beast. Ron had never been able to go into Bonner's lab without feeling frightened and sick with himself from the guilt of not setting the creature loose.

Ron knocked on the door to Bonner's office before he went inside. Bonner wasn't the sort of person you wanted to walk in on and surprise. He wasn't the sort of person you wanted to see at all, for that matter. Ron wasn't sure he was less eager to be in that room with the . . . *thing* while Bonner was there or while he wasn't. The creature was unsettling and physically repugnant, but there was something malignant about Bonner.

No one answered the door. So Ron took the big ring of keys off his belt and opened it.

The creature was waiting for him inside, quiet and pensive as though it knew Ron was coming. Maybe it did; Ron almost always cleared out Bonner's trash this time of night.

The creature was a physical abomination, pure and simple. Three heads, and seven other knotlike protrusions coming up out of its shoulders. Those heads were vaguely reptilian. Only the one in the center looked to be alive. The heads had mouths like lion maws, and most of them had horns. Sometimes one, sometimes two; ten horns in all. Its lower legs, those feet, they were the feet of a bear. And it had hands, too—but they were more like the hands of a monkey than they were like a man's.

One of the slack-dead heads had a wide, grisly scar on its neck, just below its jaw. A scar from a wound that ought to have killed any creature, let alone one so horribly misformed.

Ron tried not to look the thing in the eye, but he couldn't stop himself. *What are you?* The question rose to the top of his mind all by itself.

The creature didn't answer, but its real head, the only one with eyes that ever opened, shifted, almost as though it had heard Ron ask.

Ron shuddered, and he wondered—just as he did every night when he went to Bonner's laboratory—why he didn't find himself another job.

The worst part of Bonner's trash was all tied up and waiting for him, four neatly packaged red plastic bags. Red because the trash was contaminated waste, dangerous and infected with God knew what. The contaminated stuff Ron had to treat specially; it didn't go in the dumpster with everything else. It went out to a small, sturdy concrete shack, where you stacked the bags neatly and in the morning Adam Leitsky burned them in the incinerator. Bonner had a couple of wastepaper baskets, too, one under his desk and another a couple of feet from the creature's cage, but the four red bags were the part that Ron dreaded every night.

Sometimes Ron wondered what Bonner did that could make four bags of contaminated waste every day. Wondered what was inside those bags. But he wasn't stupid; he never wondered hard enough to actually open one up and see what was inside it.

The creature began to make whining sounds as Ron carried out the bags. He tried hard as he could to ignore the thing.

He tried so hard not to see or hear the creature that his eyes caught on Bonner's desk, and he saw that Bonner's briefcase was still on it, half open. That meant that the man was still in the building somewhere; he never left without that briefcase. Ron didn't want to see that man—tonight, he thought, he was even less up to coping with him than he usually was. He grabbed the last two red-plastic bags, heaved them up, and hauled them out to the cart in the hall. That left only the two small wastepaper baskets. He grabbed new plastic liners for the cans and started to empty them.

He was in such a hurry that he somehow managed to forget about the creature completely. He got the trash from under Bonner's desk, stepped across the room, bent over . . .

. . . and felt a *hand* touch his shoulder. He jumped six inches off the floor and only barely managed to force back a scream.

The hand stayed with him as he jumped, lightly, carefully following the arc of his motion, like it was a butterfly resting on the cloth of his shirt.

The touch itself was only part of what scared Ron half out of his mind; the sensation he felt was much more than just the gentle pressure of fingerlike claws on the flesh of his back. There was something else there, too, something electric that ran through him from one end to the other and funneled itself toward his heart. A sensation so strange and soft that even as Ron felt it he wasn't sure it was real.

"No!"

Ron heard himself shout before he even knew what he was saying. He caught his balance and jerked himself away from the creature's cage by reflex. When he turned to look back at it he saw the creature's hand groping toward him slowly, easily, almost the way a lover's hand reaches out at night.

"No," he said. *"Stop."* And the creature did stop, and that unnerved Ron most of all, because it meant that the thing understood him.

The creature drew its hand back into its cage, and it stared at him, not angry or even sullen, but not pleasantly, either. The thing was too grotesquely ugly to ever look pleasant.

"What do you want from me?" Ron asked. The creature didn't answer. "Do you want me to let you out of there, so you can be free? Hell, I know how you feel. I wouldn't want to be locked inside Bonner's office, either. But I can't let you out of there. They'd just find you again in the time it took to scream bloody murder, and once they found you they'd fire me. And what good would that do either one of us?" The creature didn't move a muscle, not a hair. "What are you, anyway? What *are* you?"

In his car on his way to get dinner, Ron fumbled around at the dash until he managed to turn on the radio and tune it to a news station.

It was time to make sure that the world wasn't going to blow up before he had a chance to say good-bye to it.

He knew that if they were going to start shooting off nuclear missiles it wouldn't make any difference whether he was listening to hear it or not. But if he was going to die like that, turned to fire and dust in the time it took to blink, he wanted to know about it.

Ron was a mile away from the institute; the announcer finally finished the sports and began to read through the headlines.

Terrorists had bombed a bridge, not a hundred miles away from here. Ron remembered hearing three days ago that somebody had set off a bomb on a college campus that was even closer. Probably, he thought, it was the same people.

A TV evangelist was announcing that he was going to run for President, *again.*

Those crazy cross-and-dove people had put on another protest in front of the UN, up in New York City. And this one had turned into a riot, too.

And the Russians weren't backing down, not an inch.

The announcer finished reading through the headlines and began to work his way through the details of the stories. Ron listened impatiently through the terrorists and the evangelist and the cross-and-dove people, wondering if he was going to be alive to wake up tomorrow. How could the radio let all those other stories come first when President Green was threatening to blow up the world?

Don't they know? Aren't they listening to the news as they read it? They had to be. It was just too important *not* to listen to. *Unless maybe they're as scared as I am, so scared that they're putting off dealing with it as long as they can.* There was something to that idea, Ron thought; it struck a chord. But it didn't feel *right,* either. He shook his head, and sighed, and waited, still driving toward town.

The man on the radio was just beginning to tell about the Russians when Ron got to town, which was annoying. Ron had half been planning to go into Denny's and get himself a decent meal, maybe a chili burger or something, but if he did that it'd mean not hearing what was going on, and Ron was feeling more and more of a compulsion to find out what was happening right *then,* before the nuclear bombs could sneak up on him and surprise him. So he turned into the Burger King, and went through the drive-through. Something by the restaurant caused an awful lot of static on the radio, especially right where you ordered from, with the lit-up plastic menu and the speaker and microphone. Even when he turned up the volume it was hard to hear. But he concentrated, and the girl inside the Burger King had to ask him three times what he would like to order tonight, because he was listening to how the Russians were saying they weren't going to take any more humiliation from the President ever again. He told her he wanted a Whopper and a Coke, and when she told him that they only had Pepsi he told her to just give him a soda. Actually he also used a couple of other words and his tone was more than a little surly, and when Ron heard himself he felt bad about it. But he didn't pay it a whole lot of attention, he mostly just drove his car up to the drive-through window.

Because he was listening to the beginning of the end of the world.

The next night, when Ron entered Bonner's laboratory, his unease was particularly intense. There was something in the room . . . singing. No, not singing; there was no sound. No noise at all; his ears heard only the dead silence of the building's empty hallways. It was an un-sound, and it wasn't singing at all, because instead of melody and harmony it had other, stranger, qualities. Analogous but not similar at all.

The beast, Ron thought. *The Beast.* It had to be Bonner's creature that he was . . . hearing.

Ron's fingers lost their grip on the doorknob, and the door eased open on its own. For just an instant—just an instant as his fingers reached up to turn on the overhead lamp—Ron thought that he could see the creature in spite of the room's darkness.

Perhaps it was a trick of Ron's mind. It must have been, in fact—there was no way Ron's eyes could see anything in a room that dark, not when they were so accustomed to the bright fluorescent light in the corridors.

But, of course, when his eyes finally finished blinking away the room's sudden brightness, the creature was exactly as he'd seen it in the darkness. And now, inside the room, the sound that wasn't sound or noise was clearer and more lyrical. It was wrong. Whatever was going on was wrong, and it was physically impossible, and Ron should have been scared. He should have been scared enough to turn around, bolt from that white-white room, slam the door behind him. Leave his cart behind him and run for his life.

He would have survived that night if he had.

But he wasn't scared. It did not, in fact, even occur to

him to be afraid. What he felt was . . . something sensual. Like a cool breeze drifting along the sweat-damp skin of his neck on a hot day. But different from that, too: intimate and intense as though there had never been such a breeze or such a day ever before in his life.

Some small shade in his heart whispered that his life was almost over. He didn't ignore it—he couldn't have ignored a whisper that quietly intense—but he didn't mind it, either. It just didn't matter to him, in that one moment, whether or not he'd still be alive in half an hour. The moment was that powerful—that seductive and important. More important than his life.

"What *are* you?" Ron heard himself ask, and he knew that he'd asked the question before, but he wasn't sure if he'd asked it out loud or in a dream. The Beast looked at him, and suddenly his heart *knew* something.

"You're . . . you're—" But the other word was missing, and he had no clue where he should look to find it.

The Beast nodded at him, and he would have sworn that it smiled, except there was no way that a mouth of that construction could smile recognizably.

"I've got to turn you loose," Ron said. "You shouldn't be in any cage. Not you."

As he spoke Ron looked at the cage, trying to figure out how he was going to get it open; there was a heavy steel bolt there where the bars met to form a door, and the bolt was secured with a padlock.

The light seemed to flicker in the Beast's eyes—no, there wasn't any light, nothing physical you could point at—the . . . *something* seemed to flicker in the Beast's eyes for a moment. Almost . . . indulgently? Tolerantly? Warmly, and with humor, and mercy, and ease. And in a way that told Ron that the idea was futile.

Then there was something in the music—not-music? —that was all around them, something understandable and almost real enough to be certain of. *You have to leave now,* it meant. *Run now, and in the moments that are left you will get far enough to survive.*

And Ron understood that, and the way that the understanding came to him made it impossible for him to doubt. But if he couldn't doubt, he could still deny:

"That's silly," he said. He said the words out loud, even though he knew it wasn't necessary. "Don't be silly. You're important—more important than I'll ever be. I've got to get you out of here. The hell with my job and everything and anything else: God didn't make you to live in a cage. No sir. Not for another instant."

Already Ron was climbing on the bars, pulling on the cage door with all the strength in his arms and legs. Down there—the weld that bound the door-bolt secure —he could feel it beginning to stress. To give. If only he had more leverage, or stronger legs, or—or *more*—

Go now, the Beast told him. *You'll still be trapped in the blast, but if you run fast enough it might not kill you.*

"Blast? What blast? What are you—*talking* about?"

A vision, then, seen with his mind's eye—or perhaps he saw it with his memory: Luke Munsen's briefcase. On the floor of Luke's lab. After Luke had already left for the airport. After Bonner had skulked into the place, when he thought no one else would see.

A briefcase that couldn't be there, since Ron had *seen* Luke leave the building with his briefcase in hand.

The latch-weld suddenly burst loose; the force of the door flying free all at once sent Ron tumbling to the floor. And the Beast, in the instant that the two of them had left to live, reached down to help Ron to his feet. Their hands had only barely clasped when the bomb Bonner had planted brought the whole building to rubble in a hail of fire and dust.

Only Ron and the Beast were caught in the blast. There were guards on the institute's grounds, but none of them close enough that the explosion could do injury.

It was twenty minutes to midnight on Thursday evening. Half an hour later the first hydrogen bomb fell, on a wheat field in western Kansas.

DON'T MISS
THESE CURRENT
Bantam Bestsellers

☐	27814	**THIS FAR FROM PARADISE** Philip Shelby	$4.95
☐	27811	**DOCTORS** Erich Segal	$5.95
☐	28179	**TREVAYNE** Robert Ludlum	$5.95
☐	27807	**PARTNERS** John Martel	$4.95
☐	28058	**EVA LUNA** Isabel Allende	$4.95
☐	27597	**THE BONFIRE OF THE VANITIES** Tom Wolfe	$5.95
☐	27456	**TIME AND TIDE** Thomas Fleming	$4.95
☐	27510	**THE BUTCHER'S THEATER** Jonathan Kellerman	$4.95
☐	27800	**THE ICARUS AGENDA** Robert Ludlum	$5.95
☐	27891	**PEOPLE LIKE US** Dominick Dunne	$4.95
☐	27953	**TO BE THE BEST** Barbara Taylor Bradford	$5.95
☐	26554	**HOLD THE DREAM** Barbara Taylor Bradford	$5.95
☐	26253	**VOICE OF THE HEART** Barbara Taylor Bradford	$5.95
☐	26888	**THE PRINCE OF TIDES** Pat Conroy	$4.95
☐	26892	**THE GREAT SANTINI** Pat Conroy	$4.95
☐	26574	**SACRED SINS** Nora Roberts	$3.95
☐	27018	**DESTINY** Sally Beauman	$4.95

Buy them at your local bookstore or use this page to order.

Bantam Books, Dept. FB, 414 East Golf Road, Des Plaines, IL 60016

Please send me the items I have checked above. I am enclosing $_____
(please add $2.00 to cover postage and handling). Send check or money
order, no cash or C.O.D.s please.

Mr/Ms _____

Address _____

City/State _____ Zip_____

FB–11/89

Please allow four to six weeks for delivery.
Prices and availability subject to change without notice.